A HARVEST OF ASH & BLOOD

D. J. MOLLES

A HARVEST OF ASH & BLOOD

BLACK STONE PUBLISHING

Published in 2023 by Blackstone Publishing
Cover and book design by Kathryn Galloway English

Printed in the United States of America
Originally published in hardcover by Blackstone Publishing in 2023

First paperback edition: 2023
ISBN 979-8-212-38989-1
Fiction / Fantasy / Military

Version 1

Blackstone Publishing
31 Mistletoe Rd.
Ashland, OR 97520

www.BlackstonePublishing.com

This one's for Tara,
who has somehow managed to make me look
like I know what I'm doing.

And the voice said, "Take the ash and eat it." So I took it and ate it, and it was bitter in my mouth, but it gave unto my body great strength, and to my mind all manner of understanding. And from the strength of my body and the understanding of my mind, I gave strength and understanding to all the men of the world. And the voice said to me, "This is your work: to give to the many what you reap from the few."

And then the flame of the light of Feor that had been unleashed from the flesh and bone of the burned man ascended into the heavens and hung upon the firmament like a star. And the voice spoke again, this time from the star, saying, "My light I bring to you. My light I give to you. Light unto light. Go and do the work I have given you."

—Beficien's Revelation

MAP OF

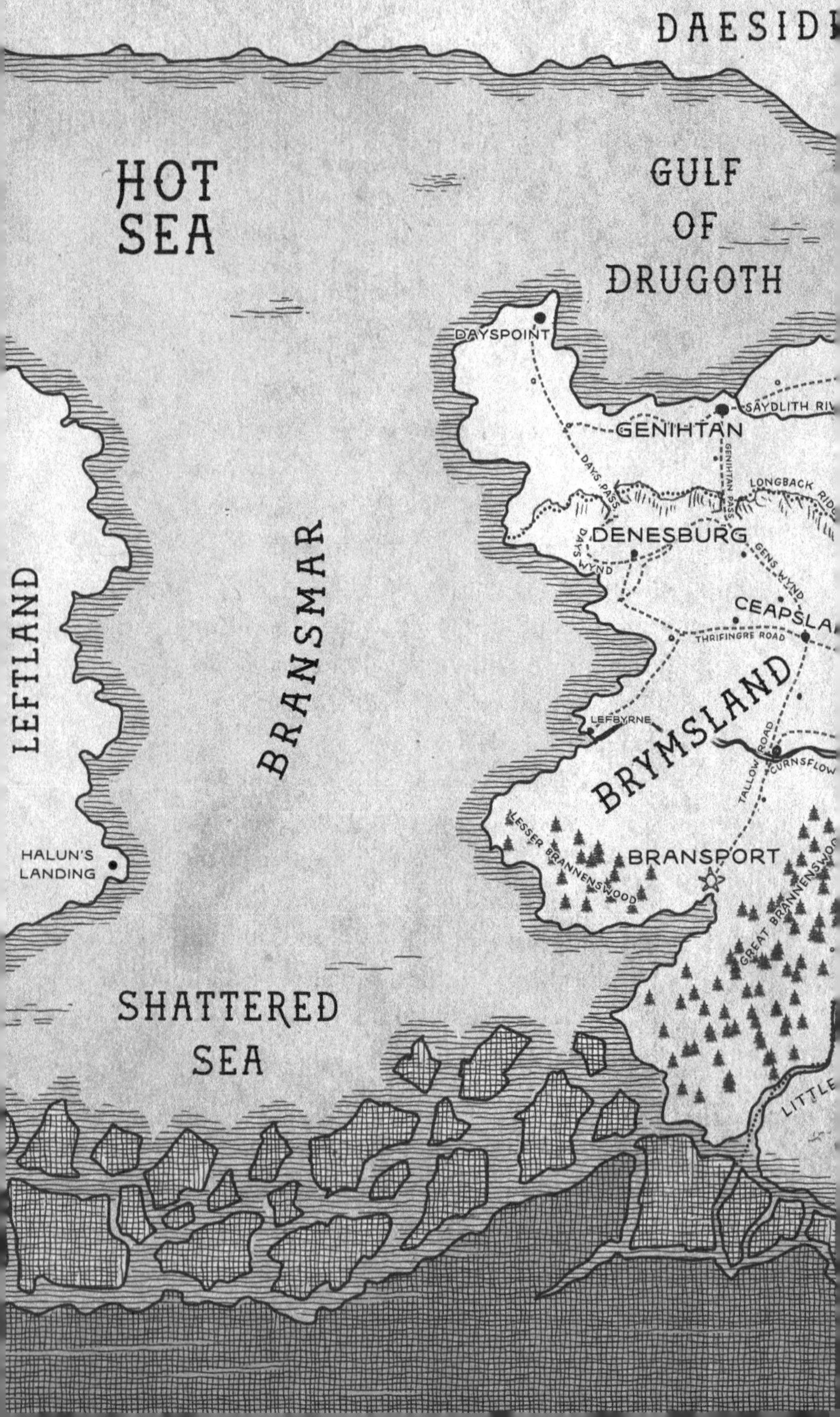
DAESIDE
HOT SEA
GULF OF DRUGOTH
DAYSPOINT
SAYDLITH RIV
GENIHTAN
DAYS PASS
GENIHTAN PASS
LONGBACK RID
DENESBURG
DAYS WYND
GENS WYND
CEAPSLA
THRIFINGRE ROAD
BRYMSLAND
LEFBYRNE
TALLOW ROAD
CURNSFLOW
LEFTLAND
BRANSMAR
HALUN'S LANDING
LESSER BRANNENSWOOD
BRANSPORT
GREAT BRANNENSWOO
SHATTERED SEA
LITTLE

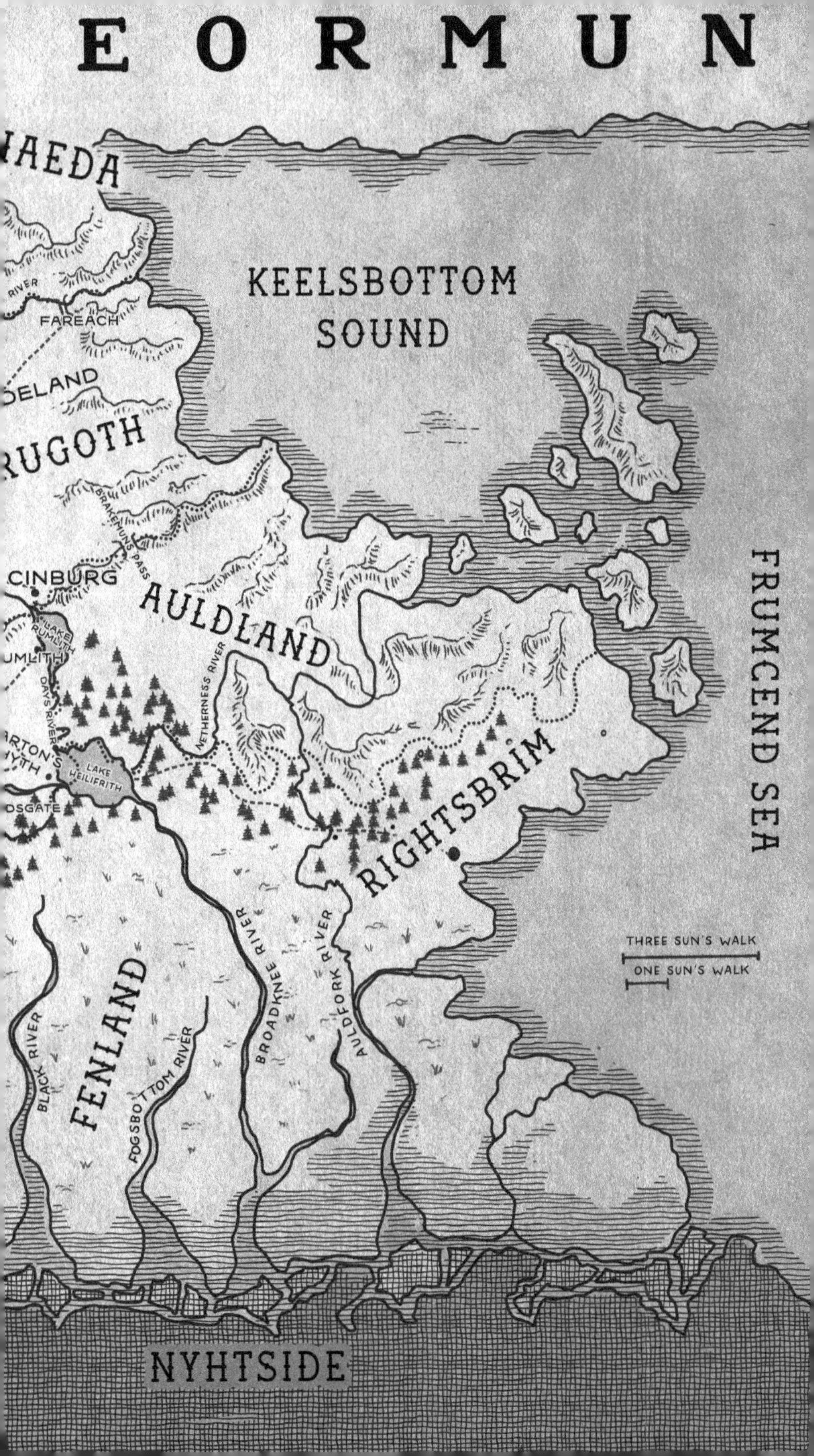
EORMUN
AEÐA
RIVER
FAREACH
DELAND
RUGOTH
KEELSBOTTOM SOUND
BRAKENUNS PASS
CINBURG
AULDLAND
LAKE RUMLITH
UMLITH
DAYS RIVER
NETHERNESS RIVER
ARTON'S HYTH
LAKE HEILIFRITH
DSGATE
RIGHTSBRIM
FRUMCEND SEA
THREE SUN'S WALK
ONE SUN'S WALK
FENLAND
BLACK RIVER
FOGSBOTTOM RIVER
BROADKNEE RIVER
AULDFORK RIVER
NYHTSIDE

CHAPTER 1

Hard to measure where a man's life takes a swerve from the common to the uncommon. For Lochled Thatcher, it may well have been the moment that he stared the girl right in the eye and wondered when they were going to burn her alive.

He stood as though struck dumb, right there in the middle of the shit-stinking streets of Bransport, across from the gated courtyard of the House of Draeids. His stomach was all slithering eels, and he couldn't tell if it was from too much drink the night before or from the image he had in his head of that girl screaming while they rendered her down to a mound of ash.

Strange how you can know that something is coming from a thousand glimpses of it in the distance, and still be surprised when it flattens you. This was a reckoning, and it'd been a long time coming.

Every evening at dusk he'd glimpsed it coming, when the city's Burners started belching smoke, and Lochled would find himself cringing as he walked through flurries of sootfall, wondering if he would hear the screams of the draeids as they burned. Wondering if he'd recognize his daughter's screams in among them.

Yes, he'd seen it coming then. And he'd ignored it.

His head pounded. Sweat tickled his eyebrows, smelling of barley spirits. Mouth sour and gums tingling from too much scaef. He didn't know how long he stared at her, that slim, pale face with her white-blond hair hanging limp about it. She sat so still, robed in white, like she might've been just as much stone as the bench she sat upon.

His Libby would've been about the same age. Was she still alive too?

All he wanted in that moment was to escape. But he couldn't seem to feel his feet beneath him. Couldn't tear his eyes away from the girl. And everything had gone dark around the edges and overbright in the center, like he was peering through a long black tunnel.

He felt like he'd stepped into a trap. He'd been a damn fool for coming this way. Had, in fact, been avoiding this street for a very long time. Terrified of exactly this.

A horrendous squeal made him jerk and spin to look behind him, his shaking hands slipping to the long-knife and hand axe in his belt. A woman stood a few paces from him, cranking a water wheel, brass keening against brass. He blinked as a bead of sweat slipped into his eye. Why was he suddenly sweating so much? And why couldn't he seem to catch his breath?

As the woman finished cranking, the pipes began to rattle. Lochled remembered a time not so long ago when you had to walk to the well for your water. Now fucking lengths of tarnished brass crisscrossed walls of wattle and daub, like cheap baubles on an old whore, and there were water wheels on damn near every corner.

Water gushed from the spout, making Lochled flinch despite himself, and poured into the woman's bucket, just as easy as you please. The woman spotted Lochled staring and trembling. She frowned at him, then looked away.

A sudden geyser of rage blotted out his mind, and he almost screamed at her: *Is it fucking worth it?* He barely kept it from coming out, issuing a strange gagging noise instead.

Behind the woman stood three others, waiting their turn. Two women with buckets at their feet, and a man with a bucket in each of his hands. This last one seemed put out that there was a line at all.

Lochled loathed them something fierce in that moment. Were they fucking daft, or did they just not care? To pull their water from the spout directly across from the House of Draeids? To flaunt it in the faces of the very children whose ashes, once alchemized, would be used to push that water through those pipes and into their waiting buckets?

Or maybe they did see it and chose to ignore it. Just like Lochled had. But a reckoning cannot be stopped by simply looking away from it. These people, ravenous for more and more alchemy—to push their water, to heat their stoves, to light their homes—would eventually be forced to confront the cost of their so-called progress.

Perhaps when it was *their* children that were sent to the Burners. You never could know, after all. Draeids were not born according to any pattern. Any young child could be one, and the parents wouldn't know it until a Seeker sensed it in them.

Yes, these people's reckoning was coming.

But Lochled's was already here.

Mouth working like a landed fish, Lochled turned back to the House of Draeids and found the world reeling and tilting as he did so that he staggered and caught himself. His breath came so hard and harsh that his throat had turned raw and dry.

The House of Draeids. Two stories of glowering, stacked

stone, and a steep slate roof almost the same color as the sky above it. They could call it a house all they wanted, but the tiny arched windows and the bars within them told the truth. It was a fucking prison. And every major city in all the Brannic Empire had one.

In the courtyard of the House of Draeids, a priestess in vermilion robes approached the girl. She stopped at the bench and bent at the waist. Said something sharp. But the girl didn't even twitch. Was she as paralyzed as Lochled was? He and her, so very different: he, battered and bearded, a swarthy Brymic; she, young as a spotted fawn and obviously a Fen with her milk-pale skin and unnerving blue eyes. And yet the both of them connected by the look they shared in that moment. A common understanding of the terror that lay ahead for her.

Clap-clap, the priestess's hands went, right in front of the girl's face. But the girl just kept on staring right at Lochled. Something wild in those eyes. Something untamed, though she'd likely spent her life behind those bars.

When the clapping garnered no response, the priestess frowned and followed the girl's gaze out, through the bars, across the street, and right to Lochled.

He jerked when the priestess made eye contact with him. Felt guilty and ghoulish for staring in at the girl. The woman's eyes narrowed at him, took in his disheveled gray uniform with the three black bands of a sergeant across its chest. She gave him a minuscule nod.

Lochled spun, gasping like he might spew, and managed to move his feet again. He refused to look back at the House of Draeids, but he could feel it there, dominating the left corner of his eye, scorching him as hot as any Burner.

His legs felt weak, his feet like blocks of wood, stumping senselessly along. He pointed himself down toward the docks, where the sea breeze would sweep away some of the stench of the city and replace it with the stench of fish.

The ocean heals all wounds—at least that's what Marna used to say. She said the clean salt air and the clean salt water and the sand and the crowing gulls—it all healed a person inside and out. That's one of the reasons she'd wanted to move to Bransport so bad—a city on the ocean, where they could heal.

But Bransport was a shattered dream. The ocean here was filthy, more sewage than salt water, the breeze more of soot and shit and fish, and the gulls swarmed the docks like hungry locusts. Nothing good had come of this place of broken promises. Everything had gone white belly to the sky, and Lochled had never been able to right it again.

"Fucking hate this city," Lochled husked as he started walking again. "Fucking hate these people."

But for all of his impotent rage at the alchemy-crazed populace, he couldn't escape the notion that he hated himself most of all. He'd fought so many battles, in so many wars. Fought for men. Fought for ideals. Fought for a bit of coin in his pocket. Fought because it was all he knew how to do.

And yet he hadn't fought for Libby.

CHAPTER 2

"Lochled, you . . ."

Lochled was sure an insult had been forthcoming, but the man in the captain's tunic trailed off when he looked Lochled up and down.

Hotsteel was the spitting image of his father—Lochled's old captain—so it gave Lochled a start damn near every time he settled his gaze on him. Just a younger, less scarred version.

Hotsteel's brows twitched together in a note of concern. "What happened to you?"

"Rough night," Lochled grumbled. "Where's my squad?"

Hotsteel jerked his head toward the docks, where ranks upon ranks of soldiers stood beneath their company banners. "They're forming up. You're late, Lochled."

"I know I'm late. Got caught up in something."

"Yes, looks like it." Hotsteel had a look about him like he was readying to have a conversation he didn't want to have. "Lochled, I vouched for you because of your history with my father—and, I'll be honest, my own admiration for you. But this isn't a good start."

"Come now," Lochled sighed, "forgive an old comrade for drinking himself to sleep the night before he leaves for war."

Hotsteel's mild expression of rebuke fell away easily enough into an amiable smile. "Fah. You and every other man in this army. Be surprised if there's a damned drop of spirits left in this city after last night."

Lochled nodded, glancing off to the docks, where the armada of barques bobbed gently in the tide, their masts and rigging creaking along to the tramp of soldiers' feet, the greedy cawing of gulls, and the gentle wash of waves.

"Still," Hotsteel edged on with his reprimand, though it had the sound of something a tad practiced, "those that know who you really are will have the utmost respect for you. It's important that you not test me. I can't be seen to give you favoritism, you know."

"Sorry, hef. I'll not take your kindness for granted. I'll make it right."

"I'll hold you to that." Hotsteel flashed him a roguish smile and bent over the table. He fluffed about a couple of sheets of parchment, each crammed full of tiny letters. Found Lochled's name in all that mess. Scribbled something illegible with a quill. "There. You're all signed in."

Lochled stared for a moment at his name on the parchment. He didn't know how he should feel about it. Seemed he was feeling several different things all at once, and none of them particularly pleasant.

How long had he been spouting that he hated this city and couldn't wait to leave it? He tore his eyes from the parchment and looked over his shoulder at the hulking gray mess of Bransport. The air above that maze of squat dwellings and shops had a yellowish tint, as though in a perpetual sunset. Except it wasn't light that made it yellow. It was smoke. Alchemic smoke.

He'd lost his daughter and his wife in that yellow-tinged

madness. One taken, the other run off on her own. Work had been hard to come by and barely paid when he found it. Which was why he was doing *this* shit. Again.

He turned and looked at the parchment once more. There it was—his name, with his captain's sign scrawled right next to it. It was for sure and certain now, and he couldn't take it back. He was going on the glorious Fourth Crusade.

He was going back to war.

But for the life of him, he couldn't make himself feel relieved to escape Bransport. So he just hung there for a moment, in some strange place between two things he kept trying to get away from but only ever managed to stumble from, one to the other, like a drunk between the walls of an alley.

"Y'aright, Lochled?"

He straightened, realizing that Hotsteel was watching him carefully.

"Steady on, hef." Lochled tried on a rickety smile. "Just getting my bearings."

Hotsteel's eyes narrowed, but a quirk came to one side of his mouth. "And have you got them?"

"Of course, hef. I'm an old hand at making the best of my shit decisions."

"Good," Hotsteel said. "Because I need you to do something for me."

Lochled could already tell by the look on Hotsteel's face—just like his father—that this was going to be something he didn't want to do. But he'd just told the man he'd make things right naught but a single minute ago.

"Piss on it," Lochled mumbled, looking away. "What do you want?"

Hotsteel leaned slightly to the side, looking over Lochled's shoulder. "Hirdman! Up here!"

Lochled twisted, didn't even see who Hotsteel was calling to until they stood up.

A girl. Maybe eighteen or nineteen rains. Dressed in a threadbare tunic and leather breeches that were far too big for her. Like she'd dressed in her father's clothes. She looked shocked to be called upon but snatched up her satchel of belongings and hustled eagerly to the table.

"Yes, hef?"

Lochled was still very unsure as to what in the hell was happening. He looked the girl up and down. Skinny. Ill fed. Broad featured and dark skinned, like she might have some Drugothan in her. Black hair pulled back tight into a braid that only reached the nape of her neck.

Gradually Lochled was able to tear his eyes away from the enigma at his side and found Hotsteel smiling at him. "Lochled Thatcher, this is Rony Hirdman—the newest member of your squad. Rony, this is your sergeant. Do what he says if you want to live. Now, does that satisfy you?"

"No," Lochled spat.

"Yes," the girl said, right over him.

"There's an archery corps," Lochled growled at her. "All female. I'm sure you'll be very welcome there."

The girl didn't seem able to hold his gaze. "They wouldn't take me. On account of I've never pulled a bow."

Lochled found himself looming over her. Didn't really want to be a cock about it, but he was entirely put off. And with good reason. "But you've killed a man in battle, uh? Hand to hand? Cleft many heads, hewn many foes? Uh?" Back to Hotsteel. "What is this? A lineman's company is no place for a cully. Unless you want her dead. Do you want her dead?" Back to the girl. "Do you want to die?"

Lochled didn't know if he was pleased or infuriated to see

the little thing jut up to him, chin raised, a spark of defiance in her eyes. "Dying's not the plan, hef. I can fight."

For a flash, he thought he saw a bit of Libby in her. Maybe in the way she had to crane her neck to look up at him. Or how the corners of her mouth were all tight as she tried to be stern.

It didn't make him want to take her to war with him. Quite the opposite, actually.

"The fuck you can," he snapped, then turned back to his captain. "Hotsteel, she's going to get killed. And Feor knows what else. You know as well as I—"

"The Brannen," Hotsteel interrupted, "in his wisdom, has opened enlistment to *all* volunteers of the empire. This little cully arrived a tad late, on account of her long journey—and being rejected by the archery corps—so she's a perfect match for you! And there's always a place for someone in our ranks—isn't that right, Lochled?"

"No. There's a place for murderers and rapists and thieves. But there's no place for a cully."

A horn bleated somewhere down the docks. Long and wounded sounding, like cattle lowing in the distance.

"Ah." Hotsteel began rolling the parchments gently onto their dowels. "The Brannen has arrived. And you, Lochled, and your new squadmate, need to get to your company. As do I."

Lochled slapped his palm down on the table. "And what's she going to fight with, uh?"

Hotsteel held up a finger. Stepped back to a wooden crate. Reached inside among the straw, and drew out an object that sent a weird mix of feelings colliding through Lochled's chest. A thrill. A beat of anger. A tinge of bloodthirst. A stab of shame.

Three feet long. A thick brass bore strapped to a wooden body rubbed smooth and waxy with the sweat and grime and blood of a hundred men's hands. Bronze hinges, tarnished slightly. The long swoop of the thin trigger bar—such a seemingly graceful piece of metalwork, until you knew what pulling it did to a man.

It had a flat back end, supposedly for putting up to your shoulder, but no man was fool enough to do that. Hotsteel slapped this back end on the table and leaned the object toward Rony. She hesitated, hands half up, like she wanted to take it but was afraid. As she should've been.

"The Leveler," Hotsteel intoned. A nod toward Lochled. "Your sergeant's favorite weapon, actually."

"Favorite's not the word I'd use," Lochled mumbled. Just because something worked well didn't mean you liked it. Especially if that work was wet and red.

But then, maybe Lochled was lying to himself. Because, as Rony reached up and took hold of the thing, he felt a pang of jealousy. Like a prize that had been meant for him had been given to someone else.

Hotsteel leaned over the table as Rony held the thing awkwardly at arm's length. He pointed to the midsection. "Push that bit there, and then break it in half."

"Break it in half?" Rony seemed surprised.

Hotsteel smiled. Nodded.

She pressed the latch. Then rammed the middle of the thing down on her knee. It split open on its hinges, exposing the thick, shadowy maw of the breech.

Made Lochled's heart do a strange thing. Like fear and love all at once.

"Good. You can break it open. That's the breech. Now close it again."

She closed it with a snap, a shaky smile on her lips. Glanced at Lochled, but quickly looked away. Lochled realized he was glaring. Cleared his throat and licked his lips.

"Now," Hotsteel said. "Put your finger on that thin bronze piece right there. Yes. Just like that. Now squeeze it."

She did. The thing made a diminutive little *clack*.

Lochled twitched. Felt a shiver down his spine.

Hotsteel leaned back, hands held wide, eyebrows arched at Lochled. "See? A woman can work a Leveler just as easy as a man."

Lochled hadn't the words to protest anymore. Found his eyes ranging back to the crate. Hungry and nauseated all at once.

"Yes, I have yours as well," Hotsteel said. Walked back. Retrieved it. Brushed the straw from it. Pushed it across the table to Lochled.

Lochled found it hard to swallow for a moment. His throat had gone a little dry. He worked some spit up. Thought about how nice a pinch of scaef would be right now. Good to harden him up. Callus his soul a bit. Get him ready for what needed to be done.

He got the spit down his throat, then grabbed the Leveler. Snapped the thing open one handed, inspected the breech, snapped it closed, pulled the trigger bar. That click again. So innocent. Until it was loaded. And then not so much.

"All settled, then?" Hotsteel asked.

Lochled glowered at Rony. Then at his captain. Turned and started walking away.

"Come on, then," he griped over his shoulder.

He felt the heft of the thing, cradled in the crook of his arms while he walked. As natural as laying with an old lover. One that was a hateful skelpie but who you just kept coming back to, time and time again.

Rony's footsteps behind him made his shoulders draw up tight as he clattered down the gangway to the docks. All along the wharf, companies of men stood about, some in formation, some not so much. A mix of professional soldiers and men simply seeking riches by way of violence. The latter far outnumbering the former.

Lochled was neither. He served no chief or Steadman. Nor did he want riches. He was just a man trying to escape Bransport. And his past. And his regrets.

"Hirdman, uh?" he growled at Rony.

"Yes, hef."

"Swine?"

"Yes, hef."

"You slaughter 'em yourself?"

"Yes, hef."

"Well, that's something. At least you don't blanch at blood, and you're used to things squealing as they die."

"I am."

"And what got into your head, uh?" He turned to glare at her up and down again. "What made you decide to do this ridiculous thing?"

"I need the money," she said, eyes dodging about as though embarrassed.

"Yeah, well, you gotta survive first." He stopped, wheeled around to face her. Pointed at the planks beneath their feet. "You're about to get in with some nasty men. And you're going to be surrounded by them for a long time. Until the day comes—assuming you somehow manage not to die—when you step back off that boat and put your feet on Brymsland soil again, just remember this: you're in hell, and everyone around you is a daemon."

Her lips tightened. A single nod. She looked down at the thing in her hands. "How's it work?"

"How's it work?" He ground his teeth together, hating every part of that question. The ignorance of it. The innocence of it.

And the fact that he didn't have a very good answer. "You point it at the other guy and blow him to pieces. Preferably you point it at *several* other guys and blow the lot of 'em to pieces."

She let out an unsteady little puff of air. "It's alchemy, isn't it?" A faint note of queasiness in her voice. "*Bairnsoot.* How do they make it work?"

Lochled leaned closer to her. "You'll have to ask a priest, though I don't think they'll tell. I couldn't tell you how they harness the magic from the ashes"—*The girl . . . my Libby . . . how many others?*—"but when it gets to you, it'll be a push charge. A canister shot." He tapped the breech of her weapon. "You put the canister in there. Then you snap it closed. And then you let it loose."

How many draeids' ashes had he fired through his own Leveler? Had they been little girls or little boys?

A terrible thought—one he'd never had before: *Maybe you've fired Libby's ashes through that wicked thing.*

It almost choked him. Almost made him drop the Leveler from his hands.

Rony was staring at him, dark eyes narrowed. "You all right, hef?"

He grunted, turned from her. "Steady on."

They continued onto the docks, Lochled all out of sorts. This was not how he'd seen the first day of the Fourth Crusade going for him. Tried not to think about it too much, because it seemed like a bad omen.

He scanned the banners that flapped above the heads of men, whose faces took on a feral cast in the sharply angled sunlight. Eyes in shadow. Mouths tight, but teeth showing—maybe grins or maybe grimaces. Most men wore the clothes that had been on their backs when they'd signed up. Only the Steadmen, captains, lieutenants, and sergeants wore the gray uniforms with their ranks on them.

But every man had a sash about his belly, just above his belt, and the colors of those sashes were the colors of their company. Lochled remembered that his own sash was improperly tied—a bit of hasty fumbling when he'd awakened underneath a tavern table. He held his Leveler in front of him to hide the haphazard knot.

He found his company banner—blue, with a white stripe in the center, just like his sash—and headed for it. He took a glance at Rony's waist and shook his head.

"You'll need a sash. Like mine. Everyone you see wearing those colors is in your company. If you ever need to find your company, just look for those colors. You know what they mean?"

"Blue and white," Rony observed. "House Brytan . . . *Fifinger*! Is Brun Brytan our commander?" Her eyes were wide, as though having such a legendary figure as her commander could somehow save her from being chewed to shreds on the beaches of Leftland.

Lochled gave her a mean laugh. "Brun Brytan is an old man now, and he hasn't left Rumlith since he got back from the Third Crusade." They said the tragedy of that ill-fated expedition had broken his spirit. Lochled could sympathize, though he left that out. "No, our commander will be his Steadman, Gunnar Thaersh. I've not met the man. They say he fought well in the Third."

Everyone fought well in the Third Crusade. Unfortunately, the Leftlanders did what no one thought they could do, and fought better.

They drew up to their company. Sharp little eyes watched them, glancing over Lochled with deference to his stripes, but landing on Rony and sparking something ugly, like a dog that's seen a rabbit. Swearnsoot, but they hadn't even left port and they were already turning to animals.

"Now, you listen," Lochled growled at her, lower now that he was within earshot of his company. "I can vouch for only one man in my squad. One of our shieldmen: Cryer. I fought in the Third with him, and in the Pan. You can trust him. The rest of them I only met last week. Treat 'em like you would wild dogs. Because that's what they are."

The Brytan Company was a thin measure of Steadmen and retainers from Rumlith poured into a barrel of ruffians from Feor knew where, who might've been sheepherders or carpenters, or pirates and brigands. There was no way to know when a man made his mark to enlist. But really, if it weren't for the fact that he had a young woman crammed into a squad where she didn't belong, Lochled would have liked the meanness of them. The meaner linemen were, the more likely they were to survive.

Lochled found a hole in the ranks where he was supposed to be, sidled up to it with Rony close behind, and found Cryer gazing down at him from his lofty height.

"Oh, *now* he shows," Cryer remarked. The massive, brown-skinned Drugothan leaned against his heavy greatshield, cheek bulging with a wad of scaef. His black eyes caught sight of Rony. "And with what? What's she supposed to be?"

"Leveler," Lochled said, pushing Rony into the ranks.

Cryer chewed twice, looking Rony up and down, then spat between his boots. "If you say so."

"Name's Rony," the young woman offered.

Cryer ignored her. "Don't care. You'll be dead in . . . how long is the sail, Lochled?"

"Five days."

"Five days, then."

"Probably," Lochled agreed. "But you and I, we're going to keep her alive until then, uh?"

"If you say so."

Rony seemed confused. "Are we expecting sea battles, then?"

Cryer grunted. Spat again. "We're expecting you to get raped and thrown overboard." He turned hard eyes on her, voice going low. "See, the New Laws made it punishable by death for a man to rape a woman who's supposed to be his comrade. But all that law accomplished is, now, after they're finished passing you around, they slit your throat and get rid of your body. There's progress for you." Cryer chuckled, shaking his head. "Ever onward we strive."

Rony's lips narrowed tight, like someone had drawn purse strings around them.

He tried not to see his daughter in that expression. It didn't work.

Lochled cleared his throat. "You got steel, Rony?"

"I've a knife."

"Good point? Honed blade?"

"Yes, hef."

"Keep it in your waistband. Stick by me and Cryer, but should you get separated, don't suffer any man to lay his hands on you. Anyone looks like they might be going that way, you stick 'em good, just like you would a hog."

"Are you trying to frighten me away?" Rony snapped. "Is that what this is?"

Lochled was genuinely taken aback. "Frighten you? No, cully. Just don't want you blind to the truth."

"Man trying to stick his pintel in you?" Cryer added. "That's the least of your worries. Now, the Tickers and their stone throwing? Those you should worry about."

Rony seemed like she couldn't decide whether to get mad or take them seriously. But eventually she stooped and discreetly drew a short knife from her worn boots. Brought it up and slid it into her beltline.

The horns blared again, this time three long blasts. Swearnsoot, but Lochled hated that sound. It never stirred his blood. Only made him cringe. Almost embarrassed for the fool blowing his cheeks out to make the damn noise, all martial pomp and bluster.

The simmering ranks of men quieted, but only slightly. Necks stretched trying to see over those in front, up to the top of the docks, where the Brannen's colors whipped in the wind about the dais they'd erected just for this occasion. The red and black of the Fyrngelts. Normally these grand speeches would be given on the morning of the battle and not five days before. But Morric Fyrngelt would be the first Brannen *not* to accompany his troops on crusade.

A tall shape rose up from the platform. Not the Brannen, one of his Steadmen. Lochled couldn't tell which one. Wasn't sure he could name him anyway. The figure strode to the edge of the dais overlooking the docks and the troops below, cupped his hands to his mouth, and bellowed something that sounded like "the Brannen!"

"Who's this cockabout?" Cryer murmured.

Lochled shrugged. "Some Steadman." Turned his attention to the pesky knot of his sash. He held the Leveler between his knees and set to tying the knot correctly.

A glance up revealed that the Brannen himself had taken the stage. Couldn't barely recognize his face from there. Just the humble white sash of his office, stark against his humble black attire.

"Ah, the Usurper himself," Cryer said, even lower. Slightly treasonous, some might say, though most men in the company likely held the same opinion. "At least the Mad Queen had the balls to sail to Leftland with us."

"He's too much a toy for the Church," Lochled grumbled.

Managed to untie the knot. Glanced back up at the dais, where he spotted the somber figures of the Elders of the Church of Alchemy. Their robes far richer and more ornate than the Brannen himself. Not humble at all.

Rony stood on tiptoe. "Is he making a speech?"

Back to his sash. Was it right over left, then left over right? Or the other way around? It'd been so long since he'd been forced to do it properly.

"If you've heard one martial speech," Cryer observed. "You've heard them all."

"I can barely hear anything." Rony almost seemed in a panic about it.

"Listen to the wind, then," Lochled put in. "It says about as much."

Rony skewered him with a look. "I've never heard the Brannen speak before!"

Lochled let out a long-suffering sigh and straightened, sash again being left to dangle, abandoned. He squinted into the distance, as though that would somehow sharpen his hearing. Morric Fyrngelt stood upon the dais, gesticulating with a sort of consciously regal mix of stoicism and passion. It all looked practiced.

"All right then," Lochled mumbled. "Let's see . . ."

When he focused past the steady burble of distracted conversation all around them, Lochled could just make out the Brannen's voice.

"I look about me at a sea of you," the Brannen was saying. "And I'm told there are many from Drugoth, from Fenland, from Rightsbrim, and from every city in our sacred home of Brymsland. I'm told this, but when I look at you, that's not what I see. I see a hard people. I see honest workers, with callused hands to prove it. I see faces as sharp as the steel in your belts."

Lochled snorted. "He sees an army of the poor and the criminal."

Rony frowned. "That's not what he said."

"It's not about what he said," Cryer said, boredly. "It's about what he means. Strip away the fancy words, and you'll see they're just goldendust on a finely sculpted turd."

The Brannen continued, getting into a rhythm now. More confident, it seemed. "I see not a man here, or a woman there, or a Drugothan, or a Fen. I see the army of the Brannic Empire! I see five thousand people from every corner of Eormun, from every trade and every station, united as one for the common good."

"For greed," Lochled and Cryer chuffed at the same time.

"I'm trying to listen!" Rony hissed.

"I see eyes that hunger for the harvest of progress." The Brannen was pacing now, back and forth. "A progress that has allowed our smiths to forge not only brass and bronze but iron and steel! A progress that has allowed our empire to spread to every corner of the continent of Eormun! A progress that, with the divine guidance of the Church of Alchemy, has allowed us to put bread into the hands of widows and orphans, ease the hard lives of our citizens, give warmth into the corners of Bransport that have been left cold from want, and to shed light into the dark streets so that a mother and her child can walk safely, without fear."

Mostly true, Lochled admitted. *Though he forgot to mention the thousands of draeids that have to be burned to get all that progress.*

"At times, this progress has been frightening."

Downright terrifying.

"It has thrust us into an age that is unfamiliar to us all. Even I look about sometimes and barely recognize where I am."

Lochled couldn't resist: "Because he doesn't belong there."

Cryer sniggered.

"So much has changed, and change is difficult, for it requires that we learn, and adapt. That we seek new resources. There are those that would say we should stay in the past. That we should plant ourselves in the mud and remain immovable, sticking to the Old Ways. But if any of those people could truly see what I see—Food for the starving! Warmth for the cold! Pure water for those that thirst!—then I think that they would know what I know: that forward is the only way. Forward, with the vigor and strength for which we are known and for which we all pride ourselves as citizens of the Brannic Empire!"

Lochled glanced sidelong at Rony, a half smile and a joke on his lips. But she was focused on the words. Seemed bewitched by them. Poor daft girl.

"Nearly one hundred rains have passed since the Church of Alchemy empowered our ancestors with the knowledge to harness the energy that had lived amongst us for so long, untapped, unused, and squandered. It was this shining light of knowledge that allowed the people of Eormun to unite as one, just as I see you all united before me now! We are Feor's chosen people, and he smiled upon us when he led my great-uncle across the Bransmar, to discover a land so full of the resources we so desperately needed."

A land full of Tickers. All the magical ash the Church could ever wish for.

"There have been trying times for all in the years since. The First and Second Crusades live in our memories as glories, but the taste of the Third is stuck on our tongues. Many of you were there for that, and you may think to yourself, How will this be any different?"

Cryer grunted. "It'd crossed my mind."

"And I will tell you how it is different. Because this time Feor is on our side! The wise Elders of the Church told my predecessor not to go, but she went anyway. She sowed bad seed in fallow ground, and she reaped blood and tears as a result. But times change. Things progress. Ever onward we strive! This time, the Church has assured me that Feor is at our backs, pushing our sails true, strengthening our hearts, and tightening the sinews of our arms! This time we go to Leftland prepared, and ready! Our armada is vast, our battlecraft strong and swift, our shields impenetrable, our arms and armor the very peak of what the great minds at the Church of Alchemy have discovered! And before us lies a rich harvest made richer by the fact that it's gone unplucked for so long. You are the reapers, you men and women of the empire! Your scythes are sharp and your minds are ready, your abilities more than equal to the task."

Lochled glanced down at his Leveler. Just another tool for the harvest.

"So put behind you now your love of peace and mercy. Summon up the savage blood of your ancestors and, for once, rejoice that your lineage was so meanly tempered in the crucible of ancient wars! Put aside all thoughts of home, but know that when you return, the women will weep at your feet and proud men will bow their heads in your honor, for what you will have accomplished will pour fresh life into our great empire! The eyes of your fathers and forefathers are upon you! The eyes of your countrymen are upon you! And the hopes and dreams of the downtrodden fly with you on the ocean winds, pushing you ever onward to the greatness of your deeds, and the greatness of the empire that you serve! Onward to the greatest harvest our people have ever known—Swing your scythes, you reapers! Ever onward we strive!"

The applause was more or less genuine. Lochled had to

admit, the last part had sounded less like a monarch blowing wind up his hindshole, and more like a field commander that knew how to rile his men. It almost made Lochled believe the bastard really *was* heartbroken not to be going with them.

Lochled managed to tie his knot in what he thought was the appropriate manner and got in a few perfunctory claps before the applause died out.

Cryer spat. "Right. So, can we go now?"

Lochled hefted his Leveler back into his arms, met Rony's gaze. "What'd you think of your first Brannen's speech? Are you moved? Inspired? Ready to die for the empire?"

Rony seemed to struggle with what to say to that. Lochled supposed he could understand. All this was new to her. And she was framed by two men for whom it had long ago lost all of its luster. He might've let her feel inspired if he hadn't been worried she'd run off and do something heroic because of it.

"I didn't understand all the words," Rony finally admitted. "But I thought it was a nice speech."

From somewhere out there, the voice of Hotsteel bellowed: "Brytan Com-panyyyyyy! *Fo-ward!*"

The mass of men and arms and armor began to move, clank, swagger, tromp and tramp and stamp. A creature all its own, slogging toward doom for many, murder for most, and quiet, haunting regrets for all.

"Yes," Lochled sighed as he fell in with the others. "They're all nice speeches."

CHAPTER 3

Ord Griman, priest of the Third Order, handpicked for this journey by the High Elder himself, squatted over a stinking hole in the front of the barque, with his fine vermilion robes pulled up around his waist, trying to decide whether he should shit first and then spew, or the other way around.

He'd discovered something about himself in the month since the Church had assigned him to the Fourth Crusade: he fucking hated boats.

Strange, seeing as how he'd grown up on them. But the still, black waters of the Fenland marshes were like glass, and the old flatboats he'd grown up on simply skimmed gently across them.

Not at all like the damn ferry he'd taken down the Curnsflow River. That wretched thing had pitched and yawed about, sending his stomach lurching and setting his knees to shaking. And he distinctly recalled thinking, as his pale skin turned green, *Surely the Bransmar won't be as bad as this.*

Turns out the Bransmar was far worse.

Turns out seafaring ships were absolute travesties.

Here he sat, with his white hind end visible to all, becoming increasingly sure that the vomit was going to come first. At this rate, he'd be emaciated by the time they reached Leftland. Between the constant lurching of the vessel and the hellacious stink of unwashed bodies and piss and shit, which permeated every rat-infested corner of the boat, he hadn't been able to keep food down since they'd departed Bransport the day before.

Despite the chill wind of the Bransmar—which did nothing to whisk away the stink—Ord found himself sweating. He kept rubbing at his forehead, because the gentle touch of his own fingers seemed to combat the growing nausea. But not quite enough to keep his food down.

He barely even cared when one of the crew sidled around him, and leaned straight over him to tie some rigging to a post behind Ord.

"Pardon, Theynen," the man murmured respectfully, pretending not to hear the squeak of a fart that Ord had just issued.

The ship hit a heavy swell straight on and seemed to launch skyward. Ord could do nothing to keep himself from toppling except grip the sides of the head on which he sat, and on which Feor knew how many other filthy souls had sat. The crewman jostled into him, his armpits in Ord's face, reeking of spoiled onions.

"Fah!" the crewman grunted. "Steady on, then . . ."

Ord's mouth watered sickly. "Ooooh," he groaned.

The ship started coming down. Down, down, down, while all the bile in Ord's gut came up, up, up. A monstrous roar of wood breaking waves as the ship plunged into the sea again. The hole on which Ord sat, being a straight shot through to the sea below, gave a warning gurgle, and Ord had just enough time to tighten his buttocks before a spray of cold seawater cleaned him out.

And then he spewed all over the deck—and the bare feet of the crewman.

When Ord blinked the tears out of his eyes, gasping and gagging, he was distantly disappointed to see the soggy bits of the single piece of bread he'd managed to swallow for breakfast now adorning the crewman's right foot.

"Not to worry, Theynen," the crewman said with a smile, shaking his foot off like a dog with water on its coat. Then he ground the ball of his foot into the wood to get the worst of the slime from it. "Seas take some getting used to. At least we've a calm day today. Captain says we might hit bad weather closer to Leftland."

"Calm?" Ord balked. "This is calm?"

The crewman moved on cheerily, finishing with his rigging and moving back toward the aft. "It's calm for the Bransmar, Theynen. Not to worry! Only three more days!"

Ord closed his eyes, but found that made the nausea worse. "Three more days," he whispered to himself. Although, in all honesty, it did nothing to help him. Because being aboard this shit-stinking, constantly tossing, barque would seem like a wonderful dream once they reached the beaches of Leftland.

At least that's what Ord had been told. He'd never been on crusade before. He was only twenty rains, and had been a priest's adept during the last crusade.

"Feor, have mercy on your servant," Ord murmured, clasping his hands tight before him. "Grant me serenity of mind and strength of limb—ungh!"

And then he finally managed to offload the baggage he'd been carrying into the sea below.

"Thank you for your sweet mercies," Ord gasped. He hadn't been able to relieve himself for two days, by virtue of the fact that he'd never had to do so with an audience. Had taken him most of the first day to even be able to piss over the rails with everyone milling about.

He was completely empty of stomach and bowel, and at least for the moment, he felt enormously better.

After cleaning himself off with a scrap of frayed rope, Ord descended from the bow of the barque, staggering along with his hand on the rail to keep himself from falling, while the crewmen bustled around him, nodding and murmuring "Theynen" to him as he passed.

The center of the barque, all around the three masts, was filled with the men of Brytan Company. Not all of them, of course. About a third, by Ord's estimate. They took to the deck in shifts, it seemed. Probably to escape the far worse stench below.

They were an undisciplined, ragged lot. Barely any of them wore a uniform. The clothes they did have were old and worn, a mix of hemp and flax and leather in a huddled mass of beige. Their beards were long and unkempt, though they religiously kept their cheeks and the sides of their heads shaved. The better to display their scars, and there were a multitude of them. Ord had yet to pass a single one of them that didn't have a nasty mark on some portion of his face or head. White eyes, mangled ears, crooked noses, and all manner of grisly slashes and puckered punctures.

Their eyes were hard little windows into base little hearts that seemed to beat for only one thing: gain. The promise of riches found abroad. The possibility of getting their name on some trinket leftover from the Old Ones that might turn out to be useful to the Church, and thereby justify this whole miserable episode with a substantial reward.

There was not a man among them that didn't have a flask of drips at his side. They all stank of it, night and day. They chewed bindles worth of scaef, and the rails on either side of the deck—not to mention the deck itself—were crisscrossed with bright red spit. They played dice and bones almost constantly, gambling with bronze fiths and coppers and the occasional cold glint of a silver. They spoke swears and oaths with such fluency that it almost seemed a language all its own. Bawdy jokes circulated through their ranks like a plague, and at night, when they got to drinking in earnest, they'd sing terrible songs about war that made Ord shiver in apprehension of what lay ahead.

And yet, Ord could not summon a single drop of disdain for them. As rough as they were, as coarse and violent and daemonic as they appeared, Ord had to admit that they made him feel safer. He thought of the horrific stories he'd heard about the crusades—the Battle of Halun's Landing, the Scouring of Leftland, the Bloody Tide—and for the life of him couldn't imagine any type of man surviving those things but the type of man he saw before him now. After all, if you're going to journey into hell, you'd best be able to dance with daemons.

Perhaps that was why the Elders had urged Morric Fyrngelt to remain behind.

To either side of the rails and far beyond, the roiling Bransmar was prickly with ships' masts. Seventy three-masted barques, each of them crawling with a company of soldiers—most of them linemen, but some cavalry as well—and four of the seventy devoted solely to the massive Battle Plows and their teams of oxen. Behind each barque was towed one of the newly designed landing craft, with their wide, shallow keels and heavily armored sides. Twenty two-masted war barges lay scattered among the barques, their great, brass siege cannons glinting in the sunlight. The whole fleet churning and splashing their way aleft, the greatest armada ever gathered for a crusade, their sails so numerous and bellied with wind that they looked like a sprawl of low-hanging white clouds.

For a moment, Ord found it so damned impressive he forgot to be sick.

He sidled up to the starboard rails, beside his unusual traveling companion.

Kayna Redstone gave him a glance as he leaned heavily on the rail. He surely looked as wrung out as he felt. She, however, seemed entirely unaffected by the voyage.

"Feeling any better?" she asked in that low purr with which she always spoke. As though every instant were night and they were always in a dim, quiet room together.

"A pinch," Ord grunted. He nodded to her. "You seem . . ."

Well, he was going to say "radiant," but nothing could be further from the truth. She claimed Fareach as her home, but her blood was clearly Haedan. Her skin dark as pitch—as dark as her black Seeker's robes. Hair cut short, almost to the scalp. Large, mysterious eyes that seemed to show a depth of knowledge about everyone else's secrets. As though, no matter who she spoke with, she knew everything about them at the moment they introduced themselves.

Ord cleared his throat uncomfortably. "You seem like you're handling it well."

She gave a minuscule shrug. "I am very far from anything familiar to me. But I take it moment by moment. This moment is a good one: I've just seen a blackfish."

She said it as though it should hold some special import to him.

He frowned. "Oh? Well, they're not exactly rare in the Bransmar. As I hear."

She turned so that she was facing him, one elbow on the rail. She was tall—taller than Ord—and as thin as the rail on which she leaned. "Aren't blackfish a good omen to your people?"

Ord felt the familiar rise of defensiveness come up from his chest. A wellspring that kept on flowing no matter how much distance or how much time he put between himself and

Fenland. It seemed everyone's eyes skipped right over the vermilion robes that he'd worked so hard for and settled on his white face. They called him "Theynen," but behind the words it seemed all they saw was a Fen.

"My lineage may come from Fenland, but they're not my people," he said, trying and failing not to sound sharp about it. "The Fens are primitive and superstitious. They hold to the Old Ways, and pray to Gasric gods. I am a man of the Church. The priesthood is my people now."

Kayna bowed her head slightly. "I meant no offense."

No one ever meant offense, but they seemed good at giving it anyway.

Ord forced a smile. "A blackfish is just a creature of the sea. Nothing more."

"Perhaps," Kayna said. "But I still feel that it is a good omen. And so this moment is still good."

"Speaking of omens might be seen as . . . unbecoming."

Kayna grinned at him, her teeth almost blindingly white in the sun. "Perhaps for a priest. But I am a Seeker. We . . . see things a mite differently."

Ord narrowed his eyes at her. Thought carefully about his next words. He'd never cared for Seekers, with their black robes and their secrets and their insistence on separation from the Church. Made him wonder if they truly believed. He supposed he would need to get more comfortable with them, as there was one assigned to each company on crusade. But still . . .

"Even so," he said, slowly. "The men about us don't see Seekers and Church as separate. They equate the two, and rightly so. It would be best if you curtailed any further religious wanderings and stuck to official Church doctrine. For the sake of the men."

"Oh. Official Church doctrine, then?" Kayna leaned back away from him, raising a single eyebrow. That damned knowing smile on her lips. "And do you stick to the official Church doctrine, Ord Griman?"

If it were possible for his skin to go any whiter, it might've. He swallowed. Felt the urge to bluster, but tamped it down. Perhaps she was only making conversation. Perhaps it was only his guilty conscience that made it feel like she was toying with him.

He managed to keep a carefree smile on his lips, even as guilt curdled in his guts. "I'm a priest of the Third Order, Seeker Redstone. One does not get to my station by flouting doctrine."

Forgive me, Feor.

Kayna raised a single hand in a surrender and seemed to back away from the topic. "Of course, Theynen. I was only conversing. Didn't Beficien say, 'Without doubt there can be no exploration of truth'?"

It nettled him a bit to have scripture quoted to him. "Indeed he did."

"Well." Kayna eyed him for a long moment, then sniffed. "We will speak of other things, then. How are you finding your sleeping arrangements?"

More than happy to diverge from the previous topic, Ord relaxed and grimaced. "You mean a straw mat crammed in with a hundred other sleeping, stinking soldiers? Splendid. Burdens are like a forge to temper the soul, trials like whetstones to hone a man's character."

"There is plenty of room in the captain's quarters."

"A generous offer, truly. But the captain gave up his quarters for a *lady*, not a man. I cannot be so low as to deprive a lady of the meager comforts afforded by it."

She gave him a strange look. "I meant that there is plenty of room for both of us."

Ord's mouth flopped open like a fish in air. He stammered

around for words, then tripped over them when he found them. "That, that, that would be *unseemly*."

She reached a hand out, and for one spectacularly terrifying moment, he thought she was going to lay it on his. He almost jerked his hand back, but then Kayna set hers on the rail, beside his.

Her face seemed guileless for once. Earnest. Her voice even a tad lower than usual when she spoke. "I know that my chastity is safe with you."

"Kind," he blurted. "A kind offer. However . . ." His throat seemed so damned dry now. Like the vestiges of his vomit had thickened into a glue, sealing it shut. "It would still be unseemly. Regardless. Regardless of intentions. Unseemly for a priest to share quarters with—uh—uh—a woman not his wife. Can you imagine the gossip?" He let out a strange titter that sounded like someone else altogether.

Kayna retracted her hand slowly. "True. Men gossip like hens in a coop. Soldiers even more so."

"Fact is," he kept going, the words coming out faster than he could vet them. "I'm a bit tired from my purge, and the little mat belowdecks actually sounds quite nice for a nap." It sounded absolutely dreadful, but he hoped Feor would forgive him this deceit. "I think I'll try to sleep. I didn't sleep much last night."

Really, he simply needed to get away from any place where Kayna could see him. And on a boat, that limited one's options.

He did a weird dance on his feet, back and forth, like he was on the verge of saying something else, recognized that this was a very awkward parting, and then decided that any more words would only make it worse.

So he spun swiftly and—somehow—managed to navigate the rolling deck of the ship and get himself belowdecks without falling on his face.

CHAPTER 4

"You should've painted it in blue," Libby said, squinting at Lochled's work.

Lochled looked down at his daughter. Only six rains, and apparently already an expert on sign painting. She stood there with one little arm crossed over her chest, the other hand perched contemplatively on her chin.

Lochled gave out a small noise of affrontery. "Oh, you think your da's a rich man, uh?"

She looked up at him, gauging how serious he was. He winked, and she gave him a pert little smile. "Blue would be *prettier*."

Lochled sighed, one hand still holding the sign upright on his work table. "And it'd cost me a pretty bit too." He laid the sign down and stretched his back. "Last time I went to market, the man wanted two silvers for a single dip of azurite."

"Gullsnatch!" Libby declared, in a fair impersonation of her mother's frequent rebuke of anyone who couldn't be haggled down to half their asking price.

Lochled chuckled and glanced over to where Marna sat by

the oven, preparing their evening meal. She caught his look with wide eyes and then frowned at their daughter.

"Young ladies shouldn't be so coarse in the tongue," Marna corrected.

Libby looked slightly confused. "But that's what—"

"I'm not a young lady," Marna cut her off with raised eyebrows.

Lochled took a gander at the meal. Four boiled carrots and a loaf of bread. A crock with a quarter pound of butter—now that was the real prize. He gave Marna a suspicious look. "And what'd you call the dairymaid when she tried to take you for two coppers?"

One corner of Marna's mouth drew up. "I called her what she is. And got the butter for one and two fiths."

Lochled smiled at his wife, but he was looking at the bread. One large, round loaf. An X split the center of its brown dome. He didn't bother to ask her if she'd gotten it from the breadlines. It was Church bread, and he knew it. Resented it something fierce, but chose to keep that to himself. No point in souring a fine evening with talk of money. And besides, if Marna had paid for the bread, she wouldn't have been able to pay for the butter.

This was just how things were in Bransport. Lochled missed their country home. He missed his life as a thatcher. He missed his small herd of swine—not them, particularly, but the pork.

Still, things wouldn't always be this bad. He was doing well as a sign painter. Had learned his letters to do it, which he was proud of, and he had a steady hand with a brush. More common folk were learning their letters nowadays, and more and more shops were putting up signs. Things would get better.

But then there was a knock at the door.

"Hef."

Lochled spun groggily awake, glaring. It was all dim wood and stink. Shoulders and hips aching from the hard deck on which he slept. Musty straw scratching at his neck, poking through his tunic.

Rony, crouching there before him, looking like the piss might start leaking out of her ears.

"What?" Lochled growled. "Again?"

Rony jerked a thumb upward. "It's our turn on top anyways."

Lochled grumbled his way upright. "Can't you just go in a corner, for mercy's sake?"

She glared at him. "If I'd a pintel to whip out and piss with my breeches still on, I'd do it. But I don't." A glance about. "Besides. I've got to use the *head*." She said it with a significance that implied it wasn't just piss this time.

Lochled caught the chorus of "Theynen-Theynen-Theynen" a bit too late. A swish of vermilion. Rony jerked, saw the priest standing there, and jolted up, pushing herself to the bulkhead. Lochled hauled himself to his feet, had to hunch over to keep his head from hitting the deck above.

"Theynen," he murmured along with Rony, casting his gaze downward, though he didn't have near the respect that the look implied. Priests were not his favorite people. And this one a Fen on top of it.

He'd expected the priest to stalk by—his bunk was farther down—but the vermilion robes swayed to a stop right there in front of Lochled and Rony's feet.

"Another woman?" the priest said, as though he'd just spotted a mythical creature. "How many *are* there on this barque?"

Lochled lifted his gaze. Took in the man standing across from him. His white skin. His blond hair, cut short. Face shaven clean. Eyes that spooky, light blue that Fens had. It was like he glowed. Like all the light that leaked through the deck above somehow stuck to him.

"Just me, Theynen," Rony said, seeming unsure about whether she should meet his gaze.

The ship gave a massive lurch beneath their feet, and the priest jolted a hand out, grabbing Lochled's shoulder by instinct. The man had stiff legs entirely unsuited for the sea.

Lochled grabbed the priest's arm in a firm grip. "Steady on, Theynen. You all right? Looking a bit green." Lochled felt his face flush—he hadn't meant any offense by mentioning the man's skin. But he could see he'd given it anyway.

The priest swallowed hard. Lips quivered. "I'm fine," he croaked. Looked back at Rony. "There's a lady in black up above. She's got the captain's quarters, and I'm sure she's willing to share." A self-conscious glance away. "She's got a privy in there as well. Should you need to use it."

Rony looked aghast. "You mean the Seeker?"

Lochled couldn't help a slight wrinkle of his lips. Like a dog starting to snarl.

"Yes, she's a Seeker," the priest confirmed. "But she's very welcoming. I'm sure she'll find it no issue to help a fellow lady." He drew himself up, looked down at Lochled's hand, as though he'd just remembered it was there on his arm. He blinked a few times at it. Seemed oddly uncomfortable.

Lochled withdrew his hand. "Pardon, Theynen."

The priest let out a squeaky cough. "Steady on, then." And he turned and marched on—or tried to, though he staggered like a drunkard every time the ship moved.

Lochled waited until he was a good ways down, then whipped around to Rony. "I don't like Seekers."

Rony cocked an eyebrow at him. "You like standing beside me while I use the head?"

Lochled flashed his teeth. Bent, snatched his flask and his pouch of scaef. Realized that Cryer wasn't around and the rest of the squad must've already gone topside. "Come on, then."

They trundled their way to the ladder, the bright square of sunlight shining down from the open hatch. Lochled took a heavy swig from his flask to settle his stomach, then packed his cheek full of scaef to settle his nerves. Rony trailed behind, watching the men they passed to either side like Lochled had told her to, right hand on her belt where her knife was stowed.

Good girl.

Ships generally stank. But being in the thick of it belowdecks, then coming up into the ocean breeze was like stepping into an entirely different world. One with sunlight and airflow and not so much foot and crotch smell.

Lochled got to the top first, spat bright red on the deck, then scanned around. She wasn't hard to find. The only person wearing black. Stuck out like a crow among sparrows. Standing there at the rails and looking out at the sea. Or maybe all the ships.

"What do I say?" Rony whispered as they crossed the deck toward her.

"How about, 'I'd like to take a shit in your privy'?"

"I can't say 'shit' to a Seeker!"

"Why not? Seekers shit too. Far as I know."

Rony stopped a few paces from the woman in black, wringing her hands about what to say, but the Seeker turned around and smiled at Rony as though she'd been expecting them.

"Well. Another lady!" A sly quirk of the brow. "And one that looks like she needs some privacy. Yes?"

Rony looked like she was about to melt with relief. "Yes . . . Theyna?"

"Seekers aren't priests," Lochled grumbled, eyeing the Haedan woman like she might be dangerous.

The Seeker stepped away from the rail and closed the distance between them, mostly ignoring Lochled. She reached out and took Rony's wringing hands in hers, a sisterly sort of gesture. "Seekers do not need titles, cully. Our parents gave us names and those work just fine. Mine is Kayna."

"Kayna," Rony repeated. Then stammered out, "Mine's Rony."

Kayna the Seeker pointed to the aft of the ship. "You know where the captain's quarters are, Rony?"

"Yes . . ." she seemed to struggle with not adding a term of respect.

Kayna smiled with those bright white teeth. Lochled had never seen teeth so clean and straight. It was almost a marvel. He caught himself staring. "Take your time, then."

Rony wasted no more words but pointed herself toward the captain's quarters and started off, moving with purpose. Lochled spat off to the side and dipped his head as he started to follow. "True thanks."

Kayna held out her hand. "You'll stay with me."

Lochled stopped, staring at that hand. "Oh?"

"She's safe in the captain's quarters. We can see the door from here. Let the girl be alone for a moment. Solitude is a rare commodity on a ship."

"Hrm." Lochled wasn't quite sure what to do with himself now that he wasn't watching after Rony. Eyed the men on the deck. Caught sight of Cryer, deep in a game of bones. He saw Lochled and waved him over. Lochled shook his head. The Seeker had said to stay with her. And while he didn't care for Seekers, she still was far above his station, and Lochled was a man that followed the orders of his betters. "So . . . uh . . . something you need from me?"

"You don't like me," Kayna said, as lightly as though she were observing the shape of a cloud. "No . . . you don't like *Seekers*."

Lochled considered denying it. But Seekers were a spooky lot. They knew things.

Then again, it seemed rude to come out and say it, especially to someone over you. So he stood there silent. Silence was always a good choice.

"Had to give up a loved one, then?" Kayna asked.

Lochled's throat thickened. A dull ache somewhere way back behind his eyes. Maybe in his brain.

"Ah, but yours is a special sort of dislike. Isn't it?" She had a way of speaking. All feathery and soft, like they were sharing a bed. "It must've been your child. A son?"

"Daughter," Lochled husked. Spat. Some of it dribbled down his chin. He wiped it brusquely with the back of his wrist.

Kayna was silent for a moment. Lochled could feel her looking at him, like her eyes were little pikes jabbing at him.

"What was her name?"

Lochled felt a flash of anger, hot and sudden. If it hadn't burned so hot, it might've lasted long enough for him to get his axe right between that skelpie's eyes. But when he spun, he looked at her, even while his hand was sliding along his belt toward his steel. And looking at her snuffed it all out.

For some reason, he'd pictured her smiling at him, taunting him. But she didn't look happy at all. Looked saddened.

Lochled felt his throat work, trying to summon his voice up to do its job. "Pardon me, Seeker. But your kind already took her from me, body, mind, and spirit. I'll not share her memory with you as well."

Kayna bowed her head slightly. "That is . . . understandable. I will say only this: hunters hunt; fishermen fish; and Seekers seek. And we find. That is our reason for being." Then she surprised him, like a well-trained fighter might parry a blow and sink their knife into you in the same move. "What's yours?"

"What's mine?" Lochled repeated, dumbly.

"Soldier is just a fancy word for killer, and killers kill, just as sure as wolves hunt deer. Is that your reason for being? To kill?"

Lochled's eyes narrowed. "Not today. Three days' time? Yes. And long after. But today? Today my purpose is to keep all the wolves around me from hunting a little doe called Rony. Drink and chew scaef to keep my mind from running off into what's next."

"Ah, a man who lives for the moment."

"The moment's all you got. We killers learn that quick. Those that don't lose their minds."

Kayna smiled, as though to tell him his jab had been well received. She turned and held her arms out to the sea. "But if you could be anywhere else in the world, where would you be?"

Back at my country home, thatching roofs, with my family still whole . . .

"I'd be right here," Lochled spat. "Which is why I signed up in the first place."

"Really?" Kayna lowered her arms and looked at him over her shoulder. "Most men pine for their homes when they're away at war."

"And they pine for war when they're away at home. But you got to have a home if you're going to pine for it."

"So you've no home?"

He looked away from her again. "There a reason you want to know so much about me, Seeker Kayna?"

"No," she admitted. "You've got scaef and a flask to keep your mind from running in circles. I've got neither. This is how I occupy myself on journeys—learning about the people I'm traveling with. You'd be surprised how fascinating even the most common man can be."

"Glad I could entertain you for a while, but I'm afraid

you've scraped the bottom of how interesting I am. You got me all pegged down. Know me like my own mother."

"Hardly."

"I'm a simple man."

"Men that call themselves simple rarely are."

Lochled searched for an escape, and found it in the form of Hotsteel, stalking up to the quarterdeck. Lochled turned to Kayna and gave her a bow of the head. "Pardon me, Seeker. I've been trying to find my captain all morning. I have . . . things to go over." And, not able to resist a parting shot: "Soldierly things. About killing and such."

Kayna smiled brilliantly. "Of course you do."

Lochled turned and strode to the aft, muttering under his breath, "Spooky fucking Seekers."

On the quarterdeck, Hotsteel and the ship's captain had huddled in a sort of urgent conversation. The ship's captain, an old gray-bearded man with the odd, goggly eyes and flat features of an Auldlander, pointed back at the sea, or perhaps one of the other vessels. Hotsteel looked, then went back to talking, his youthful face clouded into something very much like his father's glowering visage.

Perhaps now wasn't the best time to interrupt, but Lochled had now committed himself. So he mounted the steep stairs to the quarterdeck and paused there, waiting for Hotsteel to notice him.

"Very well," Hotsteel was saying. "I'll notify the Seeker and have her confirm."

"Is a bad omen," the captain said quietly. "Dunna tell the men. It'll take a fight right out of 'em."

"You handle the ship," Hotsteel said. "I'll handle the men."

He turned, hesitated when he saw Lochled standing there, then frowned. "How long have you been standing there?"

"Long enough to know there's trouble. Not long enough to know what it is."

"Rumors," Hotsteel said. "Just rumors at this point. I'm going to have the Seeker make contact. We'll know for sure after that. What did you need?"

"Well, I was trying to escape the Seeker, but it seems that failed." Lochled fell into step with Hotsteel, now moving back toward Kayna.

Hotsteel smirked. "I'll dismiss you before we get there. Ship's captain says there's bad weather been spotted alefts. Been chasing us since Bransport. Might hit us tonight or tomorrow. So enjoy the sun and fresh air while you can."

"What're the rumors?"

Hotsteel simply shook his head. "Nothing you need to worry about, Lochled. They won't affect our landing, and we've still got a job to do. You stay focused on that."

Lochled sighed. "You won't tell us until after we take Halun's Landing."

"No, I won't."

"The rumors might become more distracting than the truth."

Hotsteel stopped, a pace or so away from Kayna, and gave Lochled a hard look. "As of now, there *are* no rumors on this ship. Unless you start them."

Lochled shrugged. "Oh, then. Never you mind it. This ship will remain clean of rumors, and if I spot one, I'll be sure to smash it underfoot."

"Good man." A glance sideways at Kayna. "That'll be all, Sergeant Thatcher. Steady on."

"Steady on." Lochled nodded, and deftly slipped away.

A cry went up from somewhere in the huddled masses of men—a shout of victory, and a moan of defeat, as someone took a game of bones and all the coppers that went with it.

Lochled snapped his gaze in that direction out of instinct, even as he registered the door to the captain's quarters opening and Rony stepping out.

By the time he dismissed the gambling commotion as harmless, he had only enough time to swing his gaze back toward Rony and see the two men that'd been lounging in a spot of shade near the captain's quarters. Not even men, really. Just two boys, no more than fifteen or sixteen rains, their beards just wispy, scraggly things around their mouths. Maybe that's why he hadn't taken note of them before.

One moved up behind Rony, not in any particularly aggressive fashion, maybe just wanting some attention from a girl. But he chose the wrong one.

He laid his hand on her shoulder with a cheery, "Hullo, cully . . ."

And Rony spun, doing exactly what Lochled had told her to do—she buried her knife to the hilt in his gut.

"Get off me!" Rony shouted, completely needlessly, as the boy was already backpedaling, hands clutching at his belly, eyes gone all wide and fearful, mouth wheezing like he wanted to scream but didn't have the breath for it.

"Rony, no!" Lochled snapped, far too late, grabbed her wrist, as though he could somehow wind back the moment and keep the glinting sliver of steel from stabbing the boy.

The boy found his breath, just as his friend grabbed him up before he toppled. "You fucking skelpie!" he seethed, the words starting low and husky and ending in a high-pitched squeal, the crack of his voice driving home that he wasn't a man at all but just playing at one. "Aah! She fucking stabbed me! I'm fucking stabbed!"

All at once, the deck of the ship turned into a roiling mess. Squadmates of the two boys were rushing in, all yelling, their hands on their axes, some of them with long-knives already drawn, half their attention on Rony, half on Lochled.

Lochled mushed Rony backward with his left hand, drawing his axe with his right. Caught sight of Cryer and the rest of his squad charging through the tumult of bodies, not knowing what the hell was happening, only seeing their sergeant in the middle of a bad situation.

It all became a rush of noise—too many people yelling, the stuck boy screaming—so that it seemed no one was making any words, or at least none that Lochled could understand. He brandished his axe, bawling at the boy's squadmates to get back, red scaef juice dribbling down his beard like he'd been gut-stabbed himself.

One of the men wasn't having it, seemed intent on targeting Lochled. All Lochled could see about him in the moment was his mean little eyes and a miserly pucker of a mouth. The man had both his steels in his hands—long-knife underhanded, axe held at the top of the haft, ready to slash and parry. Lochled saw Cryer coming in strong, his own axe in hand, ready to take the other man's head off.

"STAND DOWN!" Hotsteel's voice shot through the chaos like a blast from a siege cannon—a surprising depth of fury in it for a man so young.

No one really stood down, so to speak. The steel remained out, glinting dangerously in the sunlight, but everyone froze to the spot where they were, and a weird quiet came over the whole crowd of them.

Except for the stuck boy. He kept on hollering.

"Who is that?" Hotsteel bellowed, slamming through the men with all the rage of a soldier sacking a city. He shouldered Cryer back from the man he'd been about to murder, then grabbed that man by the back of his collar and heaved him away from Lochled, sending him staggering back into his squadmates. "Who—is—yelling!"

The man with the puckered mouth thrashed himself back upright after being tossed by Hotsteel. "Our man's been stabbed by that skelpie!"

Hotsteel stopped in the midst of it all, hands up, a palm to one side and a palm to the other, keeping the two groups of men from slaughtering each other simply through the force of his presence. He looked at the man with the puckered mouth. "It's Breakwood, yes?"

"Yes, hef," the man said, weasel's eyes snapping from Hotsteel to Lochled and back again.

Hotsteel turned and looked at Lochled and saw no denial of the facts from him. Looked at Rony next.

"I . . . I . . ." she stammered.

The very faintest glimmer of pity in Hotsteel's eyes—so fast that Lochled thought he might've imagined it. "Quiet now, cully," he husked, then looked over to where the boy and his friend were huddling, the stuck one now sunk down to the ground, staring at his bleeding midsection like he was fascinated by it, his screams gone to reedy little gasps.

A brief moment of silence. Just the sea breeze and the splash of the waves. Lochled's eyes scanned rapidly about. Caught Cryer's gaze. Saw deadliness in it. Readiness to do something, though it didn't seem like he or Lochled knew quite what. Off to the side, the black shape of Kayna Redstone, watching the whole debacle with an expression of faint interest.

"Right." Hotsteel's voice assumed its command again. "Everyone belowdecks! Stow that steel, Breakwood. We don't fight our own kind. Whatever this is stays right here. Any man caught arguing about it belowdecks?" A look in his eyes that made it all too clear why he'd earned his name. "I'll hang you from the rigging myself. *Move!*"

The crowd jumped. Those that had no part in it were quick to be free of their captain's ire. Those that were involved moved a tad slower, as though they weren't quite sure if they were getting away with something. The man named Breakwood in particular. He kept trying to stab Lochled with his gaze. As though it'd all been Lochled's fault.

"Not you," Hotsteel said, laying a hand on Lochled's shoulder. "You stay up here. Rony, you too. And you—" pointing to the boy's squadmate. "Get your man to the doctor. You there! Help him."

And just like that, the deck was cleared of men, save for Lochled, Rony, and Hotsteel himself, Seeker Redstone lurking in the background.

CHAPTER 5

"It's my fault, hef," Lochled started, but Hotsteel cut him off with a sharply raised hand.

"I'll get to you in a moment, Sergeant." His eyes flicked to Rony. "You. What happened?"

Rony's dark skin had turned a strange ashy color, like sun-bleached wood. She still had the knife in her hand. A tiny bit of blood on it—a speckling of it near where her trembling hand gripped it.

"You said to put the steel away, hef," Rony managed, and Lochled was surprised to hear her voice come out with a certain dead levelness. "Should I do that, or do you want it?"

"Why would I want your bloody steel?" Hotsteel frowned. "Put the thing back where you got it and tell me what happened."

Two quick swipes on her thigh. The motion of someone accustomed to quickly cleaning bloody knives. Slaughtering pigs and slaughtering men did, apparently, have some slight relationship. Though Lochled doubted Rony's hands and knees shook this much after bleeding a sow.

She sat the knife back in her beltline. Her movements slow.

Measured. Like she had to think about everything she did. When she had it back in place, she straightened up, arms stiff at her sides, chin up, lips tight, eyes not looking at Hotsteel, but off to the side a bit. Off at nothing in particular.

"Heard footsteps behind me," she said, still in that voice as flat as a sea becalmed. "Heard a voice say, 'Hullo, cully,' and then felt a hand grab my shoulder. Didn't think about it, hef. Just knew."

Hotsteel's eyes narrowed a bit. "Knew what?"

"Knew he was . . . he was . . ." Her tongue darted out, about as dry and ashy as her lips. "Going to try to take me."

Hotsteel's frown deepened with incredulity. "So you stabbed him?"

Lochled knew he'd been ordered to stay quiet, but he couldn't let Rony tell the captain why she'd done it. It would never make sense to Hotsteel coming from her mouth. Not until he knew the why of it.

"It's my fault," Lochled repeated. "I told her to do it."

Hotsteel raised an eyebrow at Lochled. "You told her to stab the boy?"

"No, hef, not him in particular." Lochled took a deep breath to steady himself. "You assigned me a cully in a place where one shouldn't be. You expected me to keep her alive. You know the types of men we have on board. So do I. So I told her if anyone even tried to touch her, to stick them. You know . . . before it turned into anything else."

Hotsteel stood there with his jaw clenching and unclenching, blinking at the two of them. Like their trouble was a speck of dust caught in his eyes.

A whisper of footsteps. A flutter of robes in the wind.

Kayna Redstone was suddenly there, standing to Lochled's right. "Captain, is there any way I can be of service in this matter?"

For a moment, Lochled wasn't sure Hotsteel had even heard her. Then he let a sharp breath out of his nose. "Did you see what happened?"

"Yes."

"And has the girl told it true?"

"She has."

Hotsteel finally turned and looked at Kayna. "And did you see the boy she stabbed?"

"I did."

"And what do you think he was doing, running up behind her and grabbing her like that?"

Kayna's lips turned down at the corners. Like an upside-down smile. She looked at Rony, almost apologetically. "What I perceived, and what Rony perceived, may well be two different things, and neither any less true than the other. Rony perceived an attack, because she was told that it was coming, she was primed and ready for it this whole time." Kayna looked back at Hotsteel. "What I perceived was a silly boy who thought he could win a girl's attention with a poor show of acting rough and manly."

Hotsteel's lips pulled back, his bottom teeth showing. He hiked his hands to his hips and seemed again to be at a loss for how to proceed.

"If you would like," Kayna continued. "I can keep the girl in my quarters. That will give you time to gather your thoughts and make a sound judgment."

Hotsteel gave her a hooded look. "She won't disturb your . . . work?"

Kayna smiled and swept gracefully between Lochled and Hotsteel, hooking an arm through Rony's as though they were two friends going for a stroll. "I think our young cully is in a rather pensive mood at this point. I don't think she'll be very distracting at all."

And without waiting for any sort of confirmation, Kayna led Rony, following like a stunned animal on a leash, into the captain's quarters, and closed the door behind them.

The girl named Rony didn't say much, but Kayna Redstone heard plenty. That was the curse of her kind—to always hear, but to never speak of it. To take their secrets to the grave, lest the grave came for them all.

All in all, Kayna thought the girl handled herself very well, considering it was her first time putting blade to human flesh. As Kayna guided her into the captain's quarters, hands on Rony's shoulders, she noted that the girl didn't tremble. A glance at her face told Kayna that this little cully kept a tight grip on her emotions—or at least how they expressed themselves on her features. Just the tiniest little wrinkle between her slightly furrowed brows, a cinch of tension in her lips.

Ah, but her thoughts. Well, those ran as wild as panicked horses.

Kayna removed her hands from Rony's shoulders as she detected a whiff of resentment in the form of a fleeting image: Rony, jerking her shoulder away. An imagined action that Rony forestalled on account of not wanting to seem impertinent.

"Would you like to sit?" Kayna asked, gesturing to a small chair.

Rony took a long time to answer. Probably took her a long time just to realize a question had been asked. Rampant emotions could be distracting like that, Kayna knew. She waited patiently under the deluge of Rony's thoughts.

In truth, it wasn't that Kayna *heard* the thoughts, but more that she felt them. And the feelings came with images—some of them from Rony's mind, but also some from Kayna's own. And that was another difficulty in being a Seeker, besides the secrecy: learning to differentiate between the two. Learning to interpret your own thoughts in the light of another's emotions.

The knife into the belly—well, that image was damn near constant, looping around and around in Rony's mind. But with it, a feeling of disbelief—which conjured in Kayna's mind a scene of waking up in the middle of a dusty wasteland of parched and cracked rocks. A memory from Kayna's own past. But the interpretation was in the emotion behind it: *How the hell did I get here?*

"I'll stand," Rony finally said. Even as Rony imagined herself collapsing into the chair. And then imagined Kayna sneering and thinking her weak.

Kayna smiled wanly. "Well, I believe I'll have a seat myself." She moved to the other side of a small table and settled herself into an identical chair across from Rony. The girl was watching her hard. Kayna sighed and shuffled her shoulders, as though to release tension. "Things like this always stir me up. I'll wager a hard cully like you would think that a weakness in someone like me."

Rony blinked a few times. "No, Seeker. Not at all. And I'm not hard."

"No?" Kayna arched her eyebrows and laced her long fingers in front of her. "And why not?"

"First man I ever killed." Rony's words came with a wave of that same disbelief, along with many other things. Shame prominent among them. But not shame of what she'd done, really, because when the emotion struck, it wasn't the boy that she was thinking about. It was an old man with hard eyes, glaring down at her, speaking sharply to her.

That thought had a familial patina to it. Too old to be a brother. Her father perhaps?

"You've not killed him yet," Kayna sighed. "So rest yourself on that count. He'll live a while longer, though I doubt the beaches will be forgiving to wounded men."

Rony's throat bobbed. "I'll have that sit now."

Kayna only nodded.

Rony slid stiffly into the chair, her hands clasped tightly in her lap.

"Would you like a drink?" Kayna offered. "I've only water, though I'm sure you'd prefer something harder."

Rony did want it, but shook her head. "I'm all right." A long pause. Kayna let her have it, as she was clearly wrestling with whether to say what Kayna already knew she was going to say. "Is it true? What you said?"

"What part, dear?" Another difficulty: always having to feign ignorance.

A flash of a grimace. "About the boy not wanting . . . About how he only wanted to impress me, and weren't going to . . . you know . . ."

"Ah, well, one can never be certain of the mind of another." Though Kayna was certain enough. "I said what I said to keep the peace."

Rony's eyes narrowed. "And make me look a murderer and a half-wit."

A bolt of panic came from Rony the second the words left her mouth. But she had the spine to stick by them, even as she was suddenly terrified of some thunderous response from Kayna.

Oh, but she is a hard one, isn't she?

Kayna smiled to show she bore no offense, then leaned forward and rested her elbows on the table. "Not yet a murderer, as he isn't dead. And if he dies on the beaches, well, that'll be the fault of the Leftlanders. As for you being a half-wit? Anyone who looks can see that you're not, and it's best not to mind the ones that don't bother looking."

Rony glowered at the deck between her boots. "They'll think me a scared little girl."

Kayna laughed, drawing a sharp look of surprise from Rony. "My dear, they already think that. Why disabuse them when it works in your favor? A scared girl is easy to forgive—which saves you from swinging from the ship's rigging. A hard woman is an alien thing to them. And we know how men handle things that are alien to them."

Rony sat very still for a time, watching Kayna intently, her thoughts picking through everything the Seeker had said and finding it true, albeit humiliating. "How do you know these things?"

Kayna settled back into her chair, still smiling disarmingly. "Time and observation, Rony. That's all."

"Why are you here?" Rony asked quite suddenly. Sudden enough that Kayna didn't see it coming. "I mean, why are any Seekers here? It can't be for finding draeids—I hear they're all draeids in Leftland."

Kayna nodded once. "We provide a means of communicating quickly across long distances."

Rony tilted her head to one side. "How?"

Kayna only shook her head. "Secrets, my dear. Secrets. How about that water? Your lips are looking quite dry." Another challenge, but one that Kayna was skilled in overcoming: the constant need to deflect.

Deflect and feign ignorance and speak in riddles and never, ever, tell the truth. For the truth, once told, would lead every Seeker to the grave.

Or, more correctly, the Burners.

"Ten lashes," Lochled said, staring out at a midnight sea. The deck was quiet. No one allowed up top now but the crew themselves and Lochled's squad, who, in a huddle to the port side, tried to figure out what they were going to do.

Out there, the Bransmar shimmered in the low light of a million stars. Aleft, the sky was clear and perfect. Aright, shrouded and black, the water and the sky indistinguishable from each other. Seemed the storm that had been chasing them from Bransport was going to catch up to them after all.

There were nine of them in all. Ten, had Rony been there, but she was still sequestered. Ten was the usual number for a lineman's squad. Two shieldmen. Two Levelers. Two polearms. Four heavies. Those were numbers that mattered to Lochled. They were numbers that mattered to any sergeant. The numbers of survival.

The two Levelers were Lochled and Rony, should she survive her sentence. Otherwise, they might be hitting Leftland with just one—him.

Cryer was one of the shieldmen. The other was Ponts, a big Brymic boy from Denesburg. They had to be big on account of the massive greatshields they carried. Usually didn't even pull their steel unless things really went bad. Lochled wasn't so sure about Ponts. He seemed too mild to be a man at war. Would've maybe been better as a blacksmith. Lochled realized he'd already marked him off in his mind as dead.

The polearms were brothers. Trut the older, and Wen the younger. Stringy bastards from Rightsbrim. They'd been in the Pan same time and place as Lochled, apparently, but different companies. He'd heard of their work, and others vouched for their fighting. But Lochled didn't care for their hearts. They seemed like men that only did the right thing if there was something to gain from it. They'd probably survive. The nasty ones always do.

The four heavies were a mix, and Lochled knew the least about them. A pair of Brymics, like Lochled and Ponts, though he couldn't recall where from—Gonder and Effel. One Lochled remembered, on account of he was a Fen, and small to boot. They called him Licker. And the last was Jory, another one that Lochled had written off as soon to be dead, as he was far too old to be going to war. Had at least ten rains on Lochled himself, and Lochled was no spring buck. Jory was of indeterminate blood—light eyes and hair, like he might have some Fen in him, but darker skin, like there might be some Drugothan as well. Lochled wasn't curious enough to ask him. No point in getting to know someone who was going to die in the first ten minutes of fighting anyway.

And he was trying to figure out which one of these bastards would carry the second Leveler. Because he'd also written Rony off at this point. The polearms would be the least useful tools. But Lochled didn't like the idea of Trut or Wen having a Leveler in their hands. He couldn't spare either of his shieldmen. Which left the four heavies, but they were the most useful in the close-in stuff that Lochled anticipated once they got into Halun's Landing.

His unpleasant arithmetic was interrupted by a long, low growl from Cryer.

"Tiny little thing like her?" Cryer said. "Ten lashes'll kill her."

"Depends on who gives the lashes," Trut observed, spitting over the siderail. "Gonna be you, hef?"

Lochled nodded. "But I can't go light. Hotsteel would notice."

"Seems a big fuss for nothing," Ponts said in that slow, ponderous voice of his. Ponts the Ponderous. "The boy didn't even die, did he?"

"He didn't," Lochled confirmed. "Which is why it's lashes and not hanging."

"One man out of the fight already," Cryer mused. "And they make the matter worse by stripping the skin off our second Leveler's back. Puts us all at a disadvantage. Hotsteel seems an honest captain, but it's bad strategy."

"Got to maintain order," Lochled said.

"And appease the boy's squadmates," Wen put in with a knowing glint to his eyes.

Lochled nodded. He might not like the man much, but Wen was still right.

"But . . ." Wen stretched his arms out, languid, like a cat rising from a nap. Leaned on his polearm. "We all knew she was going to die on the beach anyway. Why not add some lashes to her back and keep the peace between the real soldiers? Makes sense to me."

"Mmm," Trut agreed. "If she don't die from the lashes, she might be laid up. Might not even make it on the landing craft with us." He winked at Lochled. "Give her some good strokes, you might even save her life."

"Now it might be my primitive ways," Licker announced, lounging against the siderail and looking down at his fingernails, which he was trimming with a knife. "But we Fens, ignorant pagans that we are, at least *try* and stick by our kind."

"We are sticking by our kind," Trut said, leaning toward Licker. "Men. That's what kind we are. She never was one of us. You wetfoots might let your women fight your battles for you, but that's not how we civilized folk do it in Brymsland."

"That so?" Licker still hadn't looked up from his nail trimming. "Pardon my feeble wetfoot mind, but I don't think we're in Brymsland anymore."

"Steady on," Lochled cut them off. "Let's not turn one stupid fight into two. Now I didn't call you all up here to listen to your brownspill. In a way, Licker's got the right of it. So does

Cryer. We might not like a cully in our squad, and yes, she might be dead soon enough anyways. But I've every intention of trying to get into Halun's Landing with a full squad. Rony might not be what we wanted, but she's one of the squad, and that means I need her on that Leveler come landing day."

"She won't with ten lashes on her back," Cryer reiterated. "We hit the beaches in less than three days now, possibly sooner if that storm behind us gives us a push. She won't be healed by then."

"How many lashes do you think she *can* handle?" Lochled mused.

Cryer snorted. "On that little skelpie? Ten lashes is nine too many."

Lochled's stomach did an unpleasant little flip-flop. "Same as I was thinking. Right, then. I'll give her one lash so the boy's squad can see her blood. Hearing a cully scream might settle their angers a bit." He swallowed. Hated it. But he'd known it was shaping up this way. "I'll take the rest of the nine lashes myself. Cryer, you'll give 'em to me, and no dandying about with it. You give 'em hard and true."

Cryer stared at Lochled for a long moment. Leaned forward slowly. Let a stream of red out of his mouth. "If you say so, hef. But it seems you're trading five fiths for a copper. She takes the lashes, we're down one Leveler. You take the lashes for her, we're still down one Leveler, and a sergeant as well."

Lochled gruffed, trying not to think about the slash of pain across his back. "Nine lashes won't put me out, Cryer. What kind of feebling do you take me for?"

"Maybe not out," Cryer admitted. "But not fully in, either."

"Back in Fenland—" Licker began.

"Piss on fucking Fenland," Trut murmured.

Licker gave no reaction. "Back in pissed-on fucking Fenland, the wic is family. It's all you got. Kind of like this squad here. That means you share everything between yourselves. The good and the bad." Licker finally seemed to get his nail properly trimmed and blew off the edge of his knife, twirled it in his palms. "Seems there's ten lashes. Seems there's ten of us."

"What?" Trut came upright. "Take a lash for her? You're tacking in a tailwind, ghosty-boy."

Licker finally looked right at Trut. Smiling. "What's a matter, halfie? Afraid of one little lash?"

"Not in the habit of taking punishment for crimes I didn't commit."

"Ah." Licker wagged his knife at Trut. "You know what it is? You're afraid that little Rony might stand up strong after her one lash, and you might get all floppy kneed."

"Stop," Lochled snapped before the two could spiral any further. "I'll not force any of you to take a lash you don't want to take. It's your call. One lash for Rony, if you're of a mind to. However many are left, I'll take myself."

"We'll split 'em between us," Cryer said.

"I'll take one." Licker winked at Trut. "Lashes don't hurt us ghosties. Just goes right through us."

"I'll take one," Ponts intoned. Ponderously.

Gonder, Effel, and Jory traded glances, then nods. Jory was the one who spoke for them. "We'll all take one."

Wen sighed heavily. "Don't be a flowerman, Trut. I'll take one. But for the sergeant's sake, not for hers."

Trut shook his head, looking skyward. "Fucking madness. This is what women do to men—turn 'em all dumb with honor and such. Seen it happen a thousand times."

"Don't worry," Lochled said to him. "No one suspects you of having honor."

"Good," Trut said, sullen. "And I'll keep it that way." A

sidelong glance at Wen. "But I will take a lash. For you, Sergeant. And so my brother don't forever call me a pintelsniff."

The storm hadn't quite caught up to them by morning, but it was threatening to. Looming large and dark at their backs. In the distance, Lochled could see the gray smudge of rain on the horizon aright.

He sighed. Turned back. Cinched Rony's wrists a tad tighter to the mizzenmast. Leaned in close and spoke low, just a whisper into her ear, so none of the others of Brytan Company standing all about on the deck could hear.

"I'm going to give the lash hard."

She nodded.

"Harder than I give it to the men."

She turned her head. Looked at him. That same defiant look in her eyes that she'd given him back on the docks.

Lochled pretended to fiddle with her bindings, but was looking right at her. "I'll not have anyone thinking you had the easy part of it. That'll only lessen you."

"Fine," she whispered. "Do it."

"You feel the need to cry out, let it loose."

"I won't."

Lochled doubted that. "Steady on, then."

"Steady on."

Lochled backed off, counting his steps—one, two, three. Shook out the whip in his hand so it flopped on the deck like a dead snake. Looked behind him. Made eye contact with Hotsteel and gave him a nod.

Hotsteel stood in front of the quarter deck, stiff and looking like he'd rather be doing anything else in the world at that moment, and rather peeved about it. "For the crime of severely injuring a fellow companyman, Rony Hirdman, you are sentenced to ten lashes, to be carried out by your sergeant." He looked at Lochled again, gave him a respectful nod. "Your squad has agreed to share this sentence with you. Sergeant Lochled, carry on."

All silent on the deck save for the creak of wood. The tapping of rigging in the wind. Some men stood boredly, eager to get on with other things. Others craned their necks to get a better view of the gore.

Lochled took a deep breath. Twirled the whip. Swung it wide and harsh and brought it down on Rony's back with everything he had.

Snap!

She stiffened. Back hard as a board. A sharp intake of breath. Her feet did a little shuffle beneath her, blood already welling, dripping down her brown skin.

Scream, Lochled thought, urged her. *Let them hear what they want to hear.*

But all that came out of her from the breath she'd taken was a tiny, almost inaudible groan. Like she'd just lifted something heavy. Head tilted back, looking straight up the mast she was tied to. Her right foot stamped once. Twice. And then she relaxed.

Lochled scanned the crowd. Even the bored ones were looking now. A lot of arched eyebrows. Some murmurs in the stillness.

"Swearnsoot."

"That was a man's lashing."

"Did she faint?"

"She's still standing."

Then someone called out, "Good showing, cully!"

"Quiet on the deck!" Hotsteel barked. Sounded angry, but when Lochled glanced back at him, he looked a bit proud. "That's one."

CHAPTER 6

They nursed their wounds belowdecks, while the rain slashed the ship, the waves tossing the vessel about so violently that even the seasoned deckhands staggered a bit as they bustled from place to place.

The only thing on a ship meant to keep water out was the hull. Even with the hatches battened down, the water came through to them in constant streams and dribbles. Men swore and cursed the rain. Those with oil cloaks slung them on and huddled beneath them. Some made little shelters with theirs so that two or three men squashed together could escape under it.

The wood beneath them was slippery with water, making footing even more treacherous. The straw from bunks scattered in the pathways to give some traction soon turned sodden and brown.

Quiet conversations. Outbursts of laughter. The clatter of dice and bones, and muffled arguments over winnings and losses. Sighs and grunts. The occasional belch or flap of a fart. Every kind of smell thick in the air, some pleasant, but more often not. The haze of scaef smoke, warm and tangy. Wet men, not dissimilar from the smell of wet dogs. The grassy scent of the trampled straw. Musty feet, freed from soaking boots. The sharp smell of piss underlaying everything.

Dim and dark, save for the light of a handful of alchemic lanterns that the captain had allowed to be burned swinging from the low ceiling, casting hard shadows that crawled and lurched with the motion of the barque.

Lochled stared at one of those lights, wondering again how it all worked. They said alchemy was science, but to Lochled it might as well have been witchcraft. How many draeids had to die to light a lantern for an hour? He had no concept of it. Could have been ten souls burning behind that glass. Or maybe one was enough to light the dark for days on end.

If he saw that priest again, perhaps he'd ask.

As his gaze drifted back, it caught on another man's. Gazes are like that—prickly damn briars, and the men that held them even pricklier. Took Lochled a moment in the gloom to realize it was the edgy bastard that'd seemed all too happy to split Lochled's head when the trouble with Rony had gone down.

Breakwood, Lochled recalled. Another sergeant. The boy that Rony had stuck was one of his, and he seemed determined to remind Lochled about it with every hazardous glare.

He'd been more than clear on his feelings when Lochled had trailed his squad back belowdecks only an hour before, all of them wincing and walking stiff from the split right down their backs. Breakwood had been lounging up against the rail near the hatch, packing a wad of scaef three sizes too large into a mouth hole three sizes too small.

"Don't think this solves the problem between us," Breakwood had sneered at Lochled as he passed.

Lochled had stopped before getting on the ladder below. Looked at Breakwood. "Judgment's been rendered. Punishment's been meted out. It's over now."

Breakwood only shook his head, spat over the rail. "Not for my boy, it isn't. You putting a stripe across your cully's back don't quite match up to the fact that my boy's laid up, can't hardly stand, and we're only a few days until the landing."

Lochled nodded, trying his hardest to give Breakwood his better half. "If I could've stopped her, I would have. Shame about your boy."

But Breakwood spat again, and this time it landed right at Lochled's feet, and Lochled felt that better half of him sour up mighty quick. "My boy dies in the landing?" Breakwood said. "Me and you are gonna have a debt to settle."

Lochled's eyes dragged their way from the splatter of red spit all the way back up to Breakwood's face. And he tried. He really did. Tried so hard not to let his mind go where it inevitably went. The daemons of his flesh were like mad dogs in cages, and Breakwood was sure rattling them, getting them all riled up so that Lochled was sorely tempted to let them run.

But no. Not on the ship.

So he'd swallowed down his violence like sickening medicine. Kept those daemons locked up where they belonged. For now. "Well. Who knows who's gonna make it off the beaches?" He smiled. "Might be we *all* get slaughtered, uh?" Gave the other sergeant a sharp nod and grabbed the ladder to go down.

"I know who you are," Breakwood snapped at him.

And Lochled froze there on the ladder. Breakwood at his back. His eyes fixed forward, not seeing anything in the real world but something from hell, and he had no fear of it, because it was a hell of his own making.

He almost let them loose. Oh, the temptation was strong, and it's just so easy to flip the latch on those cages—such flimsy things anyway. And the bars are so rusted and crumbling. With only such derelict restraints, it was a wonder to Lochled that people provoked what they contained. But maybe that's because they didn't know.

Lochled knew, though. He knew it all too well.

Standing there, clutching the ladder, Lochled's blood seemed to be screaming in his veins, filling his head with a strange, daemonic keening, and he had to wait for a few seconds to let it quiet down.

"Well, then," he had finally rasped. "Good for you."

And then he'd gone belowdecks, trying hard not to think of murder, trying hard to be a better man than that—but oh, how people were always testing him.

"How's your lash doing, hef?"

Lochled jerked out of his thoughts, and it took a moment for him to focus on Cryer's big face and to actually see it, rather than all the gore he'd just been picturing. Cryer was maneuvering his bulky body around to inspect Lochled's bare back.

Lochled had given out nine lashes. Cryer had given him the tenth.

"Is that what it was?" Lochled remarked. "Thought a bug had bit me."

Cryer sniggered. Lifted the wet bandage. Took a sniff of it. "Clean," he announced. "Smells like a fresh-minted copper."

Lochled glanced about his huddled squad. "Keep 'em clean. Soon as the storm passes, I'll get a bucket of seawater. Salt'll help seal it closed. Clean your hands before you muck about with 'em. Don't want the rot setting in. And don't sleep on your backs. And keep your shirts off—I know it's a chill, but your dirty clothes'll ripen those cuts faster than these pissy floors."

His gaze landed on Rony. "Except for you, cully." He managed a wink, and she managed a smile. "You keep your shirt on."

She wore her tunic draped around her neck so her back

stayed clear but her breasts stayed covered. It would just have to do.

Of all of them, Gonder had been the whiniest about it. He twisted up, grimacing. "How'm I supposed to wear my armor, hef?"

"Like a man, you feebling," Jory grouched. He'd been heavy after his flask. Played at being tough, but he sure was drinking a lot to cover pain he claimed he didn't feel. "Had worse cuts than this from a hundred battles, and fought through them."

"Oh, a hundred battles, uh?" Wen sniffed, rattling a pair of dice in his hands. "Strange, but I hadn't seen a scar on you. Your back looks as neat and sleek as the cully's."

Jory glowered over at Wen. "Tha's 'cause my scars are on the front of me, where they belong. Kind of coward has scars on his back?"

"We all got scars on our backs now," Ponderous Ponts observed.

"Right then," Wen clenched the dice in his hand, smiled meanly up at Jory. "Let's see 'em, graybeard. All these scars you claim."

Jory took a long swig from his flask. Stood up. Tottered a bit. Stuck out his chest, all bespeckled with a mat of graying hair. He started to point at his chest and stomach, though Lochled couldn't see anything but hair. "The Battle of Halun's Landing! Second crusade! And this here from the Third! That's the Battle of the Gulf. And this one's the Battle of Fall's Bluff."

"Fah!" Wen waved at him. "All I see is a wet pelt. Sit down, you old fool."

Jory looked like he might launch himself at Wen, so Lochled cut in smoothly. So much of being a sergeant was like managing children. Very strong children with bad tempers and dangerous weapons.

"You were in the Pan, then?" Lochled asked.

Jory swung his drunken gaze to Lochled. "I was. Under Caltor Fyrngelt."

Lochled gave him a respectful nod. "I was under Brun Brytan." He motioned to Cryer. "Same as him."

Jory swayed there a moment in that drunken way men have, as though they're trying to figure out if a fight is still brewing. Then he threw his head back and laughed. Started swinging his flask back and forth with a rhythm.

"OH! On through the breach, crash through the door! Oh, look! I think that I've been here before. It's already painted from ceiling to floor! Because my Leveler paints it so pretty! Yes, my Leveler paints it so pretty!"

Lochled winced like he'd been stuck. He fucking hated that song. But men down the way didn't, apparently, and a raucous cry went up from further in the darkness: "Sing it! OH, my Leveler paints it so pretty!"

Lochled held up a hand to Jory as the old man took another breath to keep on with the song. "Save it for the landing, Jory."

Jory seemed disappointed. Maybe it was the damp, but the enthusiasm died out quickly in the dimness belowdecks. A few more murmured lines from the next verse, and then all was quiet again. Jory slouched down, mirth gone to melancholy, just that fast.

That was the problem with those old fighting songs, Lochled thought. You sang them and felt wonderfully heady while you belted out the words, but in the silence after, you remembered what it meant, and then it didn't seem so great anymore.

"What about you, cully?" Trut asked, leaning forward to count the numbers of Wen's last throw of the dice. "Been in many battles?" He snickered.

She stared at him for a long moment. Lochled had an urge to step in on that too. But eventually she'd have to prove she was capable of defending herself.

"No," she said. "But I can stick a man."

"Ooooh," Trut sneered. "A boy, you mean."

She shrugged, winced at the motion. "You're right, Trut. I don't know much about war and fighting. You can correct me if I'm wrong, but seems a bit of steel goes as easily into a man's stomach as a boy's."

He turned and regarded her for a moment, smirking, jangling the dice in his hands. "That it does, Little Roan."

"Why did you want to come?" Ponts labored out.

"Didn't *want* to," she replied, a bit snappy. Then quieter: "Had to."

"She *had* to," Wen said, watching Trut's roll. Pointing. "Six-count, you flopfin. Pay me." He glanced at Rony. "Made an oath to your chief, uh? You a Steadman?" He frowned. Looked up. "Stead-woman? Stead-lady?"

Rony stared at the sodden floor between them, eyes lost in something, lips a sad line. "Got two brothers. Both older. Mother and father left us in debt trying to save the farm. Plague came through Ceapsland . . ."

Licker dotted his palms superstitiously. "Blood, tree, and son."

". . . They died, but me and my brothers never got it. Had to sell the entire herd to pay the worst of the debts, but it wasn't enough. Brothers are in debtors' prison now, on a work farm." She took a deep breath. Brought her eyes up. Gaze bouncing around to each in the squad, never lingering, maybe trying to find something in their eyes and failing. "If I can get my name on a Leftlander trinket—a good one, one that the priests want—I might be able to pay them out."

"Ah," Wen gave her a wink. "You and every man in the army."

Licker made a few intrigued noises, fished a wad of scaef from his pouch, and stuffed it into his lip. "That's something my feeble Fenish mind has never been able to grasp. Hef, you might enlighten me." He looked at Lochled. "If the Tickers are so damned dumb, why do they have trinkets that do things we've never seen before?"

"Fuck the Tickers," Jory put in. "Savages."

"Savages, uh?" Licker arched his eyebrows. Spat off to the side. "Savages that have trinkets the Church can't even figure out? Have to ship 'em back home to inspect 'em and break 'em apart and figure out what they do? Don't sound savage to me."

"They're not savages," Trut said, as though everyone else was being a complete idiot and he was the only one with the answers. "They're just not . . . people. They're just low minded. Like something between a dog and a Fen."

"Oh, low minded, are they?" Licker scoffed. "Then how'd they make all the trinkets?"

"They didn't make the trinkets," Wen answered, matter-of-factly. "The Old Ones made the trinkets. We don't know what happened to the Old Ones, but they built everything in Leftland, a long, long time ago. The Tickers were their slaves, but now their masters are gone, they just run around playing with the masters' trinkets and living in the masters' houses and cities. Tickers didn't build nothin' for themselves. They're too dull witted. Hell, they can't even speak."

"But wait . . ." Licker said, looking at the ceiling. "How's Feor get into all this? Because we're supposed to be doing his will, aren't we? That's what the Brannen said in that very pretty speech he gave us. Said the Church had assured him that Feor wanted us to go to Leftland and kill us some Tickers." Licker scratched at the side of his face, one eyebrow up. "But idn't Feor supposed to be all loving and merciful and light and life?"

"Fah," Jory sneered. "All this doubt from a man who holds to Gasric gods? You don't even believe the Church anyways."

"Well, I might," Licker replied. "If anything they said made sense."

"Oh, heresy, heresy," Wen chided. "Shame on you, ya backwards wetfoot. Don't let the priest hear you gabbing on."

Jory swirled up onto his knees, his hands upraised as though he fancied himself a priest teaching to the masses. "Everything Feor made has Feor's light in it. That's our spirit, y'see? But it's surrounded by our flesh. And our flesh can be dark and evil. When the flesh of a boy or a girl is daemonic, that clash of light and dark is what makes them a draeid and gives them powers. And it's our duty to Feor himself to burn the flesh of those draeids—*Bairnsoot*—so that his light can be set free."

Licker was peering at Jory as though he were speaking a different language. "That explains absolutely nothing about the Tickers."

Jory looked at him like he was a fool. "Fucking Gasric pagan. Maybe if you'd ever listened to the Church, you'd know these things. In Eormun, you take ten boys and girls, and maybe one of 'em will be a draeid. In Leftland, damn near half of all the Tickers is draeids. It's our duty as followers of the light to find draeids wherever they might be and put them to the flame. The fact that we're able to use that ash to harness those powers is just lobsters in the crab cage. It's Feor's blessing upon us for doing his will."

Licker appeared mystified for a moment, but then raised his hands in surrender. Looked to Lochled. "Sergeant? What's your take on it, hef? You think the Tickers is real people or just low-minded chattel, free for the taking?"

Lochled looked tiredly at the Fen. "A man with a moral conundrum about killing Tickers shouldn't sign up for a crusade."

Licker shrugged. "Moral conundrums never stopped me from trying to get rich."

Rony seemed inordinately fascinated and was now staring hard at Lochled. "What do they look like though? I never seen one. Is it true that they're just trinkets themselves? All just clockwork on the inside?"

Lochled decided it was a good time to start in on his own flask. Pain of the mind is often more pressing than pain of the body. "I'm not a priest, Rony. There's one aboard. You can ask him."

"I don't think he's ever seen a Ticker either," Ponts said.

"Just want to know who I'll be killing in two days," Rony said quietly.

"*Trying* to kill," Trut snarked. "If they don't get you first."

"Trying then," she snapped back. Then looked pleadingly at Lochled.

Lochled took a long pull from his flask, let the burn go all the way down, hot and uncomfortable, then warm and wonderful. Cleared his throat. "Old rumor. People used to say they was made by the Old Ones to be just another trinket themselves, and that they was all gears and cogs inside, and if you got close enough to a living one, you could hear 'em ticking on the inside. But . . ." Lochled stared at the sodden straw at his feet and saw . . . other things. "I've opened enough of 'em up to know their insides look much like any man's."

Then he drank.

Ord hustled along the deck as though he didn't want to get too wet, even though his robes were already soaked. He staggered into the mizzenmast and clutched at it while the boat felt like it was flying into the sky, then plummeting down. The seas so high and black around them that as the barque tilted from side to side, Ord kept thinking they were going to get swallowed up.

He was gradually becoming inured to the thought of dying at sea. At first it had been abject terror, almost too much to think through. But now, after days of it gone by and no end in sight, the possibility of a watery grave just seemed like something you might shrug your shoulders about.

Still, it did nothing to solve his seasickness.

Face pressed to the rough fibers of the ropes wrapped around the base of the mast, he let out a little burp that smelled of nothing in particular—just the bile in his stomach. But he'd already emptied himself out belowdecks, and the worst of the nausea had receded. At least for a time.

He stared at the door to the captain's quarters, breathing heavily through loose lips all dripping with rainwater and a bit of snot. Desecrated his robes of office by taking the sodden sleeve and smearing it under his nose to get the worst of it.

Right, then. Just another jaunt forward and he'd be there.

He released the mast, staggered sideways, then staggered the other way, like a ship tacking against the wind. Finally the barque hit a valley in the waves and stayed still long enough for him to bumble forward and crash rudely into the door.

Any sense of propriety now abandoned, he pounded his fist on the door. "It's Ord! You called for me!"

He briefly considered just barging in, but before he could, the door swung wide and he fell through, nearly planting his face on the deck, and would have if Kayna hadn't caught him with surprisingly strong arms, steadied him, and slammed the door behind him.

She held him at arm's length, eyeballing him with a note of concern. "Theynen, I don't believe the seas are the place for you."

He stared at her, trying mightily to come up with something clever to say back, but just shook his head. "No. They're not."

"Come in and sit. Get warm."

Warm? He hadn't even noticed it until now, but the captain's quarters were downright cheery. Warm enough to set his robes to steaming. Made him want to shuck them off and dry them out, lady present or no.

The quarters weren't spacious—nothing on a barque was spacious, apparently. It was simply a room. But the only one on the damn vessel. And sealed well from the rain. A tiny leak in the far corner was all he could spot, which seemed a trivial nuisance compared to the waterfalls belowdecks.

An alchemic lantern hung from the center of the ceiling, glowing warm and bright, and a similar brazier in the center of the room, bolted to the floor, emitted a dim red light and blessed warmth. An expensive luxury, but then again, you had to keep warm somehow, and open flames on wooden boats sealed with pitch had proven hazardous in the past.

Kayna strode to the brazier and motioned to one of the two chairs that sat beside it.

A chair! How delightful.

Ord plopped himself moistly on it and leaned forward, cold, wet hands reaching for the warmth of the brazier.

Kayna settled into her own seat. Crossed one leg over the other beneath her black robes. Nestled her hands together in her lap. "News from Bransport," she said, holding Ord's gaze.

Ord grunted. "Good or bad?"

Kayna shrugged. "Suppose that depends on your personal leanings. For our purposes, we'll call it bad."

He waited for her to continue, fingers flexing in the warmth.

"Seems the Mad Queen has escaped her confinement."

Ord's hands froze. Felt cold again. "Escaped? How? When?"

"The same day we left Bransport. As for the how, it seems she had some help from a handful of loyalists."

Ord slumped back into his seat, hands flat on his thighs.

He wasn't quite sure how to feel about this. On the one hand, he'd always had favorable feelings toward Annistis Fyrngelt. He'd never met her, but he somehow imagined her as a kindred spirit—the first female Brannen, overcoming the scorn of so many to rise to the occasion, just as he, a Fen, had overcome the specter of his race to become a priest.

Unfortunately, she'd also rebelled against the Church. Gone off and started the Third Crusade without their blessing, and they all knew how *that* had turned out. They say she'd gone mad—the stresses of war compounded by her abject failure had broken her frail lady's mind. Ord had his doubts about that, but the Elders had confirmed her state and sequestered her for her own health.

He realized he'd been staring silently into the brazier. Dragged his gaze back up to the Seeker across from him. "Are we still continuing to Leftland?" A brief moment of horror, as he imagined this miserable trip being turned around a day from landing, then having to repeat the whole journey in reverse, and all for nothing.

His fears were assuaged by a slow nod from Kayna. "Yes, the crusade continues. The Seekers have been notified and are, as of this moment, tracking her. It appears she has fled into Fenland."

Ord grimaced. Yet another hurdle for him to overcome. If Fenland offered the Mad Queen support, that would be one more mark against him in the eyes of the Elders.

"Does she have friends in Fenland?" Ord asked in his best attempt to sound like he didn't really care all that much.

"That remains to be seen. We suspect she fled there simply to remain out of reach." Kayna leaned forward. "There is some speculation that she may attempt to go to Leftland."

"Leftland?" Ord scoffed. "What could she possibly want in Leftland?"

"The Fourth Crusade," Kayna said, as though it were obvious. "And therein lies our problem, Theynen. Most of the men here fought with her in the Third. Now, no one likes the taste of defeat, but even so, a war fought together is a binding experience. There may be more loyalists to Annistis in our ranks than the Church—or the current Brannen—want to admit."

Ord brought a hand up to his face, rubbed his jaw. "It doesn't help their loyalties that Morric Fyrngelt didn't come along with them."

"No, it doesn't," Kayna agreed. "Many still refer to him as the Usurper. Quietly, of course. But the opinion is still there. And widespread."

Ord narrowed his eyes briefly at Kayna. These damned Seekers. Always knowing things that no one else knew. Or at least pretending that they did. Ord could never decide whether they truly had a handle on so many secrets or if it was all a part of their mysterious act.

"Even so," Ord said. "She can't get to Leftland from where she is. No seaports in Fenland."

"She may continue through Fenland to Rightsbrim," Kayna suggested. "The Caldefoots have always been . . . sympathetic toward her."

Ord was unimpressed. "And then? Rightsbrim's on the wrong side of the continent. She'd have to sail daeside and go by the Haedan River." He shook his head, confidently. "She'd never get through the tolls with everyone searching for her."

Kayna gave him a significant look. "She could sail nyhtside."

The old children's rhyme tittered through Ord's head: *Daeside, nyhtside, cold side, hot side.*

Daeside, past the Haedan River, was a land where the sun never set. And nyhtside, past Fenland, the sun never rose. Daeside was impassably hot, said to be filled with scorched rock and mountains that spewed fire. Nyhtside was impassably cold, nothing but darkness and ice.

Except for stories about a narrow sea lane, just below Fenland—if you were brave enough to take on a shifting maze of icebergs.

Ord found that highly unlikely. "No ship's captain is mad enough to try the Caldegrund Pass."

Kayna sighed. "In any case, speculation is useless. The future is dark and unknowable. But . . . the Church is concerned about her coming to Leftland. And so our plans have changed."

Ord sensed the crux of the issue coming at him. "The crusade will need to finish its work quicker than expected. Did they give you a timeline?"

Kayna regarded him with a cautious eye. "One month."

"A month?" Ord gasped. "I was told three!"

"And now they are saying one."

Ord could hardly summon the words. "It can't be done." He shot to his feet, did a little spin, flinging water droplets across the floor. "You say it all lightly, as though you know what I've been asked to accomplish, but you don't! If you knew, then you'd know it can't be done in one month!"

"Don't be so quick to assume what I know and don't know."

Ord was all burning fury now. Had the opportunity to catch her in a lie, prove to her that all her mysteriousness was just smoke and magician's tricks. He whirled on her. "Oh? Then why don't you enlighten me?" He planted his hands on his hips, leaning over the hot brazier to glare at her, unable to repress the little smile he had at exposing her as a fraud.

Kayna stared at him for a long, quiet moment.

"You see?" he snarled, triumphant. "Seekers don't have any mystical knowledge of the unknown. You just—"

"You're here to see how deep Leftland goes," she sighed.

Ord drew back like he'd been slapped. Mouth quivered about wordlessly for a few haggard breaths.

Kayna didn't look particularly pleased with herself. Almost annoyed. She released him from her stare and chose instead to gaze at the brazier. "One doesn't need mystical knowledge to piece together obvious facts."

"How . . . ?"

"It doesn't matter how. It only matters that it is. Your Church has overextended its use of alchemy."

"*My* Church?"

She ignored him. "They're far past the point of being able to sustain their alchemic works with draeids harvested from the Brannic Empire. They've been past that point for decades now. Which is why they need the Leftlanders. But a wise man doesn't cull cattle for a feast when he doesn't even know the numbers of his herd."

Ord's legs felt suddenly boneless, and he collapsed into the chair, arms limp and shoddy. *How had she known?* But then as soon as he asked himself the question, he knew that she was right: it didn't matter how she'd known. She knew.

He looked at her sharply. "Not exactly the sort of thing the Church wants to admit to a public that's come to rely on everything being powered by alchemy."

Kayna deigned to look at him again. "Secrecy is not something you need to request from a Seeker, Theynen. I only spoke of it because you insisted."

Ord's hands found themselves again. Fingers twisting around each other. "I've been asked to compile a reasonable estimate of the population of Leftland. Which means I need to determine how large of a tract of land it is, and how densely populated. Otherwise, we run the risk of harvesting the Leftlanders into extinction." He looked up at Kayna, all pretense of holy fury gone. Desperate now. Almost hoping she had an idea that was better than his, which wouldn't be hard, since he had no idea whatsoever. "How am I to catalog an entire land in *one month*?"

"We separate," Kayna said, as though she had it all thought out already. And maybe she did, and Ord was relieved. "Take a small escort, and move fast alefts. We don't necessarily need to reach the end of Leftland. We only need to know if there's enough of them. If we happen across more cities like Halun's Landing, then we know there are plenty of Leftlanders—or at least enough to justify an additional crusade once Annistis is no longer a concern."

Ord rubbed his face. Glanced cautiously in Kayna's direction, but somehow felt the urge to not let her see his eyes, so he jerked them away at the last moment. He almost told her about his personal reasons for wanting to go to Leftland—but it didn't seem like the right time.

Will I still have a chance to find it? he worried, chewing at the inside of his lip. Hewing their way hastily across Leftland wouldn't leave him with much opportunity to search for the thing he'd endured all this discomfort and danger for, the goal he'd spent all that political capital on to get his name to the front of the line of priests willing to go on crusade.

How could he possibly track it down in one month's time?

"Oh, everything's turning on its side." He stood up again. "Like a capsizing ship."

"Well." Kayna stood up, moved gracefully to the door. "I'm sure you'll find a way to accomplish everything you set out to do."

Ord grunted, sweeping his still-wet robes about him and preparing for another rain lashing on his run back belowdecks. "Yes. I'm sure."

But he doubted it.

So, Kayna thought, as she settled back into her chair and stared at the glowing brazier. *The priest has secrets.*

She couldn't say she was surprised. Everyone had secrets, perhaps priests more so than anyone, as they were expected to be morally superior but were, in fact, just people. She understood the need to maintain a facade. She'd been doing it practically her whole life.

Ever since she'd found out what she truly was. Ever since she'd learned that not all draeids have the ability to move things with their minds. Some had the ability to read the minds of others. To peer into their souls, and see the truth within them.

Secrets on top of secrets. Everyone holding back from everyone else.

Despite the fact that the Church and Seekers worked closely together, each held things back from the other. The Church had never made known how exactly its alchemists were able to harness powers from draeids' ashes, and the original Seekers, not wanting to *be* ashes, had never made known that they themselves were draeids. Nor did the Seekers offer any hint as to how they were able to find and identify their fellow draeids. The Church was content to use the Seekers for their own ends, and the Seekers were content to keep their lives, and be paid handsomely for it.

Deflect. Speak in riddles. Feign ignorance.

It'd worked so far. But of late the abject lack of trust between the two parties had caused relations to become . . . brittle.

As for Ord, Kayna did not think his secret was a Church secret. Which was both disappointing and fascinating. No, Ord's secret was personal. His mind had been flooded with images of sick and dying people, many of them Fens. And a little village on stilts—what the Fens called a wic—burning brightly, its flames reflected on black, marshy waters.

Something concerning the plague, then?

Kayna steepled her fingers and pressed them softly to her lips, remembering the images and the feelings that had flown through Ord's mind. Devastation. Grief. And . . . betrayal. Betrayal from some quarter of Ord's life. Something very dear to him.

Something wrapped in vermilion.

How fascinating, Kayna thought, letting her eyes drift closed. *And possibly useful?*

Possibly. There was no denying that it would be useful for the Seekers to have an ally in the Church. But Ord was still conflicted—*that* she'd sensed in cartloads. Conflicted, and therefore not yet ripe. But still, there was a *possibility* there.

A priest that feels betrayed, Kayna mused, picking at the idea even as she drowsed. *By his own Church. How very, very fascinating.*

CHAPTER 7

Four boiled carrots. A loaf of bread. A crock of butter.

Thoughts of money—or the lack of it—pushed away because Lochled didn't want to spoil the evening with his wife and daughter by being surly. And besides, things would get better . . .

And then there was a knock at the door.

The sound of it sent a note of alarm humming through Lochled's chest. He glanced at the door, then frowned at Marna. "It's an hour after last lights." It was unheard of to go about knocking on folks' doors after dark . . . unless something bad had happened.

"I'll get it," Libby offered up, scampering toward the door.

Lochled caught her before she reached it. Only had to reach out to do it—his worktable and the stove and the two chairs and stool were all crammed into the same tiny room, barely three strides from end to end. A ladder in the corner led to the small loft where the family bed lay.

"Easy now," Lochled said, pulling her back from the door and staring at it suspiciously. "Don't know who's knocking on doors at all hours. You stand back with your ma."

Libby seemed to finally sense the tension, sidestepping out of her father's arms and into her mother's.

Lochled moved toward the door. Four planks nailed together with a simple drop latch to secure it. A gap nearly two thumbs high between the door and the dirt floor. He'd been meaning to fix that before the weather got cold and the rains came.

His eyes went to the left of the door, where his old long-knife and hand axe were balanced on two wooden pegs. He chose the long-knife and held it in his left hand. Raised the latch with his right hand and pulled the door open just far enough to see out.

A man stood there, barely more than an arm's length from Lochled. That it was a man was the first thing Lochled noted, and it made him tighten his grip on the long-knife, holding it in the usual way—underhanded, with the blade hidden behind his forearm. The second thing he noted was that the man was a bit slighter of frame than himself, and a hand shorter, and Lochled thought, *I could kill him if need be.*

The last thing that Lochled noticed was the black robes.

"Seeker," Lochled uttered in shock, unconsciously opening the door a bit further and wondering if he should offer a bow or a salute. How were you supposed to greet a Seeker? He'd never met one before. Only ever seen them from a distance.

Lochled was entirely flummoxed. Why was a Seeker here? At their home?

The man in the black robes offered the barest of smiles—little more than politeness. "I am Seeker Gehret," he said, his eyes never leaving Lochled's. The glow from the oil lamp on Lochled's worktable glimmered dimly across his tan skin. He was Brymic, but he shaved his face for some odd reason. Dark eyebrows raised, disappearing in the shadows of the hood he wore. "And who are you?"

"Uh—Lochled Thatcher," he stammered out. "But we've no draeids here, Seeker."

That small, polite smile again. Just the mouth. Nothing in the eyes. "May I be welcomed into your home?"

Lochled almost swung the door wide simply out of reflex. A Seeker was comparable in station to a priest, or even a Steadman. The idea of not obliging him was almost unthinkable. And yet, he hesitated. Cast a glance over his shoulder at Marna.

She was standing with her back to the wall and both her arms around Libby. Her eyes were wide. She mouthed "Seeker?" in a way that told Lochled she did not want the man in her home. But what was Lochled to do?

He could feel the moment drawing tight. If he hesitated any longer, it might be seen as impertinent. He turned hurriedly back to the Seeker and pulled the door open wide, stepping out of the way and doing his best to hide the knife behind his back lest he be thought threatening to his betters.

"Of course, hef," Lochled said, then winced. Should he have called him that? Or was it best to only refer to them as Seeker?

The Seeker didn't seem bothered by it and nodded a soft "True thanks" as he stepped into their home . . .

If you want to find a madman, simply walk among an army in the small hours before a battle. He'll be easy enough to find: he'll be the only one snoring peacefully.

Lochled was not fortunate enough to be a madman. It wasn't the dream he'd had of that Seeker stepping into his home. More a memory that he went over and over in his mind while he tossed and turned all through the small hours of the morning.

After a while, he gave up on even the pretense of sleep and lay with his eyes open, hating everything and everybody. Hating his squad. Hating this ship. Hating these wars. Hating the great men that forced them on the little men. But mostly hating himself.

By now, some men had begun to shuffle about, being quiet so as not to wake others that were likely already awake. Gradually they were joined by their fellow wakeful squadmates, and the noise continued to get louder and louder until no one gave a shit anymore, because it was only the madmen sleeping by then.

Lochled sat cross-legged on the floor with his satchel in the hollow of his legs, packing it tight, pulling the thongs closed and tying them off with an eager sort of vigor. It was good to get moving. Time to leave all that dark night behind. Time to lose himself in the coming destruction.

"Satchels tight," Lochled croaked, his voice still rough and phlegmy from waking up. Rony was beside him, half watching him, half trying to mimic how he was packing. "Chance you might go over. Might have to swim for the shore. If you pack it tight, it'll help you float for a little bit before it gets waterlogged. That little bit might save you from drowning."

"Do the landing craft not land?" Rony worried, frowning at her own satchel as she rammed her meager belongings into it.

"Well, we'd sure like them to, but remember this: everything you'd like, the Tickers would like the exact opposite."

Cryer was chewing scaef with unusual zeal. Already packed up. Squatting. Stretching. Couldn't stop fidgeting about. "The landing craft in the Third got stuck. Keels drew too much depth, and the Tickers had made a jetty of rocks all across the landing point, just under the water. Landing craft got caught on it." Cryer looked dark and still for a breath before he shook his head and started wiggling again. "Anyways. New landing craft are flat bottomed. So, hopefully that won't happen again. But you never know what the Tickers might try to pull."

"Sounds like the Tickers is not quite so low minded as the Church claims," Licker put in.

"Enough of that shit!" Lochled snarled, getting to his feet and slinging the pack onto his back. The nervous energy was grasping him tight now, and it wasn't going to let go today. For the journey, he might've kept the peace between his squad. But for the fighting, there was no room for niceness. "No more talk of what's got a mind and what doesn't. *You* don't have a fucking mind. Not today you don't. For today, you don't think about morals or home or the precious little whore that's going to gobble your pintel when you get back. There's nothing of that now. Now there's only killing. You understand that?"

"Yes, hef," they all murmured.

A shout from the front of the boat: a crewman, hanging off the ladder, bellowing into the dark hold, where all the soldiers were milling about in preparation. "First wave is off!" he shouted to the right. "First wave is off!" he shouted to the left. "Standby belowdecks!"

"Fuck." Cryer had his massive greatshield, was jamming his knuckles into the steel plating, not hard enough to crack bone, but harder than looked comfortable. "Fuck. Fuck. Fuck."

"Why can't we go topside?" Rony asked.

Fuh-WHOOM!

The whole ship rocked, quaked, shuddered.

"That's why." Lochled cringed, not able to move, because now everyone was up and about and there just wasn't room to move. He was stuck in one spot, overloaded with energy. And now all there was to do was wait. "Those are the war barges." *Fuh-WHOOM!* "No point being topside when those big cannons are going off. They'll call us up as soon as we leave them behind and start advancing on the beach."

"Yes," Trut hissed, exulting in the sound of the cannons.

"Fuck 'em. Kill 'em. Hope the whole fucking lot of 'em is buried in rubble by the time we hit the beach, and all we gotta do is harvest ash and get rich."

Lochled couldn't take it anymore. He had to do something—even if it was just talk—or he'd devolve into a fit of shakes. "Right then, fuck it. Get in here. All of you." He waved his arms rapidly, as though they had no time, though who knew how long they'd have to wait? The squad squeezed in tight, shoulder to shoulder, faces drawn, eyes as sharp as cats', lips so flat and bloodless you'd think they'd never known how to kiss or speak a kind word. "Rony's new, so I'm gonna say it, but you all might listen as well."

"Doesn't hurt to be reminded," Cryer agreed, fists clenching and unclenching rapidly.

Lochled jammed his hand at Cryer and Ponts. "My big boys. Watch your fucking feet, uh? Don't lift your fucking shields too high. I know the sand is a bastard, but you're no good to us if your legs get chopped out from under you." He circled his hand. "The rest of you, stay as close to Cryer and Ponts's hindsholes as you can squeeze yourself. Stay low. Stay close. Watch your elbows and feet—and your fucking heads! Keep your fucking heads down, for mercy's sake, uh? Don't get stupid, and remember you got to survive the fucking beach before you can start killing. Get off the fucking beach, get into the city. That's all I want you to think about. Off the beach—into the city." He looked about them. Thought of a hundred other things to say, but none of them really needed to be said. "Right, then. Listen to me, and do what the fuck I say. And that's it."

A tumble of feet down the ladder, then a loud bang. Hotsteel had descended, then chosen to simply jump because he couldn't be bothered with the last few rungs. He looked a completely different man somehow. His shoulders were all hunched and tight, brow beetled over his eyes so that they looked like dark holes, like the maws of two Levelers. The sides of his head had been freshly shaved. His hair in a tight braid. Looked like all the other savage men, except he wore the captain's tunic.

"Right then!" He barked, stalking down the center of the deck, arms tense, fists clenched at his sides. "You want to survive? You got to get mean. How down and dirty in the mud and filth are you willing to get? That's what this is about. Who are you then? Who's going home? You, who worked and sweat and bled for what you have?" Stabbing his fingers out at an unseen land. "Or that Ticker that's little more than a beast? Who's gonna win that fight? It's gonna be me! It's gonna be you! Because we're the meanest fucking things to ever crawl out of an ocean, and there's no measure to how deep I'll dive in the fucking mud, so fuck 'em! Let's go!"

The men raged, and Lochled raged with them. Growls and spits and curses and mad laughter. Everyone was doing it. Made it all right. Made it easy to get lost in the chaos. Rony must've felt it too, the weird safety of it, how you could almost do anything in that moment, and no one would balk. There was nothing too insane, because they'd all flatly lost their minds. She must've let out a scream, but Lochled couldn't hear in all the ruckus, just saw her mouth open, teeth bared, cords standing out on her neck.

Hotsteel, cupped his hands to his mouth. "To arms! To fucking arms!" Pushing men toward the ladder. "Topside! Topside!"

They were all caught up in the crush now as every man in Brytan Company—and one woman—milled their way toward the ladder, pressed in tight, chest to back. Pain from his lashing, but it was dim in Lochled's mind, hardly something to worry about at this point. Death and destruction were hurtling fast toward him—who gave a fuck about a little strip of skin missing from their back?

It was hot and heady in that crowd. Everyone was talking,

but no one's words made any sense, hopes and prayers with oaths and curses mixed into them. Asking Feor for mercy in one breath, help in murdering the enemy the next. The profane and the sacred always made odd dance partners, and battles seemed to be where they liked to dance best.

Cryer and Ponts got their shields on their backs, barely fitting through the hatch with the damn things. Lochled clambered after Ponts, his head pushing on the big man's rear. Cleared the hatch into dim dawn, a breath of fresh air, sea breeze, then the heavy, clotted stink of alchemy billowing out of those siege guns and tainting the air yellow.

"Leveler!" a man in a lieutenant's tunic shouted, and pushed a loop of twenty charges into Lochled's chest.

"Gimme two!" Lochled demanded.

The lieutenant gave him two. It was an odd request—a loop of twenty charges already weighed a man down, and most men don't want extra weight on them when drowning's a possibility. But Lochled didn't plan on drowning today, and it was better to sweat for the weight than to bleed for the lack of it.

"Leveler!" the lieutenant yelled at Rony, then thrust a loop in her arms too.

"Can I get two?" Rony tried.

Lochled snatched her by the arm and jerked her along. "You fucking mad, woman? Two loops'd be a third your own weight."

"I can handle it!"

Lochled grabbed her by the front of her tunic. "No arguments today, Rony. You do what the fuck I say, when I say it. I won't warn you again."

He didn't wait to see what reaction she had to this. Didn't want to see it. Might make him feel a little like a human again, and that wasn't where he needed to be. Not now. Not with the landing craft being drawn up along the port side of the barque.

Breath shushing in his ears. People jostling into his arms. The hammering of the war barges now a little ways off as the fleet crept closer to shore, the screech of the massive stone projectiles splitting the air over their heads, seeming close enough to knock the masts off the ship.

If Lochled stood on tiptoe and peered out past the fore of the ship, he could just make out the rocky outline of Leftland and the sprawl of structures that was Halun's Landing. The sky was getting brighter, but the sun hadn't quite risen yet, so he could still see fires in the city. Hundreds of fires, twinkling in the darkness, some of them small, just guttering pinpricks, while others seemed to swallow whole sections of the city.

"Lochled! Lochled!" Hotsteel, barged through the bustle.

Lochled didn't respond verbally, just stared at the man as he approached.

Hotsteel grabbed him around the back of his neck. Rough with affection. "First wave is getting thrashed. I want you up front on the second, uh? I need a fucking Brytan man to stick a shield on that fucking beach, or we'll all be floating by the time the sun gets up." A squeeze. Hotsteel rocked him back and forth. "First boat out. First shield on the beach. I know you can do it. If even half of the tales my father told me about you are true, then I know you can do it."

Lochled found himself nodding. "Fuck it then, hef. Uh? Fuck it, I'll get that shield on the beach."

"Good man."

Lochled spun when Hotsteel released him, started grabbing his squad as he went for the port side. "On me," he snapped at them. "On me."

Funny how everyone was all piss and stamping hooves, but there was an empty spot at the portside railing. It was obvious that no one wanted to be the first squad on the landing craft.

"I'll go!" Lochled roared at the fuckers as he passed them by. "I'll fucking go first! Me and my squad'll get you on that fucking beach, you bunch of pintelsniffs, don't you worry!"

Haggard smiles and a weak cheer of encouragement from the others, relieved they wouldn't have to be the first in.

A pair of crewmen slipped past Lochled, towing the landing craft up from the aft and bringing it alongside, bumping noisily against the barque's hull. "Got a stiff wind to carry you to shore," one of the crewmen hollered at him. "We'll raise up the sail for you!"

Lochled leaned against the railing and looked aleft, toward the beaches of Halun's Landing. A great crescent shape of bone-white sand, the city stretching all around it, so that when they hit the beach they'd be encircled by the city. A city filled with Tickers, using their powers of push and pull to rain destruction on them.

Lochled pointed to it, speaking to Cryer. "By the time we get there, the entire daeside of the city'll be backlit by the sun." He pivoted so he was pointing to the other end of the city. "We'll go nyhtside, that way the sun's in their eyes, not ours. But you'll need to keep our backs covered."

"Do my best," Cryer said, staring hot irons at the beaches.

Lochled frowned into the gray light, black waves, charcoal shoreline. He could make out a handful of small, white sails bobbing rapidly in the surf, approaching the beaches. That would be what was left of the first wave. He counted maybe a dozen sails.

"There should be more landing craft hitting the beach," Lochled growled. "Where's the rest of—"

A warbling sound. Lochled stood there dumbly listening to it, not a clue in the world as to what it was, but a vague sense that it was bad.

The sea, not four boat lengths ahead of their barque,

erupted. A mountain of white water leapt into the sky, and every man on board let out a girlish yelp and ducked.

"Fuck! Was that our cannons?" Cryer snapped.

Lochled shook his head. "That came from Halun's Landing."

"Damn near hit us! They've never been able to hit our ships from that far!"

"Seems they learn a new trick every fucking time."

That same noise again. And now, knowing what it was, every man in the boat—and probably in the fleet—tucked their necks in tight to their shoulders like a bunch of turtles, knowing well it wouldn't do them any good, but unable to help it. Like a flinch response.

Boom! Crash!

Another geyser of seawater, this time right between their ship and the next one over to port.

The captain of the ship shouted something about not being able to get any closer.

Way off in the other direction, three ships over from the starboard side, a barque simply shattered into splinters. Three masts went jutting up into the sky like missiles, while the fore and the aft of the ship went tilting into the water, sails and rigging fluttering like feathers off a savaged bird.

"Soot, fire, and child," Lochled whispered.

Their ship began to turn sharply. Lochled staggered against the port railing. The whole thing was leaning hard, the deck like a hill now, and all the men upon it struggling to keep their feet as the captain of the ship turned his wheel madly about, shouting orders to his crew that meant absolutely nothing to Lochled.

A panorama of ships as they slowly spun about, the seas churning and crashing and erupting all around them with whatever it was the damned Tickers were sending at them. All the ships in the fleet were turning about, unable to get any closer.

"Guess we know what happened to the *first* wave!" Licker shouted.

Hotsteel came charging up again. "Can't get any closer! As soon as we get out of range, you'll have to board the landing craft and go from there!"

Lochled stared at the rapidly growing distance between them and the beaches of Leftland. "That's damn near two thousand-stride!"

But Hotsteel slapped him on the shoulder, already walking away. "Good thing you have a stiff wind to carry you to shore!"

CHAPTER 8

When they flipped the ladder over the side and down to the waiting landing craft, Rony felt her insides turn to water. Seemed to want to flow out of her pretty bad, but she couldn't—*wouldn't*—do that to herself in front of the others.

Up until that moment, it had all been about being brave and keeping her chin up and learning the ropes, and everything about the landing had just been some far-off worry because there'd been more present things to deal with, like what bastard was going to try to grab her in the dark like a goblin.

But Cryer had been right. Who was trying to stick their pintel in her was the least of her worries. It all came down to this here, right now, staring at that ladder and knowing that she had to go over.

Too late to turn back now. But, oh, the temptation was awful strong. To just shake her head and step back. Fact was, probably most would just laugh at her and say they knew it all along. Except she'd be the one laughing at the end of the day, when she was the only one left alive.

Only, her feet were moving forward. A pair of tan arms were

reaching out for the ladder, one of them with a Leveler gripped in it, and she realized with a shock that they were hers.

Why was she doing this? Weren't there a million other ways to try to pay off debt? They'd all seemed terrible when she thought of them before. Now they seemed bright and shiny, attractive. Anything was attractive compared to this.

She threw one leg over. Then the other. Looked down. Crashing seas. Lochled below, already in the boat, waving at her hastily, eyes gone all weird and inhuman, like he'd been possessed.

Why couldn't she stop herself? What was animating her limbs? It was like she was watching herself, rather than actually controlling her movements. Like her mind had simply become an audience to her actions, and her body was trundling along on a preset course to doom.

"Come on then, Little Roan!" A voice from the deck. She looked back. Trut was standing there, shoving the haft of his polearm at her. "Get the fuck on with it!"

And down she went. Hand over hand. Foot over foot. The rocking of the barque. The swinging of the rope ladder. The crash of waves—no, not waves, it was the crash of whatever the Tickers were hurling at them, battering the seas and any craft unlucky enough to be in the wrong spot at the wrong time.

She'd seen what it had done to that other barque. If one of them hit the landing craft, it would . . . just not be there anymore.

Strangely, she drew some comfort from that. When every road around you seems to lead to inevitable death, it's the one with the quickest, cleanest, least painful death that grants you comfort.

The siege cannons from the war barges, constantly going off, constantly whining over their heads. And the shouts of men coming from over the water, coming from the other ships. So much chaos. How could it get worse than this?

Just before her feet hit the deck, she felt hands grab her up like a wayward child and yank her from the ladder. Lochled's voice in her ear: "Gonna have to move faster than that if you wanna live!"

"Yes, hef." Her own voice barely audible, like she was speaking underwater.

Live. That's all she had to do. Seemed a relatively simple thing for the other eighteen rains of her life. But today it would be hard.

The boat rocked and thumped as Trut landed and immediately took a position out of the way. At first she thought he was staring at her, but then she realized he was looking past her at the beaches. She wanted to turn around and look herself but then hesitated. Wondered if she actually wanted to see what was ahead or if it would be better to simply close her eyes and hope to make it to land.

Hard. You've got to be hard.

She twisted around and looked.

Every minute, the sky was becoming lighter. The seas were pitching the landing craft about, and the swells were rolling by them, blotting out the shoreline so that she could only get glimpses. She could see a few white sails. Looked like they were coming back. She couldn't see enough of the beach to know if there were men on it.

The massive shotstones from the war barges whistled overhead, and Rony realized that you could see them when you were watching for them—little gray streaks in the morning light that ended in a cloud of dust somewhere in the city of Halun's Landing, and sometimes a gout of fire.

Swearnsoot, they were pounding the city to rubble. And

yet the Tickers were still fighting, still hurtling their own shots down in the water while the harried landing craft tried to scurry back to the fleet so that they could make the trip again with a new squad.

What was it like on the beach?

"Watch out now!" Cryer snapped at her, kneeing her out of the way as he swung his greatshield around to the front of him and posted it on the fore of the boat. Ponts was right at his side, did the same thing, so that the prow of the landing craft was an armored wedge.

Lochled pulled himself up into the middle, right between Cryer and Ponts. "Everyone, get in tight!"

There was a scuttle for the front end, Gonder and Effel clambering over one another, clambering over Rony, to get a spot nice and deep behind the shields. Rony found herself smashed into the middle of the wedge, her face against Lochled's thigh, Gonder nearly laying on top of her.

Dead ahead, there was a little crack between the shields. Clutching her Leveler, Rony leaned hard against Lochled's leg, partly for the comfort of it, partly to see out of the crack.

There was a creak, and a rumble. The sound of squeaking pulleys. Then the heavy flap of sail fabric unfurling. A snap as it suddenly filled with wind, and then the landing craft shot forward, and the barque that had been her home for the last five days rapidly retreated behind her.

"Steady on!" Lochled called out. "Sides of the craft are armored, so stay low behind 'em. We'll get this fucker close as we can to the sand, but when I say 'bail,' you fucking bail any which way you can. Find a shield and get the fuck behind it."

Rony stared through the crack, breath coming faster now. Tongue dry. Wishing for water. There were so many commands Lochled had issued, she couldn't keep them all in her head.

Find a shield. Survive. Get off the beach. Get off the boat. Get *to* the beach. Stay on Cryer's rear. Move quicker. Which one was she supposed to do first? Which one was she supposed to be doing now?

A glimpse of the beach as they crested a swell. She still couldn't see any men on it. Had the *entire* first wave been killed?

Hands a bit unsteady now, she shuffled the Leveler about in her grip. Worked the latch and broke it open. Fumbled for one of the charges. The loop of them was just a wide strip of leather, with the charges tucked into a bunch of slots. She shucked one of them out and stared at it.

A big brass cylinder, maybe a hand long, a few thumbs thick. On one end, a little hole with what looked like a tiny cork snugged in there. On the other end, the brass looked like it had been cut six ways, so there were six little triangles of metal that were holding something in. When she looked, she thought she saw dark little spheres rattling around in there.

Those must be the shotstones. Twenty of them, Lochled had said. Each one big enough to kill a man by itself. Or a Ticker.

She started to slide the charge into the breech as she'd been told, but a rough hand came out of nowhere, slapping the charge away from the Leveler.

"Not yet!" Lochled barked at her. "Not when we're all fucking crammed together! One nudge on that trigger bar and you'll rip us all to shreds!"

Rony wasn't sure which she was more terrified of—the Tickers or the weapon she was supposed to use to kill them.

FWOOM!

A pillar of water jetted into the sky, just in the wake of their craft, sending Rony's eyes wide as she watched the top of it tower over them. Feor's mercy—the size of the stones they must be throwing!

The craft jolted and rocked in the shock wave, back end rising up so the damn thing was almost vertical for a breath, the armored crewman at the tiller looking ahead with eyes peeled wide behind his helmet, mouth puckered into a little O, shoulders all scrunched up while he tried mightily to keep the craft from squirreling sideways and capsizing.

A wash of water, like a sudden deluge, swept over them. Cold. Ice cold. Everyone gasped. Swore. Spat seawater.

What to do? Was there anything *to* do?

Lochled had the answer: "Nothing to do now but pray! Don't give a fuck if you pray to Feor or Nyht and Nyhtson, but fucking pray! We're in the thick of it now!"

FWOOM!

The seas erupted all around them.

FWOOM! FWOOM!

Behind them, in little glimpses as their craft rocked violently up and down and side to side through falling water so thick it felt like rain and mist mixed together, Rony could see dozens more sails, dozens more shielded prows battering their way through the waters.

There was another mountain of water, and one of the landing craft simply disappeared into the waves, not a scrap of sail or a shred of wood to show where ten men had died.

"Light unto light," someone was murmuring, sounded like Jory. "Feor, have mercy on your servants in our time of trouble. Only let us make it to the beach, so that we can do your will and free you from the prison of those fuck Tickers. Swearnsoot. Swearnfire. Swearnchild."

"Soot, fire, and child," someone else agreed, sounded like Trut, or maybe Wen.

Licker was murmuring a Gasric prayer just on the other side of Lochled's legs, eyes locked onto Rony, it seemed, but then again, maybe not seeing her at all. "Nyhtson, intercede for us." He kept saying. "Nyhtson, intercede . . . intercede for us . . ."

Lochled screamed out, "Come on, you fuckers!"

Rony had no idea who that was directed at. The squad? The Tickers? Feor and the Nyhtson? Maybe all of them together?

"Almost there!" Cryer called out.

Rony peered hopefully through the crack, expecting to see the beach just ahead. She was crushed to see that it looked like they hadn't gotten any closer. Somehow they seemed to have retreated a thousandstride from the safety of the barque, and yet gotten a thousandstride more distant from the beach.

A stone struck the water ahead of them, no more than ten strides. For a blink, just a little sliver of time, she watched the water welling up into that great plume and thought it odd that it looked tinted red, wondered if maybe the dawn light had finally shown itself but then saw the shapes of bodies in that water, ghostly silhouettes all mangled and torn up.

The craft bucked wildly as it hurtled into the spot that had just been struck. A wash of seawater blanketed them again. A fish flopped into Rony's lap. She jerked, surprised, looked down at it.

Not a fish. An arm. A man's arm. With a faded tattoo on the wrist.

Her heart beat wildly, breath caught in her lungs, but she couldn't really figure out what to do at that point. A dead man's arm in her lap. She couldn't scream about it, though she wanted to. Didn't want to rise up enough to toss it overboard, though she desperately needed it out of her lap.

So she grabbed it in the crook of its elbow. Passed it to Licker.

The Fen frowned at it for a moment, then shook his head, passed it on to Jory, who tossed it overboard with a grunt and a swear.

"Keep your wits, cully!" Cryer boomed from over top of her.

She craned her neck up to see the man's dark face smiling down at her, backlit by the brightening sky so that all she could see were the whites of his eyes and the stretch of his grin.

"My wits are right where they're supposed to be!" she snarled at him.

Ping!

They all jerked, Cryer included. Mirth gone from his face. Everyone's eyes were whipping this way and that, trying to figure out what the sound was and whether it was dangerous. Seemed everything was dangerous, so why not that sound?

Ping! Ping!

Evenly spaced.

Then a flurry: *Ping-ping-ping! Ping! Ping!*

"The fuck's all—?" The crewman at the tiller looked terrified for one brief moment before a red hole suddenly appeared in the center of his chest, as though by magic. Like a bit of his heart had burst out of his chest.

The entire squad had seen it, and they all cried out at once, instantly terrified and yelling curses. The crewman, though, seemed a bit confused. Looked down at his chest. Let go of the tiller so his trembling hands could poke at the hole.

"Whassat, then?" he gurgled, a bit of blood dribbling out of his mouth as he said it.

And then the top of his head came clean off, the metal helm half crushed, half sheered. He pitched backward, legs kicking aimlessly.

"The fuck is *that*!" Trut was screaming, cramming himself up against Jory like a scared kid to his father. "What are they throwing at us?"

Ping-ping-ping!

All across the shields. Rony realized she could feel the impacts on her back, she was pressed so tight to the shields.

"Shotstones!" Lochled shouted with his back against Cryer's chest, the two of them curled around each other like a man and his lover. "Always something new with these fucks!"

It seemed Ponts's ponderousness did not cease under the threat of death. Crunched in there with all the others, he calmly pointed to the dead crewman and the tiller which was banging wildly back and forth.

"Going to lose control of the craft once we hit the surf," he spoke out, carefully enunciating over the clamor of the shotstone plinking off their shields, sparking off the edges of the craft's armored sides. "If we wash sideways, we're fucked."

Another crash of water. Another barrel's worth of bloody sea dumped over their heads. A chorus of metallic percussion, like a madman at a steel drum.

Licker spat saltwater tinted pink. "Go ahead, you big goff! You wanna get your head shot off, then go for it!"

Ponts shrugged, started to labor forward, as though Licker had given him an order. Lochled's arm shot out, grabbed the big man's shoulders, and rammed him back into place.

"Don't you fucking think about it, twank!" Lochled roared. "I'm not carrying that fucking shield when you die!"

"He's right!" Cryer called out. "We're drifting sideways!"

As though to prove the point, the ping-ping-pinging of the shotstones seemed to migrate to the port side of the craft as it yawed to starboard. Jory's elbow exploded. He yowled, back arching, squirming into a tiny hollow behind Trut and Wen's bodies, feet stamping out angrily at the deck.

"My arm! My fucking arm!" Jory was holding it up. Below the elbow it flopped, hand and fingers dangling uselessly.

Effel, who hadn't done much but cling to Gonder, was now

trying to snake his foot down the side of the boat, kicking at the tiller, though Rony reckoned his mind must've left him, as the tip of his toes was at least two strides from the tiller.

"We're almost to the breakers!" Cryer shouted. "Somebody right this fucking boat!"

Though no one seemed inclined to.

The sound of the shotstones pelting their craft intensified, almost so that you couldn't tell one impact from another, all one big ringing bell, and the entire squad was in it, cringing, barely able to hear a damned thing. The Tickers knew they had this craft. They could see it turning broadside to them, exposing the fleshy innards behind the armor, and after that they'd be done for, just a bit more blood in the water.

Rony elbowed out, caught Lochled in the chest. "Hef! Flip the fucking boat!"

"What?" Lochled's eyes widened. "You mad?"

Rony stamped her foot on the deck. "It's armored!" She pointed to the air above their heads. "That's not!"

"Capsized boats still float!" Cryer observed. "We can cling to the underside!"

"Ah, my arm! My arm!"

"Shut up, you fucking feebling! You got to take it like a man!"

FWOOM!

SPLASH!

Ping-ping-ping!

"Fuck it!" Lochled shouted. "On my call, everyone on the starboard side!"

CHAPTER 9

A good idea is a good idea. Sometimes leaders get their pride all caught up in it, can't take an idea they didn't come up with. Lochled didn't give a fuck about all that. He'd take anything that kept them from getting shredded by shotstones.

"We're gonna capsize the boat and walk it into shore!" Lochled shouted at his crew, trying to make sure that the whole squad heard. Jory was still wailing about his arm, probably wasn't paying attention.

"Jory! Jory, you fuck!" Lochled screamed at him.

Trut, who had Jory all draped over him, started slapping the side of the man's gray head. "Listen to the sergeant! Fucking listen if you want to live!"

Jory turned a haggard, snarling face on Lochled. "Give the order then!"

They were damn near broadside to the beach now. A flurry of shotstones chewed the tiller up to splinters, and did worse to the dead crewman beside it.

No time for a countdown. "Now!" Lochled shouted. "Everyone on the starboard side! Tip it! Tip it!"

One big mass of humanity, crawling, scrambling, shoving, kicking, grappling for the starboard side of the boat, Cryer and Ponts working the straps of their greatshields onto their shoulders without moving the shields themselves, knowing that if it didn't work, they were going to sink to the bottom like rocks.

Lochled rode the wave of bodies, all of them surging to the starboard side, heaving themselves against it. The clatter of shotstones. Then the wet *smack* of one hitting flesh, and Lochled wondered if it was him, but he couldn't feel anything.

The deck of the craft lifted. The port side coming out of the water.

Rony went slithering fully overboard, clinging to the side and shouting, "Pull! Pull!"

Cryer and Ponts were up now, their shields out of position. A shotstone slipped through their unprotected front, skimmed across Licker's back like another lash from the whip, making him startle and screech, but he didn't stop working.

Lochled was on top of Trut and Wen now, Jory was on top of him, and Cryer and Ponts were on top of them all, keeping them covered as best they could. Rony, Gonder, and Effel were already in the water, and Licker joined them with a flailing splash.

The craft hit its tipping point and capsized, all the squad trying to keep a handhold so they didn't plunge to the bottom, all their legs kicking, hoping against hope to find sand beneath their boots, and having their hopes dashed—they were still in deep water.

All the way over now, everyone gasping, everyone snarling, everyone yelling random things about how to not die, and no one listening to anyone else.

Sudden darkness, as the boat entombed them. Lochled couldn't see a thing but the water beneath him, just a bunch of wet, cold gray in the middle of all the blackness. The noise was thick, though. Overpowering in the enclosed space. Huffing, spitting, swearing. Arms and legs hit each other as they desperately tried to tread water against the weight of weapons and armor, hands slashing about for something to latch onto.

Lochled found the sturdy bench that ran the length of the landing craft and hooked his fingers on it. Seawater filled his mouth, his throat. He coughed it up, trying to talk, but couldn't for a moment, even though he was desperate to get the words out.

Finally, "Cryer! Cryer, you with me?"

Slightly dimmer now, but still very insistent—the plume of the giant shots hitting the water. Still the clank and tink of the shotstones, all across the armored walls of the craft. And then *ponk*-ing through the wooden keel, letting in little spears of light.

But no sound from Cryer.

"Ponts!" Lochled shouted, the fact that his friend might be dead only a peripheral concern to having at least one shieldman if they should somehow, miraculously, find themselves on the beach.

"Here," the big man gurgled.

Something clamped onto Lochled's ankle. He cried out, almost jerked away from it, thinking of what terrible things might be slithering about this foreign seabed, but then knew they were hands. Big hands.

He held on tight to the bench, even as the weight threatened to pull him from his roost and drown him. Groaning against the effort.

Finally the hands worked up to Lochled's shoulders and a great gust of spluttering breath hit the side of his face.

"Cryer, that you?"

"It's me," he coughed, right into Lochled's eyes.

"Grab the bench! Get off me!" He searched the darkness.

Pock! Pock!

Two more holes in the wooden keel. Two more streams of light, but not quite enough to make sense of the jumble of bodies and splashing water.

Cryer managed to get himself on the bench, clung to it, gasping for air.

"Everyone here?" Lochled demanded. "Trut! Wen!"

"Here!" they called out from somewhere in there.

"Rony, you with us?"

"Yes, hef."

"Good fucking idea!"

"Are you serious?"

"We're alive, aren't we? Gonder! Effel!"

"Hanging on, Sergeant!"

"Jory! Licker!"

"Here," Licker responded.

"Jory? Jory?"

Nothing.

"Fuck it. We lost the old man," Lochled said.

"Are we going towards shore?"

"I sure as fuck hope so!"

Now that he could take a moment to think about it, Lochled could feel the rise and fall of the surf, the heavy rolling crash of it, the way it bears you up for a breath, then thrusts you forward.

"We're in the surf! We're past the breakers!" Lochled felt a pang of terror and regret. It had been almost peaceful in the darkness underneath the capsized boat. And besides the handful of shotstone that got through the keel, it seemed the Tickers thought they'd drowned. Weren't giving the craft much attention.

That would change when it hit the beach and grew nine pairs of legs.

Lochled let out a string of curses. "Any second now our feet are gonna touch bottom. Now, listen to me. Everyone take a deep fucking breath and open your fucking ears, uh?" He gulped air himself. Peered around in the darkness. Thought he could see the dim shine of wet faces. "We're gonna walk this boat in until the prow hits the sand. Then we're all going to slip out the back, Cryer and Ponts first, and the rest of us after. Cryer, Ponts, don't get turned around under the water. Get your lungs a nice whiff of air, go under the backside of the boat, turn around completely, and then come up. You hear?"

"Yes, hef."

"The rest of you stay tight with me . . ." He trailed off as he felt his feet hit the bottom. Shocked him a bit.

"Sand!" Wen cried out. "I can feel the sand!"

"Right then, get ready! The rest of you stay tight with me, get behind a shield, and hope we're not the only sad fucks on the beach."

All of a sudden the water was starting to run out. Their feet were solidly on the bottom now, treading forward into shallower and shallower surf until the weight of the craft started to bear down on them and the hull finally crunched into the sand.

"Shieldmen! Go!" Lochled shouted, taking a series of big breaths and preparing to follow. Clutching his Leveler, patting the two loops of charges. Ready to go. Ready for the beach. Or at least as ready as any man could be for it.

Cryer heaved toward the rear, sucked in air, then went under. Ponts was right behind, and Lochled followed in his wake.

Down.

Under the water. Blessed peace. Just the sound of the water rushing, crashing. Lochled wished he were a fish, wished he could breathe that briny Bransmar and swim away in it, never get caught up in people's brownspill again . . .

Up.

Water draining out of his ears. Chaos filling in behind it. The whistle and whine of shotstones splitting the air, splashing into the water, chewing up the beach in little eruptions of sand. Smoke in the air, heavy, stinking, pouring out of Halun's Landing from a thousand strikes of their siege cannons. The city rose up above them, like a cliff face, all the buildings that made it seemingly coalesced into one threatening mass, like a wave itself, always on the pinnacle of crashing down on them.

Shields. Shields. Where were the shields?

There.

Cryer, slogging out of the water with his shield up. Hefting the massive thing, pacing forward a few steps, then plonking it down.

Ponts must've gotten turned around, he was ten strides to the right of Cryer and a bit behind, trying to get himself up abreast of his fellow shieldman.

Go. Move.

Shotstones flickered, splashed, guttered in the water about him.

Lochled surged forward, having the urge to fire his Leveler back, but knowing it would do no good. It wasn't for long ranges. Lochled wasn't sure how the hell the Tickers were managing to hurl shotstones at them with such force, over such distances, but that was a matter for later pondering—they were doing it, and Lochled's job was to not get hit.

He thrashed out of the surf, the weight of his body, the weight of his sodden clothes and weapons getting heavier and heavier, while his boots sunk further and further into the sand. His whole world shrunk down to the onerous task of getting one foot in front of the other, each step a minor victory in the grand goal of getting to Cryer's shield.

Out of the water completely now. Salt on his tongue, down

his throat. Sand in his crotch and every other crevice, roughing his skin raw with every movement. The sand fought him, tried to snag his tired feet, tried to fill his boots, cake them on the outside, weigh him down to a standstill. But he wouldn't stop.

He collapsed, right into Cryer, nearly knocked the big man over. Cryer posted his shield to keep himself from toppling, then sagged against it, heaving hard. White sand coated the entire left side of his dark face. Made him look oddly terrifying.

I made it! I made it onto the fucking beach!

A brief wash of elation.

Ping-ping-ping! All across the shield.

Fuck. What now?

Get off the beach—no. Get his *squad* off the beach. Into the city.

Spitting and cursing, Lochled swept wet tentacles of his own hair out of his eyes, tried to find a clean finger to wipe them out with, but everything was coated in sand. Set to blinking the seawater out instead. His vision cleared enough to look right, then left, up and down the crescent beach.

Maybe fifty strides down, another squad had made it. Both shields posted, soldiers straggling out of the surf. One of them lurched backward, spinning ribbons of red out of his neck, then flopped around in the surf.

He spotted Rony, charging up to get seated behind Ponts, who was still trying to work his way to connect with Cryer. The rest of the squad, all spread out over a handful of strides, drool and snot and seawater stringing out of their mouths and noses.

One of the big, ship-killing stones smacked into the beach, as big as a barrel, rolled through the surf, squashing Wen flat, and sent up a wave of sandy water that swallowed Trut in the midst of a shriek.

Licker struggled past them as though it weren't worth noticing.

Trut came up, still shrieking, all covered in sandy mud, a gaping mouth in a white blob, arms flailing, trying to see.

Licker paused, panting. Shotstones smacking all around him. Looked back. Saw Trut staggering around in circles like a blind man, arms held out, reaching for something, anything.

"Come on, Licker!" Lochled shouted at him.

He meant for Licker to get to the shields, but instead, Licker slogged back into the water, seized the shoulder of Trut's light armor, and started dragging him toward the shields, moving no faster than an old man's exhausted walk.

A body flopped about bonelessly in the water, moved only by the waves. Face in the sand. Lochled couldn't tell who it was. Spotted Gonder on hands and knees, crawling for them, so the dead one must've been Effel.

Just behind their abandoned landing craft, another squad hit the beach, their boat striking the massive stone that had just killed Wen, tipping, and then spilling out the men inside. Two were caught by shotstones, crumpling as red mist sprouted out of them. Lochled was fine with that because it gave Licker and Trut a chance.

The two of them fell into cover, right on top of Rony's legs. Ponts had managed to post his shield side to side with Cryer's now, and Rony was up against it, just to Lochled's left.

"Can't fucking see!" Trut was screaming. "Got it all in my fucking eyes!"

"Hold still!" Rony snapped at him. "Tilt your head up!" He obeyed her, wheezing and whining, while she snatched his flask from his belt, uncorked it, and dribbled spirits over the man's clenched eyes. "It's gonna b—"

"Ah fuck! It burns! Is that my drips?"

"Fuck your drips, you need your eyes more!" Rony stuck both her thumbs in her mouth, sucked the sand from them, spat it off to the side, then rammed them into Trut's eyes and wiped them clear. "Open your fucking eyes!"

Trut blinked rapidly, still cursing, but scrambled his way in tight to the shields.

Gonder came in like a mad animal, flinging sand every which way as he clambered up Lochled's legs and rammed into the shield, shivering hard. "Where's Effel?" he was whimpering. "Where's Effel?"

"Shut up," Lochled grunted at him, thrusting him out of the way and seizing Trut's flask from beside Rony's leg. He upended it into his mouth. Drank it straight to empty. Slapped it into Trut's chest. "Right then! We got to the fucking beach! Now it's time to get *off* the fucking beach, uh?"

"I'm all for it," Cryer agreed.

Lochled rolled onto his knees, keeping his body low behind the shields. The air over their heads kept whistling and whining. But the shots seemed to be coming from everywhere. Maybe the whole damn city was hurling stones at them.

"What's it look like?" Cryer grunted, adjusting his grip on the shield.

"Looks like shit. Can't see a damned thing. No idea where all the shots are coming from."

"Sounds like it doesn't matter, then."

"Reckon it don't." Lochled twisted back around. Another landing craft hit the beach behind them. Then another. The first rays of sunlight were making it over the city of Halun's Landing, spearing the pall of smoke with glimmering shafts.

A pair of shields were inching toward them from the surf. Looked like they were angling to Lochled's left, which would put them daeside. He didn't want that. If they tried to make the shield line running daeside to the city, they'd have the sun in their eyes, and something told Lochled the city's defenders were high up, raining their shotstones down. Lochled didn't intend to give them any more advantages.

"No!" Lochled shouted, waving his arms the other way. "Nyhtside! Get on our nyhtside! You fucking bastards, do you hear me?"

They didn't. Tramped up, shotstones clattering over the shields and peppering Lochled's legs with shrapnel—harmless but stinging. The squad got their shield in line with Ponts, and Lochled swept the contingent of them until he found the soaking gray tunic.

Lieutenant's stripes. Shit.

"Lieutenant!" Lochled shouted at him. "We need to line up nyhtside!" he jabbed his finger to the other side of the crescent beach, where a few other squads were managing to form up under the withering fire.

The lieutenant looked down the beach with that blank sort of expression of someone who's near to losing it. "No. Daeside is better."

Lochled balked. What fucking reason did this twank have for saying daeside was better? "Hef, I gotta disagree. We'll have the sun in our eyes if we—"

"We're going daeside!" the lieutenant suddenly screeched at him, face gone ruddy, veins bulging. But he'd stood up a bit too much in his rage, and a shotstone took the top of his skull off just as neat as you please, a little white cap with some scalp attached gone spinning away into the sand.

The lieutenant gave no reaction to it. Just seemed to wither on the spot. Weird though, he didn't crumple. Sort of laid himself down, all curled up like a child gone to sleep in the cold, the red and white interior of his head showing.

"Solves that fucking problem," Lochled grunted. He pointed to the shieldmen. "You two! Other side of us! We're working nyhtside!"

They didn't seem to care one way or the other. Shrugged and got to it, trampling over their dead lieutenant, then forming up on the other side of Cryer.

More squads poured in from the surf. Didn't seem like the Tickers were sending any more ship-killers out into the ocean. Maybe they'd run out? Or maybe whoever they had hurling the bastard things had been taken out by the war barges. Didn't really matter. What mattered was that the entire horizon of the sea was now dotted with little sails, pushing landing craft toward the beach.

"What do we do now?" Rony asked.

Lochled shifted positions, always diligent to stay small, and stay very tight up against the shields. "Now we load up and get ready." He raised his voice to the others. "Get water if you have it. Drips if you need it. Check your weapons and armor. Get the sand out of your boots. Be ready to move fast—there's no more rest once we get into the city."

"This is *rest*?" Rony cried out, as a dozen or so shotstones rapped an insistent rhythm on the shield against her back.

"Nothing we can do until the shield line gets made," he said, fishing around his waist for his flask. Felt a little bad about taking all of Trut's. He'd save a bit of his own for him. "You wanna spend it all tense and tire yourself out further, you go right on ahead. But I'd advise a drink, shake out those legs, catch your breath, and get your Leveler ready. Uh?"

He found his flask. Upended it into his mouth. Took a big gulp. Passed it to Trut.

"Licker, how's your back?" Lochled called, glancing sideways as he slung his satchel around to his front.

The Fen spat sand and salt water out of his mouth. "Fucking scratch is all, hef."

"Good." Lochled ripped the top of his satchel open. A handful of tiny seashell fragments and sand came tumbling out of the creases.

More shotstones raked the shields. Lochled stopped and listened to them. Quirked an eyebrow at Cryer. "That sound different to you?"

Cryer nodded. "Slower."

"Running out of shot, or just taking their time?"

Cryer shrugged. "Won't know until we kill 'em."

Lochled had to agree. No point in speculating. He didn't even know how they were doing it. They'd thrown stones at the Third Crusade, and while it had been devastating because the landing craft had all run aground on the jetty, it hadn't been this intense or this accurate. Nor had it reached half as far.

He frowned, dove into his satchel for his pouch of scaef. Ripped a shaggy pinch out and stuffed it into his cheek. More landing craft were coming in, more soldiers, more shieldmen. And they seemed to get the right idea—form the wall moving to the nyhtside of the beach.

Hurling rocks is one thing. The Tickers were almost all draeids, so they could push and pull objects all they wanted. That was no surprise. Made sense that they'd use it to toss things at their attackers. Even a dumb cow will lash out with its horns to keep from being eaten by wolves.

But to make shotstones? To send them as far and as accurately as they were?

The Tickers had to have *made* something to do that. They had to have *invented* something. Something that not even the Church knew about. And that didn't sound low minded to Lochled. Not at all.

CHAPTER 10

"Line's ready!"

"Line's ready!"

"Line's ready!"

Lochled could hear the call come from all the way down the beach, but each man in that line of shields, huddled and dripping and sodden and exhausted, still dutifully turned their head when they heard it and shouted it on down the line until it finally reached Cryer.

"That's it then," Cryer gruffed. "You ready, hef?"

Lochled had gotten to his knees when he'd heard the call coming a few seconds ago. Pack already on his back and cinched tight again. Worst of the sand dumped out of his boots, though he suspected he was about to get more.

He twisted, spat scaef juice, and pointed to Rony. "You're up front with me. Levelers lead the way. Heavies, behind us!" Though it was just Gonder and Licker at this point, Gonder looking drained, and Licker wounded, but still in the fight. "Trut! Fuck the polearm, grab a Leveler if you see one with a dead owner, and be ready with your axe and knife until then!"

"But I like my polearm!"

"You see any fucking armies coming out to clash with us, you dense fuck?" Lochled roared. "Now ditch it!" Then he turned to Rony again, head still throbbing from screaming. "Go on and charge it up, cully. Now's the time."

Rony nodded, focused. Broke the Leveler open. Seated a charge. Every movement slow and deliberate, but that was good. Rushing things made you fumble. Lochled would rather she be slow and get it done, than fast and drop it in the sand.

When she snapped it closed, he patted her shoulder. "Good girl. Don't touch that trigger bar until you see something needs shredding. You ready to run?"

She grunted.

Cryer and Ponts had already turned their backs to their shields, looped their arms through the carrying straps so now they looked like a pair of strange turtles with enormous shells, standing on two legs.

"Got the longest rest, but now we've got the longest run!" Lochled cried out. "On me!"

Lochled took off, hunched at the waist, keeping his head below the line of shields. Steel whizzed by him. Shotstones whistling. Chips of them nettling his face and neck, making him growl and curse.

Faces watched him go. Eager faces. Downtrodden faces. Hateful faces. Faces with no expression at all. Flashes of color, marking every point of the Brannic Empire—pale Fens, tan Brymics, brown Drugothans, black Haedans. Some of them cheered him on. Some of them didn't say anything—lost in their own little worlds of chaos and terror.

Dead ahead, the city loomed. Now that he'd had a moment to clear his head, it wasn't the dark monstrosity that it'd seemed when he'd first crawled out of the surf. He'd never been this close to it before. The first and last time he saw it was from a distance of nearly a thousandstride, clinging to a piece of his shattered landing craft.

It wasn't dark at all. In fact, most of the buildings were as white as the sand on the beach. Metal roofs, the green of weathered copper. Nearly all of them. He almost staggered to a stop trying to wrap his mind around that. The pure opulence of it. Bransport was the wealthiest city he'd ever seen, and the roofs there were thatch—slate if you were rich.

A tower, straight ahead. Something glinting in one of the top windows. Then he saw something streak through the air, ending in a puff of sand, just a few feet from him. Didn't think about it much, just yanked his Leveler up, holding it at the hip, and let loose.

There was a small sound when he pulled the trigger bar, like a cork popping. And then a big *fuh-BOOM* that nearly set him to staggering. The twenty shotstones came hurtling out of that maw, trailing a plume of bright yellow smoke, and clattered all across the tower and around the window.

Whatever had been hanging out that window quickly retreated inside.

"That tower!" Lochled gasped—barely had the air to keep running his cramping legs, let alone talk while he did. "They're in that tower!"

Breaking the Leveler open while he ran. Pace flagging. Breath ragged, every intake a desperate rattle, every exhale a painful wheeze. The loops of charges jangled all around on his chest. He managed to snag one. Rip it free. Into the breech. Snapped it closed with a grind of sand caught in the hinges.

The line of shields suddenly disappeared. He'd been so focused on reloading he hadn't even realized they were there at the end. Just a small section of open beach now, and then there was the city.

Into the city! Into that tower!

But every step was turning into agony. If he were fresh, he might've been able to walk faster than this. Rony was beside him and had one hand on his shoulder, and for a second he thought he was dragging her but then realized she was pushing him on.

"Almost there!" she said—certainly out of breath, but not dying of it like Lochled.

Might've felt a little pang of hurt pride if he'd had the energy for it. As it was, he accepted her push, thankful that at least one fuck on their squad was fleet of foot.

Up ahead, a stone seawall separated the beach from the city. It wasn't all that tall, but when you're exhausted to the point of staggering, five feet starts to look like it might as well be a cliff.

Lochled slammed into it, then immediately went to his knees, hacking and coughing. Swallowed a bit of scaef juice, which burned all the way down. Decided to dig the rest out with his tongue before he caught a fit of vomiting from it. Spat the wad into the sand at his feet.

"Here," he labored out, thrusting his hands out and into a stirrup. "I'll hoist you." Pretty much because he was too tired to climb the wall at that precise moment. He needed another few breaths. "Stick your head up and clear the other side—make sure there aren't any surprises."

Rony bit her lip, looking scared, determined, and just a bit savage herself. She thrust her boot into his hands, and he grunted as he heaved her up. She got her arms up, shouted, "It's all clear!" and then scampered over.

The rest of the squad came piling in after that. Lochled would have liked to stay right there, against the relative safety of a stone wall, but he couldn't leave Rony on the other side. So he swore, thrust himself upright—a slower move than he had hoped for—then forced a tiny, lackluster jump from his legs, caught the top of the wall, and started trying mightily to get himself over. Would have completely failed if a few hands from his men below hadn't shoved him over.

He rolled over the top of it, then fell, only two feet, crunching onto cobbles.

And just like that, he was in the city of Halun's Landing.

Rony was shaking all over with every single thing that could make a person shake. Fear of death. Horror at watching so many others die. Exhaustion in every muscle. Not enough air in her lungs. Leveler too heavy in her arms.

Jittering, she spun, left to right, as Lochled came tumbling over the wall after her. Her mind was blank with the inability to truly take in all that she was seeing. The city was massive—much bigger than Bransport, but she'd known that from peeks of it on the landing craft. But it was *taller* too, not just wider and deeper. The buildings looked carved from the very ground, not a seam or a joint to be seen, no mortar anywhere, and they all towered into the sky over their heads so that her neck hurt trying to see the top of them.

In Bransport, the tallest building she'd seen was the Brannen's Keep, at four stories tall. Seemed *every* building in this place was *at least* four stories.

It struck her as terribly beautiful. Beautiful because of what it might've looked like before. Terrible because of what they'd done to it. Smashed these great white buildings to rubble. Darkened the sky with smoke. Thickened the air with the sound of men's screaming and shouting . . .

But where were all the Leftlanders?

Right over her head, she registered a noise she'd never heard before: a *zzzip*, almost like someone ripping fine cloth. It was followed by a sound she'd become intimately familiar with in the last hour: the *pock* of a shotstone hitting something hard.

Didn't realize the shotstone had been meant for her until the spray of shattered stone caught her up the left side of her face, making her yip and jump away.

"Rony!" Lochled was yelling. "The tower! Right above you!"

She wrenched her gaze up. Saw the white walls towering over her, saw the window way up toward the top, the glint of something long and brassy hanging out of it, waggling around, trying to point at her.

"Fuck!" she belted out, raised her Leveler, and fired it off for the first time.

She thought the damned thing had exploded. It went off in her hands, and it was all she could do to hold onto it. It bucked backward with the force of a mule kick, nearly ripped her shoulders from their sockets, belching smoke as yellow as goldenrod blooms.

She'd barely cleared her head from the sudden sound blast and jarring to her bones when she caught Lochled, yelling again: "Get on the wall! Get right underneath it!"

She jolted forward, only remembering that her Leveler was discharged when she realized how far she was from the safety of her squad—all the way across a wide street that seemed to run along the seawall.

She slammed her back against the white stone wall, tried to break the thing open, but it was being stubborn with all the sand in the hinges. She grunted and growled at it and finally rammed the thing down on her knee like she'd done the first time in front of Hotsteel, and that worked.

Across the street, Lochled snapped a fresh charge into his Leveler, standing up with his eyes and his Leveler pointed at the top of the tower while Gonder, Licker, and Trut came piling over, running straight past their sergeant and crossing the street to Rony.

Trut was shouting, pointing to her left: "Watch the corner, you half-wit!"

She realized she was just standing there, watching all of this with the empty charge still in her fingers, just shucked from the breech. She jerked at the order, dropped the empty charge. Looked left and saw the corner of the tower, a few strides from her. Fingers crabbing about for another charge. Grabbing it. Seating it. Snapping the nasty thing closed again.

Edging toward the corner. Suddenly terrified of what was beyond it. Terrified of what might be done to her. Terrified of what she might have to do.

Lochled's Leveler roared out again, but Rony couldn't rip her eyes off the corner she was edging toward. A second after his Leveler went off, Rony felt a smattering of debris trickle over her head and shoulders, getting down her collar.

Licker was right behind her, shoulder snugged in tight to her back. "Go on, then, cully! You hit that corner and rip up anything that idn't one of us!"

Right. Yes. She could do that.

Almost there.

Out of the corner of her eye—Lochled running to catch up to them. More soldiers pouring over the seawall. That harsh zipping sound again, followed by a sickening thud and a squeal from one of the men.

Licker's hand on her shoulder. "Don't creep corners, Little Roan. Hit 'em hard so they don't see you coming."

Right. Well. She was there.

Lochled's voice: "Rony! Go!"

She spun around the corner. Froze. Couldn't take in anything about the narrow street—only saw the figure right there in the center of it, not ten strides from her. Everything else faded to grim impression, but that figure speared its way into her, and she saw every detail in a flash.

It was olive skinned, that was the first thing she noticed—just like a Brymic, except so olive that it was damn near green. And tall! Tall and lanky, like a Haedan.

Then she noticed it wasn't wearing a scrap of clothing—had some baubles and jewelry about its neck and waist, but that was it. And it had no weapons in its hands.

Hands. Just like people's hands.

Feet, just like people's feet.

But oddest of all was that it had not a single hair—not on its head, and not even around it's . . .

Pintel. It was a man-Ticker.

She opened her mouth to speak but got nothing out but a croak.

"Ah!" Licker shouted in her ear. "Fucking get it!"

But it don't have any weapons—

The thing snarled at her, showing rows of tiny, flat teeth. Then it brought its hands together in a clap, and the next thing Rony knew, her hearing had gone out like someone had poked her ears with a needle, and she was flying backward into Licker. The two of them tumbling to the cobbles.

No sound after that. Just a harsh ringing in her ears.

Vision swimming around, dark, then too bright to see. She felt the Leveler still in her grip. Had she fired it off in the tumble? She had no clue. No way to know.

Someone was slapping her.

Then grabbing her.

Sound began to bleed its way in again.

She was being hauled up. The city swirled around her, white stone, massive towers, piles of rubble, pillars of smoke, the morning sun blazing through them . . .

"Rony! Rony!"

"Wha . . . ?" She goggled about, saw a dim, fleshy smudge in front of her. She frowned at it and that seemed to help her focus a bit. The face cleared up, pale blue eyes looking scared for her, or maybe for all of them.

"You with me?" Licker asked.

"Yeah . . ."

He was pulling her back. Back around the corner. She got a glimpse of Lochled snarling something at her, face all contorted with rage. He was on the corner now. He swung around it and let loose with his Leveler, but the noise barely bothered Rony this time.

Back against the wall. Her lungs were aching, and she couldn't breathe. Tried to tell Licker, but couldn't get the words out. He started slapping her back, hard, right on the lash mark.

She managed to suck in a breath of air. Coughed.

"There you are, cully," Licker soothed.

"Leave it to a fucking girl to not be able to pull the fucking trigger!" Trut cackled madly. "Never get a cleaner shot than that!"

Lochled stormed toward her, reloading his Leveler. Grabbed her by the front of her tunic with his free hand and jammed her rough against the wall. "Didn't I fucking say they were draeids? Uh? Don't fucking wait for them to use their powers, just fucking kill 'em!" He yanked her off the wall. "With me!"

Around the corner. Stumbling. She looked down at her Leveler. Broke it open. The charge inside was unspent. She looked up.

On the cobbles was a mess. She could tell it'd been the Ticker she'd seen only because it was in about the same spot. Other than that, it had been mangled beyond recognition.

Cryer and Ponts, side by side with their shields deployed, edging along the bottom of the tower. Lochled let go of her tunic, hustled to catch up to them, and Rony followed.

"Need to find a door into this tower," Lochled seethed, like the tower itself made him furious, and finding a way in was all the vengeance he craved.

"There, hef!" Cryer nodded ahead as they maneuvered their little wall of shields down the cobbles.

To the left, a narrow doorway. A wooden door hanging open.

"Think they're still inside?" Ponts said.

"Don't matter," Lochled spat. "We take the tower. Anyone in our way"—he looked viciously at Rony—"get's fucking *Leveled*."

Rony nodded, still struggling to get enough air to talk after that tumble.

"Shields won't fit through that door," Cryer observed as they came abreast of it.

"Fine!" Lochled pushed the shields out of the way. "Post on the bottom. Licker, Gonder, Trut! Knives and axes! Get ready to clean up!"

Lochled turned, and for a moment, Rony thought he was going to take to the doorway, but instead he used his Leveler like a baton and shoved Rony through it first.

Out of the blazing daylight and the reflection of white stone. Into dark shadow. She couldn't see shit. Almost triggered her Leveler right then and there at the darkness. Just in case.

She stayed frozen with her shoulder to the inside wall, breathing hard, waiting for her eyes to adjust.

Lochled came in behind her. Hesitated, maybe for the same reason.

After a few seconds, Rony could make out a source of light from above. She was looking at a spiral stairwell cut straight into the stone of the tower.

Rony kept the Leveler at her hip, angled it up, and started on the stairs. Foot over foot. Tread over tread. Her sodden tunic rubbing and squelching along the stone. Arms burning. Legs aching.

That zipping noise again, coming from above them.

She glanced down at Lochled. "It's still up there!"

Lochled simply nodded. His eyes were fixed on the horizon of those stairs, waiting, fingers trembling right next to his trigger bar.

Up she went. More zipping. Other sounds she couldn't identify. Didn't matter. At the top of these stairs, there would be something there. Maybe even more than one. And she wasn't going to hesitate this time. No. She was going to sweep into that room like death itself and level anything that was standing.

The daylight was getting brighter now.

A glance down again. Back behind Lochled, there was Licker and Truts and Gonder. Axes out. Knives out. Looking ready to use them. Not men anymore at all. Not even animals. At least animals aren't malicious. These men were daemons.

And she was one of them.

All too soon, she saw that last tread falling away, revealing the room beyond as she slunk higher and higher. A blaze of daylight coming in from an open window. The form, much like a man, backlit by the window. Not a scrap of clothing on it. Maneuvering some sort of contraption with a big, long pipe on it that was sticking out the window.

Zzzzzip!

He was firing down at someone. Another soldier. Another person. One of Rony's people.

The thought made her angry.

She screamed as she barged into the room, Lochled hot on her heels. The second she was clear of the narrow doorway and had her feet on flat ground, she pointed her Leveler at the shape near the window and yanked the trigger bar.

She knew about the noise. Was ready for the bone-jarring jerk of the thing in her hands. Ready for the spew of bright yellow dust.

Was not at all ready for what it did to the creature before her.

It seemed to fall apart. Like it'd been made of old pottery. Bits of it got everywhere, and there was a giant wash of red, like someone had smashed a cask of wine against the wall. A whole wave of it went splashing out the window, coating the white stone.

And down below there was a cheer.

Then there was screaming.

She whirled around, thinking it was a Ticker, but then remembered that the Tickers didn't talk—some said they didn't even make noise; they were as mute as they were stupid.

There *was* another Ticker, but it wasn't the one doing the screaming. It was laying against the far wall, looked like its leg had caught a few shotstones from her Leveler, though she hadn't even seen the thing until now. Trut was on it, howling like a wolf at the sky, and hacking away at it.

It raised its hands up, maybe to use its powers, or maybe just an instinctive attempt to ward off the coming blows, and Trut's axe went right through the wrist, sent the hand spinning across the room where it wedged against Rony's foot.

A delicate hand. Long fingered. Looked like a woman's hand.

Rony looked up, struck dumb by all that she saw, and in the mess of hacking and flailing, she saw the sag and jiggle of breasts. A woman-Ticker, then. Didn't seem to matter to Trut.

Didn't seem to matter to Licker, either, or Gonder, because they got in there and started kicking at it and cursing it until Trut finally cleft its head in two.

"Yeah," Rony husked out, not even sure what she was saying. The same animating power that had led her over that ladder and into the landing craft seemed to be moving her mouth all on its own. "Kill that fucker!"

Then, when she tried to speak again, her mouth filled with vomit. She doubled over and spewed on the floor and on the delicate hand that lay dead at her feet.

CHAPTER 11

"Good girl!" Lochled growled at Rony as she doubled over. He gave her a dismissive pat on the back as she vomited and strode past her, eyes fixed on the contraption hanging out of the window.

What the fuck is that thing?

Not the Ticker. That was just meat at this point. He grabbed what was left of it, gumming up the corner of the window, and heaved it out. Gave a peek to watch it fall. Saw the men below, faces looking up and watching that big chunk of Ticker plummet to the ground. Their faces were happy, chagrined, mournful, ecstatic, enraged.

The piece splattered, and another cheer went up below.

"We got the fucker!" Lochled bellowed down to them, then pulled his head back inside, rapidly scanned the room to see if there was anything else of use, but there wasn't much. The tower had a few other windows. Those might provide some good vantage points on the city.

Finally, he turned to the contraption, frowning at it, heaving air past a dry tongue as his eyes went over it from top to bottom and side to side.

"What is it?" Rony asked.

He couldn't even begin to guess. Barely even knew how his own weapon worked, let alone this foreign thing. "Something that throws shotstones harder and farther than our Levelers. And I don't like that one bit."

Rony's eyes had a feverish look about them. Didn't seem to be able to rip them from the contraption. "Think it'll fetch a price with the priests?"

Lochled shrugged. "It may. But we got work to do before we start worrying about all that." He threw a hand at it as he stalked across the room. "Besides, it's bolted to the floor."

"Right. Well." Rony's voice faded behind him, Lochled only half paying attention, eyeing those other windows now. "I, uh . . . I claim this."

Breathless and mocking, Trut giggled at her. "You don't claim it like that, Little Roan. Besides, if anything in this tower fetches a price it's split between the squad. Don't reckon you found it by yourself, now did you?"

Lochled worked his way to the window, exceedingly conscious of the fact that the Tickers had more of those things, given the volume of shotstones thrown at them on the beach. Last thing he wanted was to make an easy target and get his head punched out just when things were starting to look up.

He said as much to his squad, and they all got small, seeking corners.

Lochled angled this way and that, inspecting the other buildings around them, but nothing seemed occupied. When he finally reached the window and looked out, his breath caught in his chest, and for a very brief moment he thought he was going to sob.

You bastard fucking animal . . .

Halun's Landing stretched tall and imperious around the

crescent of beach. Rose up into the mountains from which it seemed to be carved. A place with so many back alleys and sections it was like multiple cities all bundled together tight like a sheaf of wheat.

And the towers! Feor's mercy, he'd never seen such lofty things! The beauty and craftsmanship of them so far beyond anything he'd seen in the Brannic Empire that it almost made him balk at what they'd done to it. Shattered those great, ancient buildings with their siege cannons. Reduced so many of them to rubble. And they'd never be able to put them back together the way they'd been—because they didn't even know how. There was no stonemason or architect in all the empire that could rebuild what they'd just destroyed.

And it wasn't all just white stone—seemed every level of every tower had a terrace overflowing with plant growth. Long tendrils of green vines and splashes of red and yellow and pink flowers. Some of the terraces even had trees growing on them, many covered in bright white blooms. It all seemed so oddly pristine amid the roiling smoke and flames.

Between several of the towers that still stood, Lochled saw what he thought were great lengths of rope that ended on either side in wide, open balconies, as though to connect the towers. But then he saw the way the sunlight glittered off those ropes and realized they weren't rope at all. They were . . . metal?

How does one make metal ropes? And to what end?

He realized he was just standing there, marveling at it all. Swore under his breath and shook his head to clear the awe from between his ears. Forced himself to look at all that magnificence with a soldier's eye. Tried to make himself feel vindicated by the destruction of all that beauty—vengeance for all the lives they'd lost. But then he remembered that they'd been the ones to attack.

Find the Tickers, you half-wit.

He leaned into the window, eyes narrowing.

There was a little spot, toward the center of the city, where the buildings were spaced out enough to see a massive thoroughfare at ground level. Reminded him of the market streets in Bransport. It wasn't the wideness of the street that he noticed, but that it was filled with Tickers. A river of them, all flowing away from the beach and out of the city.

That's where they all went!

"Hey, we got—"

The stone to the left of his head shattered.

"Fuck!" He dropped in place.

"You all right?" Trut called to him, back flat against the wall. "They get you?"

"Nah, fucker missed." Lochled wiped sweat and grit off his face. Hiked a thumb over his shoulder. "Tickers are fleeing the city!"

"Uh?" Trut grinned. "Guess they remember the Second!"

Lochled shuffled on hands and knees, keeping below the windows until he got to the one with the contraption mounted in it. He sidled up, leaned over. Found a mass of men and shields below, all milling about like they couldn't figure where to go from there. Probably thinking what they'd all thought when they got over the seawall: Where the fuck are all the Tickers?

"Hey!" he shouted down at them. "They're fleeing alefts, out of the city! Pass on the word! Cut 'em off! They're fleeing alefts!"

There was a scream of rage and triumph, a howl that shook the rafters and the stones. Men charged down the street, axes and knives and polearms and Levelers all waving about, shieldmen lugging their greatshields and trying to keep up. A few men conscientiously passed the word down over the seawall and back to the hordes of soldiers crawling all over the beach like ants on a corpse.

He watched it happen. Had seen it in the Pan, so many times. And everyone knew that this was when the slaughter happened: the rout. As soon as one side gets to running, the other goes mad, chasing after them like hounds on a rabbit, and there's nothing that can stop the murder.

He could see the word reaching the men on the beach. Saw them suddenly abandoning caution. Streaming out from behind the shield wall, surging toward the city.

On the streets, howling and screaming. Men darting every which way with no apparent purpose, just looking for something to destroy. Slipping in and out of alleys. Any semblance of order or strategy or training simply gone—gone, and it wouldn't be back for some time.

A fleshy shape darted out of an alley. A male Ticker. That was all that Lochled could tell from his vantage point. It kept looking behind it. Made it across the street to the seawall, as though it thought the beach might be an escape.

Men poured over the seawall right in front of it. No hesitation—they just started hacking away at it.

It never made a sound. Just died there, writhing in pain.

Lochled stepped away from the window. His right hand crept over his beltline. Shaking fingers touched his flask. He wiggled it in place, felt the slosh—there was still a mouthful in there. Meant to save it for Trut, but he *needed* it now.

"Hef, we going or what?" Gonder whined. Like a kid that couldn't wait to get to a festival.

"Uh." Lochled took another step back from the window. But no matter where he positioned himself, there was still a view of a city being sacked. Ravaged. Raped. And he'd done it. He didn't have to tell them that the Tickers were fleeing down the center. But he did. Seemed like a good, soldierly thing to do, to let your comrades know where the enemy is.

The stink of spirits made him quiver. Took the last mouthful. It didn't even burn. Tasted almost like water, it went down so easy. And he desperately wanted more. But that was it. He capped it. He had a little longer yet to let the daemons of his flesh run amok.

He was just beginning to wonder if he was willing to pay the price on the back end.

Things to think about later.

He secured the flask to his belt, spun about. "Right then, fuckers. Down we go."

Down, down, down.

Down the steps. The clatter of feet becoming a wild tumble the closer they got to the bottom. Gonder and Trut breathing hard and heavy, like men fucking. Lochled feeling lost, half in and half out of this world.

They burst out into daylight.

Cryer and Ponts were still there, looking antsy.

"Fuck took you so long?" Cryer griped at him.

"I'm here now, aren't I?" Lochled set off across the street, pace picking up again. If he kept moving, he wouldn't have time to think. Feor help him if he had time to think. Time to think was time to doubt. Doubt made you hesitate. Hesitation made you dead.

They were charging through eerily abandoned streets. Every once in a while, they'd slip into an alley and see another soldier down a ways. Once, Lochled thought it might've been a Ticker, but it disappeared too quick to be sure.

The Leftlanders had been ready this time. Ready to put in a fight, but also ready to retreat if their defenses broke.

Movement from a doorway to his left. He whipped his Leveler around, almost unleashed it, but saw a hand axe emerge from the shadows within, then a long-knife, and then an eager face grinning from ear to ear like it was some hell of a revelry, though the man's eyes looked sunken and sick.

"Copper pots!" he yelled at Lochled. "*Copper* fucking *pots*!"

"Get on, then!" Lochled barked at him, heart pounding at almost having killed a comrade.

All around them the white stone loomed, pristine—that is, except for where it'd been splattered by blood, pockmarked by shotstones, or completely crumbled by the siege cannons. One thing Lochled noted: he hadn't seen a single damn pipe. In Bransport the pipes coursed all through the city, and it was technology that they'd stolen from Leftland.

So where were all the water pipes? And where were the water wheels?

The squad trooped into a narrow intersection, half blocked by an object so odd that it drew them all to a stop, every member of the squad staring at it wonderment, and no small amount of avarice.

"Heyo—whassat?" Trut murmured, tilting his head to one side as though trying to make sense of what he was seeing. "A carriage of some sort?"

By Lochled's estimation, that's exactly what it was, though how it worked, he couldn't tell. That it was a fine piece of craftsmanship was obvious—all neatly milled carpentry and fine metalworking to join it all together. Two large wheels on what must've been the front, based on the orientation of the open seats. One small wheel on the back that jutted out and seemed to be able to swing freely from a metal strut. At the midpoint of that strut was another seat. Reminded him of how a boatsman sat in the rear of their landing craft, manning the tiller to steer it.

But . . . no yoke for animals to pull it.

"Best not get your hopes up," Lochled advised Trut, nodding to the handful of other soldiers that were already climbing all over it, poking and prodding. One of them saw Lochled and his squad and glared, hands wringing the haft of a polearm. Like a wolf standing over his kill.

"Best be moving on!" the man growled at them.

"Come on, then," Lochled said, giving the strange carriage and its finders a wide berth as he skirted the intersection.

On they went. Pace slowing now. Getting toward the center of the city.

Another odd thing that Lochled noticed: he'd never been in a city that didn't stink of sewage. And maybe it was just that the stink of smoke—both from wood and from alchemy—covered it. But no matter which street they went down, Lochled hadn't spotted a single gutter for effluent to flow through. Not like in Bransport.

Hell, down in certain sections of Bransport, like Rotsbottom, they didn't even have gutters—just tossed it out into the street.

So, what did the Tickers do with all their piss and shit?

The smoke was getting thicker, as were the sounds of destruction. From every corner, the crash of pottery and the clanging of metal. Shouted words that meant nothing. Wails and screams. Some fighting, Lochled thought, by the sound of things being hurled—big impacts as the Tickers threw stones it would take a catapult for a man to get into the air.

CRASH! Something big hit a building up ahead. The top crumbled, and a few men inside went flailing out, screaming.

They passed a building completely engulfed in flames—one of the few structures that looked like it'd been made of wood. Looked like a chief's house, it was so nice. Except for the flames consuming it.

A man came out of a doorway, hauling two dead Tickers by their limp arms. Slumped them up against the wall outside.

Stomped one in the head, crushing its skull for no apparent reason. "Two more for the Burners!"

Lochled's pace had flagged, but still he kept on, and his squad with him. And dead ahead, the street they were on opened up wide. Looked like that main thoroughfare in the center of the city. Men were scurrying back and forth. Objects were being thrown, presumably by the retreating Tickers, as they all seemed to be going one way. A shield line was forming up in the street, the soldiers getting behind it, all gnashing teeth and wide eyes. Levelers poked out of the top, fluming yellow dust.

A squad of men scampered around the street, one of them shouting, "Go, boys! Take 'em from the side! From the side!"

Lochled was still striding toward it, but he didn't want it. Would have liked to be anywhere else in the world, if he were being honest—

"Hef! There!"

He jerked at the sound of Cryer's voice. The big man was pointing to an alley on their left.

"Swearnsoot, I just saw that door close, like someone didn't want us coming in."

Trut let out a blast of curses. Took off across the street toward the door. "We'll see about that!"

Gonder was right behind him. Lochled was following too. Hell, the whole squad was moving now, churning toward that door. They would've stopped if Lochled had told them to, but he didn't. Couldn't. It wasn't time for that. Not yet.

Trut stomped to a halt in front of the door, rapped the flat of his hand axe against it. "If you're one of us, best speak out! If you're a fuck Ticker, don't say nothing at all!"

No sound came from beyond the door.

Lochled got to the door and sunk into position, right on the hinge side, Leveler ready. Ready to breach and kill.

On through the breach, crash through the door!

Rony was there, right next to him.

"I'll go right, you go left," Lochled whispered, then nodded at Trut.

Kept telling himself that it was because there might be Tickers in there with some of those contraptions like the one in the tower. Knew those thoughts for lies as soon as he had them. Didn't matter who was inside there, Lochled meant to kill them.

Trut kicked, and the door burst open.

Lochled and Rony, jammed in shoulder to shoulder, barely fitting through the door—would've been comical, the two of them jockeying around each other like a pair of imbeciles, if their intentions weren't so dark.

Lochled got through, swept right, and instantly triggered the Leveler. Rony did the same. Two big blasts in the enclosed space, setting his ears to ringing again. Dust sifting through the air, yellow, and stinking of sooty alchemy.

The rush behind them. Screams and yells. Men kicking things, axing things, throwing things, just to watch them break.

Lochled cursed, coughed, spat. Lunged through the misty yellow air. Found splatter all across one wall. *Oh, my Leveler paints it so pretty!*

"Got one!" Lochled yelled, his voice breaking.

A great, wild cry in all that madness—the swirling yellow, the dark, looming shapes of bodies, the flash of steel. The sound of an axe thunking into a skull.

"Rony got half, I got the other half!" a triumphant Trut proclaimed.

Lochled followed the wall, came across another Ticker body not too far from the first. A big squiggle of red, like someone had dragged a paintbrush across the floor. It was a male Ticker. Must've caught a few shotstones in the hip and thigh. It was trying to pull itself along with its arms. Eyes gaped fearfully up at Lochled. They were oddly round, making them look perpetually shocked. Its hand started to move. Maybe to beg for mercy or maybe to use its powers to hurl Lochled through the wall.

He rammed the flat end of his Leveler down hard on the Ticker's face, mushing half of it into red porridge. The thing collapsed on the ground, but wasn't quite dead yet, or maybe was just twitching. Lochled wasn't taking chances.

Growling, lost in the moment, the pure maliciousness of it, almost a panic, Lochled wrenched his Leveler open, thumbed the spent charge out. Heard it clatter to the floor—*tink-tink-tink*—slammed a fresh one in, snapped it closed. All quick and shaky, so he almost fumbled the whole weapon out of his hands in the doing, but then leaned back and shoved the maw of it close to the Ticker's upper body, cringing and squinting one eye so he wouldn't get blood and bone fragments in it.

Yes! My Leveler paints it so pretty!

Tears in his eyes, and he told himself it was just the thickness of the yellow dust.

He swung away from the mess he'd made, recharged the Leveler, hid a sob with a cough but chose not to think about that too much—not yet, anyway.

"What's this then?" Gonder's voice sneered.

Lochled could barely see more than a foot in front of him, the air was so thick with yellow. He lurched through the fog and happened upon a cluster of dark shapes hovering in the corner of the room. Something about the way they all stood terrified Lochled. All hunched and greedy, like all they wanted in the world wasn't just the riches of Leftland but simply to murder freely, wildly, with abandon.

The daemons of their flesh had taken control of them. But they were doing Feor's will, so that made it all right.

Lochled barged through the ring of bodies, morbidly curious as to what they were all gibbering on about. Gonder and Trut had their axes up, kept raising them threateningly, then laughing uncontrollably. Cryer and Ponts were staring down, blank and empty.

Only Rony was looking right at him. Eyes wide, like the only one among them that was holding onto a shred of her humanity. Poor, daft girl. She didn't know any better.

Lochled found what everyone was carrying on about: two Tickers. But young. Very young. One a boy, one a girl. Huddling there against the wall with their hands upraised, crying their little round eyes out. But not making a sound while they did it.

Gonder giggled at it. "They really *are* mute! They can't even wail like real children!"

Every time Gonder and Trut raised their axes, the two young Tickers cringed back. Gonder and Trut were having a grand time of it. Or at least looked like they were. Though there was a madness in their eyes that said they knew they were plummeting into hell and could only deal with it by fully committing to the insanity, even as the descent terrified them.

"All right then!" Rony suddenly shrieked, her voice shrill and jarring. "Just do it! No need to torture the poor fucks!"

Trut leered at her. "Well, if you're so keen on it, then go ahead, Little Roan."

There was a bad look to Rony's face. The life had gone out of her dark skin. Turned near black around her eyes, and a washed-out gray in her cheeks and around her tense mouth. Looked like she'd been bled dry, and for a second, Lochled eyed her up and down to see if she really was wounded.

She let out a little noise: "Ah." Then raised her Leveler.

"Don't do it," Lochled vomited the words out. Uncontrollable.

Watched himself lean across and redirect the maw of Rony's Leveler off to the side. Felt everyone's attention shift to him.

A shiver ran through him head to foot as he turned his eyes on his squad, feeling like the wounded wolf in a hungry pack. Spat on the ground and bared his teeth at them. Couldn't look at the two Tickers, but could still see them jittering about out of the corner of his eye, they were shaking so hard.

"Let's not be dense about it," Lochled said, trying to scramble back to the top, find some words that made sense, that wouldn't seem weak. "The priests might have some interest in the small ones. Besides. Our own draeids can't be harvested for anything worthwhile until"—he almost choked, because, dammit, he glanced at the Tickers and saw Libby instead—"until they've grown into their pintel and sheath." He waved a hand at the two, ripping his gaze away and feeling like he left bits of himself behind. "These two obviously haven't. Even if the priests aren't interested, you might end up mixing dud ash in with the good. Right? I dunno. Just being cautious."

Cryer was watching him carefully. Lochled didn't like that look one bit. Trut and Gonder had expressions like they fully believed Lochled had lost himself. Ponderous Ponts didn't seem to care one way or the other, just had those gloomy eyes of his fixed on the Tickers.

"Sergeant's right," Cryer suddenly said. "These two little ones aren't worth killing. Not yet, anyways. Not until we're told so. Like the sergeant said, be best to wait and see if there's interest in 'em."

"Right. Yes." Lochled waved a hand in front of his face, blinking rapidly. "Fucking dust. Take these two young'uns outside, clear the rest of this shit heap, and let's move on."

Trut and Gonder grumbled about it but complied with the order.

"That your mum, uh?" Trut teased the girl-Ticker as he hauled her up. "Look what we did to her! More than she deserved after what she did to all our boys on the beach!"

Gonder dragged the boy outside by the neck and shoved him roughly against the wall. "Sit down!" He pointed, and the boy slumped to the ground, face in his hands, shoulders quaking. "Well, whaddaya know, Sergeant!" Gonder marveled. "These Tickers understand Brymic! He-he-he!"

Lochled coughed again. Damned dust was drying out his throat and wetting his eyes at the same time. He waved his Leveler irritably at Gonder. "Go on then! Search the house!"

Fingers, scrabbling about for his flask. Only remembering it was empty when he touched it.

"Swearnsoot," he griped, still with his back to the Ticker children. Didn't want to turn around. Rony was over there, on the other side of the alley, her back to the opposite wall, watching them with an expression of complete confusion.

Lochled went for his pouch of scaef instead, trying to will his fingers to be still enough to do it. "What's wrong with you, uh? You look confused. What are you confused about?"

"They're . . ." Rony turned her head, like she wanted to look away, but her eyes stayed stuck to them. "They're crying for their parents."

Lochled glared at her. Didn't need Rony adding to his troubles. He was having a hard enough time keeping it together as it was. Stupid, daft skelpie. He managed to get his scaef pouch open. "Lots of animals cry out for their parents when you kill 'em. You ever seen a blackfish harvested, uh? The calves'll follow the boats with their parents in 'em getting peeled, whining and crying the whole time. Follow 'em all the way back to Bransport." He jammed some scaef into his mouth. Then more. Then more. Until his cheek nearly hurt from being stretched. "That's how it is with most whales, actually. Doesn't make 'em any less a dumb animal."

But what about . . . ?

"No!" Lochled roared at nothing, bits of scaef and spit spurting out of his mouth. "NOT FUCKING YET!"

Rony didn't even twitch at his outburst. And he checked himself, feeling ashamed, feeling like he'd lost himself, maybe to the point that he wouldn't find himself again when he needed it. What if he was in this state forever? What if he'd been in it for so long that he couldn't come back out?

"Sergeant Lochled Thatcher!" The voice came booming down the alleyway.

Cheek bulging ridiculously with scaef, lips quivering and dabbed red with it, eyes manic, still glistening with tears, Lochled watched Hotsteel come stalking from the main street, a squad of heavies trundling along after him, knives and axes unbloodied, but eyes looking eager to remedy it.

"Captain," Lochled croaked.

Hotsteel was grinning broadly, as happy as a cat in a fish market. "Brytan Company! First on the beach! I *knew* you would do it!" He slapped Lochled hard on the shoulder, damn near made him stagger.

"We weren't the first on the beach," Lochled mumbled.

"First to survive," Hotsteel said. "First into the city, I hear!" Then he caught sight of the two Tickers. One of them moved its feet, and Hotsteel whirled on it, hand axe coming up, then hesitating. "What's this, Lochled?"

Hotsteel's squad of heavies all came trooping in close, half a dozen grown men with steel in their hands, glowering down at the two children as though those helpless figures were the most threatening things in the world.

Lochled wished he had some scaef juice to spit, but honestly, his mouth was so dry, and whatever moisture there was had been soaked up by the wad. He spat anyway—just a globule of pinkish froth.

"I think they're too young to use their powers," Lochled said.

"Doesn't matter. They all go in the Burners."

"Well, I thought if they didn't have their powers yet, maybe we didn't want their ash mixed in with the others."

Hotsteel gave him a strange look, like maybe he thought Lochled was having him on. "We don't have time to sort through every Ticker and see which ones are worth harvesting." A slightly confused smile. "And could you imagine how slow our work would be if we had to? No, our job is to kill as many as possible, burn 'em, and send the ashes back to Bransport. Let the priests sort the rest of it out."

"Right, well," Lochled was getting flustered now. "The priests, yes. I was wondering if maybe the priests would be interested in a few live young ones."

Hotsteel's eyes crinkled up at the corners, like he was looking into the sun. "What are you on about, Lochled?" He smiled again, but it was hesitant. "You catch a stone to the head or something? What use would the priests have for young Tickers?"

"I don't know," Lochled could feel his heart battering at his ribs like a madman in a cage. "To learn something about them, maybe."

Hotsteel's face flattened out. Like all the things that made him a man were simply rubbed out and he was stone as smooth as river rock. "There's nothing more we need to learn about the Tickers. The Church has told us everything we need to know. All that studying and learning—that's the job of the priests." He pointed a finger at Lochled. "You're not a priest. You're a soldier."

"Right. And a soldier's just a fancy word for a killer."

Hotsteel tilted his head to one side and his voice got quiet.

"I've tried to speak reason to you, Lochled. Will you make me give you a direct order, then?" Something in his eyes, as stony as they were, seemed hurt by that.

Lochled was as still as the ice in Caldegrund. What would Hotsteel's father think if he saw this now? His son, Lochled's captain, having to give Lochled orders as if they were common soldiers with no history between them. Hotsteel having to use the threat of force just to get a man who should've been his greatest ally and asset to do what he was told?

Lochled felt a heavy load of guilt laid across his shoulders, and he averted his eyes from Hotsteel's. "Sorry, hef." Lochled muttered. Closed his Leveler. Turned it on the two Ticker children, and did what he'd been ordered to do.

The plume of yellow. The blast of red.

It's already been painted from ceiling to floor! Oh, my Leveler paints it so pretty! Yes, my Leveler paints it so pretty!

A heavy hand on his shoulder.

Hotsteel's breath, hot on his cheek. "Good man."

CHAPTER 12

Ord actually felt a little adventurous at the prow of the landing craft as it bobbled its way toward the beaches of Leftland. It didn't last long—just a bit of relief that came upon him like a break in the clouds during the rains, shining a smidgen of light on him before slipping back into a downpour.

But for that brief moment, with the wind at his back, looking ahead to the burning city of Halun's Landing, he pictured himself as he might appear on a tapestry: *Ord Griman, priest of the Third Order, arriving in Halun's Landing, Fourth Crusade.*

Then he heard a thump against the hull of the craft, and when he looked down, he realized they were skimming through a patch of dead bodies, all bobbing along in the same spot by some coincidence of current. Some of them facing up. Some of them facing down. Must've been mostly Levelers or polearms, he noted distantly. The shieldmen and the heavies would've sunk to the bottom.

He had no visceral reaction to it. He seemed drained dry of visceral reactions, after all morning long with the pounding of the war barges and the shouting of men preparing for battle.

The horror of watching the Leftlanders take out entire barques with massive throwing stones. Seeing the men go pinwheeling into the air, screaming. Seeing the landing craft go under in giant plumes of seawater. Heavily laden men slipping under the surface, hands clawing for air. Huge fogbanks of yellow smoke from their siege cannons, drifting about the fleet.

Worst of all was how every man on the boat seemed to change, and he was the only one left the same. They all went to a place he didn't even know existed. And he was left standing there, wondering where their minds had gone.

Funny. He'd always pictured these great battles happening with some semblance of honor, the smash of forces together more like sport than anything truly malicious. Yes, a certain amount of manful anger toward the enemy, but otherwise, still as civilized as slaughter could be. Efficient almost. A machine made up of men doing their little parts to make it churn forward. And if they won, it was "Steady on, men! We've taken the field!" and if they lost, it was "Steady on, men! Take courage!"

He'd pictured a lot more grand speeches, like the one the Brannen had given before their departure. Men cheering bravely. Then bowing their heads for prayers. Maybe even asking him to say a prayer for them. Some encouragement between the men: "Be brave, and the day will be ours!" and other such things.

Basically, he'd expected all of these people to act like . . . well . . . people.

That had not been the case.

He'd gone to bed that night on a ship full of men—hard men, sure. Rough men, definitely. But men just the same. And when he'd woken up they'd all gone. Their spirits had left them. Any light of Feor that might have been in them seemed to have died in the night, and all that strode about the deck were their wrathful corpses, seething toward wanton destruction.

And then it had occurred to Ord Griman, priest of the Third Order, that the horror of war was less in the doing, and more in the spirit in which it was done. The spirit behind the Fourth Crusade seemed a foul one, but no one else seemed to notice, not even Kayna Redstone. Everyone just seemed to accept it without mention, and Ord could only conclude that this was normal. This was how things were done. This was what war looked like.

And that was about the time his spirits sort of withered.

So now, when he looked down at the floating bodies that his landing craft was plowing through, like a patch of seaweed detached from the ocean floor, he didn't feel much at all. Just another confirmation of his worst fears.

How could this work be the work of Feor? How could mangling men's souls to the point that they were willing to mangle others' bodies have anything to do with goodness and light? It all felt twisted up on itself, like a fishing net that's gotten tangled in a reef.

Did Feor simply forgive them for succumbing to their daemonic flesh because they were unleashing his spirit from the Leftlanders? Was it the men's fault for being so base about the whole thing? Were there, perhaps, soldiers out here who had fought and conducted themselves with honor?

So far, he hadn't seen any.

"Oh, look!" Kayna chirped out cheerily behind him.

He twitched, looked around, saw what she was pointing at: a wide, flat-keeled barge, trundling its way toward the beach, with what looked like fifty or so horses on it.

"If we'd waited another twenty minutes, we wouldn't have had to walk through the sand."

Ord grunted, in no mood for chirping or cheer. "A sacrifice I'll accept to be free of boats twenty minutes sooner."

She regarded him with a hand up to shade her eyes. "You don't look as bad as you did the rest of the trip. Seasickness leave you?"

"It was replaced with a different sickness."

She licked her lips, and gave him a look he didn't care for. Like she was humoring him. "Oh?"

Ord waved a hand about, not leaving a single direction out of his accusation. "All these men. Purged of reason and . . . and . . . debased of their humanity! Running amok and slaughtering like beasts, and being slaughtered like beasts in return."

"Mmm." Kayna indelicately picked something from the corner of her eye, inspected it, then flicked it away. "Imagine how the men feel, having to debase themselves just to survive."

Ord glanced at the crewman at the tiller, but he either hadn't heard or didn't care. "They made choices, Kayna."

"Yes. Everyone makes choices. You make choices. I make choices. Some of those choices lead to good things. Some of them lead to bad things. But everything good, and everything bad, always started with a choice. And that's the thing about choices: sometimes we make a good choice that leads us down a bad road. And so often we never see it coming until we're in the thick of it." She sighed. Shrugged. "What can we do? Such is life."

"Hold steady, Theynen!" the crewman called.

Ord had just enough time to look forward, see the wave bearing them rapidly toward the beach, and grab onto the sides of the prow before it thumped into the sand.

"Whoop! Good showing, Theynen." A somewhat cautious glance at Kayna. "Missus." The crewman hopped over, up to his waist in the water, and began to heave the boat steadily toward the shore. "Steady on. Almost there."

The shoreline was choked with bodies. The tide would come in, stir them about a bit, then leave them beached again.

Some of them were streaming little lagoons of red in the sand. Others, apparently, had been there long enough to completely bleed out. Already some crabs were darting in and out of the surf to snatch morsels from the men's softer bits, and the gulls were winging around in great white clouds, filling the air with their gluttonous keening.

Ord hopped out. Thought he'd be ecstatic to be on dry land again. Had pictured himself kissing the sand. But the sand looked a bit less wonderful now, washed with waves tinted red, a faint smell in the background, like ripening meat and shit, the latter of which Ord was shocked he could even smell after five days on that barque.

Oddly enough, the sudden cessation of constant motion made him feel a little topsy-turvy, and he almost staggered. Eyes had a bit of trouble adjusting, they were so used to tracking so much movement up and down. All this stillness was making him nauseated again.

He had the urge to laugh, but thought it would be inappropriate among so many dead.

"Seasickness turns to . . . what?" he looked around at Kayna. "They have a name for when being on land makes you sick?"

She smiled. "Landsickness, I presume."

Ord's lips made something like a smile, though it managed not to be cheerful at all. "Of course. Landsickness." He turned back toward the beach as the crewman helped Kayna from the boat, the Seeker conscientiously holding her black robes above the ankle-deep water until she was able to take a few steps onto dry sand.

From the left side of the beach, a small contingent of men were approaching, led by a man in a gray uniform tunic. Lieutenant's stripes. Hand axe and long-knife in his belt. The others mostly with Levelers.

Ord glanced past them, spied the shade flapping violently in the wind, just on the beach side of what appeared to be a seawall that ringed the entire strand. That would be where Steadman Gunnar Thaersh had erected his command post. Distantly, Ord could make out a man a solid head shorter than everyone else around him, yet all the men spun and bustled around him as though he were the hub of a wheel, and they the spokes.

The lieutenant reached them, red faced and sweating. Squinting against the sun so hard he only had one eye open. "Theynen Ord Griman?"

"Yes?"

The lieutenant glanced at Kayna. "And Seeker Kayna Redstone?"

"That is what they call me." She smiled prettily. The only pretty thing in this wash of ugliness.

The lieutenant averted his gaze from her, as though embarrassed at his appearance before a lady—breeches sodden, caked to the knees in white sand, hands tinted with blood, a bit of it speckled on his face, stripes of it looking black on his gray tunic.

"If you'll follow me." He spun stiffly and began marching back the other way.

Ord and Kayna followed behind, Kayna smartly sticking to the slightly wet sand that was solid and compact, while Ord stubbornly stuck to the soft stuff that took twice the effort.

"Why not use the buildings?" Ord asked the lieutenant.

"What's that, Theynen?"

Ord pointed. "Why not put the command post in the buildings? I'm sure it would be far more comfortable than the beach." And Ord could have done with a bit of comfort right about then. Wanted it bad, like a man wants water when he comes in from working the plow.

The lieutenant gawked at him like he was mad. Then a flicker of a smile, as though he had suddenly decided Ord *must* be joking. "Well, Theynen . . . you . . . uh . . . don't want to be inside the city at a time like this." Somewhere in there, he'd realized Ord was indeed *not* joking and had whipped back around. "It'll be a bit heady in there through the night. Best to stick to the beach. But perhaps in the morning. When things have calmed down."

Ord glanced about the expanse of Halun's Landing. "Seems fairly ca—"

A great ruckus suddenly spilled over the seawall, rather close, Ord thought—only a few hundred strides from the post. The shouting and whooping of men. Then a single nude figure came hurtling over the seawall and landed in the sand. Its complexion looked almost green against the white sand.

A Ticker! Ord's heart went into paroxysms of sudden terror and not a little bit of excitement. It was running *toward* him! And it was . . . a woman?

A polearm chased her, hacking madly through the air, then being thrown at her like a javelin. She dodged and rolled through the sand, sending gouts of it flying.

Nearly twenty men suddenly hit the seawall and started clambering after her, baying like a pack of hounds. Steel glinted in the sun. Plumes of yellow dust erupted from a handful of Levelers, and a moment later, the sound of it came in big pulses that Ord could feel in his chest.

The female Ticker somehow wasn't hit. She managed to dance and weave in almost impossible ways, and when she came upright she reached out with both hands toward her pursuers . . .

"Feor's mercy," Ord gasped, as he watched the nearest of the men go launching off the face of the earth like he'd had a siege cannon's push charge strapped to his hindquarters, his body spinning off into the side of a nearby building and then dropping bonelessly.

The others kept charging after her. She sent another slamming into the seawall, where his head burst like an overripe fruit, and then another was simply tossed into the air and landed a hundred strides away in the sand, not moving after that. But eventually one of the men managed to maneuver around her side and brought down a polearm like he was chopping wood.

Ord heard the *thunk* all the way across the beach. Straight down through the Ticker's shoulder, nearly down to her belly. She waggled about, still standing, as the man with the polearm tried to yank his weapon out of her, struggling with it, apparently.

One of the other soldiers ran up and triggered his Leveler, and the woman-Ticker broke like an old wineskin dropped out of a window.

Ord jerked when he saw that happen. Shocked. And he waited for the feeling of revulsion. Gave it time to bubble up. Was that it? No. Maybe that was just the "landsickness," making everything unsteady. What about that uncomfortable feeling in his gut, right there?

With a note of horror, he realized that what he'd just felt was hunger.

Mercy, he was starving.

He frowned, knowing that the Tickers were barely more than animals. And should he feel anything to watch a butcher slaughter a calf? Of course not. That animal was there to feed man. That was its purpose. These animals were here to give them their ashes. That was *their* purpose.

"Well," the lieutenant said, voice a little thready, wiping at his brow. "Like I said. Best to keep out of the city until things have fully calmed down."

The lieutenant was walking again, and Kayna was following. Ord moved his feet along, but his eyes stayed out there where the Ticker had fallen. Watched one of the men stand over her and spit on her. Yelled something at the body. Ord couldn't tell what he'd said but was fairly sure it was profane.

Do you spit on the calf when you kill it? Do you curse it?

Something about that felt wrong to him. But then again, the calf likely hadn't just flung your fellow butchers into a stone wall. Ord supposed that could make the men a little edgy.

Maybe if they could trick the Tickers into cooperating more?

He imagined neat little lines of Tickers, standing there all nice and orderly, while one soldier with a hand axe hacked his way through the lot of them.

Probably unrealistic to hope for. But perhaps something to ponder. The Church was always seeking innovations. More efficient ways of doing things. Mounting crusades like this and throwing thousands of men into walls of shotstones . . . well, that didn't seem very efficient to Ord.

They were at the command post now, near to the shade, and all the milling bodies. All the captains in their tunics and sashes, and the Seekers assigned to each company in their black robes, creating a wall, so Steadman Gunnar Thaersh could not be seen. But he could be heard. His voice was harsh and deep, a little raspy. His accent so quintessentially Rumlith that one didn't need colored banners and sashes to know where he came from.

"One of these days they'll let us build a fucking harbor and stick around after we're done, uh? 'No, no,' they say. 'Go and then come back.' Now, where's the sense in that? We've taken the fucking city. Why not keep the fucking city? Fah! The fucking Church"—Ord broke through the wall of captains and Seekers, and Gunnar caught him with a single glance and deftly pivoted his words—"knows what they're talking about, though, uh? Suppose us soldiers should stick to soldiering. 'Sides. If we didn't have Halun's Landing to take over every three to five years, the lot of us might actually live to grow old, and no one wants that shit!"

A hearty laugh from the captains—the Seekers remained predictably aloof. Sounded more like a laugh because they loved Gunnar than it did because they loved the joke. Then again, maybe they'd seen the switch he'd done and were backing up their beloved commander now that a priest was present.

Gunnar looked at him, acted surprised. "Ah! And there he is! Ord Griman, priest of the Third Order. Did you see that shit?" he said, pointing to the spot on the seawall where the woman-Ticker had made her last stand. "Bitch-Ticker done smacked the men around like a monger whacking fish heads. These fucking animals. Swearnsoot, most of 'em are dumber than cow turds, but every once in a while you come across one's got some stank to their fighting, and gives you a bit of trouble."

Ord tilted his head, taking Gunnar in while he spoke. He felt almost confused. Had to turn and look at the others who were also listening to Gunnar go on, and found his confusion doubled: the looks on their faces were of genuine admiration. And yet, how could that be? For Gunnar had the pale blue eyes of a Fen. Granted, not the milky skin or white-blond hair of Ord, but—

"Ah, I see you've found me out," Gunnar said, interrupting Ord's thoughts. He leaned in and pointed to his eyes. "I got the spooky blues, uh?" he cackled, and his men cackled with him, not an ounce of sneering in their laughter. Almost like . . . they didn't care that he had Fen in him. "I'd ask you if working with a half Fen would bother your sensibilities, but . . ." Gunnar made a face, and motioned to Ord, up and down.

The men burst out into guffaws.

"So," Gunnar sighed, hands on his hips, grinning like his men's laughter was a filling feast. "Got a half Fen for a commander, and a full one for a priest. Swearnsoot, one might say this crusade was doomed from the start." A wink at Ord. "And yet, here we are."

"Yes." Ord managed to return the smile. "Here we are."

"And I suppose you'd like to get started? There's already a fair amount of tallying to catch up on." Gunnar squinted up as though counting in his head. "Four hundred fifty-two, last I checked. And more coming in all the time."

It was tedious work, counting all the dead Tickers. Ord barely bothered to look up from his ledger as he worked the numbers, but he could see the piles growing in the corner of his vision. Now that they'd gotten the horses in, they were hauling wagonloads from the center of the city, where the harvest was best.

Luckily, he didn't have to count them himself. All he had to do was sit on a little wooden stool under the shade and add up the numbers he was given by whoever gave them. Mostly lieutenants. Sometimes a captain.

"Sixty-eight, Theynen."

"Fourteen, Theynen."

"Fifty-one, Theynen."

Wild variances. Sometimes just a few bodies would roll off the cart. Sometimes they were piled so high they'd tumble off before it even came to a stop. Soldiers stripped to their breeches, bloody up to their shoulders, would dive in and haul the bodies out, grunting and heaving and cursing and spitting scaef juice while they did.

"What the fuck you want me to do with an arm?" Ord heard one of them call. "Fucker got shredded by a Leveler. I mean, what's that? A fifth of a body? Or more like a sixth or a seventh?"

"Look. Toss it over here. We'll add pieces as we find 'em until we've got more or less a whole body, then we'll count it as one."

"Ah, right. That's good sense."

Strange. It was all just becoming numbers to Ord. Bodies in, and soon, pounds of ash out. They'd pack the ash in barrels and weigh them then, two bales a barrel, give or take. They'd only just begun bringing in the Burners—probably wouldn't get any ashes until after dark.

This was more like what war *should* be like, Ord thought. Neat and orderly. Efficient. Everyone doing their little part to make it all work.

Momentarily distracted, Ord let his gaze wander up from his ledger. Across to the wagon now backed up to the seawall, not too far from where Ord sat in the shade. Two soldiers, drenched in sweat, smiling and joking their way through the grim work.

The two soldiers jostled about, climbing up onto the spokes of the wagon wheels to start peeling away the top layer of bodies. One of them was younger, barely more than a boy, and not yet hardened off—muscles more like a rangy colt than a stallion.

But the other . . . now, there was a hardened man. A flush of sun and effort across his tan chest. Sinews bumping and writhing as he swung about with the strange sort of grace belonging to men who know how to do hard labor. Forearms tensing, traveling up to sculpted biceps, shoulders standing out in stark relief as he heaved, shining like a well-lathered horse.

What would it be like to put my hands on those shoulders?

Ord jerked as something thumped into his table, his heart stammering about like a thief caught in the act.

"What's that?" he ejaculated, hands pattering about the ledger for the quill that should've been in his hand. There the bastard was, wiggling toward the edge of the table, caught in a breeze. He snatched it up, sat erect, and only then, when he felt he looked enough like a priest, did he look around and see Hotsteel standing there, gazing down at him with a queer look in his eye, his hand still upon the object he'd dropped on the table.

"Theynen," Hotsteel said cautiously. "Pardon me if I've interrupted your . . . meditations."

Ord waved him away and added a few dismissive noises. "What's this then, uh?"

Hotsteel shoved the item closer to Ord. What looked like a box made of tightly woven hemp perhaps. Or some maybe type of straw? Certainly the box itself wasn't heavy enough to make the thump it had made. It must contain something quite weighty.

"Found it in a house," came another voice. He leaned forward to peek around Hotsteel's frame and discovered a man in the most soiled uniform tunic he'd witnessed on a live body so far. Sergeant's stripes barely even visible under all the crisscrossed splatters of blood dried black.

Ord almost didn't recognize him—last he'd seen of him, he'd looked entirely different. When he'd been the first to board the landing craft that very morning, his uniform had been unsullied, but his eyes and his face had told of unutterable desecration.

Now his eyes had a sort of stillness to them. Reminded Ord of the dull, depressing days of constant drizzle that followed the rains. That sort of chilly quiet that came along with it. And his skin—the normal tan of a Brymic man, but coated in yellow dust.

"Ah," Ord said, a little stiffly, still taken a bit off guard by the change that had come over the man. Or perhaps more accurately, his return to humanity? "Sergeant Lochled Thatcher, first on the beach, I'm told!"

Lochled blinked slowly. "We weren't the first on the beach."

Hotsteel was quick to bolster his man. "First *off* the beach then, which is even greater a feat: first into the city." A slap to Lochled's shoulder, which Lochled returned with a sidelong glance that he held a little too long, a little too still. "Shows the prowess of a Brytan Company man!"

"Yes," Ord said, glancing uncertainly from one man to the other until whatever was passing between them had subsided and their attentions returned to the table. Ord mustered up an amicable smile. "And what might this fine piece of basketwork contain?"

Hotsteel flicked a finger under the lid and opened it.

Ord leaned forward, frowning at the contents. He reached in. Grabbed one of the little round gray objects. "We appear to have . . . a collection of . . ." he glanced up at Hotsteel and Lochled, entirely confused as to why they would bring him something so mundane. "Marbles?"

"Shotstones," Lochled uttered, emotionless.

Ord let the one between his fingers fall back into the pile. Must have been a few hundred in the woven box. But it still didn't make sense to him. A connection wasn't being made. And it appeared the two soldiers standing over him weren't inclined to make it for him.

"Shotstones, uh?" Ord nodded. "You'll pardon me, gentlemen, if I'm not certain why you've brought these to me."

"Your Church have any record of shotstones being found on previous crusades?" Lochled said, not exactly accusatory but leaning that way.

Ord tapped his finger on his ledger a few times, trying to think. "I don't recall ever reading any record of shotstones, specifically. However, stones of all sorts were hurled at each crusade. Except for the First, of course." Because during the First, the poor stupid fucks hadn't realized they were about to be harvested. Hadn't figured out how to fight back yet.

"Stones are not shotstones," Lochled said, voice getting a little edgier now. He leaned in, grabbed one of the spheres. "Shotstones are polished and round. Made for shooting. Stones are just stones. Now a creature like a Ticker can find stones to throw anywhere they look. But shotstones have to be made."

"Ah." Ord leaned in. "I believe I see what you're getting at. However, Leftland appears to be full of all kinds of relics left over from the Old Ones. I suspect these shotstones are another relic of their civilization. Interestingly, they probably weren't used for shooting at all, as our records indicate a marked lack of weaponry in their civilization. The Church believes the Old Ones were a very peaceful race."

"Oh, peaceful, uh?" Lochled grunted. Let out a rough chuckle. "Well, there's something you should see."

Ord could feel the defiance in Lochled, trying to leak out around his dutiful respectfulness. And he didn't like it. He didn't like *doubt.* People that wallowed in it only succeeded in pulling others into the mire with them. Faith was a narrow path, his mentors had taught him, but a solid one.

"I'll be happy to inspect anything you bring and document it for the Church's records."

"No, you'll need to come with us to see it," Lochled said. He jerked a thumb upward. "Don't worry, it's not far. Right over our heads, actually. Top of that tower there."

Ord stood up and leaned out of the shade, squinting against the blinding white stone of the tower that Lochled had gestured to. Seemed like a long way up. And besides . . .

"Unfortunately," Ord sighed. "I have work to do. Still counting, as you can see."

"I can continue the count," Kayna's voice said from behind him, making him jump yet again. Feor's mercy, but that pitch-skinned skelpie needed to stop sneaking up on people like that.

Ord swung around to her, flashing an unpleasant smile. "That's quite generous, but it's important that the tally is *accurate*, and I must ensure—"

Kayna completely ignored him by sliding onto the stool he'd just vacated. "Oh, settle yourself, Theynen. I know my numbers backwards and forwards. The count will be accurate. Or is it that Fens fancy themselves better counters than Drugothans?"

Ord's smile became rigid. Such a casual dismissal.

"I cannot speak for all Fens," Ord grated out. "But I know that *my* counting is beyond reproach."

"As is mine," Kayna muttered, as though bored with the whole topic. She didn't even look at him when she said it. Just flittered her fingers at him, eyes already upon the ledger.

Ord's blood heated so rapidly that every muscle in his body tensed, and for just a moment, for just a tiny speck of time, he thought he saw how men like Lochled could succumb to the madness of violence.

"Of course, Seeker Redstone." Ord turned stiffly to the soldiers. "Lead on, then. I will follow."

CHAPTER 13

Lochled stamped his way steadily up the tower, his muscles tight and hot from the day's labors, clenching and cramping at this final effort. He should've had more water, but a fresh flask sounded better.

Behind him, the priest huffed and puffed, trying to keep up. Damn fool hadn't even had to do anything hard that day. But Lochled supposed priests were not appointed for their physical prowess.

He reached the top of the stairs and led the way into the room that overlooked the beach. The contraption that he'd been unable to figure out earlier still sat where it had before, too bulky to move. The Tickers' bodies had been removed, but their blood still shone black on the white stone.

Hotsteel entered second, frowning at the thing in the window, then giving Lochled a long-suffering look as they listened to the gasping of the priest and the slow, exhausted footfalls of his final steps into the room.

Ord leaned against the wall with one hand, pale face flushed red and sweaty, breathing heavily through his mouth.

"Right then," Ord eked out. "What's this you so badly want me to see?"

Lochled strode to the object. Laid a hand on it. The top of it swiveled smoothly with a light touch, well balanced on a series of hinges and fulcrums. "Not completely sure, Theynen. That's why I wanted you to look at it. All I can say is I'm fairly certain this thing was hurling shotstones at us on the beach. Same as the ones in the box we brought you."

Ord looked across the room as though the ten strides it would take him to get to the contraption were an impossible distance. He huffed a few times, gathering himself, then crossed the room with as much priestly aplomb as he could summon.

"Interesting," the priest said, taking a step this way, then that, inspecting the thing from all angles before putting his hands on it. "But you say you never saw it in use?"

Lochled frowned at Ord, feeling like the priest was already trying to maneuver his way around the evidence. Priests had a habit of doing that, and Lochled had no intention of letting Ord get away with it.

"Depends," Lochled grunted. "Saw it from below, clear enough, firing shotstones down at us as we scaled the seawall. By the time I made it into the room, the Ticker that had been using it had already been killed."

"So you never saw the Ticker actually using it?"

Lochled felt the tightness of anger in his chest, but it was slight. Only so much rage you can have in a day before it leaves you feeling bled out. "No. Can't say that I did."

"Interesting," Ord said again. Finally deigning to lay his hands on it. Pale hands, long fingers, and fingernails longer than any working man should have them—and clean too. No grime under them. No calluses to speak of.

"We appear to have a brass bin on the top . . ." Ord stood

on tiptoe to peer into the box. Surely saw what Lochled had already seen inside. "Which contains shotstones," Ord said, a bit mystified. He bent down. "It seems the shotstones feed into this long section here." It was open on the back end, a shotstone sitting cradled in what looked to Lochled like a breech.

He said as much to Ord.

"A breech, uh?" He seemed doubtful. "Like a small version of our siege cannons, then?"

"That's what I suspect."

Ord squinted at the opening, stuck his finger in, and hooked the little shotstone out. Another fell in behind it and took its place. Ord made an intrigued noise and poked at the new shotstone a few times, ramming it an inch or so into the long pipe.

Lochled stepped closer. "Suppose the Tickers use their powers to push the shotstone down this bore here." He gestured to the long pipe that still stuck out the window.

"Hmm. I suppose you may be right."

"They were able to throw those shotstones far and fast. Were hitting us with 'em when we were still past the breakers. And even at that distance, they were hitting hard enough to punch through one of my men."

"Hmm." Ord stepped back. Finger to his lips in thoughtful repose. Frowning at the thing. Then frowning at Lochled. Then frowning at Hotsteel. "Very interesting. And I suppose you wish to know the value of the thing?"

Hotsteel stepped in. "If it has any value, the reward should be split amongst Lochled's squad. I can give you their names."

"Very well," Ord said, nodding. "Provide me with the names once we return to the ledger. If the Church finds the item of use in their research, the men of your squad will see their rightful rewards from it."

Ord made to turn and take to the stairs again, as though

their business were concluded. Hotsteel seemed to think it was too.

"Wait," Lochled said, a little irritably. "That's not all there is to discuss."

Ord sighed. Turned back around. "And what else might you wish to discuss, Sergeant Thatcher?"

Lochled put his hands on his hips, fingers touching his long-knife and hand axe. "You said the Old Ones didn't use shotstones for shooting. But this thing here is clearly made for shooting."

"Yes," Ord admitted. "It certainly appears that way, although there's really no way to know for sure."

"No way to know for sure?" Lochled scoffed. "If you'd been on the beach and seen what it did to our men, maybe you'd be a tad surer."

"I'm not doubting that the thing was used to shoot at your men, Sergeant. I'm simply saying, there's no way to know whether it was designed for that purpose or not. As I stated before, the Old Ones were not a warlike people. We've never seen any weapons amongst their relics."

Lochled narrowed his eyes at the man. "Are you saying it would be impossible for the Tickers to've designed it themselves for that purpose?"

Hotsteel made an uncomfortable noise, low in his throat.

Ord glanced about, seeming uncertain for a breath, and then contorted his face into something like a patronizing smile. "Ah. I see. You wish to challenge Church doctrine on the Leftlanders."

Lochled took a step toward the priest—not really trying to be menacing, but the priest looked briefly frightened anyway. "No, Theynen. I'm not a man to challenge. I just wish to know the truth. I wish to know what I'm fighting out there. We're the ones putting our lives on the line. And knowing your enemy is half the battle."

"And you *do* know your enemy," Ord said, a little brusquely now. "Savages. Low-minded beings. Possibly the former slaves of the Old Ones, or perhaps they simply took over what the Old Ones left behind when they disappeared. But not *thinking* creatures, Sergeant. Not creatures capable of designing, let alone *building*, something like this."

"But smart enough to take this item of unknown purpose and use it against us?" Lochled raised his eyebrows. "Whether they designed it is not the question. Repurposing it shows just as much intelligence, doesn't it?"

Ord's face took on a distinctly defensive cast. "Theories abound, Sergeant. Yours and a million others that think they know better than the great minds of the Church of Alchemy, who have done far more research into the origins of the Old Ones and this breed of Leftlanders you call Tickers." Ord held up a hand, cutting Lochled off from a response. "Imagine, for just a moment, that the Leftlanders were the slaves of the Old Ones. They would have perhaps seen the Old Ones use a contraption like this—and perhaps it was even used for hurling shotstones! Perhaps it was used for hunting! We don't know. In any case, if you imagine that, is it so hard to see that the Tickers may have had some memory of this thing being used, and making a dim, animalistic connection in their brain that they could use it to defend themselves just as they do when they throw regular stones at us?"

Lochled pulled his head back like he'd tasted something bitter. "Seems like you're conjuring very complicated answers when a simpler answer would do just fine."

"Lochled," Hotsteel uttered in a warning tone.

"It won't 'do just fine' if it flies in the face of Church doctrine!" Ord snapped.

"And what if the Church is mistaken?" Lochled growled back.

"Lochled!" Hotsteel barked.

Everything got still. Lochled stood there, frowning at Ord, while the priest sweated and flushed and tried hard to look like he was in charge. And who the fuck was he? Lochled could just as easily toss the dandy fuck out the window like he'd done to the Ticker . . .

"Captain Hotsteel," Ord proclaimed. "It seems you should teach your man here about what all is considered heresy, and to guard his tongue and his thoughts from it." Ord turned dismissively away from Lochled. "Now, if there's nothing further?"

Hotsteel shook his head. "No, Theynen. I apologize. Heat of the day. Heat of battle. I'm sure you understand." He cast a hard look at Lochled. "Sergeant Thatcher is simply not himself. A common malady after a hard day of fighting."

Lochled stared back at Hotsteel, old histories and old friendships clashing with old angers and deep-seated doubts.

"Very well, Captain," Ord said. "I'll expect those names, then. Carry on. I have other duties to oversee."

And with that, Ord left them, trundling his way down the stairs with floppy footsteps and huffing breaths.

Hotsteel and Lochled. Still staring at each other. Like two men unsure if the next action will be more words, or if they'll skip straight to a fight.

Hotsteel spread his hands. "What was that about, uh?"

Lochled hung his head, suddenly tired about it all. Disappointed that he'd put himself at odds with his captain. The son of an old friend. Someone Lochled should have backed with unquestioning loyalty. "I'm not a faithless man, hef. I know the Church has studied the Tickers. And I'll not call them liars. But I wonder if they've seen it all? If something was missed? Because this?" Lochled gestured out at the city around them. "The things I've seen the Tickers do today? I don't think they're low minded."

"Not low minded?" Hotsteel's jaw dropped like he'd never heard such nonsense in all his life. "Have you gone through the day blindfolded, Lochled? Have you not seen 'em?"

"Oh, I've seen 'em."

"And what've you seen, then, uh? Savages. They don't have the minds to even talk! They don't even wear clothing! The men of 'em running around with their pintels wagging, and their women with their teats out and slits showing?" Hotsteel's volume was getting higher as his incredulity mounted. "What more evidence do you need than the evidence of your eyes, man?"

Lochled turned away, shaking his head. Hotsteel had a point. But Lochled believed he did too. Why couldn't he make it as obvious to others as it seemed to him? All across the breadth of Eormun, the peoples there looked different, dressed different, ate different, had different customs. The Fens and the Auldish were looked down upon as being savage, but were still regarded as men—capable of thinking, of creating, of *being*. Was it such a stretch to them that these creatures from another land would also have things about them that seemed alien? So they didn't talk. So they didn't wear clothes. Was that evidence enough to call them low minded?

And worse than all that: What dangers would they expose themselves to by underestimating their enemy?

Lochled heard Hotsteel's footfalls behind him. A gruff laugh, trying to bridge the gap between the two of them. A hand on his shoulder. A squeeze.

"My father always said you had a thinking side to you," Hotsteel muttered quietly. "That you could get a bit pensive from time to time. Prone to questioning the why of it. I only wish he'd told me how he got you to come around."

"Mostly he threatened to run me through if I didn't shut up."

Hotsteel chuffed. "And did it work?"

Lochled smiled. "Might've, if I didn't know it was all bluster." His smile fell. He looked away. "I was too useful to him."

Hotsteel seemed to miss the thoughts beneath Lochled's words. Or maybe he didn't know. Maybe his father hadn't told him everything. Maybe his father had never told him the truth about that little village and the day that Lochled had earned his hated byname. Because he patted Lochled on the shoulder and said, "And you're useful to me too, Lochled."

CHAPTER 14

Night came upon the city rapidly. A skein of thick clouds skirted the daeside horizon, taking away the hours of dusk and plunging Halun's Landing straight into an unnatural darkness stabbed through with firelight.

Torches. Packs of them roaming about the city. Flickering between buildings, searching out corners, illuminating the rooms behind unshuttered windows.

Fires. So many of them that the smoke made a stinking haze across the city and blotted out any stars that might've been seen from the cobbles below, where chaos and madness were blooming like some noxious weed gone fertile for a single night, spreading its pollen as far and wide as it could in those dark hours where no man ruled, and anything might happen.

Buildings blazing into towering pillars of furious orange and yellow. If any house or structure was found to have a frame of wood, it was swarmed by a sort of feverish excitement, every dark figure beneath a torch seeking to be the first to set it alight, as though wood were an evil that needed to be purged from the place so that only charred stones remained in the morning.

And piles. Piles of wood, stacked upon abandoned carriages of strange construction, along with tables and chairs and woven straw baskets—anything that could be burned, really. Chucked out of open windows. Dragged through the streets by men in the grip of some mania. Beautiful things, ornately carved, or carefully woven. All piled high into flaming mounds that belched blackness at the sky, and all around the consuming glow of those fires, scarred and bearded faces leered and grinned and laughed and cursed.

It was through all of this that Rony ran, both hands clutching her Leveler and pumping it back and forth as she went. She was one of a pack—Cryer and Ponts, Trut, and Gonder, and Licker. And her. In among them.

They were all of them drunk. No two ways about it. Entire barrels of drips had been offloaded from the beach and quickly pilfered by the army gone mad. Commanders, captains, lieutenants—not a one of them tried to stop it from happening. None of them held sway, and they knew it. Rony had simply watched them when they and a handful of other squads had seized the barrels. Watched the officers watching them, as though this was all to be expected.

"Price of getting men to do your dirty deeds for you," Trut observed as he hacked away at the top of the barrel. "This is our reward for winning!" He grinned wildly at her as the wood gave way and a splash of drips caught him across the belly, immediately started steaming off him. "They'll not fuck with us tonight! Tonight, we're the gods!"

And they'd all filled their flasks and drank freely. Rony'd never had it without water to milden it. It was harsh and felt like it was stripping the softness of her throat straight to leather. But the glow when it started in through her veins . . .

Running. Stumbling around corners. Knocking things out

of the way for no apparent purpose. Shattering what could be shattered just to watch the pieces fall apart.

Rony staggered up to a door while the others rushed past her. Had the notion of firing her Leveler into the shadows, even though she didn't know what was in there—man or Ticker, or maybe nothing at all.

"Rony, you rotslit!" Trut snapped at her. "Come on! You want your fucking throat cut?"

"Fah!" she grunted, then triggered the Leveler. A plume of yellow, caught by a nearby fire, spearing into the darkness. She looked around at Trut, wild eyed.

He was grinning at her but still waving his hands. "Come on, then, you mad skelpie!"

She giggled, started running again, shucking the charge out. She had no idea where they were going. It seemed they were following Cryer, who'd ditched his greatshield now and had only his axe and knife in his hands while he ran. He seemed to know where he was going. Or maybe he was just running for the hell of it.

Why were they running in the first place?

She stuttered to a stop in the middle of a street dimly lit by an ochre glow—a fire at each end of the street. She was having trouble getting the new charge seated.

"Rony!" Trut was yelling at her again.

Then there was a tumble of footsteps from around the corner she'd just cleared. She spun in time to see a haggard band of faces she didn't recognize, and in this time and place, the only friendly faces were those of her squad.

They all had knives and axes out, a few with polearms, one with a Leveler.

Rony didn't actively think about it. She just saw the man with the Leveler and knew beyond all reason that he was going to try and rip her to shreds with the thing, so she snapped her own closed and did it to him first, splattering him across the corner and sending his comrades screaming and diving for cover.

"Ah!" Rony gasped. "Ah! Ah!" She was backpedaling, but all she felt was a sort of low sickness in her gut, but it was so dim beneath the soaring elation of being alive.

Trut grabbed her by the arm—she knew it was him without having to look. He yanked her, started pulling her along with him. He was laughing breathlessly, nearly doubled over while he ran, eyes squinted, tears streaming.

Rony could do nothing but join in with him.

"Right then, you magnificent cunny!" he wheezed out. "You taught 'em what us Brytan boys are all about!"

They were running again.

Why were they running again?

Seemed other soldiers were chasing them, but she didn't know what for.

She set to recharging her Leveler. Didn't think she'd been about it so long, but when she looked up, she couldn't see the others.

A small seed of worry began to germinate in her, but surprisingly enough, it wasn't worry for herself. She wasn't afraid of the darkness and the fire, and the mad men all about. She had her Leveler and half a loop of charges left. There was no man could get in arm's reach of her if she didn't want them to. Not while she still had something in her Leveler.

No, she was worried that they'd gone and left her behind. Gotten into something without her. Abandoned her. Didn't want her anymore. She'd find them later and they'd all laugh and tell her she should have been there.

"Trut? Licker?" she called out, eyes jittering around the street—mercy, she couldn't quite seem to focus on anything, and her eyes weren't tracking normally. And though it was the last thing she needed, her mouth was feeling a tad dry, and she wanted to wet it. So she propped her Leveler on her hip and went for her flask again, still with a bit of drips sloshing in the bottom.

Took a sip and coughed.

"Gonder? Ponts? Cryer?"

Still making her way down the street, turning, turning, turning, like a dancer in slow motion. But less graceful. More staggering. What street was this anyway? It wasn't like she had a map of the city. She had no idea where she was. Couldn't see the ocean. Couldn't see the sky for the smoke in it. Couldn't see anything but buildings.

A man dangled out of a third-story window, laughing madly about it. Firelight from the window. Voices in there, cursing and shouting at the man, who with a great war cry, let himself fall to the cobbles below. He struck the ground with an unsurprising *crunch* of bones breaking. Rony could actually see some bloodless white sticking out of his lower leg.

"Ah, fuck!" the man suddenly shrieked. "Fuck! Help!"

Someone stuck their head out the window he'd just fallen from. "What'd you mean by it, you daft fuck? Serves you right!"

Rony turned away from them and slid into deeper shadows. She already wanted another sip from her flask, but when she raised it to her lips she only got a drop. She cursed it, considered throwing it away, but then knew she'd want it in the future.

A man ran by on the opposite side of the street, and she damn near scattered his parts about, as he was naked from head to toe and she thought him a Ticker. Except he had a beard, and hair on the top of his head. He also apparently thought he was Ticker, or was having a grand time pretending to be one.

"I'm a Ticker!" he was shouting. "I'm a naked fucking Ticker!"

Someone was going to kill him for that, whether they knew him for a man or not. It was only a matter of time, Rony thought.

She turned about again, and looked back and forth between the fires at both ends of the street. One was much farther away than the other. She decided to head for the closer one.

There were figures around the fire. Was that her squad? She couldn't tell. They were all just black silhouettes, like the painted cutouts in a child's show, all of them leaping and dancing around the fire. Whooping and laughing.

She was drawn to that. Thought maybe she could hear the voices of her squad in all that ruckus, but more than that, she wanted to be near the fire. She wanted to leap and dance too. Wasn't sure why. There was something in the air, and it was catching.

She strode into the glow of the firelight. One big, burning monolith of chairs, tables, doors, and chests, the fire so hot you couldn't get closer than ten strides from it. She could feel the heat of it already puckering her skin, drying her sweat at first, but then making her sweat harder than ever.

They were Brytan Company men, she realized, spying a sash that wasn't worn about the waist anymore, but had been tied around a man's head while he jumped, squatted low, and shimmied about, whooping while he did it.

Another man was holding a woman-Ticker's body to him, dancing with it, slow and intimate, alternately acting as though he were entranced and in love, and then looking to his squadmates and laughing. The body dangled limply, feet dragging carelessly on the ground as he sashayed about. The bald head split right down the middle by a bloody canyon.

"Rony!" someone shouted.

She jumped, turned, saw Cryer around the horizon of the

fire, waving at her, his face wearing a big, welcoming grin. And she felt light and wonderful all over. Head to toe and back up again. So she started walking toward him, and only halfway there did some caution reassert itself. Reason still trying to be heard, even while it was drowning in drips.

Watch yourself. Don't get carried away around them. They're not your friends.

Was that still true, though? It had been true on the barque, but now things had changed. Everything was different. The world was different. She was different.

She swaggered in around the fire and found the whole squad standing there. Well. Except for the dead ones. And Lochled—he'd gone off to do sergeant things. Didn't seem to have a mind to help them sack the city. Or maybe he didn't have the stomach.

They all cried out when they saw her. Genuine excitement lit their faces. And she felt that wash of belonging again, blotting out reason once and for all.

"Where'd Little Roan gallop off to, uh?" Licker said, stilting his way unsteadily toward her. He had something in his cupped hand, was holding it up in front of his face.

"I don't know," Rony admitted.

"We thought they'd got you!" Trut called.

"Fucking nonsense!" Licker roared, turning around to face Trut. "This little cunny don't get got by no one! Uh?" He spun back around to her. Lifted his hand to her face. "Here."

She stared at it. A small pile of some sort of powder. Couldn't tell if it was golden because of the firelight, or if that was the actual color. "What is it?"

Licker scoffed, like he couldn't believe she didn't know. "It's fucking goldendust, cully! That's what I took from that dead man! Why you think his squadmates were chasing us all over the city for it?" Licker cackled madly to himself. "I don't know who the fuck he was, but this shit is far beyond his pay. Have you ever?"

"No."

"Well you do tonight!" And Licker took a big breath and puffed the dust into her face.

She started to cringe back from it, but he seized her shoulders.

"No, no!" he said, urgently. "Breathe it in, cully! Breathe it in!"

So she did. Because why not, at this point? Why not take a step further down the road? She'd already gone so far down it.

It tasted like sugar one second and gall the next. Stung the back of her throat like pepper, made her nose tickle like she might sneeze. Heat around her eyes, making them water. And she almost coughed, but then all of a sudden it seemed to sink into her, and she could see it, in a way, in her mind, plummeting through her body and exploding, kind of like a charge from her Leveler, and what it was Leveling was everything that might make her stomach twist, so that all that was left when it had burned through her from top to bottom was a blissful state she hadn't felt since she'd been a child in her mother's arms.

"Oh, mercy," Rony breathed.

Licker's face, swirling and grinning before her. "Yes! Good girl!"

She felt like she was tilting, tilting, tilting backward, like she might as well be laying on the floor, but nothing in her vision had changed, so she figured she was still upright, and what did it matter anyway? Trut suddenly loomed up in front of her. She couldn't make sense of his facial expression, but then realized he was smiling at her. Not the sneering grin he'd given her on the barque. An actual smile. With warmth, and depth of feeling.

He hooked an arm around her neck. "You. Cully. Rony." He shook her back and forth. Turned to the others, poking a finger into her sternum as he talked. "This fucking skelpie! Did you see her in the fucking tower? Nah, nah, fuck the tower. Did you see her on the street naught but a few moments ago? Blasted some fucking doxie that was after us! No fucking heart at all, this one! She's a mad, coldhearted little slit, but she's ours, uh?" Shook her again. Planted a big, wet kiss on her forehead. Grinned at her. "You made your bones today, cully. Blood-bounded now—we all are. Uh? *UH*?"

Next thing she knew she was prancing around the fire, Leveler waving wildly about. Sweat dripping down her skin. Fire hot, but she could get so much hotter, she could be as hot as that fire, and she was, on the inside, she was all burned up. Tongue dry, aching for more drips, but it was a good ache too, because everything was somehow good all of a sudden. Everything was going to be fine.

Someone was singing, and she only knew the chorus, so when they came to it, she screeched it out at the top of her lungs, and the men around her—her men, her squadmates—they shouted it too, and they laughed at her and with her, and they all danced.

"On through the breach! Crash through the door! Oh, look! I think that I've been here before. It's already painted from ceiling to floor!"

And Rony screamed: "Because my Leveler paints it so pretty! Yes my Leveler paints it so pretty!"

Swirling, dancing, fire, death.

"Back in the alley, I saw an old hag. Stalwart, defiant, she waved the wrong flag. The colors needed changing, so I turned her to slag!"

"And let my Leveler paint it so pretty! Yes, my Leveler paints it so pretty!"

Hand in hand with Cryer now. Him grinning down at her,

Rony not feeling threatened by his size at all, just swinging around him like a child around a tree.

"Now blue's a fine color, as blue as the sea. And green's like the leaves of a Brannenswood tree. But red's the best color, the right one for me!"

"Because my Leveler . . ." Rony fell into a coughing fit.

Hands slapping her back. Bearing her upright. Pulling her along. No rest. Not now.

"Paints it so pretty!" she wheezed, breathless. "So pretty!"

"Well life can get gloomy when you enter the fray. The smoke from the hellfires turns the skies gray. So, just liven it up with a bright crimson spray! And let your Leveler paint it so pretty!"

"So pretty . . . Leveler . . . paints it . . ."

Then she was standing over a dead man. It was cool, and dark. She was no longer around the fire. She didn't know if she'd killed the man, but somebody had. She could see her squadmates ahead of her, trooping slowly down the street. Cryer stumbled into a doorway and began kicking it until it shattered. The others rooted for him. He went inside, and Ponts followed him in. Licker and Trut and Gonder passed what looked like a skin of wine around.

Wine! Her mouth felt ashy and windswept.

Wine, and where in hell did they get it?

She knelt over the man, and took what he had—his flask, his hand axe, and his long-knife, because she figured she could use them, and he sure as shit didn't need them.

Robbing the dead?

The attempt of her conscience to accuse her was almost laughable. In fact, she did laugh. A solid snort of amusement, which hid a great depth of horror. Covered it up like leaves over a pit left behind to ensnare her at some other time.

This was a different world now, and she a different person. It didn't matter what you did anymore, because you'd already done your worst. You'd broken every code that'd ever been in your head. You'd gone as low as a person can go, done things no person should do. There was nothing left for you back in the world of men, where rules matter. Your place was here, and here there were no rules because they'd all been slaughtered on an altar to a god no one could quite put their finger on. A place where all you were ever going to get is whatever you wrung from it with your own two hands, and since you had no more boundaries, there was no length you wouldn't go to in order to wring out more.

It was a place of perfect freedom. Perfect chaos. Magic. And death. Because what you've wrung will be wrung from you too, in time. Because that is the way of things. That is the law of the lawless.

There was a great ache behind her eyeballs, and she realized that reality was slowly encroaching, while the goldendust was slowly giving way. She staggered over to the others, seized the wineskin, and upended it while they laughed and cheered her on.

Her next moment of clarity, she was screaming, weeping, inconsolable. She was looking at the sea, had caught a glimpse of it between two buildings, and it all hit her—all the thoughts that she'd been ignoring in order to stay sane and strong and capable—they all landed on her at once and took the mirth right out of her in a deluge of panic.

"I don't wanna be here anymore!" she was sobbing, reaching for the sea like a child. Someone had their arms around her, was alternately cursing her and trying to comfort her.

"Get your fucking head on, you pintelsheath! It's all right, it's all right. We've got you."

"I don't want you to get me! I want to go home! I'm too far away!"

"Settle now. Settle now." She realized it was Cryer holding her back from running for the sea. "It's far away across the Bransmar, cully. You gonna swim it all in one go?"

"I need to see my brothers! I need to see Gwint and Sander!"

"Hey, hey." He had her face in his hands now, forcing her to look at him. The others were there too, she noticed. Off to the side, watching her, and not with malice, she realized. Watching her the way you watch someone endure a pain you've long ago learned how to cope with. "Fuck Gwint and Sander, uh?" Cryer said. "We're your brothers now! The lot of us! We're your Leftland brothers, and we're with you now. Blood bound."

Rony sniffed, felt suddenly mortified to have shown so much weakness, though the shame was somewhat dulled by the vestiges of goldendust and plenty of fresh drips working through her gut.

"What about my pigs?" she murmured.

And then they all laughed.

It all bled together into a rush, and yet, somehow, she knew that she'd never forget this day, or this night. The wild dichotomy of the moments, an entire lifetime of ups and downs, wrongs and rights, all smashed into a single rising and falling of the sun. She felt ancient and newborn. Sick and yet animated to near giddiness by some force that had her caught up in it, as impossible to fight as the tides.

The moment when you're so sure that you're going to die, squashed in snug with the next moment, where a man that might've raped you and killed you two nights ago now clings to you like his mother, cringing and shivering in the salt spray of a landing craft while shotstones clatter over your heads. And the very next moment, a man you thought would never think you higher than dirt gives you a savage wink and you know that you're blood bound despite it all.

How do you encapsulate that day? How do you store it away in your mind? Is there a place in there big enough to fit the breadth and depth of it? Or do you have to take it all down to pieces to get it through the door?

Here: Ponts with his hand in her hair, mesmerized by it. "You've beautiful hair, Rony."

There: Gonder, crying on her shoulder, and she with no idea why. "I should've taken it when I had the chance! I'm such a fucking half-wit." And Rony, not knowing what he was talking about, patting his head. "It's all right, Gonder. You did the best you could."

Now: Trut tossing her a piece of art he'd ripped from a wall. Looked inlaid with gold. "Put it in your satchel, and don't let anyone else see!"

Then: Still and quiet, staring up—all of them staring up—at a little piece of the sky that'd just been opened by a stiff breeze parting the clouds of smoke that hung over the city, and they could see the stars, the same stars they knew, no different here, and to the daeside, a graying of the sky—it was already approaching the graylit hours.

Who could you ever explain this to? How each moment was a world in itself, and all of them made something that seemed like a moment stretched out across months? How the repugnance of one moment was the birth of acceptance in another. How do you explain the goodness of that acceptance when, after, there is only carnage? How do you explain that the good moments bled into the inhuman ones and gave them all a veneer of wondrous clarity and beauty, the likes of which you'll yearn for the rest of your life? How do you explain what a single day has made you become?

Then, somehow, she was inside a house. Didn't know how she'd gotten there.

Licker and Trut were in front of her, framing what looked like a metal box on the wall. They were arguing, both of them quite drunk.

"Look'ere," Licker announced, pointing. "This'n pipe goes in, and that one comes out the other side of it and goes to that basin there. See?"

"I can see the fuckin' pipes," Trut slurred, swaying on his feet. "But how's you know they carry water?"

Licker blinked at him for a moment. "'Cause they go to a fucking spigot over a basin, you twank!"

"Fah!" Trut waved at him. "And what's the box for, then, uh?" He kicked it, then swore, favoring that foot.

"To heat the water!" Licker yelled like it was just so obvious. "Make a fire in the box, and then it heats the water! Sootyhell, man! How daft are you?"

"Me daft?" Trut glared at the Fen. Looked like he might start swinging but then broke into gales of laughter, holding his belly. "You're the daft one, thinking the fucking animals need hot baths like a chief's wife!"

"Ah, fuck it then!" Licker roared, and began bludgeoning the box and the pipes with the back of his axe-head. Trut watched him dumbly for a moment, then joined in. They went at it for a time, as though it'd somehow offended them. Soon the box was all dented and mangled—must've been a thin bit of metal—and they'd tired themselves out.

Panting, Licker took a pinch of goldendust and snorted it. Then turned and seemed surprised to find Rony there. But he smiled friendly at her.

"Here," Licker said, getting another pinch of goldendust between thumb and forefinger as he stumbled up to her. She didn't stop him, and he shoved it up her nose. She breathed it in—sweet, hot, bitter, stinging—and then everything was all right.

Then she was tumbling along walls, bouncing off them, somehow attached to Cryer. They were laughing. Tripping over each other. They'd just done something, but she couldn't remember what. Only that she felt elated. Accepted. Like she could never do anything wrong again—not with these men. Nothing was wrong to them, and so she was free.

Then she was reaching up and grabbing Cryer's neck, pulling him down. Kissing him. Tongues lapping at each other, smelling of drips and scaef. Both of them stinking and filthy and bloody, but neither of them caring. Everything tingling like goldendust. Tiny shots of horror, like needles piercing the veil of ecstasy, when she would realize what they were doing and where they were doing it, but it was just so easy to brush aside at this point.

They were pulling off breeches. Yanking at laces. Unconcerned with anything except getting the necessary parts uncovered. Best way to do it was yanking down her breeches, pushing her up against the wall. Spinning her about so he was behind her. He moved her like she weighed nothing, and it frightened her in little moments where her stomach would pitch like a boat on waves, but he wasn't mean. Rough and clumsy, yes, but they both were.

There was no rhythm to any of it. He swore and stumbled, having to get so low because of the difference in their heights. She was tense for a bit, having just enough time to drunkenly consider the foreign concept of consequences, but that didn't last long, because then he was slipping in and it was too late anyway, and she liked it more than she didn't, she realized, liked it a lot in fact, fucking *needed it* . . .

An undercurrent of fear at first. Did nothing to chill her—made the heat even more searing, aching, wanting. He was threatening. Could kill her so easily if he chose to, and she, in a dark alley, somewhere in a war torn city. And where was her

Leveler? Oh, she couldn't think about things like that! No, there was only this—this thing that was making her feel like everything would be fine, just like the goldendust, and she needed them both.

She realized she could control *him* as well. She could do things that made him lock up or lose himself or groan like he was about to die. And the feeling of power that it gave her was exquisite—just as power always is, especially to those who've never had it.

He'd seemed so hard and distant, so unassailable, so invulnerable, she couldn't believe he was now huffing, breathless, caught up in her, as defenseless as a man will ever be while awake. And that, to her, was what kept her wits at bay, kept her going when she knew she should have stopped. Because none of it mattered anymore. Not rules or laws or the crusade or the farm or debts and debtors or even her poor, sad brothers.

No, the world had changed in a day.

And so had Rony.

She awoke with someone kicking her. Not hard, but enough to get her reeling upright, drool running down her face, head pounding, stomach quaking. Sticky wetness in her crotch . . .

Memories like dreams churning by in a swollen river of consciousness.

There was a distant sound, like someone fiercely blowing their nose. And where were they? She looked around, saw toppled and broken things, white stone walls, decorations ripped down and shattered to pieces. Light streaking in from a window—the first lights of dawn.

It was Cryer that was kicking her, she realized. Looked up at him with some confusion in her face, wondering for a moment if what she thought she remembered had been real or simply a drunken dream fueled by drips and goldendust.

Cryer didn't speak a word. Looked tired and worn. She probably looked it as well. In his eyes was only a dim recognition of anything they'd done. But more than that, there was a sense of absolution in them.

She realized there'd been a part of her all wound up about what she might think of herself in the light of dawn. But looking up at Cryer, she realized it didn't matter anyway. No one cared what she'd done. There was no need to regret any of it, because it wasn't real, wasn't talked about, wasn't mentioned. An unspoken agreement to let it live in their minds only, because speaking it would make it real.

That noise again. Long and sad and slightly wounded sounding.

The horn, she realized. *They're calling us back.*

Slowly and painfully, they all rose to their feet. Rony frowned around, counting heads, and realized one was missing.

"Where's Gonder?" she croaked out.

No one answered her. Trut leaned against the wall and spewed red wine all over the floor. Wiped his mouth, then staggered out the door.

She looked to Cryer with a question in her eyes, but all he did was shake his head once as everyone got up and started moving. The only words that were said among any of them were simply a litany of swears, by which they all knew that each of them was suffering as mightily as the others. But not one of them uttered any word of regret. And no one said a damn word about Gonder.

She couldn't even remember what had happened to him. He'd been there in some memories of the previous night. But whatever had happened to him, she couldn't recall. Just one more life swallowed up by the city like it'd never even been there in the first place.

They slowly tramped out into the dawn. The sun just peeking over the summits of the crescent of mountains Halun's Landing was built out of. Bright. Bright on the white bricks. Bright on the shimmering water. Too damned bright. They all groaned and squinted. Started walking in the general direction of the beach.

Cool air would gust past. Followed by warm, humid air. Followed by sniffs of woodsmoke. But the morning was clear. Not a trace of a cloud in the sky. The ocean seemed to stretch out so far that she wondered if she could see Brymsland from here if she had a spyglass.

At first it was just Rony and her squad. Like all the world had gone and died and left them alone in the ruins. But slowly, slowly, others trickled in. Men from other companies. None of them speaking. Too tired. Too drunk. Too sick.

They all started to melt together as they trooped toward the beach. Men that might've slit each other's throats only hours before in the darkness and firelight of a city being sacked, back to being comrades now. Back to following orders. Back to heeding the call of the horns and to rank and rules and laws.

Whatever had possessed them all the previous night simply flittered away like the last embers of a watch fire burning out into a single tendril of smoke. They trickled out of the city, forming up into companies by force of habit. Lines of them trundling steadily on, putting one foot in front of the other, even while still half-drunk and mostly asleep. Like ants finally deserting a carcass they've picked clean, right down to the bone.

Behind them, the city just a shell.

Lochled hadn't slept all night. Had tried, but the faraway noises of mayhem had kept him awake. The occasional screams that made him wonder if it were one of his squad that was screaming while another fought them over something idiotic.

When he saw them all come drifting out of the city, gray and sooty, bloodied and yellowed with discharge, eyes fixed on the ground before them, and eerily silent like a procession of ghosts, he hooked the wad of scaef from his mouth and spat one final time into the sand.

He stayed there, just outside his tent, watching the hordes of them silently responding to the call of the horn—not a call to war this time. Just a call to return to order. They would be useless until that evening, at the very earliest. Finally, he thought he spotted Cryer, his dark brown head towering over the others.

That was enough for Lochled.

"Finally. Get some fucking sleep," he growled, and pushed his way into his tent.

CHAPTER 15

It was shaping up to be a beautiful, clear day, so naturally the army had to ruin it.

Ord watched as the first of the four Burners was activated with a giant thrum, rattle, and cough, and then began belching black smoke into the otherwise perfectly blue sky. It took two heat charges to run the thing for an hour, but as long as they were steadily feeding it bodies, the return on investment was worth it. You had to use ash to make ash, after all.

His nose curled as he watched the black smoke climb into the sky and gradually begin to thin into wavering tendrils. The first bodies were being fed in, and for a moment, the smoke stopped. Then, when it started coming out again, it was heavy and pale, almost like steam, except for all the little particles of soot that came spewing out with it.

He squinted at the Burner, his brain analyzing and picking the problem apart. How much ash was strewn into the air by the Burners? Was it negligible or was it significant enough to begin thinking about ways to keep it from floating away? How would he even go about testing that?

He sighed heavily, letting the thought die unborn. He really should've been in the Church's Office of Patents. He was quite good at analyzing and figuring things out. He had no doubt he could figure out any Leftlander trinket that was brought to him and then develop a way to replicate it with the materials they had on hand.

But that was not his job. He had been assigned to the Fourth Crusade, and that was a great honor, so they told him. He really shouldn't be ungrateful. And besides. If he worked for the Office of Patents, he would never have had the opportunity to come here and find the one special thing that got him interested in this duty to begin with.

And honestly, it wasn't all that bad. The misery of the journey was behind him now and already starting to fade. The madness of the day before had been startling, but after sleeping—more like starting awake every ten minutes due to some drunken soldier caterwauling in the city—he felt like he had a better grasp of the insanity.

If there were a turd floating in Ord's leisure pool, however, it was Kayna Redstone.

Even now he was having to wait on her. In the sand. In the hot sun. Sweating. Undignified.

He huffed. Tried to focus on the glittering sea. But he couldn't ignore the tickle of sweat down the side of his face. And he wasn't even wearing his full robes. Only a vermilion tunic today, as the robes were still wet and sandy from yesterday. And hot. Very hot. Leftland, it seemed, was a slightly warmer clime than he was used to.

And, oh yes, that fucking skelpie Kayna.

He rolled his eyes toward her tent and glared at it.

Black. Black, just like her robes. Just like her skin. Mercy, it must've felt like an oven in that tent, all closed up and baking.

But then again, she *was* a Haedan. Maybe she found the heat pleasant.

He almost called out to her, but he wasn't sure how all this worked—the Seekers, and how they communicated across such vast distances. The lot of them were very tight lipped about the whole thing. Seemed a mite dodgy if you asked him, but no one had.

Some sort of secret ritual, perhaps? Some dancing about and calling upon Gasric gods? Feor help them if that were the case. He could only imagine if the Church's single source of long-distance communication turned out to be a bunch of Gasric witches and warlocks.

That was, actually, the one thing that the Seekers *would* say about themselves, and were quite adamant about: they were not draeids or magical in any way. But that was all they would say. And the Church needed them, so really, how much did one want to poke around? If a man gives you a fish, do you ask him where he caught it?

Not magical, the Seekers said. And yet able to freely communicate over the breadth of the Bransmar and all of Eormun beyond.

Seemed unlikely. But perhaps they had some secret alchemy of their own.

The flap of her tent rustled, making Ord huff a fresh breath of irritation, ready to give Kayna a solid verbal barrage the second she emerged. Except that she didn't emerge.

Ord took a hesitant step toward the tent. "Kayna?"

Her voice came slithering out: "Come in, Theynen."

"Yes, well . . ." *This fucking doxie! Who does she think she is?* "I'd much rather speak in the fresh air, if you don't mind."

"I do." No edge to her voice when she said it. Just a simple statement.

Really? That was it? As though she were the one in control?

It's because you're a Fen, Ord seethed to himself. *She thinks that just because her skin's darker than yours, she can tell you what to do.*

"It's the light," her voice came again, sounding resigned and tired. "It's too much for my eyes right now."

"Fah. Piss on it," Ord grumbled, then stomped through the sand and ducked down and into her tent.

The second he stood up, his brain felt like it'd turned to liquid and was about to slosh out of his ears. He felt unsteady for a second, and everything in the tent was so dim, and his eyes were so used to the brightness, that he could barely see anything but the sparkling of stars in his vision while a strange, heady, earthy smell overwhelmed his senses, felt like it was yanking him, mind and soul, like a bull being hauled by the nose ring, back to . . . back to . . .

He couldn't quite tell. The smell reminded him of something important—something so significant that he was shocked and dismayed that he couldn't suss it out from the confusion of his thoughts.

"Well, don't hold your breath," she said calmly, sliding in behind him and letting the tent flap fall shut again. "That'll only make it worse."

He jerked his head in her direction—hadn't been expecting her to be so close, but what else was new? He wanted to ask her what the smell was, but then hesitated, wondering if it was some sort of odor that had something to do with women and their private quarters. He didn't know about these things. Thought it best to let it go. And the headiness was leaving him. Clearing out. Eyes adjusting to the darkness.

"Feor's mercy," he husked. "It's hot as a Burner in here."

"Black tent. Full sun." Kayna strode around him, and only then did Ord realize that she was not in a state of proper dress.

"Oh." He jumped, made for the flap, then thought that would be silly—a little too boyish. She wasn't stark naked after all—had the important bits covered up. But still, looking away seemed the priestly thing to do. "I apologize."

"You apologize?" she asked. She sounded half-asleep.

"I did not realize you were . . . in a state of undress."

"No, you didn't. But I did. And I invited you in. So there's no need to apologize." She sighed heavily. "Is it a bother to you, Ord? Can you manage to look at me so close to my natural form, or will your eyes begin to bleed?"

He frowned at the black fabric of the tent. Gruffed a few noises out that were meant to sound manly and confident but reminded him of a boy trying to act like he knew about girls.

"Very well," Ord said. Then turned around. Eyes avoiding her at first. Then slowly catching glimpses. Then looking at her full on. He cleared his throat. Swiped a waterfall of sweat from his brow.

She'd sat down in the center of the tent. Cross-legged and leaning back on her hands. A thin band of undyed cotton over her breasts. A pair of cotton braies covered her unmentionables, but only just. Every inch of her black skin was covered in sweat, so she seemed to have been rubbed with oil.

He studiously focused on her eyes. She was, shall we say, not to his tastes. But there was a certain intriguing quality to seeing her laid out like that in front of him. He wanted to let his eyes range over her. Analyze her. Like a fascinating trinket or an interesting sculpture.

"So," he said a bit thickly, "news from Bransport?"

Kayna had her eyes closed, head tilted back. She dragged her head back to level as though it weighed a hundred stone, and opened her eyes. Was it just the dim lighting, or did they seem blacker than usual? Deeper?

"Yes," she managed. Leaned forward. Eyebrows twitching inward at some secret discomfort. She worked her neck. Slumped over herself. Looked up at him again. "The Brannen has put a reward on the Mad Queen's head. Five hundred gold whales. Alive, preferably. But dead is acceptable if there is no alternative."

Ord frowned. "So, dead, then."

The ghost of a smile lifted one side of Kayna's mouth, a flash of white teeth at the corner. "Yes. Most likely." She reached across the floor, her movements slow, as if she were underwater, and grabbed a skin, which she upended quite suddenly and savagely into her mouth, throat working at it, water dripping down her cheeks.

Ord took that moment to snatch a glimpse of her. The shape of her thighs. The speckling of curls the closer his eyes wandered to the braies. And under her arms too. Fascinating. He'd thought only men had hair in these places. Or maybe that was only Drugothan women?

She gasped as she put the waterskin back down. Very unladylike. Wiped a wrist across her mouth like a barbarian. Ord wasn't sure what good it did her—her wrist had as much sweat on it as her mouth had water.

Eyes back to him. "They've no further information on her whereabouts." She waved a hand. "It's not important at this juncture. The Elders have confirmed their desire for you to catalog Leftland in one month's time, and have further agreed with your recommendation that you should take a small contingent of soldiers and separate from the main body."

"Wait." Ord frowned. "I never recommended that. *You* did."

"I did. And you agreed. And so do the Elders, apparently. So that is what we're going to do."

"Fine," Ord said stiffly. "I'll speak with Steadman Thaersh and request a few squads to accompany us."

"There's no need." Kayna rose, letting out a soft groan. Stretching her back. "I've already spoken with Captain Hotsteel."

"Hotsteel?" Ord felt his stomach get all tight with indignation. "I don't know if I like the length of leash he allows his men."

"Nonsense," Kayna said, walking toward the flap of the tent, nudging Ord to the side as she did. "We are already familiar with Brytan Company. No purpose having to establish new rapport and learn new names."

"He'll recommend Sergeant Thatcher," Ord sneered. "A faithless man."

"You're right, he did. And I accepted. Along with two other squads." Kayna ripped open the flap. Daylight blazed in. Damned, but the second he'd gotten his eyes adjusted to the musky darkness, she went and brightened it up. The air that gusted in chilled his sweat, made his arms and neck pimple up like a plucked goose.

Kayna stood there, breathing heavily of the fresh air, her stomach working in and out, glistening in the sun. Arms up and hands still clutching the upper corners of the tent's opening. A few soldiers passing by looked and gawked for a moment, nearly tripping themselves to the sand, but they quickly averted their eyes and moved along.

Ord edged to the side—the better to catch a bit of that breeze as it wafted past Kayna. "You know, I'm beginning to believe you just enjoy making my life miserable."

"Oh? Why would you say a thing like that?" A glance over her shoulder. "Wicked accusation to level on someone."

"The man Lochled," Ord said, frowning, troubled. "He's got no great love for the Church, and that seems to mean he's decided to hate me along with it."

"That, or he hates your pale skin," Kayna pointed out.

Ord looked up sharply at her. "Possibly." Cleared his throat. "He has issues specifically with the Church doctrine on Leftlanders. Keeps insisting they're actual thinking beings. Damn near opened me up over it yesterday while we were in the tower."

Kayna began tying the tent flap off to keep it in place. "Were you aware that they found cannons last night?"

Ord blinked at her. "Cannons?"

She nodded, still standing in the opening of the tent. "Several. Odd design, as they report. But they suspect that is how they were able to launch such large stones and strike at our ships from such a great distance." She glanced over her shoulder at him. "Interesting, don't you think? Perhaps the Old Ones made those cannons as well. For some other purpose than war. Since they were not warlike."

Ord wasn't entirely sure how seriously to take her. There was a part of him that suspected she was having him on, but he couldn't fathom for what purpose. Had they really found Leftlander cannons in Halun's Landing? And what did that mean for Church doctrine?

What if the Church is mistaken?

Kayna turned, looking like the fresh air had greatly revitalized her. Flashed him a full smile. "As for Sergeant Thatcher—perhaps your piety will inspire him. All the more reason for you two to spend more time together."

Ord felt his heart do an uncomfortable shimmy in his chest, wondering if Lochled already knew about the cannons in Halun's Landing—if, in fact, Kayna were telling him true—and what he might say about it. "If he doesn't go off and kill me first. A most dangerous man, I sense."

"Dangerous men are good for dangerous work." Kayna put one hand on her hip, gestured outside with the other. "Halun's Landing is massive. Even after the sacking last night, there are sections, up near the top, that I don't think anyone ventured into. Too much effort to get there."

"Ah, but not for us, uh?"

"No, not for us. We'll set up camp there, at a place that gives us a view of the land beyond the city."

Ord quirked an eyebrow at her. "Seeker Redstone, are you giving me orders?"

She blinked innocently at him. "Of course not, Theynen. I'm simply observing the smartest plan of action. I'm sure you were about to agree, as you are a smart man."

He waved her off. "You use flattery like a bludgeon." He stepped to the opening and peered out at the rising mountains that housed the city. What was beyond those jagged peaks? The Second Crusade had seen wide open pastures, grasslands as far as the eye could see, like a whole world made up like Ceapsland. But he'd never seen it with his own eyes.

He cast a wary glance at Kayna as she began gathering up her robes. "There is another matter. One of significant personal importance to me."

She stopped. Looked at him. Stood very still for a moment. "Oh?"

He worried about telling her. Worried that she was going to tell him no. But how ridiculous was that? He was the damned priest. He was the one who made the decisions.

"I've something of a pet interest in the research from the Second Crusade."

Kayna draped her robes over one arm. Waited patiently.

Ord frowned. "Right, then. There's evidence from the Second about some sort of medicine left over from the Old Ones. Claims about it being an elixir of life. Men with limbs gone foul fully recovering. It seems to stop corruption." Ord sniffed. "According to accounts."

"Mm. Wild accounts from drunken old men babbling on about the Second."

Ord narrowed his gaze. "I don't need you to be convinced, Seeker Redstone. I simply need you to be informed. The Brannic Empire is dealing with the most deadly plague ever recorded. Now, I don't know if this fabled medicine of the Old Ones even exists, and if it does, whether it works, but I have every intention of finding out."

Kayna tilted her head to one side. "The plague is a commoner's curse. Isn't that what the Church says?"

Ord almost lost his breath. His belly went all tight like it wanted to press the air out of him, but he held on. Let out the tiniest little groan of effort.

Thinking of his wic. Thinking of the people he'd known from birth. Thinking of how their eyes had been hollowed out by it, their bodies eaten away. Thinking about how it had simply run up on them, an invisible monster, and laid them waste. Thinking about how the wic had looked as it burned brightly on its stilts, the firelight almost perfectly reflected by the glassy, onyx marsh waters.

"Yes," Ord grated out. "That is what the Church says."

Oh, but they didn't stop there. No, the Church had much to say about the plague. They said it was a curse upon the common folk. A curse upon them from Feor himself, on account of the fact that one in ten commoners was a draeid. Because only the common folk produced draeids. Royalty need not fear the plague, because royalty was specially blessed by Feor. And blessed royal blood did not produce draeids.

But why would the god that Ord had so faithfully served curse the people of his wic? None of whom had produced a draeid. They were good people. How could this plague be an act of Feor? An act of vengeance from a god that was supposed to love them?

Unless . . .

What if the Church is mistaken?

Kayna was still watching him carefully. "It is kind of you to take up a cause for the common folk."

Guilt curdled in Ord's chest. Was it kindness, or was it rebellion? If the plague was a curse from Feor, then Ord's attempts to fight it were tantamount to rebelling against Feor's will. The only way it was *not* rebellion was if the Church was . . . wrong.

"Or have you lost folk to it as well?" Kayna asked, voice soft and slippery.

"Yes," Ord managed, then swallowed hard and gathered himself. "Well. I'll be enlisting the eyes of the men to keep a look out for anything that might match the accounts of this substance. It will not detract from our original mission. I only wanted you to be aware."

"Very well, Theynen. I am aware."

They stood there for a moment. Her with her robes over her arm. He standing at the door, not quite sure if she was waiting for him to exit in order to get dressed, but that didn't make much sense, seeing as how he'd seen her spread about with nothing but her dainties on.

He nodded to the robe. "Are you going to dress, then?"

"No."

"Of course not."

"Bodies have mostly been cleared," Kayna said, making for the exit. "And the waves look much less pink this morning. I believe I'm going to have a bathe."

"Oh," Ord said as she brushed past him. "You're going to have a bathe. Of course."

The comedown from being in communication wasn't unpleasant to Kayna. It was just . . . odd. Something akin to the feeling of waking midway through the night after drinking yourself asleep. Mouth parched. Skin hot. Everything itchy and jittery. And yet, unlike with too much drips, this comedown came with a dull glow of euphoria that rapidly retreated until her mind was fully back in the realm of mortals.

It was the gest that did it. A clear, bitter liquid derived from alchemically altered draedic ash. Like oil in a fire, it enhanced her natural abilities. Allowed her to extend herself across immeasurable distances and touch the network of Seekers, no matter where they were.

Unfortunately, it was also an easy thing to find yourself craving, even when there was no need to stretch your mind across time and space. Easy to begin craving how it made you feel when you were in it.

Kayna had set out on this journey with twenty phials of gest. She still had seventeen because she was rigorous in the exercise of her self-restraint. Sometimes she'd lay them all out and stare at them. Wait for that hot, insistent desire to come over her. And then deny it. Just to prove to herself that she could. That she was still master of it, and not the other way around.

It did different things to different Seekers, depending on their individual natures. Most often, those who ingested it became uninhibited. In someone like Kayna—someone with, shall we say, voracious appetites—that lack of inhibition tended to make them a bit . . . overamorous.

When she was in her right state of mind, she did not find Ord attractive. And she knew he wasn't one to crave the attentions of women. And yet, coming down from the gest she'd used to make contact with Bransport, she'd damn near thrown herself at him.

Good thing she practiced self-restraint.

She knew he'd been irritated to be kept waiting, but she also knew that, had she let him into her tent a few minutes earlier, things would have gotten interesting.

Well. They already *were* interesting.

She'd swum out past the breakers and now treaded water in the gentle swells, facing back toward the shore, her arms steadily fanning back and forth through the water. The ocean cooling her skin like a worked piece of steel being quenched.

A priest with a personal mission—one that she'd correctly intuited he'd kept secret from the Church. A priest conflicted by doubts as to whether the Church was telling the whole truth.

And what would he do if he found out they weren't?

And what did that mean for *her* mission?

She'd inquired about this when her mind had been in that strange place above this plane of existence. Unlike the normal constraints of their abilities, when two Seekers bolstered by gest brought their minds together, they could actually hear each other's thoughts as clearly as though they were being spoken in the ear.

What would you have me do with him?

There had been a long pause in the flow of communication, and Kayna had perceived a low, background rumble, as though the Seeker she was connected to had pulled back from her. Was, perhaps, discussing the matter with others.

Only wait and observe him closely, the answer had finally come. *Lines are being drawn all across Eormun. Lines between chiefs and the Brannen. Between the Brannen and the Church. Between the Church and the Seekers. It would do us well to make him an asset to us. But not while his loyalties still lie with the Church.*

I fear his loyalties may not change, Kayna pointed out. *He remains conflicted, even when confronted with obvious evidence.*

In his heart, he wants to believe they are right. That type of zeal is not so easily turned.

Perhaps it is not a question of turning him, the other said, *so much as a question of . . . helping him.*

Encourage his pursuit of the truth? Kayna mused. *Subtly prod him in the right direction?*

Tread carefully, Seeker Kayna, the other warned. *The minds of the zealous cannot be turned by force. They must be allowed to venture to their own inevitable conclusions. If he perceives that you are manipulating him, he may plant himself more firmly than ever.*

I do not manipulate anyone. I simply smile on them when they find the truth. And hold my peace when they do not.

Kayna had held her peace for a very long time. But peace, much like the receding euphoria of gest, would soon be only a memory.

CHAPTER 16

Lochled had let the Seeker into his home. A very small part of him screamed to know why he had done such a stupid thing. But what was the alternative, then? Turn the Seeker away in the course of his lawful duties?

Part of being a good man was doing what you were told. Bad men flouted the law and did whatever they pleased, became the very outriders and brigands that'd forced Lochled to move his family out of the countryside and into this city.

Good men upheld the rule of law. Good men followed their orders. And after all that he had done in service to his superiors, there was nothing Lochled craved more than to believe himself a *good man.*

Lochled could no more disobey his betters than he could choose to sprout fins and gills and swim away in the briny Bransmar. He'd seen what happened to men that disobeyed. They were strung up. Shot full of arrows. Beheaded. And worse than all that—they were dishonored.

And despite Marna's look of terror and her clear desire *not* to have the Seeker in her home, what did they have to fear? They'd done nothing wrong. They harbored no draeids here.

Lochled pushed the door shut and let it latch, still trying to conceal the long-knife in his left hand. He glanced at Seeker Gehret over his shoulder, saw the man was looking about their tiny domicile, and tried to discreetly place the knife back on its peg.

When he turned, Seeker Gehret was watching him.

Lochled pulled his hands away from the steels and stood up straight, heat washing over his scalp. "My apologies, Seeker," Lochled murmured with a small bow. "I didn't know who it was knocking on my door."

That same small, polite smile again. "One can't be too careful," Seeker Gehret observed. Then looked at the steels. "Have you fought for the empire, then? Or did you come by your steels another way?"

"I fought," Lochled said quickly. "In the Pan. And during the revolt of Medeland before that."

The Seeker brought his gaze back to Lochled. "A truehearted Brymic, then." The Seeker tilted his head back as though to look at Lochled from a different perspective. "A true servant of the empire."

Lochled swallowed. Glanced to Marna, whose expression had not settled. "I do my part."

Seeker Gehret inspected him for another moment. Then turned to Marna and Libby. "And this is your . . . lovely family."

Lochled moved toward them. Wanted to hover protectively over them as Marna was hovering over Libby, but didn't think it would do to seem scared of the Seeker. What did they have to be scared of? And it might be insulting to the man.

"My wife, Marna," Lochled said, keeping his voice steady and trying hard to be amiable. "My daughter, Libby." He shifted uncomfortably, resting a hand on Marna's shoulder. He could feel the tension in it. A slight tremor—but was that her body or his hand?

After a long moment, wherein the Seeker simply stared at Marna and Libby, Lochled cleared his throat. "I hope you won't think this impertinent, Seeker, but . . . I'm not sure why you're here."

The Seeker sighed steadily through his nose and crossed his arms over his chest. "No, I don't suppose you would." He locked eyes with Lochled again. "Did you serve with honor, Lochled Thatcher?"

"Yes, Seeker. I like to think that I did."

A quirked eyebrow. "You like to think you did? Well, did you do what you were told?"

"Yes."

"Even to your own detriment?" the Seeker pressed, his eyes narrowing.

Lochled felt a bit defensive at the question, but managed to keep it from his face and his tone. "Yes. Even to my own detriment."

"Even when you knew it would cost the lives of your fellows?"

Flashes of steel crashed through Lochled's mind. Memories of blood. Memories of screams. Memories of men he'd considered brothers, trampled in mud, baked into dust, and hewn into pieces.

"Even then, yes," Lochled answered.

"And are you a man of faith?"

Ah, now there was a tricky question. But part of dealing with your superiors was knowing how to tell them what they wanted to hear while not actually lying.

"I hold to Feor," Lochled answered carefully.

"Hmm." The Seeker brought his arms down from his chest and clasped his hands behind his back, gazing at the dirt floor. "And do you believe in Beficien's Revelation? That it is the true word of Feor, spoken to man?"

Well, Lochled didn't really know, on account of he'd only just learned his letters and so had never read it for himself. Only heard what snippets the priests chose to share when they stood on their street corners to preach.

He didn't *not* believe it, so he said, "Yes."

Seeker Gehret began to pace, very slowly. Not much room to do it in. Only a plodding step or two toward the door, then a slow turn, and a step or two back. "In his revelation, Beficien learned that the light of Feor came to all mankind, raising them from mere animals into the thinking beings we call men. But there is something foul that remains inside all of us. It is the daemons of our flesh. And in some of us, these daemonic forces are strong. And when the daemonic forces rage against the light of Feor that has been bequeathed to us, what results is a surge of . . . unnatural powers."

"Seeker," Lochled dared to interrupt. "I understand. But we've no draeids here. Nor have we harbored any. I'll swear an oath on it that it has only been me and my family in this dwelling."

The Seeker looked at him again. "I know, Lochled." He said it so gently. Almost sadly. "I know that you are a good man. I know that you would not knowingly harbor a draeid." He stopped pacing and held up a finger. "But how would you know?"

Lochled tried to swallow again, but his mouth was dry. He realized his heart was slamming in his chest. His fingers had gone cold. His palms sweaty. "I . . . I would not. Only Seekers can know."

"So it is," Seeker Gehret agreed. Then he took a great breath and turned back to Marna and Libby. But Lochled could see the angle of the man's eyes. Knew that they were fixed upon his daughter.

No. No, it can't be.

Despite himself, Lochled's eyes shot to the steels on their pegs. Only a quick glance, an errant thought of desperation. And then a heavy tidal wave of guilt and shame. Surely there was some mistake. Rebellion would only compound the issue. Best to do what he was told and let the Seeker realize his own mistake.

The Seeker squatted down, his black robes pooling around him like shadows made physical. He smiled at Libby and extended a hand. "Come, little one. Let me see you."

Marna reacted by wrapping her arms around Libby even tighter, a small gasp escaping her as she did.

Seeker Gehret looked sharply up at Lochled.

It felt like lightning coursing down his spine. Lochled twitched. His hand upon Marna's shoulder tightening. "Marna," he said, sharper than he'd intended.

She gawped up at him, disbelieving but wordless.

It couldn't be what it seemed. It just *couldn't*. They say that only Seekers could sense who was a draeid, but for mercy's sake, this was their daughter! Their one and only child. And they were Libby's parents. And who knows a child better than their own parents?

Libby had never shown even a hint of oddity. She'd always been a kind and happy soul. They might say that everyone had daemons of the flesh, but if ever there were a child so free of their influence, it was Libby. She could not possibly have such strong daemonic forces in her as to render her a draeid. It was beyond comprehension. It simply made no sense.

"Do not test the man's patience," Lochled said, even as he felt his throat getting tighter and tighter.

And Marna, who had ever been a good wife, seemed to wilt under Lochled's glare. And her arm retreated from around Libby.

"There you are," the Seeker cooed, as though coaxing a skittish animal to eat from his hand. "Come. Let me have a look at you."

Libby, uncertain of anything—except for the fact that, surely, she had nothing to fear in her own home, with her parents standing right behind her—stepped forward.

The Seeker smiled. "Will you take my hand?"

A frown crossed Libby's gentle face. She glanced over her shoulder. Not at Marna, but at Lochled.

And this is what he said to his daughter: "Go on, then. You've nothing to fear."

So she took the Seeker's hand.

"Sergeant Fucking Thatcher!"

Lochled rolled awake with no concept of where he was, what time of day it was, or who the fuck was yelling at him, but certain he didn't like it. His heart was already pounding, his head full of rage, his heart full of grief, and he came up out of his bedroll in the tiny little tent he'd made out of his oilskin.

Thrashed his way free of it with his long-knife and hand axe ready, nostrils flaring, chin jutting, eyes wild, because he wasn't quite sure if he was back in Bransport with Marna and Libby, but if he were—

Sand.

Lochled looked down.

Ah. Right.

Sand. Beaches. Leftland. Halun's Landing.

"There he is!" Sounded like Trut.

Head still spinning loose of the dream, Lochled turned and saw his squad a few tent rows away.

"Piss on you!" one of the tents yelled. "Trying to fucking sleep here!"

"All right," Trut frowned at the tent as he edged past. "Loosen your breeches, you twank. It'll be all right."

Cryer. Rony. Licker. Ponts plodding along in the rear. That was all of . . . Wait!

"Where's Gonder?" Lochled husked, voice rough and dry.

His eyes naturally went to Cryer when he asked the question, but Cryer seemed to be avoiding his gaze. "Didn't make it."

"Didn't make it?" Lochled repeated. "The fuck happened?"

"Don't know."

"Well, that's not a lot of help."

Cryer finally met his gaze, and Lochled could see that the big man was feeling guilty—not the shady guilt of a man who'd done a crime himself, but the sorrowing kind when a man thinks he could've prevented something but didn't.

"Found him stabbed full of holes," Cryer finally said. "Don't know who did it or why. Just found him that way." A minuscule shrug. "It was a sack."

"Well, shit." Lochled worked his tongue around his mouth, trying to summon some spit. Took a gander at the sky, the location of the sun. He'd slept through the whole damn day. "Fucking time is it?"

"Two hours past the middle, hef," Cryer said. "And we've work to do before dark. So says the captain."

It was shaping up to be a shit day, so naturally the army had to make it worse.

Lochled stomped his way through the loose sand—hating sand, hating sun—trying to keep up with Hotsteel's longer stride, the captain seeming to glide across it with only enough effort to make him look heroic.

Lochled definitely didn't look heroic. He had a downright thunderous scowl, was breathing too hard, trying to get a bit of his hair out of his face and back into his braid, but it was all matted and uncooperative.

Lochled's squad definitely didn't look heroic. Their shoulders were all slumped, looking positively downtrodden. All of them breathing through their mouths though they were going no faster than a march. Long night of wrecking a city will do that to you.

Up ahead, sitting there in the middle of the semicircular beach, looking suspiciously like something Lochled didn't want to get involved in, were two other squads, and it seemed that's where Hotsteel was heading. Near the two squads stood Ord Griman and Kayna Redstone. Lochled's two most favorite people on the whole fucking continent.

"Is this punishment, then, uh, hef?" Lochled grumbled at Hotsteel's back. "Because of what I said to the theynen yesterday?"

Hotsteel looked at him with a frown. "Theynen Griman requested Brytan Company's three best squads. You're one of them."

Oh, well idn't that just fucking dandy. "Maybe a reward for our efforts would be better than extra duty."

As though Lochled hadn't even spoken: "You'll hold your tongue today, Lochled. Behave. You've no excuse not to today."

On the contrary, Lochled thought he had a myriad of pretty damn good excuses, not the least of which was the simple fact that he just didn't like the little flowerman the Church had sent.

He'd hoped that once they'd landed he wouldn't have to see the self-righteous fucker again. Now it looked like they'd be stuck together once more.

Hotsteel slowed a bit, looked over his shoulder at Lochled. "Did you hear me?"

Lochled managed a respectful half salute as he finally got his hair out of his face. "Yes, hef. I'll mind my tongue." His eyes flicked over to one of those squads. "That Breakwood's squad?"

Hotsteel stopped. Hands on hips. Eyebrows up. Looking a bit like his name again. "Will that be a problem, then?"

Lochled bit a piece of dry skin from his lip. Spat it. "Not if that bastard fuck doesn't make it one."

A squint. "You're in a mood today."

"I've been in a mood since we left Bransport," Lochled grumbled, and started walking again. "Go on, then. Let's get it over with."

Hotsteel stopped him by grabbing his arm. Shot a glance over to Lochled's squad, but they were probably too miserable to care or notice the tension in front of them.

Lochled looked at that hand on his arm. Felt his stomach sink. Looked up at Hotsteel's face. Felt it sink a little further. Damn it, he'd gotten ahead of himself there, and he knew it. They both knew it. That was one of the toughest things about soldiering: when you were tired and pissed, you still had to eat shit and smile about it.

"Sorry, hef," Lochled said, keeping his tone even.

"I allow you a lot of leeway," Hotsteel said in a hard tone barely above a whisper. A tone that told Lochled things had shifted very rapidly out of friendship and into business. "Because of your history with my father. But where we are going, we are going alone—just the three squads. I cannot afford to lose control out there. Do you understand me?"

Lochled frowned. "We're going off on our own? Away from the army?"

Hotsteel just kept staring at him.

Lochled nodded. "Yes, hef. I understand."

"Good. Steady on."

"Steady on."

So they steady-on-ed their way up to the two squads and the one priest and the one Seeker, and Hotsteel disconnected from Lochled just as they neared the gathering and a few eyes turned to them. Naturally, Lochled's were all over Breakwood's, the scheming bastard, with his ugly little pucker of a mouth, like his face didn't have an opening so someone had had to poke a hole in it so he could feed. The two of them stared at each other appropriately long and hard.

The gathering was mostly standing, mostly in a circle. A clear line between the squads, with empty sand between them like some unspoken no-man's-land had been decided upon. But that's the nature of things. You get close to your squad, and you don't mind rubbing shoulders with them, because you piss and shit and sleep next to them. But other squads? Fuck them.

Hotsteel skirted around to where Ord and Kayna were standing, while Lochled and his squad tramped to a stop. All three squads sized each other up. It was so automatic that it had the feeling of ritual, like this was just what happened when groups of soldiers met.

Lochled wisely positioned his own squad away from Breakwood's, so that the third squad was between them. He noted that Breakwood's squad was only missing one—the boy that Rony had stuck in the gut. Rankled him something fierce that he'd lost so many men and Breakwood hadn't. Rankled him because he knew that Breakwood was looking at Lochled's five and thinking what a shit sergeant he must be for having lost so many. Rankled him because there hadn't been shit that either of them could have done about it. It was pure chance that Breakwood had most of his men still standing and Lochled didn't.

So, not only did Lochled have to endure that pintelsniff Ord for however long this mission would take, but he'd also have to deal with Breakwood. And they were detaching from the main body of troops. Which meant they were likely to be in more danger, but worse than that, they wouldn't have access to the amenities that being in the main body of the army afforded a man to stave off his misery, such as barrels of drips. Were they even taking drips with them? Who was going to carry it? Did each man have to carry his own? Because Lochled wasn't sure if he could shoulder the amount necessary to get him through.

He was already starting to sweat just thinking about it. Breakwood. Ord. Kayna. For an unknown amount of time. And possibly he'd have to do it sober. He hated this mission already.

"Right then," Hotsteel harrumphed up some attention. "We'll get on with it. We've a special request from the Church itself, by way of Theynen Ord Griman." Hotsteel raised his eyebrows at Ord, inviting him to take over.

"Yes. Well." Ord shuffled a bit. A sidelong glance at the Seeker next to him. "We've been given a special task. One of the utmost importance to the Church." His eyes flashed to Lochled's. Lochled stared back, deadpan. That's what Hotsteel wanted, after all. "We'll be detaching from the main body of forces and pushing straight through Leftland in an attempt to discover how large of a land it is."

One of the men from the squad between Lochled and Breakwood's leaned in, face all screwed up. "Pardon, Theynen. Are you saying we're going to be a *mapping detail*?"

"No, not exactly. Although I will be drawing some maps.

But, as I said, the purpose of the expedition is to learn how large Leftland is."

Rony leaned close in to Lochled, whispering, "Whycome we don't know how big Leftland is already?"

Lochled shrugged. "Always get all the harvest we need from the coastal cities and villages," he murmured back. "Never had a need to go in deeper."

Another man spoke up, voicing the question likely on everyone's minds: "What we need to know the size of Leftland for?"

Ord blinked a few times. Maybe he hadn't been expecting many questions. But you can't swoop in and upset everyone's plans for a glorious crusade of being drunk and scaef addled while pillaging a foreign country to your heart's content, and not expect to field some questions.

"To . . . ascertain . . . the size of the landmass . . . from which I can calculate a reasonable . . . uh . . . population."

Lochled lowered his chin and narrowed his eyes at the priest. Did he really think that talking around in circles like that was going to get him free of the truth?

"Population?" the same soldier asked.

"Swearnsoot, man," Hotsteel snapped. "The population of Tickers. Try and keep up."

It seemed to do the man no good. His brain was still in knots.

Lochled knew he'd been told to behave himself, but Hotsteel hadn't told him he couldn't speak the truth. So that's what he did. Nice and level and without too much teeth behind it. "The Church needs to learn how many Tickers are in Leftland. Otherwise we might hunt 'em all dead. Like we done with the whales back in Bransport."

"Oh."

"Sergeant Thatcher." Hotsteel's voice.

"Yes, hef?" Lochled met his eyes. They were, predictably, glaring. Lochled held up a hand, and looked to Ord, managing to appear convincingly innocent, he thought. "That is what you meant, right, Theynen? I was only attempting to put it in words that a simple soldier can grasp."

Ord hesitated for a moment. But then nodded. "Yes. That is the idea."

"So we won't be with the main body?" one of the men in Breakwood's squad asked.

Hotsteel huffed, stepped forward. "That's enough questions. How's about you let me get all the facts of the matter out and *then* you can ask a question, if they haven't already been answered, uh?"

A few desultory *yes, hefs*.

Lochled snorted softly and looked away at the beach for a moment. Every soldier in those three squads was thinking exactly what Lochled had just been thinking, and really not liking the shape it was taking. Made him feel a little vindicated, actually. Let Hotsteel see for himself that it wasn't just Lochled being sour—no one wanted to do what was being asked of them.

"We'll be going mounted," Hotsteel said, hands on his hips, looking them in the eyes as though challenging the three squads to say something untoward. "We'll need the mobility as this is a time-sensitive mission. We've one month to find the approximate dimensions of—"

He was already getting drowned out by a chorus of "One month?" Hotsteel stopped talking and simply stared at them until they all got quiet again.

"To find the approximate dimensions of Leftland," he labored on. "That means we're going to need to travel fast. You'll be expected to care for your own horse. Does anyone *not* know how to handle a horse?"

Silence.

Hotsteel offered them the gift of a tiny smile. "Buncha true-hearted Brymics you are. Excellent. We'll be afforded a single wagon for additional supplies. Yes, we will have a cask of drips aboard and enough scaef to go around." An audible sigh of relief from all gathered. Hotsteel shook his head. "Come now, men. What kind of a captain do you think I am? Can't be expected to fight without food, drips, and scaef."

"Pardon, captain," Breakwood sounded off. Speaking of scaef, he was in the process of cramming a wad of it into his puckered little mouth hole. Reminded Lochled of something else at the other end. Made him sneer in disgust. "This all the men we're taking with us?" A glance toward Lochled, then Rony. "Well . . . men and one girl, anyways."

"It is."

Breakwood nodded. Spat red. "Not many. Certainly won't be able to take on much more than a small village, if that."

"You are correct, Breakwood. We'll be avoiding any larger settlements. Cost of staying fast and mobile."

"Yes, hef." Breakwood seemed to be drawing something in the sand with the toe of his boot. "Quite a cost, though." A murmur of assent at that—and not just from Breakwood's squad either. Now that the more immediate concern of drips and scaef had been handled, they were on to more long-term matters. "Most of us agreed to come on crusade hoping for a commission on a good trinket that takes the Church's fancy."

"Yes? And?"

"Well, hef, if we can't take on nothing more than a little village, then we probably won't find many trinkets worth getting our names on. Now, we're not a cowardly bunch—we fought our way onto the beaches, and many a man died doing that. Died for it because they thought they could get something out of it, make their lives better, pay off a debt, or win a wife, or feed a family. Without that, seems like there's a lot of danger for not much reward."

Well, they'd all been thinking it—Lochled included—and even though he'd sorely like to ram his fist into that puckered hole where Breakwood's words came out, he had to admit they were true ones.

Hotsteel, however, had the appearance of a small mountain threatening to turn into a volcano. His face was getting all red, like his veins were running with lava, like those ugly black hills in the Pan, ready to spew burning rock on everyone.

It was Ord that kept him from exploding, though. He stepped forward with a gentle hand on Hotsteel's shoulder and spoke just as the captain was opening his mouth, forcing him to snap it shut again and swallow his bubbling officer's rage.

"It is an understandable concern," Ord said with a thoughtful look on his face, like he didn't really understand it at all. "And I may have a solution to the problem."

"Theynen, you do not need to bargain with the men to get them to do their duty," Hotsteel glared at Breakwood, and even though Lochled agreed with what Breakwood had said, he still felt a little eager to see if he would get punished for it. "These are soldiers, and if they don't follow orders, they get executed."

"Yes, I understand that, Captain," Ord responded. "However, it is something that is mutually beneficial. It will assist me, and it will provide, hmmm . . . motivation."

Hotsteel allowed it by standing there, silent.

Ord turned his attention to the squads, making a good effort of completely avoiding Lochled's gaze. Fine by Lochled. Would be even better if they didn't have to see each other at all. "I've something of a personal interest in a particular item, and I will pay any man directly should he find it."

Much more interest now.

"What is it?"

"I've only a few texts from the Second Crusade to go on, but from that I can offer you the very general description of a glass phial filled with yellowish powder. It is a . . . medicine of sorts, according to what I've read. My interest in it is personal, and not a matter of the Church, so I will pay you myself." Ord cleared his throat, looking a little nervously at Kayna, though she only stood there and watched him, still and silent. "Ten golden whales to the man that finds it."

A rush of excitement.

Lochled's jaw nearly dropped. It wasn't quite the sum you might get if you got your name on a valuable trinket, but it wasn't too far off either. Men had risked their lives for a tenth of that, and probably less. Lochled certainly had. Sad fact was, he'd risked his life for nothing at all on more than a few occasions, and if you asked any of the squads, you'd probably find the same. Fighting men are prone to fighting, after all, and if there isn't a good reason for it, they can always make one up.

"Ten golden whales," Rony breathed from behind Lochled, right along with every man assembled.

Ord held up his finger. "But . . . it must be the substance that I'm searching for. Which I must confirm for myself before I reward the finder."

Normally, a man would need more assurances than that, but Ord was a priest, and even if you didn't like the Church, you still generally trusted the word of a priest. So there was a whole lot of nodding and half smiles that would've been full smiles, but the men didn't want to seem too much like they only cared about coin, even if that was the truth.

"So," Ord said, smiling, clapping his hands together. "It won't be such an issue to avoid large settlements, then?"

Breakwood nodded respectfully. "None at all, Theynen."

Hotsteel cleared his throat and spoke up again. "Well, then. We'll plan to camp at the edge of Halun's Landing before dark. Get a peek at the countryside beyond, and then head out at first light. There's the horses coming around—gather your things and saddle up, and let's not waste time, uh?"

Lochled looked back at Rony, whose eyes were wide and mouth open, like a starving woman looking at a whole roasted hog. "Ten whales, then. Would that free your brothers?"

Her eyes flicked to his, then away, almost guiltily. "Very nearly."

"And with your name on that shooter in the tower," Cryer put in, looking thirsty for the gold himself, even as he imagined Rony getting it. "Even though you split it with us . . ."

"More than enough," Rony almost whispered.

"Steady on," Lochled grunted. "You haven't found it yet. Don't go booking passage on dry-docked ferries."

"Right," Rony said. She was in the process of turning around, and then there was a mad shuffle of limbs from the back of Lochled's squad and she said, "Uh?"

Something about the tone of it. Something about the sound of tussling. Lochled knew something bad was happening even before he turned around, and when he did, he saw Trut in a full sprint. Didn't know what the hell the man was after until he looked and saw the line of horses being led up, and the one in the middle of the pack, a big piebald mare, had decided she didn't like something and was letting her handler know about it.

Her handler didn't like it either and was letting her know about it too, cursing and smacking her in her great big jaw with the haft of his axe, which was only making her panic worse.

It wasn't too hard to see the endpoint of Trut's heading. He was churning through the sand like a madman, the horse handler whacking away at the disobedient animal, and he didn't even register Trut coming until he was right behind him and yelled, "You fucking twank!"

"Aw, shit," Lochled spat, and started after him, Cryer and Rony close behind while Ponts and Licker simply watched on in confusion.

The horse handler turned at Trut's outburst, his eyes going wide, his mouth going into a shocked little pucker, not unlike Breakwood's, and then Trut landed both elbows in the man's face and sent him sprawling in the sand.

There was all sorts of yelling—Lochled heard Hotsteel in there, but he was yelling himself, a flurry of insults at Trut and various commands to stop, but with everyone going on, nothing seemed to break through to Trut. Maybe wouldn't have stopped him even if he could have heard it.

Trut had already snatched the axe out of the man's hand, and he was mounted atop him, leaning back so that the man's grasping claws couldn't get at his face, while Trut had one hand holding the man's head down by the jaw and, with the other, was beating him across the side of his face with the haft of the axe.

"How do you like it, you pisser?" Trut raged on, *smack-smack-smack*. "How do you like being beaten, you fuck?"

"Ah! Gah! Fuck! Get off!"

"Trut, you mad bastard!" Lochled roared at him, pulling up short just in time to snatch Trut's wrist, started hauling him backward off the horse handler.

"It's a fucking living creature, you fuck!" Trut screeched at the handler, kicking futilely at him as Cryer lent his muscle to Lochled's efforts and together they dragged Trut back a few strides. "It's got fucking *feelings*! You can't just go around beating it, you fuck! I'll fucking kill you I ever see you do that to a—"

Lochled gave him a quick jab to the mouth to shut him up before he said something he couldn't come back from. "That's enough, then!" They spilled him backward onto the sand and stood over him, breathing hard.

"Oh!" Trut winced, hands going to his face, rubbing his mouth. Eyes watering, looking angrily at Lochled. "The fuck'd you do that for, hef?"

Lochled thrust a finger at him. "You just shut your mouth before I have Cryer cave it in, you half-wit."

Boos and jeers from behind—Lochled wasn't sure who was jeering, and whether it was directed at him or Trut or the horse handler. Hotsteel was suspiciously quiet, which tweaked Lochled's panic, made him imagine the captain stomping up right behind him, so he spun. Found Hotsteel still standing where he'd been, not so much angry as disappointed.

The horse handler was writhing to his feet, spluttering and spitting and mad as a winter bear—he was about as big as one too. Lochled was briefly surprised that Trut even took him down, but even big men go down when hit on their blind side.

The handler slashed through the sand, looking for his axe and not finding it, the horse forgotten and trotting away toward the beach like it might just swim its way back to Bransport and leave the sorry two-leggers to walk their own sad bodies about. The handler gave up on his axe and yanked his long-knife out, stomping toward them.

"You stupid bastard!" he roared, steel glinting in the sun, but his face was almost confused, like he couldn't quite figure out what had just happened. "What the fuck was that for, then?"

Trut squirmed to his feet, produced his own axe and knife, and stood ready to use them. It gave the handler pause—a little flash of reason making it through all the anger. And in that pause, Lochled and Rony and Cryer had produced their steel as well.

The handler, now clearly outnumbered, backed off a step. "The fuck's the matter with you all? You let the horse get away!"

"Good!" Trut snapped at him. "I'd want to get away from the likes of you as well! Means she's a smart horse!"

"Fah!" The handler waved the knife at him, but his eyes were still jigging back and forth between Lochled, Rony, and Cryer—kept coming back to Cryer, who might not have outweighed him but was plenty big, just the same, and awful mean to look at. "Right then, you mad fuck! You want the horse so bad, you can go get her!" He pointed to where the mare was trotting uncertainly along the hard sand near the surf.

The handler slapped his knife back into his belt, stared shotstones at Trut, and spat dryly onto the sand. "Soot, fire, and child, I hope she throws you and you break your back!"

Trut spat right back. "Fuck your burning child! I hold to the Old Gods anyhow! Blood, tree, and son!"

"All right, all right," Lochled was towing Trut backward and waving away the handler. "That's enough from both of you."

In all the heavy breathing, Lochled barely made out the taunting voice from behind: "Old Sergeant Thatcher. Can't fucking control a single man on his squad. Or a single skelpie."

Lochled didn't even turn to look or respond to Breakwood but got mad about it just the same. Took it out on Trut because he was the cause of the whole thing. Grabbed him by the collar of his leather jerkin and shook him hard.

"You stupid twank!" he hissed. "Captain Hotsteel says he needs to keep control, and the breath from his words is still hanging in the air when you decide to act like a fool over some damn horse?"

Trut started to pull away from Lochled, but then something hard and sly came over his face. His eyes flickered up over Lochled's shoulder. To the other squads that were watching them, probably thinking what a pack of idiots they looked like, and no wonder they'd lost so many on the beaches yesterday.

Trut turned very still. Looked at the hand holding his jerkin. Looked at Lochled. "Yes, hef. Some damn horse. My horse now."

"Fah!" Lochled shoved him away. "Go get your fucking horse, then!"

Trut stumbled, recovered, sheathed his knife and axe, then, with a smirk, turned toward the beach and the mare that had finally stopped and was standing there in the ankle-deep water, huffing and bobbing her head.

Rony still had her steels in her hand. Lochled frowned at them. When had she gotten steels? Only had the little knife last time he'd checked. She spun in a slow circle like she couldn't figure out which way was daeside and which was nyhtside.

"What's got into him?" she breathed, not looking at Trut, but at Lochled and Cryer.

"Fuck if I know," Lochled growled. "Mad fucking bastard's just lost his mind."

"Lost it yesterday, I reckon," Cryer intoned, staring out at Trut while he slowly put his weapons away. "Reckon it went with Wen."

The words seemed to form a little needle that stuck Lochled straight in the gut. "Ah, fuck." His shoulders drooped. Head hung guiltily. Why hadn't he remembered about fucking Wen? It'd all happened so fast, the whole debacle from getting on the damned landing craft to making it into the city. Wen and Effel and Jory. He hadn't spent much time thinking on any of them. Was almost like they'd never existed. Grieve for every man who dies under you, and you'll soon lose your stomach—and your courage with it.

But Trut had lost a brother. A man he'd grown up with and fought with in a half-dozen skirmishes and two wars—that Lochled knew about.

"What?" Cryer eyed him.

Lochled shook his head. "I should've . . ."

"Should've what? Stopped the shotstone from poking Wen's heart out?"

"No." Lochled rubbed the stubbled back of his head, watching as Trut approached the horse ever so slowly, hands up. "Should've said something about it. Should've had some words for Wen."

"Wouldn't have done Trut any good. He was in the city last night, not moping about the camp like you."

Lochled pressed his lips together, still feeling guilty despite Cryer's offer of absolution. Out on the beach, Trut was now standing within two strides of the animal. The mare had lowered her head now, seemed to be curious about him. Lochled could see Trut's lips moving, but couldn't hear the soft words. One hand out. The mare sniffing at it. Shaking her head. Whinnying and snorting.

Cryer put a hand on Lochled's shoulder. "Tonight, then. Say some words tonight. Give the man a chance to grieve before he locks it up." A soft, disdainful chuff. "Wind up getting us all hanged with another outburst."

Lochled started to glance over his shoulder but then decided not too. He didn't need to look to see everyone's bad feelings directed at him—he could feel them just fine, prickling at the back of his neck. Fuck, but he was constantly getting in trouble for his squad's half-wit actions. Why couldn't the lot of them just control themselves?

Lochled grumbled a few curses at them under his breath. "Go on, then. Get the rest of the squad ready and mounted. And take Rony with you. I'll deal with 'Trut the Horse Master.'"

Cryer sighed, but did as requested. At least one of Lochled's squad was reliable.

He stood there in the sand, sweating, squinting against the sun, waiting for Trut to get a hand on the wayward horse's dangling reins. Dumb thing was already saddled, just needed to calm down enough for a man to get on it.

Trut continued to ease forward, gentle as can be, so kind and gentle to this animal that you'd have thought he could talk to horses and they could talk back, tell him all their supposed feelings. The mare stopped tossing her head so much, eventually let him touch her nose, and then everything was fine from there on.

Lochled fished out his pouch of scaef as he walked toward Trut, not wanting to advance too quickly and get the stupid animal all spooked again. Lochled knew how to ride horses—any good Brymic man or woman knew that—but he'd never cared for them. They were awfully large animals, and they had minds of their own. Lochled didn't like the fact that he never knew if the thing was going to go mad and kill him on a whim.

Then again, you could say the same for the men around here. Maybe Lochled was just better at reading men than he was at reading horses.

He packed a mouthful of scaef, brushed his fingers off on his tunic. Stopped about two strides from Trut as he gently looped his fingers through the mare's tack and turned, not leading the horse at all, but making her *want* to follow him.

Lochled stared at him, hands on his hips. Spat juice into the sand. "You done being an idiot yet?"

Trut didn't look at him. Kept his eyes on the horse. But it looked like his eyes were a little wet. Maybe he'd gotten sand in them. He ran a hand under the horse's thick, muscular neck. "War horses," Trut said bitterly. "A shame is what it is."

"Oh? How's that?"

Trut just shook his head, walked the horse right past Lochled so that he had to turn and keep step with him. "Never understood why we have to take something so beautiful and make it do ugly things for us."

CHAPTER 17

Things you do in the small hours of darkness rarely seem so great in broad daylight.

Maybe it was the fact that the broad daylight was pushing angrily at Rony's eyeballs, but that sense of connectedness she'd felt with the men around her, the experience of their acceptance and how it had washed away the guilt of all she'd done . . . well, that turned out to be as fleeting as the sweet taste of red wine, now turned to bitter vomit on her tongue.

The shod hooves of the horses created a slow, even clatter across the cobblestones of Halun's Landing, bouncing off the white walls that glared at her, reflecting the angry sun. The perfect polish of those white stones had been wrecked in places by shotstones from Levelers—a hazardous, chaotic series of patterns that seemed so random, and yet were unmistakable. In other places, buildings lay crumbled from the impacts of the siege cannons. Gutters lay sticky with black, beginning to smell like meat left out in the sun, and torrents of flies scoured across the stones. Bright red splashes across walls. The bodies of both men and Tickers were becoming more frequent as they ventured further into the city than the body collectors had reached.

Oh, the bodies, the bodies. How she tried to look away from them but always found her aching eyes drawn back to them, like her mind was gluttonous for the torture of it. Pain cleanses, they say. But Rony wasn't sure she could be scrubbed clean.

She would've liked herself better if she'd keeled over and spewed at that point. But she didn't. Wasn't even close. Reacted to it all with a dim sort of horror, like it wasn't her that'd had a hand in doing it, but some other person.

And all of this destruction around her—had she really pranced through it all like a blissful maid in the Festival of Flowers? Had she really run through all of this, laughing and drinking and . . .

Fucking?

What kind of a person was that? To do all that she'd done as though you're in some innocent revelry, when in fact you're dancing in the blood of thousands, and some of it from your own damned comrades? Only devils did things like that. And yet she'd done them. So she must be a devil herself.

Strange. She'd never thought of herself as an evil person. Sitting there, swaying to the rhythm of the horse between her legs, staring blankly at the back of Cryer's head sticking up above the greatshield on his back, she tried to remember some clue, some warning sign from her youth that would have foretold how foul her spirit truly was.

She was certain it was there. She just couldn't think of it right now.

And what of the others? Did they feel anything at all about what they'd done?

They'd laughed and joked about things they'd done during the day, during the landing and the fighting. Somehow they made light of the things that Rony thought would haunt her forever, and this rendered some sort of sorcery on her brain: she no longer felt guilty about it, because it was clearly all laughable.

But no one had mentioned last night.

Her hands resting on the pommel of her saddle, obsessively squeezing at the leather like she could milk an answer out of it, Rony tried to think of a way to bring it up. But no matter what she came up with, all she could imagine was them turning around and giving her a look. A terrible look. One that said, *We thought you were one of us, but clearly we were wrong.*

No. She couldn't do that. The only thing keeping her mind from dropping its sails in a leftwind was the sense that she was *together* with them. That they had accepted her. That, even though she was so far from anything she knew, she wasn't alone. They were her brothers now. They were blood bound.

She refused to endanger that.

She had no real idea why she wanted to talk about it so badly. Specifically, wanted *them* to talk about it. Perhaps because remaining silent seemed to confirm that what they'd done was wrong. And maybe, if she could get them to talk, they'd reveal to her some magical rationale for their actions that would make them honorable or righteous. Or at least a little less evil.

"So. Cryer," she started, though she still didn't know what she was going to say.

He looked over his shoulder at her. "Uh?"

She landed on the topic just before the pause became awkward. "Doesn't it strike you as a little odd how much Captain Hotsteel lets Lochled get away with?"

Cryer's heavy profile frowned. "No, not really." And then he faced forward again.

Damn it. And double-damned for the fact that her sad little heart wilted a bit when he turned back forward. What did she think? That because he'd gotten his pintel in her he'd take her up in marriage? She was being a silly girl. That wasn't even how things worked back in the real world, and certainly not here in hell. Of course he didn't give a shit. Her cunny wasn't so special.

She shook her head, irritated at herself, though much more irritated at Cryer. "Well, it seems that way to me. I mean, I'm fine by it. Works quite nice for our sergeant to be in good with the captain. But it just . . . struck me as odd."

"Clearly," Cryer said, without turning around.

Now, was she being oversensitive, or was he being deliberately dismissive?

She clicked her tongue, urged her horse up abreast of him. Gave him a look that she believed worked on most men. Cryer glanced at her. Tried to look away but got sucked into it sure enough. She didn't even know what it looked like—something to do with the lips and the eyes. And it took a few moments. But then it worked.

Cryer smirked, like he knew what she'd done. "Right, then." He nodded ahead, where Lochled was riding at the front of the column. "Lochled goes back aways with Hotsteel's father, Othis. Back to the Pan, and before that, the Third."

"Oh." Rony was disappointed with how succinctly the story ended. Didn't give her a lot of opportunity to merge the conversation into what she wanted. "What about the Pan?"

Cryer's face darkened. "I was in the Pan myself. With Lochled. We were under Othis. He was our sergeant then." A long, uncomfortable pause. Then he took a breath. "In fact, that's where Lochled got his byname."

"I didn't realize he had one. Why doesn't he go by it then?"

"Never cared for it. Gets mean when you try to use it on him, so most people don't, if they know what's good for 'em. Lochled'll get bloody for the sake of not hearing that name."

Cryer looked briefly amused. "Which is somewhat ironic, if you think about it."

Rony felt like she was missing something. "I don't know what you mean. What's his name?"

Cryer looked at her with his eyebrows up. "Ah. Right. You didn't even know he had a byname, so I suppose you wouldn't know what it is. Sorry, it's just that . . ." he trailed off, smiling, but something in it all wrong. Off. Turned, like a day-old fish. He seemed about to say something, but then shook his head and looked forward. "Fah. Just don't mention it around him. Ever."

"I won't. Tell me."

Cryer leaned toward her, lowering his voice. "Redskin."

Rony burst out laughing. He'd gotten her pretty keyed up for that one. Lochled turned in his saddle, frowning at her, so she put her hand over her mouth and stifled her laugh with a cough. And only then did she glance to Cryer and see that he was glowering like she'd belched at a burial.

Her mirth died to a snicker, which itself seemed to give up in midair, flopping down between them like a lame bird.

"What?" Cryer grunted. "What's that then? Your laughing. What's that about?"

She stared at him for a long time, her mouth poised for another smile, another laugh, while she waited for his stern countenance to crack and show her that he was only billying her about.

It didn't happen. He kept waiting for her to explain herself.

She reared back. "Swearnsoot. You're serious."

"Yes. And?"

"He can't be."

"He is."

"Redskin?"

"The same."

"No."

Cryer shook his head. "Well now, you could just go ask him about it, but I reckon he'll kill us both."

"You're having me on." She glanced back at the others, found them involved in their own conversations, though she'd half expected them to be all in a knot, giggling about the trick being played on her.

"I'm not," Cryer sighed.

"But Redskin . . . I've heard of him! They sing—"

"Shhh."

She was getting loud with a combination of indignation and excitement. Glanced around, but no one was paying attention. Back to Cryer: "They have *songs* about Redskin!"

"There is *a* song about Redskin." Cryer held up a finger. "And I'd advise you never to sing it. Least not with Lochled in earshot."

"Well, what the fuck is he doing here?" Rony hissed. "He could be a Steadman with a name like that! He could be *leading* this company!"

"He wouldn't."

"Well, obviously he didn't." She frowned at Lochled's back, several horses up from her. "Why don't he like his name?"

Cryer gave her a sidelong look. Dipped his head. Then shook it. "He's never said much about it. But I suspect . . ." He squinted at Lochled's back, right along with her. "I suspect he don't like it because of what he did to get it, uh?"

Redskin. Funny, she'd never really thought about the name. Only the courageous deeds attributed to it. Never thought about what it must've been like to do those deeds, or why, after the doing, other men looked at Lochled and decided he'd be called Redskin . . .

Rony swallowed hard. "What about you?" she croaked.

"Me?"

She looked at him. "Cryer's not a byname?"

He tried to look taken aback, but he wound up smiling. It faded fast, like a morning flower once the sun hits it full on. She kept watching him, his hesitation only making her more curious.

He sighed heavily. "First real battle I was in was Falls Bluff, up in the Pan." A glance at her. "The First Haedan War, not the Second. Though I was in that too. I was fifteen at the time. Not filled out yet. Not big enough to carry a greatshield. So they had me running foot with axe and knife." He paused for a long time, staring at nothing in particular. Then a wan little smile crossed his lips. "Oh, I cried my eyes out the second the battle was over. I dunno. Maybe I'd started crying while I was still fighting, but I don't recall. Just couldn't help myself. Cried like a baby till I couldn't cry no more, and then still sobbed for a while after. All while going about my normal duty, finishing off those too wounded to be healed or held captive. Gathering up weapons." A strange little titter, awfully high pitched for such a big man. "Just blubbering the whole damned time."

He gave a weird shudder. Worked his shoulders. Seemed to come back to himself. "Well, anyways. That was my first battle. Never happened again, but everyone remembered it, the big brown-skinned bastard weeping his eyes out while he went along, axing wounded men in the head."

Rony stayed silent for a while, picturing it, just as she'd pictured Lochled as Redskin, except in her mind she saw him only as he was now, grizzled and massive, sobbing his eyes out. She felt like there must be something vaguely amusing about it, but the thought only made her sad.

"Why do you go by it then?" she asked softly.

"Why wouldn't I?" He seemed genuinely curious.

She shrugged, a bit lamely. "I dunno. Thought maybe . . . maybe you might feel ashamed about it. Not that there's shame in it."

"Huh," he grunted, thoughtfully. "No. No shame in it. And I've never minded the name. Maybe it serves me well. Reminds me that I'm still human on the inside, no matter what I do on the outside."

"Do you . . ." she trailed off, biting her upper lip, unsure what to say, or how to say it, and whether she'd reveal herself as the fraud she knew herself to be. And then they wouldn't want her anymore, wouldn't accept her as one of them. And she didn't think she could be here all alone.

"What?"

She struggled mightily, the words like anchors. "Do you think that ever goes away?"

"What? Being human?"

"Yes. In war. Do you think you can do so many bad things that you stop being you? Stop being human?"

Cryer chuffed lightly. "Well then, what would you be if not human?"

"A devil," she mumbled.

"No, no." Cryer shook his head. "Don't matter what you've done, we're all humans, and we all have hearts. Even the worst of us. You never stop being human."

"Piss on that," a voice remarked behind them.

Rony and Cryer both twisted to find Licker riding just behind and between them.

"Oh, the wetfoot has some wisdom then, uh?" Cryer smiled, steered his horse to make room for Licker. "Tell us all about it, swamp man."

Licker looked pleased with himself as he nudged his horse up between Rony and Cryer. "Indeed the wetfoot does. We marsh dwellers are very wise, especially compared to you half-wit sod kickers. And I say piss on that. You can lose yourself in dark deeds, for sure and for certain. I've seen men who it's happened to. Not all men that go to war have it happen to them, for it's not about war, it's about who you are and what you do, but it seems who you are changes in war, and there's always plenty of opportunities to do bad things." Licker cast his spooky blues on Rony. "You can lose yourself in it. You can."

"Fah. You're mumbling night stories," Cryer dismissed him with a wave. "That's all."

"Puffy," Licker said. "Puffy Blackroot."

Cryer pointed in a random direction. "Shiny. Shiny White-stone. See? I can say words too."

Licker sighed in his usual, theatrically put-upon manner. "Puffy Blackroot was a coldhearted killer. Fought with him in Medeland, and he'd just as soon hack a man to death as say a word to him. In fact, I seen him do it. He never cared a shit for whether or not the person he was killing was the person he was *supposed* to be killing. Fact is, I seen him kill some of our own boys in the heat of battle, I think just for the fuck of it, but I never said nothing about it, 'cause I didn't want him killing me!"

Licker laughed uproariously. Tapered off with a slap to the thigh. "Anyways. I knew Puffy as a child—he's a wild, blackwater wetfoot like myself. And I can tell you he was a sweet boy. Quiet, for sure. But mild with the boys and sweet with the girls. Gentle with the creatures. Couldn't barely bring himself to gut a fish, he was that soft. Old Puffy." Licker shook his head. "Then he went off and started killing and got all twisted up inside and weren't normal no more. Still quiet as ever, but he didn't have nothing in his eyes no more." Licker pointed two fingers at his own wide eyes, peering eerily at Rony, then Cryer. "You know how you can see a man's heart through his eyes? Not Puffy. He'd lost his heart somewhere along the line, and his eyes were just as dead as shotstones. Not hard, mind you, like the young men try on when they want to look like they've been blooded. I mean *dead* dead. Gone. Nothing in 'em. Just . . . nothing."

They clip-clopped in silence for a few horse's strides.

"Anyways," Licker said suddenly, straightening. "That's why I say, 'piss on that,' when you claim you can keep your heart no matter what. You do enough killing, it'll rot your heart to nothing eventually. Just depends on who you are and how you kill."

"Oh, so there's a special way to kill that makes it all right, uh?" Cryer snorted.

"There is," Licker said solemnly. "Killing to eat. Killing to protect yourself or someone else."

Rony was expecting a third instance, but Licker just rode along in silence after that.

"Well," she ventured. "What about the Old Laws? Halun's Laws?"

Licker scoffed. "What? That it's all right to kill if your Steadman or your chief tells you to? Tsk tsk, Little Roan, I'd taken you to have a better mind than that."

Rony felt abruptly sick. She could feel the blood running out of her face like someone had opened a tap in her foot.

"Don't mind the blowhole," Cryer gruffed, casting a glare at Licker. "Pale-faced twank."

"Char-skinned halfie," Licker tossed back.

Cryer looked to Rony. "Soldiering means following orders. When you agree to be a soldier, you leave your morals behind you. You take on the morals of the men who lead you. You're not responsible for what they tell you to do. You're just a tool at that point. A weapon. So you go where you're told, and you do what you're ordered, and you kill whoever or whatever they want dead."

"Right you are," Licker agreed. "Except that after all that killing, you lose the little light inside of you that makes you human." Licker laughed again, then reached out and patted Rony on the leg. "But don't you worry, Little Roan! You've not killed any man yet. You've only killed animals. And I reckon you have to kill a lot of animals to lose your heart, you know?"

Rony tried to swallow, but found her mouth pasty. "I've killed animals before," she said. "And it didn't feel like this."

Licker's voice suddenly dropped low. "Oh, now. Steady on, cully." Looking about as though he hoped no one else had heard her. "You don't talk about *feeling*, all right?"

She stared at him, completely blank. "What?"

Cryer cleared his throat meaningfully and looked away. But Rony wasn't sure whether whatever he'd left unsaid was for her or for Licker. She was too confused. It was like they could talk about almost anything—murder and crying in your first battle and Lochled's secret byname. But mention having a feeling on the killing of Tickers, and everyone went quiet and strange.

"But . . ." Rony stammered. "What about Trut?"

Both Licker and Cryer didn't answer, now riding with their eyes deliberately anywhere but on Rony.

"Right, then. What about him?" Cryer mumbled, his tone still low.

"He had feelings for the fucking horse, but I can't have feelings for a Ticker?" Her eyes flashed rapidly back and forth—Licker, Cryer, Licker, Cryer. "They're both animals, according to you."

Licker scoffed quietly. "'According to you,' she says." He shook his head. Pulled his reins and fell back behind them, leaving the air tense and heavy, like the conversation had been strung up by the neck and Rony was watching it kick its way to death.

Cryer sniffed. Spat off to the side. Pulled out his scaef pouch and wangled it open.

Rony stared hard at the side of his face, still wanting a damned answer, thank you very much. But the anger had stilled her trembling hand at least. And it made her even more thirsty for some drips—though her head and her stomach didn't particularly agree. She uncorked her flask and took a pull from it. Her anger made it easy to grit her teeth and deal with the acid burn that roiled up in her throat when the drips splashed down. Few more of those, and she might start to feel a bit better.

"I don't understand the difference is all," Rony said.

Cryer got the scaef into his mouth. Cinched the pouch shut. Spat again. Sighed like she was a child asking too many damned questions. "Trut don't have feelings for horses. He done what he done because Wen did. Wen loved 'em like they was people. So Trut did what he did because that's what Wen would have done."

Cryer finally deigned to lay his eyes on her, cheek bulging, his words sounding weird and hollow around it. "People . . . sometimes they try to keep their lost ones alive by acting like them. It's a fool's journey, but everyone has to come to that realization on their own."

Rony thought of her father right then. Thought of what he'd told her before he died. Thought of how much she tried to be that thing. Like in doing so she kept the spirit of her father alive. And there was something about it that she still needed, so she didn't like Cryer pointing out that it was a fool's journey.

She huffed and looked away from him. "Still don't answer the question. Wen or Trut, it don't matter. A man had feelings of mercy and compassion for an animal. Am I so wrong to have it for a Ticker?"

"Wrong? No. Stupid? Yes." Cryer nudged his horse forward, leaving Rony feeling abandoned, but calling over his shoulder: "That's yet another fool's journey. But you'll come to that realization on your own."

Rony bared her teeth at his back. Then spat at him. Then went back to her flask.

A few more of those, and she might start to feel a bit better.

CHAPTER 18

Seemed everyone was comfortable sitting one of these beasts but Ord. He'd thought maybe it was a Fen thing, as horses aren't much use and can't be kept in the marshes of Fenland. But when he glanced back, the Fen named Licker was comfortably astride his horse, looking as easy as any Brymic or Drugothan.

Ord grunted and idly patted the neck of his own horse. "It's all right, girl. We'll get along."

A twitch of the ear was all the horse gave him for acknowledgment.

He shifted about in the saddle, trying to ease the tension in his back. How did everyone else manage it? They strode along all loose hipped, like their lower bodies were disconnected from their upper. Or perhaps just connected to the horse. Moving with it. Naturally.

Difficult.

Ord tried to get the easy rhythm down that he saw the others using, but felt he was humping the horse, so he stopped, slightly embarrassed, both for her and for him.

He heard the burst of a woman's laugh from back in the

column. Twisted to look, curious who would be so cheerful as they rode through so much carnage. Of course, it was Rony. Who else would it be?

He turned back forward and caught the tail end of Lochled glaring at her. The sergeant's eyes flicked to Ord's, probably just because Ord was looking at him. They didn't rest there long. His nose twitched—a sniff or a sneer, Ord couldn't tell—and Lochled faced forward again.

Ord frowned at his back. At first, just sour because Lochled was sour. But then Lochled's words went rambling through his head again, mischievous, prickling: *What if the Church is mistaken?*

Made that sourness turn to a queasy sort of dread.

Guilt, I think is what that feeling is called.

"Bastard," Ord whispered to Lochled's back. "I'm starting to think like you."

But hadn't he been entertaining those thoughts long before he'd met Sergeant Thatcher? The constant struggle between what he *felt* was true, and what he was *told* was true. But where did man's sense of truth come from, if not from Feor himself? Was Ord's sense of truth not simply the light of Feor that burned brightly inside of him? But if so, why would Feor's truth oppose the statements of the Church?

"Fah." Ord choked on it like gristle. Kicked the thought out of his mind like a penniless drunk from a tavern. He was playing a dangerous theological game with himself—something that his mentors had warned him about.

Dangerous because if the Church was wrong about one thing, then what else were they wrong about? Everything? If you called into question one slice of it, did that make the whole thing bad? Or could you pick the bad parts out, like a bit of mold on a loaf of bread?

But who's to know which is which? Who's to say you're

not just picking at the parts you don't like, like a wealthy child might decline to eat the crust of his bread but devour the soft inners? You couldn't simply make up a religion to justify whatever suited you.

And that was why you had to have faith.

But who should Ord place his faith in? The priests and priestesses who claimed to know the mind of Feor? Or his own sense of truth, which supposedly came from Feor himself?

The long and short of it was, Ord had all of these thoughts but no one to say them to, because no one wanted to hear a priest have doubts—priests were supposed to be the ones that assuaged *other's* doubts.

Which brought him, in an inevitable circle, back to where he'd started, like a goat chained to a stake: Lochled Thatcher.

That man was infuriating, it was true. But why? Because he said the things that Ord couldn't bring himself to say. Because he put strong voice to the tiny whispers that kept Ord up at night, staring at the ceiling and wondering if any of it mattered.

Maybe Ord wasn't even mad at Lochled. Maybe he wasn't even arguing with the man—maybe he was arguing with himself.

Maybe he had the overwhelming urge to keep speaking to Lochled, despite their animosity, in the hopes that some tortuous dilemma of philosophy would suddenly resolve itself without Ord having to say anything directly heretical.

Maybe he was using Lochled as a mouthpiece for his own doubts, and then acting appropriately indignant about it.

Ord frowned.

No. Couldn't be. He wasn't that downright petty. Was he?

But he found himself urging his horse forward anyway. Awkwardly, mind you. And somewhat confusing for the horse, who looked back at him as though she couldn't believe his utter ineptitude or her bad luck in being assigned to him.

Lochled saw him coming up and stiffened. Mouth going all flat, eyes too. Almost like he'd been ordered not to behave badly, but found it a terrible strain.

Ord rode there for a moment, staring at Lochled. Somewhat amused by his stiffness. Somewhat pained by it. It wasn't like he'd gone off on crusade hoping to make soldiers miserable. It just kind of happened that way.

"You know," Ord began, as gently as he could manage. "I don't think I've ever seen you *cheerful*, but you do seem unusually dour today. If our days stuck on a shit-stinking boat are anything to go by."

"Not sure I should answer that, Theynen," Lochled muttered.

"Why not?"

"It might offend you."

"Offend me, then. You've already done it before, why be shy about it now?"

"Can't."

"No?"

"Orders."

"Shame." Ord blew a breath that flapped his lips. "Well, fuck your orders."

Lochled snapped his head around, glaring. But also a little surprised. Which was satisfying for Ord. "What's that, then? What're you on about?"

Ord looked forward. Breathed deeply through his nose. "I'm afraid you've caught me at my worst, Sergeant Lochled. And for that, I would like to apologize to you. A ship is no place for me. Nor is a war. And yet, here we are."

"Mm-hmm."

"I spoke . . . poorly to you. And I may have gotten you in trouble with Hotsteel."

"Mm."

"So. Back to my original question: May I ask why you're so glowery today? And I promise, I won't report you to Hotsteel, or do anything that would get his attention. Just a soldier and a priest talking. Nothing more."

Lochled sniffed. Spat off to the side. Took his time with his flask, taking a sip, corking it again. "Might be I'm glowery 'cause I got stuck with you."

"Hmm." Ord pursed his lips. Looked straight ahead.

Well. Had he expected anything different?

Out of the corner of his eye, he could see that Lochled was looking at him, evaluating the effect of his words. He took a long time at it, letting Ord stew in his juices. But Ord supposed he'd earned that. So he took it bravely.

A small grunt, as though Lochled had measured something and was satisfied with it, but only just. "Then again," he said, hiking a thumb over his shoulder. "Maybe I'm glowery 'cause of those bastards back there. Not sure if you're aware, but one of Breakwood's crew is the one Rony ran off and stuck. He didn't do well in the landing. Didn't make it. Now Breakwood's got it in for me. Or Rony. Or the whole squad. Not quite sure."

"Oh." Ord raised his eyebrows. "I wasn't aware there was so much . . ."

"Backbiting?"

"Yes."

"Cartloads of it." Lochled sighed through his teeth. "You know the difference between criminals and soldiers?"

"What's that?"

"Criminals have rules."

Ord sucked on that for a moment. "Yes. I'm beginning to see that."

"Which brings me to a third reason for glowering. If you still have the stomach for it."

Ord huffed. "Why not? Go on, then. Have at it."

Lochled snorted. "You offered ten fucking golden whales to a pack of soldiers, for finding some fucking item you don't even know exists."

Ord tilted his head, trying to see how that was a problem. He'd thought he was being quite generous, not to mention wise. "I offered it because it seemed the men needed some motivation since I was taking them away from the potential of finding good trinkets."

"Oh, yes, you motivated them, for sure." Lochled clucked his tongue. "You know how I was just saying criminals follow rules and soldiers don't? And now you've gone and promised ten whales to three squads of men hardly better than cutthroats. Do you see the problem?"

Ord felt his face pinch up. "I see."

"Ever occur to you how in the world a few Steadmen can keep an army of men like these in check while gone off to a foreign land on crusade?"

Ord nodded, now seeing his error. "Because they don't get paid until they get back."

"Mm-hmm. And now you've gone and taken away their reason for staying civil until we get back to Brymsland, *and* told them you have at least ten golden whales in your effects."

Ord looked at Lochled sharply. "You don't think . . . ?"

Lochled shrugged. "No, I don't think they would. Most men won't have the stomach to kill a priest. Too superstitious. But if the temptation is strong enough, I could see them robbing you."

"Well, shit."

"Indeed. But you can't go back on your word now. That'd cause even more problems."

"What am I supposed to do, then? Just hope for the best?"

"More or less. And be very careful. Now, maybe someone

finds what you're looking for, maybe they don't. If they don't, no harm done. If they do? Well, maybe you take your time inspecting it." Lochled gave him a meaningful side eye. "Maybe you have to take it back to the Church in Bransport to confirm what it is. That way you don't have to pay them until we're back to civilization."

"Won't they suspect?"

Lochled shrugged. "Maybe. But you can lie about it."

"Priests aren't supposed to lie."

Lochled chuckled. "Oh?"

Ord frowned at him, but didn't answer.

"No," Lochled went on. "You tell 'em whatever you want—you lost a magic . . . thing . . . that would have confirmed the substance. It doesn't matter. These men don't know how alchemy works anyways. I certainly don't. You could say almost anything, and I'd have to believe you 'cause I don't know any better."

"Right, then." Ord shifted in his saddle again. "I'm sure I can figure something out."

"Theynen?" Lochled said, swaying easily along with the horse's gait, not looking at Ord, but around them, over at a building that'd been crushed by the siege cannons.

Ord leaned away from Lochled, suspiciously. Like he might up and take a swing at him with his hand axe. His tone had that kind of leading, conniving quality to it. "Yes?"

"Why would Tickers need or even know about medicine?"

And here they were. Back on the doctrine. And Ord couldn't decide whether what he felt was a thrill of possibility, or a stab of defensiveness. Maybe it was both. So odd how he kept poking about at Lochled, but when Lochled rose to the occasion, all Ord wanted to do was shut him up.

Conflicted, I think is what that feeling is called.

"Obviously," Ord began, carefully, "the Tickers didn't *make* the medicine themselves. If it exists, it will certainly be a leftover from the Old Ones."

"Strange how we keep finding the leftovers from the Old Ones," Lochled mused. "How long have they been gone now? Does the Church have an opinion on that?"

"Impossible to know."

"But they *know* that it idn't the Tickers."

"How do you mean?"

"I mean, what if there were no Old Ones, Theynen? What if it's just the Tickers, and always has been the Tickers?"

Ord felt that old indignation bubble up—damn it, it was almost beyond him to control it, like jerking your hand away from something hot or slapping at a fly when it bites. Lochled's words made him worry. But they also made him intensely curious.

He took a breath, sorting through a list of not-so-diplomatic responses and settling on something a little more open ended. "All right, then. You're a man who wants evidence, not faith. I can understand that. But let me ask you first, Sergeant, Do you have faith at all?"

Lochled looked at him sharply. Held his gaze for a long moment. "I suppose I do. I like to believe in Feor. Or maybe Nyhtson. Something. Something's got to be at the root of it all."

"That's very broad."

Lochled shrugged. "I try not to act like I know things when I don't."

"And you think the Church does?"

Lochled nodded. "I think the Church makes too much money *not* to. If they didn't claim to know everything, people might start to wonder about alchemy. Might start to think it's an ugly business. Only reason they don't think it now is because the Church assures them it's all fine. And it's an easy lie to swallow, that this whole burning business is Feor's will. Because we get so many fancy things from it." Lochled waved a hand about. "The people—they're drunk on it. Mad with it. Gone off the boat with their excitement for more, more, more. And the Church can give it to them. And all they have to do in return is look the other way when the fires are belching soot and the children are screaming." Lochled faltered there, his bottom teeth showing, grinding. "Look the other way when the Seekers come to take their little ones."

Ord's heart was pounding at that point. Mostly with offense. He was trying to tamp it down, but it was boiling harder than ever. Tough not to get carried away with it. The man was taking Ord's lifework and throwing it in the mud, calling it all lies and manipulation. Belittling the Church. Belittling the great works they'd done with alchemy. Even as he toted the damned Leveler he loved so much—and which never would have been possible without the alchemy that he claimed to despise.

But Ord had made him a promise. So he did his level best to keep that offense to himself. To sit there in it until the boiling anger subsided, like a pot needs a minute to cool after you take it from the fire.

"You're a very cynical man, Lochled Thatcher," Ord said, as even-keeled as he could manage. "And I suppose you've a right to be. But I wonder—you've killed so many Tickers, why are you so adamant about trying to prove that they're like men?"

Lochled gave him a hooded look. "I've killed plenty of men too."

Ord found himself earnestly curious. "Wouldn't it be easier to believe they're animals?"

"I suppose it would be," Lochled admitted. Sniffed and spat. "Probably about as easy to believe as Feor wanting my little girl burned to ashes, to . . . 'release his light.'" He said it about as bitter as a man could, then turned a stony gaze on Ord. "Just because something makes you feel better, doesn't mean it's the truth."

Ord had to turn away from him. Couldn't look him in the eyes any more. "You seem to know a lot about Church doctrine, Sergeant. Particularly for a fighting man. Most fighting men don't bother with such things."

"Most fighting men can't read."

Ord snapped back to Lochled, shocked. "You read?"

Lochled nodded. "Had to learn my letters in order to paint signs." He let out a humorless chuckle. "Signs. What a flagon of brownspill. Wasn't too long ago that a sign wasn't worth much to the regular folk, as the only people could read it were rich folk. Now most all the young folk are learning to read. And everyone has clean water, and everyone has free bread from the Church, and everyone's forgetting what it was like when *we* were children and you had to work to eat, had to find a bit of land to toil on, to bring up. That's all gone now. Or going. Dying out." A long slow sigh through his nose. "Alchemy's easier. Easier to punch a heat charge than build a fire. Easier to push water about the city in pipes, than to walk to the well for it. Easy, easy, easy. What's it end up like, then? All of us just sitting around, doing nothing? An alchemic charge for everything we might need?" He shook his head. "I don't understand what happened to the world. Seemed like it made sense when I was a boy. Now it's gotten all cocked up."

He took a sip from his flask, then looked at it, smacking his lips. "Fucking drips." Looked at Ord, shaking the flask at him. "Your father or mother have a flask of drips?"

Ord shook his head.

"'Course they didn't. It was special. Cost too much. I remember I seen my father have it once—just once. Special occasion.

Made a big deal out of it." He scoffed at his flask again, but took another sip. "Now a man's not fully dressed until he has a flask on his belt. Drips is cheaper than scaef now."

"It's progress," Ord commented, a little lamely.

Lochled gestured about at the smashed buildings around them. "Ah, progress. The Old Ones had progress too, it seems, uh? Didn't save them now, did it? All their fancy progress . . . maybe it made 'em weak. Maybe that's why we're here stealing all their shit. Just wonder who's going to do it to us once we've gone weak too."

"Uh." Ord thought about that for a minute. "Probably the Auldish."

Lochled peered at Ord. Then cracked a smile, which turned into a grin. Ord found himself grinning back. Lochled gave him a nod. "Probably the Auldish."

They rode in silence for a bit. At first, the little flash of companionable humor carried them a ways, but gradually it wore out and left Ord feeling like he needed to come up with something to say or find a way to disengage.

Lochled solved that for him: "What would it take, Theynen, for you to be convinced that the Tickers are the real Leftlanders?"

"You mean that they're thinking beings? Like men?"

Lochled nodded.

Ord frowned ahead of them. They were passing an empty shell of a building. No, actually—not empty at all. A few limbs were sticking out of the rubble. Funny, but if he didn't know this was Halun's Landing, he might've believed those limbs belonged to people.

But what kind of a creature runs around naked? What kind of a civilization is that? And they didn't even speak! How could you be a thinking being if you couldn't even communicate with each other? It was impossible. Words enabled men to think.

Without them, men would be animals. And without them, that's exactly what Tickers were too.

"I'll be convinced," Ord said, resolutely. "When one of them looks me in the eye and speaks its mind."

"Ah, I see," Lochled said, smirking to himself. "So even a priest's faith has limits."

Ord looked away from the sergeant. Found himself disconcerted all over again. That seemed to be how he ended every conversation with Lochled. This one wasn't going to be any different.

"Thank you for your thoughts," Ord said suddenly. "I'll keep it in mind about the gold."

And with that, frowning at the back of his horse's head, Ord fell back into the column.

Ord and Lochled were on about something, but Rony couldn't hear what. Didn't really care either. She was still lost in her own thoughts, still angry with Cryer, with Licker, with the whole damned lot of them.

Her anger scared her. Because what if she mouthed off again? What if she broke the fragile bond that they'd built? Then where would she be?

Alone. Friendless. Abandoned.

They were nearly halfway through the city when Rony saw them. Wasn't sure why they caught her eye—she'd seen enough death and gore, that was for sure. Seen enough yesterday, and had a long encore by traveling through it today.

But they did catch her eye. Gave her heart a little jump, though she knew they were dead. Found herself pulling the reins back, steering the horse to the right, where the two bodies lay.

She got out of the column and murmured softly to the horse, got it stopped right there, right over top of them.

Two Tickers. A male and a female. They lay there on the side of the cobbled street, with their heads together, sightless eyes filled with crawling flies. Flies going in and out of their noses. In and out of their mouths. Their arms wrapped around each other. Legs splayed out behind their bodies, each pointing a different direction. And in that direction that their legs pointed, two long ribbons of rusty brown. Come from all the way down the street in both directions. Like they'd crawled for a thousandstride just to touch each other.

Had they known each other? Were they mates? Did they mate for life, like some birds do? Or were they more like the other animals and just mated when it suited them?

Or had they not even known each other until the moment they met, both on death's doorstep, and just decided to stop and to put their arms around the other? Maybe to feel some warmth before they died? Maybe to offer some comfort? Or to take some?

"Odd that they seek comfort," a ponderous voice came from beside her.

She looked up and found Ponts slumped in his saddle, eyes staring down at those two figures. Face weary and sad.

She looked back at them. "It is."

"Doesn't seem like something an animal does."

Rony swallowed, realized her throat was thick. Gritted her teeth and wheeled her horse around, tearing her eyes away from them as she did. "Some animals do," was all she could get out.

CHAPTER 19

It was the first hour of graylight when Lochled looked up at the towering peaks that guarded the Mountain Gate of Halun's Landing. The name, as with everything in Leftland, was given it by the men of the First Crusade. No one knew what the city was called, nor the single gate out of it, a narrow gash cleft into the mountains. Leftlanders couldn't talk, so men made up names of their own.

The Mountain Gate.

Lochled pulled his horse to a stop as Hotsteel raised his fist and called for a halt. But Lochled's eyes were still swimming with what was before him. To either side of the road, massive columns of that same white stone had been hewn from the gap in the mountain. The road itself, still immaculately maintained cobble, led on through the pass, and out into a distant land beyond. Perhaps wide enough for two wagons to pass each other, but not by much.

"This place would be impregnable from a land attack," Hotsteel said as he trotted up to Lochled, neck craning to take it all in. "And they don't even have a real gate."

"The Old Ones were peaceful," Lochled commented, dropping his gaze and noting that Hotsteel was right. Not only were there no actual gates on the thing they called the Mountain Gate, but there was no evidence that there had ever even any. No great hinges. No vestiges of wooden planks that might've been used to shut the world out. The columns that were carved there seemed to have no purpose other than to be beautiful. And they were.

"So much the better for us," Hotsteel commented as he waved their small column back into movement, as though just a few moments of glancing about was more than enough time wasted.

Lochled felt a strange thrill as he moved through the massive archway. A strange terror. All he knew of the Mountain Gate and what lay in Leftland beyond were snippets of tales from old men who'd fought in the First or Second Crusade. Lochled had fought in the Third, and they'd never made it through Halun's Landing. The whole thing had been bungled right there in the water, and they'd had to sail around with the vestiges of their shattered armada, trying to find another place to make a landing. They'd taken a handful of small, coastal villages by landing party but never made it any further inland.

And now he was here. Here at the Mountain Gate, with Halun's Landing smoking and ruined at his back and all of Leftland laying before him, just a little ways further through that gouge in the mountains—no more than a thousandstride to get to the other side. Maybe even less.

He felt victorious but, all at once, small and insignificant. The mountains seemed to glower down at him, their gray-streaked faces like an old man's frown. He felt like a grave robber who'd successfully made his way into a tomb of legend—a burst of excitement, followed by a frightening sort of awe and a distinct feeling of being a trespasser.

He'd would've liked to have felt a bit more elation. Tried to summon it up, thinking heroic thoughts about achieving what he'd set out to achieve or avenging the defeat he'd suffered years ago and various other loads of brownspill. But none of it worked.

"Fah," he grunted to himself. Dropped his eyes to earthly matters.

The first inkling he had that something bad was about to happen was that warbling noise again. Didn't click for half a beat, and then it did, right before the massive chunk of rock slammed into the face of the mountain and came tumbling down.

"Fuck! Look out!" Lochled yelled—pointlessly, as everyone was looking by this time and now scrambling out of the way as the chunk of white came slamming down. A man from Breakwood's squad was trying to pull his horse away, but the thing was spooked, rearing, didn't want to go where the man was going, so he let go of the reins and leapt away. The horse got free and bolted, but not before the stone clipped its hindquarters, sending the big beast spinning like it weighed nothing.

After that it was a mad scramble, and too much yelling to make sense of.

Lochled wheeled his horse around, his mind's eye tracking what little he'd seen of the stone's arc and knowing that it'd come from Halun's Landing. He heeled the horse into a gallop, then pulled up tight next to Hotsteel, who was looking around with wide eyes like it might be the sky itself raining rocks on them.

"Came from the city!" Lochled barked at him, trying to manage his horse and get his Leveler broken open and charged, for all the good it would do.

"Fucking bastards!" Hotsteel vented through clenched teeth. "Keep your heads up!" he bellowed at the troops, and then started galloping toward the city, Lochled fast behind him.

Lochled posted in the saddle, let the beast work hard beneath him, his own legs burning with the effort of staying stable with all that movement. Managed to hook a charge out of his loop and get it seated in his Leveler but didn't close it for fear a nudge on the trigger bar would end up with a lot of spent horseflesh.

Another warbling noise, barely audible over the clatter of hooves. Lochled's eyes darted up, caught the streak of white through the air, saw it impact higher up the mountain than the first and start bouncing its way down. The soldiers on the ground were already anticipating where it would land and doing their best to get out of the way.

No clue what would come next. No idea what he actually intended to do, nor what Hotsteel might order them to do. But riding hard toward whatever was trying to kill them was better than sitting there.

Hotsteel pulled up just on the side of the mountain pass where the road angled steeply downward for a ways and the city began. Lochled reined his horse in hard and angled to Hotsteel's left to keep the horses from jostling each other. The rumble of hooves behind them.

Lochled scanned the cityscape and saw it happen this time. "There!" he pointed.

A half-demolished building, maybe a thousandstride from them. One of the top pieces simply lifted off all of a sudden and went soaring into the air, gaining height rapidly, then seemed to hang in the air right over their heads, before it started coming down again with that hair-raising noise.

A mix of squads came jumbling up behind them—Breakwood and Cryer in the lead, followed by a handful of others.

"Thought you killed all the bastards in the sack," Hotsteel said, glaring at the men as though they could have prevented this by being more murderous the previous night.

"Big city," Breakwood noted. "Hard to check everywhere, hef!"

The last thrown rock hit the mountain again, right about where the second one had crashed, and started coming down.

"It's not too far," Cryer urged. "We can charge it—take the fucker out!"

He seemed about ready to heel his horse into a charge, but Hotsteel held up a hand. "Steady on, there, Cryer. Look."

He pointed down toward the beach, where the army was splayed out all over the sand and the first row of buildings behind the seawall. To the right of the city, not too far from the first tower Lochled had climbed, he could see the specks of men swarming about two of the huge Battle Plows, whipping the oxen to wheel the brass cannons around.

Hotsteel let out a grim laugh. "Thaersh is no fool. He planned for this. Let him do the work. We'll just mind the falling rocks."

Lochled's eyes kept switching back and forth, and he felt less like a soldier under attack than a man watching a stage play—first eyeing the building to see if another rock was coming, then glancing over to the Battle Plows, where the crews were loading the massive cannon charges. Wondering which was going to strike first—the Ticker with its stones, or the oxen with their cannons.

Lochled saw the plume of yellow a few seconds before he heard the heavy *fwoom* of the charge going off. First one cannon, then the other—two on each of the three Battle Plows. A much higher-pitched noise, like something screaming.

And then *boom*. Right into the top of a building, not too far from where their attacker was. A gout of white dust, a spray of rock. Three more impacts, closer together. Then more and more. All pounding that same spot, over and over. By the time the last cannonstones hit, the Battle Plows were blooming yellow again.

Back and forth. Back and forth.

Plume. Fwoom. Screech. Boom.

"Fah," Breakwood huffed. "Got all angsted up for nothing."

After that comment, they didn't say anything at all. Maybe ten of them, just sitting there, watching it all play out. The Battle Plows didn't let up—easier to simply pound the suspected area to rubble than to send men in to seek out the hostiles. It went on for a bit longer. Maybe five minutes, and then all of a sudden it was done.

The silence around Lochled seemed to ring in his ears. Then he realized it was the shrieking of a horse. He winced when he recognized it. One of the most terrible noises he'd ever heard. Worse than a wounded man. Probably because you know the man was a guilty shit, but the animal was innocent—simply doing what its masters told it. Just like Trut had said. Making beautiful creatures do ugly things. And then, every once in a while, an ugly thing is done to the beautiful creature, and it seems such a terrible mistake.

Lochled looked back over his shoulder, but he knew what he'd find. The horse that'd been tossed by the first stone was lying on its side, head reeling around, letting out that awful noise, but its hind half wasn't working. Maybe it got its back broken.

"Somebody shut it up," Breakwood hissed, though he had no malice in his voice. More like a pleading.

One of Breakwood's men slouched up to the horse like a man that had drawn the short straw for a shit duty. He had a Leveler in his hand, and he put it against the horse's head and scattered its brains across the stone. The shrieking ended. The man shook his head. Turned and slouched away.

"Well then," Hotsteel grunted. "Quarter the horse and let's get out of this fucking pass."

Rony ate horseflesh for the first time that night. She wasn't overly pleased about it, but was even less pleased when she realized she liked it. Seemed she was finding out all kinds of horrible things about herself.

But as Trut had observed when he sneered at the charred slab of it—smoking, fresh from the fire—and took a big, determined bite: "Meat's meat."

They ate, packed in around their fire, a few hundred strides from the mountain pass that they'd come through. Licker and Ponts had drawn guard duty, so it was just Rony, Trut, Cryer, and Lochled, with all that darkness surrounding them, closing them in so tight that Rony couldn't even see the sides of the mountain they were against. Three other fires glimmered at intervals—Breakwood's squad, Hamfist's squad—their leaders in the center of it all, up against the wagon—then the Seeker, the priest, the captain, and the three boys they'd taken with them for menial chores.

There were periods of time where the night suddenly rumbled with violence, cannons belching in the distance, smashing down some section of the city or other where they'd encountered some Tickers holding out. The sound of it reverberated to them through the mountain pass, gaining a haunting echo as it did.

"How long will they be at it?" Rony asked during one of these periods, wiping the grease from her fingers and taking a drink to wash the meal down—water this time, instead of drips. She was damn tired of drips at this point. Was fairly certain she'd never drink it again. At least not until she needed to. Probably tomorrow.

Lochled was ruffling about with his bed things, making old-mannish sounds, like every movement was a battle of willpower over pain. "I suspect until there aren't enough bodies to make it worth it anymore. Then they'll move on."

Rony's own bedroll was already laid out behind her, but she didn't feel much like sleeping. Body exhausted, but mind alive with worries and suspicions. The strangeness of the place kept looming over her, making her feel so far away from anything familiar. She kept having to look at the fire to keep her head from spinning and her heart from pounding. Because the fire was familiar. The smell of woodsmoke. The smell of cooked meat.

Trut had already rolled over onto his side and looked like he might be asleep. Cryer was steadily sinking lower and lower into his bedroll, though his head was still cranked up by his satchel, eyes glistening in the fire. Sometimes looking at the flames. Sometimes looking sidelong at Rony.

Lochled made a final, exhausted push of effort and flopped his oilskin over his body for a blanket. Grumbled something unintelligible, then cleared his throat and spoke. "Might want to get some sleep, cully. Long days and long journeys and all that shit."

She nodded at the fire. "I will." But she wasn't sure when.

Wasn't long before Lochled was snoring softly. She'd become used to the sound of it already. First night in the boat, she hadn't slept a wink with all the snoring and farting and grunting and groaning, like being packed in with a bunch of swine. Compared to that, just hearing Lochled snoring was almost peaceful.

She leaned back. Her body wanted to lie. She resisted it for a moment, feeling too fidgety, but eventually gave in. Rolled onto her side, facing Cryer. He was still staring at the fire but seemed to notice her looking at him.

"Something on your mind, cully?" he asked softly, after a long spell of her staring at him to the point of awkwardness.

As a matter of fact, she did have things on her mind. Just couldn't figure out how to say them. She could feel them, clear and plain. It was just getting them into words that seemed to be the problem. She kept starting to say something but realizing it was all wrong and closing her mouth again.

"Look," Cryer sighed. "If this is about last night—"

"It's not about last night," she said quickly, and knew she'd told the truth.

"Oh." A frown. Confused, as though he were struggling to imagine how it was not about his pintel. "All right. What's it about, then?"

"My father," she started haltingly, not really sure of herself but feeling compelled to speak and hoping she could simply find her way to the truth of what she was feeling. "He was as a Brymic swineherd. My mother was a Drugothan tailor."

Silence.

But what else would there be? She hadn't said anything, really.

Cryer shifted his back around. Laced his fingers across his chest. "I'm guessing there's more than that."

"Ceapsland is where my father had his land. Long way from where my mother came from—Genihtan."

"Oh?" Cryer perked up with a small smile. "I'm Genician as well."

She already knew that. Simply nodded. "Genician tailor isn't much use on a swine farm, and my father wasn't shy about letting her know that." She frowned at her own memories. "She could've done more. But she didn't. Just let my father and my brothers do it. If it weren't fabric, it was beneath her. Didn't make it fine, all the things my father said to her. But in a way he was right. And I knew it. Even as a girl, I knew it."

Cryer took a deep breath. Nodded. "So who do you take after? Your father or your mother?"

She would've liked to say she took after her father. She'd certainly put in the work. Certainly had the calluses. Certainly had spent enough time knee deep in mud wallows and pig shit. But somehow none of that seemed to count.

"I dunno," she admitted. "I tried hard. But trying's not doing."

"You're doing a lot now, though, uh? I don't see your brothers out here fighting for the coin to save your farm."

Kind of him to say so, but completely off the point.

What was the point again?

"My father once told me . . . he said, 'Rony, there's two kinds of people in this world: those that add to your burdens and those that lighten them.'"

"Hmm." Cryer's eyebrows cinched closer. "Can't say I disagree."

"He was talking about my mother. And me."

"He was just trying to give you a lesson. That's what fathers are supposed to do."

She was silent for a time after that. Scrunched in tighter to herself. It wasn't cold, but she felt the need all the same, as though a frosty wind were blowing. She could tell that Cryer noticed. Didn't want him to, but couldn't seem to relax enough to act like it was all fine.

She had her hands all balled up in front of her face, so that when she spoke next, it was muffled. "Never felt I was a part of it. The family. You know? The family was my father and brothers. Working hard. And me and my mother were just the cullies. Supported, but not supporting. Adding weight, instead of taking it away." She tried to laugh, but it came out sounding almost like a sob, though she wasn't crying. "And here I am, all the way over in Leftland. Still trying to fucking prove that I belong to a family that doesn't even exist anymore."

Cryer turned his head and looked at her full on for a moment. She avoided his gaze because she could see the pity in it, and that's not what she wanted. She reviled it. Wanted to roll over and turn her back on him because of it. But she didn't.

He took a deep breath and sighed it out. "Right, then." He lifted one arm up toward her, exposing his big side. "Come on."

She frowned, head pulling back. "What? You want me to cuddle with you?"

He shrugged. "Do I not look comfortable?"

"I don't need your comfort."

"Well." He raised an eyebrow. "Maybe I need yours."

Pride made her want to scoff and turn away. But damn it. It did sound inviting. Sounded like something that would make all this hovering darkness go away. Make it feel a bit more like home.

"My father told me something once too," Cryer said, arm still hanging out there. "He said, 'A burden shared is a burden lifted.' Now you don't have to go on trying to be heroic, 'cause it's not about how much weight you can take but how much weight you can share. That's why we work in squads. That's what a family is, if you ask me. Not a competition to see who does the most. It's a sharing of the burden." He sniffed, watching her. "Now come on. My arm's getting tired."

Rony sat up. Torn. On one hand, she didn't believe it—all that nonsense about shared burdens. How could she? She'd believed the opposite for so long it had kind of stuck in her head. So she had to frame it in a way that made her feel like she was doing the work.

"Well," she said, sliding closer to him. "If you *need* the comfort . . . I suppose . . ."

Cryer chuffed, but reached up and took her by the shoulder very gently, not pulling her but kind of guiding her in. She was tense at first. Thought it might be awkward. But his body was warm. The smell of his sweat seemed familiar. The curve of his chest and the hollow of his shoulder.

"There." She couldn't help herself. "Be comforted."

He gave a small chuckle, barely audible but for the fact that her ear was pressed to his chest. The slow rise and fall of his breath. His palm on her shoulder. None of this very soldierly at all. But it was very human. To seek that touch from another. To be comforted by it. And she was, despite herself.

She looked up—couldn't see much but his chin. "So you boys cuddle like this when you need comfort, uh?"

His silence surprised her. She'd expected a laugh. Instead, she saw his chin move up and down in a nod. "Sometimes. Some of the worst times. Yes. But you see, we boys are too prideful most of the time. Can't admit that we get anything out of it, 'cause we're all so tough. Kind of like you, Rony. Always trying to prove that we're stronger than everyone else. But every once in a while, when it's been bad, and all your pride's gone . . . yes. I'm not ashamed to admit it. I've held a man before. And been held. Rocked like a baby."

He cleared his throat, sounding like he was suddenly uncomfortable at having revealed too much. "But, you know," he continued, voice a little more cavalier, a little less vulnerable, "a woman has something special. And no, I'm not talking about your cunny."

She snorted softly. "Special, uh?"

"Yes," he said, earnestly. "Something special. Maybe it's because we all loved our mothers at some point. We were all boys once, with skinned knees, needing a woman's touch to make ourselves feel better. Then we grow older and meaner, and the skinned knees turn into bloody fields, and the woman's touch becomes a thing to be conquered and bragged about." He snickered in a melancholy sort of way. "Ah, but maybe we're all just hurt little boys if you dig down deep enough."

Their whispers fell silent for a time. Just the low murmur of others who were still awake, still talking themselves into sleep. The fire crackling low now, hot at her feet, warm across her face. Cryer's body warm against hers.

A wind picked up, blowing through the mountain pass and teasing the flames of the fire, scattering embers. It brought with it a faint smell of the sea. And then something else—the sooty stink of the Burners. Just a whiff of it, there and then gone again. Softly keening in the crags of the mountain, shuttering out for a moment the quiet sounds of the others.

When the wind subsided, she heard something else, from close by: a wet sniff. Almost made her jerk until she realized what it was.

She leaned up from Cryer, frowning across his broad chest.

All she could see of Trut was the gray of his oilskin, lumpy with the shape of hips and shoulders. She stared at it for a time, wondering if the shadows of the guttering fire were tricking her eyes, but no—those shoulders were shaking. A low noise, not unlike the keening of the wind, but strangled off. The sound of grief choking a hard man's throat.

She started to rise but stopped herself. She had an idea of what she should do—what a *good person* should do. But she resisted it. Who was she to act good? She wasn't good anymore. Maybe she never had been. Felt like a great hypocrisy for some reason. To have her heart lurch for a man like Trut, like she could offer some solace when she was just as befouled as he.

But it wasn't a competition, according to Cryer. It was a sharing of burdens. Didn't matter whether she was better or worse or just the same. It mattered that when one staggered under the weight of something, another helped pick him up.

She glanced at Cryer. He had a soft, mournful look in his eyes. Gave her a slow nod, and a gentle pat on the shoulder.

So she rose up, feeling a bit foolish as she stepped over

Cryer's long legs and padded quietly to Trut's side. She didn't say anything to him. He might've heard her coming, because he gave a violent sniff and his body seemed to clench up, trying manfully not to let those shoulders shake.

But a woman has special powers, uh? Something in her touch, perhaps. Something that couldn't be explained, only felt. Seemed ridiculous for a moment, standing over the shape on the ground. But then her heart and stomach hurt for him. And maybe that's all a shared burden is. Maybe you take up some of that weight just by feeling it and letting the other know that you did.

She stepped over him so that she could see his face, all tucked in under his oilskin. Red, glistening eyes blinked up at her, then away, ashamed. Burrowed a little deeper, as though trying to hide.

She lowered herself to the ground, sitting right there at his head. Kept expecting him to say something sharp, tell her to be gone. But he didn't. So she scooched in closer, until her hips were close enough to him that she could feel the man's heat through her breeches. Reached out and laid a hand on his head, cautious, like he might bite. But he was still. Very still. And quiet now. Breath evening out. So she rested her hand on the side of his head. Let her fingers run across the stubble, soft, caressing.

She looked to the fire, because she didn't think Trut would like her looking at his sodden face. Took a slow, deep breath, and started to sing, very soft, barely more than a whisper:

There is a place on a Ceapsland hill,
Where the sun shine's warm and the grain
grows tall,
And the streams flow cool
In this place on a Ceapsland hill.

And in this place on a Ceapsland hill,
The boys call you brunny and the pretty girls
Smile sweet, and they'll dance with you
In this place on a Ceapsland hill.

And in this place on a Ceapsland hill,
You can rest your weary soul and never take up
your steel,
For there's never been a war
In this place on a Ceapsland hill.

Trut never said a word. But his body relaxed; she could feel that. Felt strange but right. So she stayed there while the fire burned lower and lower, no more than coals now, red and swimming with heat. Stayed there beside him while her own eyes got heavy and her steadily moving fingers grew slower and slower, finally forgetting to move and just resting there on the side of his head. His shoulders no longer shook, and his breath became level and even, the breath of sleep. And she wasn't far behind.

CHAPTER 20

"There," Lochled said, squinting against the strong morning sunlight and pointing into the great expanse of Leftland that lay before them.

It was he, Hotsteel, Ord, Kayna, and the two other sergeants, Breakwood and Hamfist, positioned now at the edge of the mountain pass where it all opened up and the road out of Halun's Landing led down a much gentler slope on this side of the mountain.

"I see it," Hotsteel said, peering into the distance.

The landscape of Leftland was like something out of a dream, or a painting by some artist's wild imagination, and yet it wasn't imaginary, it was all right there. Huge, sprawling grasslands, like those around Ceapsland. Gently rolling hills. But all in among those rippling waves of green, there were trees, giant stands of them.

It wasn't that Lochled had never seen trees before. He'd just never seen them like this. Daeside of the Curnsflow River, there weren't trees. Nyhtside of the Curnsflow, there was the Brannenswood, but that was a big, sprawling mess.

These stands of trees seemed far too ordered. They stood in circular clumps, at even intervals across the landscape, almost like they'd been placed there on purpose and their edges carefully maintained. He'd never seen anything like it.

But that wasn't what he was pointing at.

"Ah," Hamfist rumbled, perceiving it now: a shadowed gouge through all that perfect grass. A meandering trail that began where the Halun's Landing road ended. Not a road itself, but a path that had been trampled by hundreds or thousands of fleeing feet, cutting their way through the grasslands like a stream, heading aleft into the distance. "So that's where all those fuckers went."

"Escaped, uh?" Breakwood menaced. "Well, not for long."

"Our purpose isn't to hunt 'em down," Hotsteel reminded them. "So banish your bloodthirst for now. No point in running after 'em anyways—we don't have Burners and no way to get the bodies back here."

"The captain's right," Ord put in. "However, that *is* the direction we need to go. So . . ."

"Right," Lochled leaned in his saddle, drawing his pointing finger along that path through the grass, all the way out to a small point between two gentle hills. "You see that though?"

"Hrm." Ord frowned. Fumbled around in his saddlebags until he came up with his spyglass. Held it up to his eyes. Some irony there, Lochled thought, seeing as how the spyglass was yet another technology that'd been stolen from Leftland. "Ah. I see."

Lochled hadn't seen it the previous night, but with the sunlight shining, the white stones stood out starkly in the landscape: a small cluster of buildings in the distance. Made of the same stone as Halun's Landing, but squatter, and only perhaps twenty of them.

Hotsteel produced his own spyglass and confirmed the

sighting before snapping it closed again. "So, it's a small place. Reckon we could head that way."

Ord looked at him with a bit of doubt on his face. "If thousands of fleeing Leftlanders headed in that direction, it might not be a wise option. Besides, we're supposed to *avoid* cities, not seek them out."

Breakwood made a low, ornery noise. "It's not a city. It's a fucking hamlet. And even the Tickers aren't stupid enough to camp out only a few hours' stride from where we just whipped 'em."

"I tend to agree with Breakwood," Hotsteel said. "It's the direction we're heading, and if we encounter any resistance, it won't be much. Besides, Theynen," he looked at Ord. "Won't have much luck finding this medicine of yours if we avoid every smattering of buildings we see."

"I agree as well," Hamfist said, his big, wide face all scrunched up in consternation, as though he were viewing a violent battlefield and not an idyllic countryside.

Lochled had no desire to agree with Breakwood, but he didn't *disagree*, so he kept his silence.

Ord made a few more desultory noises of uncertainty but eventually shrugged. "Well, then. It's the way we need to go anyways. We can follow the path they've beaten out. But if we take on stiff resistance," he looked sternly at Hotsteel. "We will go around."

"Stiff," Hotsteel echoed, with a small smirk.

Stiff was relative.

"Right then," Hotsteel gathered his reins. "Sergeants, to your squads. Let's push on and see how far this place goes. With any luck, we'll find the edge of Leftland in time to rejoin the army and make some more profitable ventures."

"The more I see, the less I believe," Lochled said, swaying gently to the movement of his horse as the column moved slowly along the trampled path through the grass. His squad was in the middle of the column, Hamfist's behind, and Breakwood's up front with the wagon.

Rony and Cryer were beside him, Ponts just behind, and Licker and Trut trailing.

They were passing close to one of those forests, and the closer they got, the more certain Lochled became that these were no random sprouting of trees over time. His neck was getting a crick from staring to the left, into the shaded woods.

"How's that then?" Cryer asked.

Lochled nodded toward the forest. "Where's the brush? Where's the undergrowth?"

Cryer squinted at it and shrugged. "There's parts of the Brannenswood look like that."

"Only because people work through it, scraping up every piece of deadfall."

"Well," Rony sounded uncertain. "Could be the Tickers do that as well. If they know how to throw stones out of those contraptions, is it such a stretch to think they know how to build a fire?"

Lochled grunted, squinted around at the sun, bright and warm. Not as hot as Drugoth, but certainly warmer than Brymsland. "This seem like a place needs fires to warm it?"

Cryer shrugged. "Even Drugothans use fire for cooking, even if they don't need it for warmth."

"Hmph."

Cryer sighed. "You and Rony. Two fish of a shoal."

Lochled frowned at him, then at Rony. "How's that, then?"

Cryer shook his head, looking irritated. "Why are you trying to make them into men, hef? You and Rony both. I just spoke to her about letting it be. And here you are, putting doubts in her mind about it."

Lochled saw the look that Rony gave Cryer—sharp as a needle.

"I'll have my own doubts, as I have my own mind," she snipped at him.

"Difference is," Cryer said, leaning forward in his saddle to give her a stern look. "Lochled don't let himself get all torn up about killing the fucks, do you, hef?"

Lochled had the distinct sense that he'd stumbled into the midst of an ongoing battle that he had no place being in. Didn't care for it. So he stared straight ahead now. "It's a job. It's orders. I follow orders. Keeps things simple."

"Oh, yes, simple," Rony huffed. "Like all your simple nattering with the priest?"

"I have my reasons," Lochled tossed back. "Do you?"

She didn't respond, so he hazarded a glance. Saw a bleakness in her face that made him feel like he'd smacked a child. Didn't care for it. So he stared straight ahead again.

"I'll have my own doubts," he gruffed. "As I have my own mind."

"Now look at that!" Licker's eager voice came bobbing up along with the clop of his horse at a canter. Lochled turned in his saddle, saw where Licker was pointing, his face all alight with glee. A tree near the edge, hanging thick with heavy green fruits. "We can pick a fucking bushel in no time! Let me pick a few . . ."

He started to wheel his horse toward the woods, but Lochled snapped out a harsh sound to stop him. "Don't go picking it, you fucking half-wit! You don't even know what it is!"

Licker looked heartbroken. "Looks like fruit to me."

"Yes, and there's plenty of fruits in the world that make

you shit your breeches and die. Is that what you want? Go on crusade and wind up dead from a fucking fruit? I can hear the noble songs now." Lochled waved him fiercely back into line. "Back in your place, you goff."

Licker looked hurt and rubbed his stomach. "Hef, my delicate wetfoot constitution's all besmuttered by that horsemeat. Need some green things to get the flow going, you know? You want my guts to be all tangled up?"

"All right, fine." Lochled waved at the trees. "Go on and eat one, then. But don't cry to me about it if you wind up bleeding from your hindshole."

Licker frowned at the trees, hand still on his stomach. "Fah." He leaned low in the saddle and swiped up a stem of grass. Stuck it in his mouth. "See what you've reduced me to, hef? Eating grass like a horse."

Cryer cast him a look over his shoulder. "How's you know the grass idn't poison too?"

Licker's eyes crossed looking at the stem of grass in his mouth. Then he got a petulant look about him and made a great show of chewing it and eating it.

"That how you got your name?" Rony asked. "Tasting random objects by the wayside?"

Licker flashed her a lascivious grin. "Oh, no, cully. I've a taste for other things."

Rony rolled her eyes and looked away.

Cryer snorted. "Pintels is what he means."

Licker tittered. "Come now, big boy. You've never complained before."

Cryer shrugged. "What can I say? Nights is lonely."

Licker winked and sucked a kiss at him. Cryer returned it.

Licker leaned over and grabbed another stem of grass. "Hef, how come you never joke around?"

Lochled frowned. "What?"

Cryer waved it off. "Now, don't whittle the sergeant over his lack of a sense of humor. He's sensitive about the fact he wasn't born with one."

"I have a sense of humor," Lochled asserted.

"Yes, of course you do, hef," Cryer replied placatingly.

Lochled glanced around for support, but none was coming. "I have a sense of humor," he claimed again. "It's a very *fine* sense of humor. So fine, in fact, that you brash fucking donkeys would never understand it."

"Oh. What?" Cryer looked about as though confused. "Was that it there? Was that humor? I couldn't tell."

Lochled nodded. "My point exactly."

"Tell us a joke, then, hef," Licker called.

"Oh, you want a joke?" Lochled shot over his shoulder. "What happens when a Fen with a stiff pintel walks into a wall?"

Licker grinned. "What?"

"He breaks his nose."

Licker squinted skyward as though muddling it out, then shook his head. "I don't get it."

Lochled sighed. "Just think on it."

"Do I have a big nose?" Licker asked. "Is that what the joke is? I don't understand."

"I believe," Ponts said slowly. "That the sergeant is implying that Fens have small pintels."

"Thank you, Ponderous Ponts," Lochled growled. "Sharp as ever."

"Ponderous Ponts!" Licker guffawed. "Ah, see? The sergeant *does* have a sense of humor!"

"Ponderous?" Ponts asked. "Why Ponderous?"

"Look at that," Cryer smiled back at the big man. "You've earned a byname."

"But why Ponderous?"

"Don't worry, Ponderous," Cryer sighed. "You'll get there. Eventually."

"Fuck!" Trut suddenly yelped.

Lochled twisted to look behind him, the panicked tone of Trut's cry making the skin tingle up his spine and down through his fingers.

Trut was flapping his hands about his face, eyes wide and brows furrowed. "Did you see that fucker?"

"What?" Lochled demanded, his voice hoarse from the sudden surprise.

Trut twisted this way and that. "Biggest fucking fly I've ever seen just buzzed right past my fucking face!"

Lochled's clamped breath exploded out of him in a cough. "You fucking dandy! Don't fucking scare me like that over a damned bug!"

"You didn't see the size of it!" Trut exclaimed fearfully, while the others devolved into laughter.

Lochled was still staring angrily at him when Trut's throat sprouted a hole and started squirting red.

For a flash, Lochled's eyes could see nothing but that, the suddenly growing bib of blood slaking the man's chest. His eyes were wild, hands scrabbling up to his neck and poking at the hole while his mouth opened and more blood dribbled out.

"Trut?" Ponts's voice had a whining, childish quality to it. "Are you good?"

"Gah!" Trut choked, reeling in the saddle.

Lochled's shock suddenly dissipated, and he wheeled his horse violently around, screaming with the last of his breath: "Trees! Get into the fucking trees!"

Lochled swung his horse up alongside Trut and heaved him

across the front of his saddle, the man's legs kicking out aimlessly, blood pouring everywhere. He pointed his horse for the trees and spurred it into a gallop.

Cryer's voice bellowed out: "They're shooting at us! Get into the trees! Into the trees!"

Lochled barely heard it over the thundering of his horse's hooves, could barely think past the need to get to a place of safety, the need to get his hands on Trut's throat and try to stop the bleeding.

"It's all right, Trut!" Lochled gasped, though he knew it wasn't. "Stay with me!"

"Guh," was Trut's only response. "Guhng . . ."

The forest loomed up in front of him. Not seeming so alien now—it was the only conceivable point of safety, in among those trees with their thick trunks for cover.

Out of the bright sunlight, into the dappled dimness.

"Whoa!" He yanked the reins, nearly made the horse rear, which would have been catastrophic for both he and Trut. The horse stamped to a stop in the midst of the trees, and Lochled wasted no time lashing his feet from the stirrups and swinging himself over, Trut's body coming with him.

He tried to hold the man but wasn't braced for the weight of his body and found himself toppling backward, Trut landing on top of him, his eyes staring down at Lochled so wide that he could see the red-veined whites all around while Trut coughed and spluttered blood into his face, and the hole in his neck spewed it all over Lochled's chest.

Lochled heaved, groaned, rolled the man over onto his back, then straddled him and pushed him onto his side, only thinking how the blood might drown him. He had to let the blood out of Trut's throat so he could breathe . . .

The trample of other horses. Whinnying. Screaming.

Shouting. Lochled could barely tell which noises were beast and which were men.

"Try to get it out," Lochled said, nonsensically. "Try to breathe!"

He was shaking Trut's shoulders, as though that would do a damn bit of good. Trut's head lolled about, his eyes getting hazy, crossing, red-tinged lips loose and flopping. Oh yes—he needed to plug the hole. Plug the hole. Plug it . . .

Lochled jammed two fingers in the ragged wound. Felt all the muscles in Trut's neck contract around them. Trut's eyes got sharp again with sudden agony. Hands grabbing at Lochled's arms like claws, fingers biting and squeezing painfully at his flesh. He could feel Trut's rapid heartbeat in his fingers.

"What are you doing!" someone yelled, crashing down into the dirt and leaves beside Lochled, sending a dusting of brown speckles across Trut's face.

Lochled wrenched his gaze around and found himself staring at Rony, her hands seizing him by the wrists, as though she thought he were choking Trut instead of trying to save him.

He shook her violently off, shoved a shoulder into her, and toppled her sideways. "I'm fucking stopping the bleeding!"

"You're killing him!" she screamed as she thrashed upright again.

"Find cover!" Lochled roared in her face, his vision sparkling with the effort.

"Into the trees!" someone else yelled, as though they'd just come up with the idea.

Lochled whipped his head up, peered through the trees to the pathway they'd been on, now tossed into confusion. The wagon was trying to complete a circle, trying to turn for the woods. It was the big boy at the reins. One of the smaller boys was flopping around beside him, clutching a bloody hole in his chest.

"Agh . . . ffffugh . . ."

Lochled's gaze landed back on Trut. Tried to make eye contact with him but couldn't because the man's eyes were swimming about, looking in two directions at once. His body was stiffening under Lochled, heels scraping divots in the dirt, chest heaving, retching.

He wanted to say something. Wanted to tell Trut that he would be fine, but now realized he wouldn't.

"You'll see Wen," Lochled choked out. It was the best he could come up with. "You'll see Wen again. Riding horses. Can you see it?"

Trut's head flopped over to the side. Looked like nothing so much as a landed fish spluttering on a deck. His thrashing was getting slower, weaker.

"There he is," Lochled soothed, one hand with fingers in Trut's throat, the other trying to stroke his face, but too hard, only mushing him. He didn't mean to do it. Seemed his hands weren't doing what he wanted them to. "There he is. You can see him now."

Maybe Trut nodded. Or maybe he'd simply convulsed.

A pair of hands grabbed Lochled by the shoulder, hauling him up. His fingers sucked out of the open wound, and then he was on his feet, being pushed toward the thick trunk of a tree. He flailed against whoever had him, registered Cryer's massive frame huddled against him, and then was slammed into the trunk with Cryer right over him.

"Take cover, hef!" Cryer seethed in his ear. "There's nothing you can do for Trut now!"

"Get off me!" Lochled pushed against him, but he might as well have pushed against a stone wall. "Cryer, you fuck! Get off!"

The weight came off him, and Lochled spun, heaving for the air that he'd deprived himself of with all his yelling. His hands went for his steels, but what good would those do? Eyes searched for his Leveler—still strapped to the saddle of his horse—but what good would that do either?

Eyes up. Taking in what was around him. The panic hardening off now, actual sergeant's thoughts making it through the chaos of his brain: *Where's my squad? Where's everyone else's squad? Where's the enemy? How do we kill them?*

Cryer, right there. Looking whole—no wounds. Rony, huddled near a tree, a dozen strides away, Trut's body between them.

"Ponts!" Lochled yelled. "Licker!"

"There, hef!" Cryer pointed, and Lochled saw them, a bit further into the woods, both their horses side by side behind a huge, gnarled tree.

Good. He had his squad. Or what was left of it.

The wagon clattered narrowly between two smaller trees, the boy with the wound finding some air in his lungs to start screaming out a high-pitched wail. Other people yelling for him to shut up, or yelling for someone to help him.

Hotsteel came tearing in right behind the wagon. "Sergeants! To me!"

Orders. Lochled's feet were moving, almost on their own. He ran for his horse, who didn't seem to like him running at her, but he got his hands on the reins and swung himself up into the saddle.

"Lochled!" Hotsteel was bellowing. "To me!"

Lochled snarled angrily—at Hotsteel, or at his horse, he wasn't sure. Breakwood and Hamfist already there with Hotsteel. Lochled skidding up to them just a few beats after.

"Shotstones!" Breakwood declared, as though he'd discovered the finding of the century.

"Where from?" Hamfist grunted. "I didn't see shit!"

"How far away?" Hotsteel demanded. "Did anyone see?"

"Captain," Kayna called out, her voice loud but not overstressed. Her horse cantered up, then pulled to a smooth stop; it seemed to share its rider's unruffled attitude.

"What, Seeker?" Hotsteel said, as though she were interrupting great military matters.

Kayna hunched low, so that she was looking out from under the limbs all around them. She pointed. "It came from the hamlet. You can see the top of one building, just there between those two hills."

"The fucking hamlet's a thousandstride away still! No way they can hit us from there!" Breakwood snapped at her.

"It's that fucking contraption!" Lochled said. "Same as on the beaches!"

"A thousandstride?" Hotsteel glared at him.

"They hit us past the breakers," Lochled nodded. "That was more than a thousandstride."

"Right, then," Hotsteel turned his attention to the direction that Kayna had pointed. Leaning low to see what she was talking about, and then all the sergeants doing the same.

She was right—it was there, just barely visible between two small hills: a little protrusion of white stone in the sea of green grass.

"We'll split up," Hotsteel said, his voice becoming low and hard. "Charge the hamlet from three different directions at once, meet in the middle and wipe out whoever's throwing stones."

"Captain Hotsteel!" Ord's voice shook as he bounced around on the back of his horse.

Hotsteel's face got brittle. "Theynen?"

"You're not planning to attack it, are you?" Ord said breathlessly. "We should go around!"

The boy in the wagon started screaming again. Lochled hadn't even registered that he'd stopped until he heard it again. The other boys were all huddled over him, trying to shush him, as though whoever were shooting at them didn't already know where they were.

"Yes, I'm planning to fucking attack it!" Hotsteel answered.

"But you said—"

"Stiff resistance is what we agreed upon," Hotsteel barked over him. "Three men down, taken by surprise. I don't call that stiff, I call that a lucky ambush, and now they're going to fucking pay for it."

Breakwood made a weird doglike sound of excitement, like a hound on the leash, ready to tear after a rabbit.

Ord didn't seem to have anything else to say, just gawked at Hotsteel like he couldn't make sense of how he'd suddenly been so stripped of all authority and, worse, didn't know how to get it back.

Kayna put a hand on Ord's shoulder. "Trust the captain."

Hotsteel turned back to his sergeants and spoke rapidly: "Breakwood, go left. Hamfist, right up the center. Lochled, out to the right. Ride hard, storm the hamlet on horse, then dismount and clear it on foot. Use your shieldmen. Use your Levelers. Make sure it's a Ticker before you pull the trigger on one of our own. Steady on?"

"Steady on," came the three responses.

CHAPTER 21

Green grass, lashing past, coating Lochled's boots in seeds and prickers. The huffing of his horse. The pounding of hooves. Flights of bugs exploding out to either side of his horse as it charged through the meadows, sunlight flashing off their wings.

Cryer just ahead of him, his horse churning up dust and grass, speckling Lochled's face, making him taste the dirt on his tongue.

A glance behind: Rony, then Licker, then Ponts—all in single file.

"Guide right!" Lochled yelled ahead to Cryer. "Around the hill to the right!"

Cryer gave no verbal response, but his horse angled for the right of the hill, Lochled and the rest following after. The heaving breath of his horse becoming more and more rapid. A thousandstride was a long ways to run the poor beast so hard.

The hill seemed to shift slowly as they moved rapidly around its slope, the horizon of it sinking lower, exposing the tops of a few buildings, and then more and more.

Lochled's eyes scanned the buildings as they came into

view—all close together, narrow streets and alleys between. Lots of dark windows facing him. Made him worry about stone-throwing contraptions hiding inside. But orders is orders, and his orders were to ride in hard, and that's what he was going to do.

Shapes on the far side of the city. Olive skin almost blending with the shine of the sun on the green grass. Tickers, and plenty of them, fleeing out of the hamlet and into the meadows.

The temptation of those running figures was apparently too much for Cryer to resist, because he started angling toward them.

"No, Cryer!" Lochled shouted over the hammering of the hooves. "Straight on!"

Cryer twisted in his saddle so that his eyes peered over the edge of his greatshield—wicked and wrathful, like they belonged to someone Lochled had never met. But war makes strangers of all men.

Cryer straightened out, heading now for one of the buildings on the outer perimeter. Looked like they were all about the same size, about the same construction. Neat little cubes of white. With thatched roofs . . .

A flicker of movement from a rooftop. Not from the building directly ahead, but from another behind it. Sunlight glimmering off a long piece of brass as it swung around to face them.

There was no flash of yellow dust. Just a dark little streak in the air and a sound like a horrifically large bee buzzing past his ear. He let out a yelp at the feeling and sound of the near miss, then twisted to look behind him, but Rony, Ponts, and Licker were still in their saddles, still riding hard.

Back forward. Close enough to the first set of buildings now that the Ticker on that rooftop couldn't see them anymore.

"Whoa!" Cryer shouted at his horse, yanking it around so

it nearly toppled into the side of the building. He was already swinging out of the saddle by the time Lochled got his horse stopped.

Two big windows in the side of the building, Cryer standing right between them, lugging his shield off his back.

Lochled hit the ground as the others piled in and dismounted, gasping for breath, thighs burning from the hard ride. The horses twisted and turned, not sure what to do with themselves.

"Get your shield on that window!" Lochled yelled as he ripped his Leveler free of the saddle and charged it, snapping it closed as he bolted for Cryer.

Cryer hefted the shield and planted it against the window so it covered the whole thing. Lochled crashed into the shield beside Cryer, took a moment to catch some wind and get his bearings. Rony sprinting up with her Leveler opened, juggling a charge in her hands, Ponts laboring to get his shield off his back, Licker with long-knife and hand axe at the ready, pale face flushed red with effort and bloodlust.

"Ready," Lochled said as the remains of his crew piled into the wall. Not stone like they'd thought, Lochled noted, absently. It looked like wattle and daub. A big section of it ahead of him, and then the second window. He pointed his Leveler at it in case any Ticker got brave enough to poke its head out. "Rony, you're on this window. I'll take the next. We'll blast whatever the fuck is in there and come around to the door. Ponts, get ready to get in front of me. Licker, you stay right behind me and get ready to split heads."

Licker spat to the side, nodded.

"Yes, hef," Ponts gasped out, finally wrestling his greatshield to the front of him and planting it in the dirt with a *thunk*.

Rony got her Leveler charged, closed it, and stood with the

maw pointing toward the window on the other side of Cryer's shield. She glanced at Lochled and nodded. "Ready."

"Now!" Lochled sprang for the second window.

Cryer shifted his shield to the side, and Rony stuck her maw in, unleashing a blast of yellow dust in the darkness, shotstones clattering around inside. Lochled reached the second window a heartbeat after and did the same, the Leveler jumping in his grip, and then broke it open before he'd even stopped moving, ducking under the window and heading around to the front of the structure.

"Ponts! Get ahead of me!"

Ponts huffed and stumbled his way in front of Lochled, who grabbed his shoulder as they reached the corner. "Hold!" He seated another charge. Readied his Leveler. "That fucker on the roof might have a line on you when you come around, so hold that shield strong, we're right behind you!"

"Yes, hef."

"Go!"

Ponts lugged himself around the corner, his big frame scrunched tight behind the greatshield, blocking any view that Lochled might have had, but also blocking shotstones—bit of a give and take. Lochled peeked around Ponts's shield and saw a doorway to the right. What looked like curtains hanging, instead of a door.

Fucking curtains. He hated curtains. Had the tendency to wrap you up like a squid when you tried to move through them. Ponts stopped just before the doorway, and Lochled snugged in tight to him, glanced over his shoulder, and confirmed that Licker was right there behind, ready to slash and hack.

Lochled nudged Ponts forward. "Push through those fucking curtains!"

"Door's too small!" Ponts moaned.

"Fuck! Fine! Licker, on me!" and Lochled plunged through them. The fabric whipped at his face, dragged at the maw of his weapon, and then he was through and into the dimness made dark by his sun-dazzled eyes.

He immediately pulled his trigger bar and sent a flume of yellow into the room. Dust and death and chips of something skittering about. He cringed, whipped around, dropped his Leveler, and snatched up his axe and knife, blinking rapidly, sucking air that tasted of ash.

A shape in the dark, and he almost planted his axe into it before he realized it was Licker charging past him, then running almost headlong into a wall. He let out a grunt, pushed himself off. "No fuckers in here, hef!"

"Out!" Lochled barked, already spinning for the door, seating his axe and knife and snatching his Leveler up. "Cryer! Rony! Come around!"

Somewhere out there another Leveler went off. Then another.

Out into bright daylight again, blinding his confused eyes. Tearing around the corner and right into Ponts's huddled hind end.

"Which building were they shooting from?" Ponts asked, peeking up over his shield. Lochled had to nearly jump to reach the man's head and smack it down.

"Stay in cover!" Swearnsoot, did Lochled have to do the man's thinking for him?

Cryer and Rony barged around the corner, rejoining them.

"Ease it forward," Lochled said, pushing on Ponts's back. "Nice and easy. No need to rush. Time's on our side." Seemed a nice calming thing to say to the big bastard, but he didn't know if it was true.

Ponts lugged it forward until they reached the other corner of the building. Lochled squeezed around him to get a view down the other side. An alley plunged straight through the heart of the hamlet, clustered on either side with more buildings, all identical. Dirt streets. Not cobbles like in Halun's Landing.

Fwoom! Fwoom! More Levelers sounded off. Maybe killing. Or maybe just poking holes in walls like Lochled had.

Movement. Straight down the alley. A Ticker darting out from around a corner, its back turned to them, sprinting away.

"Ah!" Lochled snapped his Leveler up and triggered it. The shotstones clattered across the road, kicking up dust, but no blood. "Bastard!" Lochled roared, and took off after him, not even thinking about it, just seeing the thing run from him and somehow knowing that it was the Ticker that had killed Trut.

Someone called out for Lochled from behind, but he wasn't listening. Wouldn't listen. He wasn't about to let it get away—not after what it'd done.

He flashed past more alleys, taking only bare seconds to glance down them, but they were empty. He fought his Leveler open again, stumbling as he did. Ahead, the Ticker ducked left, down another alley. Lochled staggered to a stop right at the corner, seated a fresh charge. Took a deep breath, then plunged around it.

Nothing. Another alley, with more square buildings, and more alleys between them. The Ticker could've gone down any of them.

"Shit, shit, shit." Lochled forced his feet forward, the spur of anger now tempering into something closer to caution. He cleared one alley, didn't see a thing. Cleared the next—nothing again. Started picking up the pace, started feeling frustration boiling up. The next alley. Nothing again.

He chose the next alley and turned down it for no reason other than he knew the fleeing Ticker was trying to get away and had to have gone down one of these damn things. He was running again. No real idea of where he was in the hamlet—it all looked the same, like getting yourself lost and turned around in the woods.

Stop. Stop and think.

Lochled pulled up to the side of a building, mashed his shoulder against it, chest heaving, palms slick with sweat, Leveler trembling in his grip. He scanned left and right and all around and found nothing but white walls everywhere.

A thunder of hoofbeats made him jump. Looked down an alley just in time to see three of Breakwood's men thunder past on the outskirts of the hamlet, heading in the direction the Tickers had been fleeing.

After that, it was just the sound of his breath, harsh in his ears, dry in his throat. He swallowed on nothing. His spit like paste in his mouth, gumming up his tongue. Where to go now? Where had the Ticker gone?

He held his breath, even as his lungs burned for more air. Listened.

A shatter of glass. Close.

He jerked off the side of the building, ears pricked, Leveler swinging side to side. He eased himself around the corner. Where had that noise come from?

A shuffling sound. Like someone rummaging through things.

Lochled fixated on a door only five strides from him. He was almost certain the noise had come from in there. But who would be rummaging?

Lochled stepped toward the door. "If you're a man, say so!"

The noises of rummaging ceased.

The door, now just two strides away.

He held the Leveler at his side, fingers quivering under the trigger bar, ready to yank it. Then he held his breath and charged into the darkness.

The first thing he noticed was the smell—like a heady mix of dried herbs—and then he saw them all dangling from the ceiling, tickling the top of his head as he moved under them: herbs indeed. The next thing he saw was the Ticker—a woman-Ticker—skin shiny with sweat, mouth open and breathing hard, eyes staring at him wide. The third thing he noticed was the woven satchel in its hand, looking heavy.

Lochled realized he was frozen, standing in the middle of this little wattle-and-daub hut, staring at a Ticker, and it staring at him, just as frozen.

Its eyes snapped to the side—toward a window.

Lochled wasn't sure what he was doing or why he hadn't killed the thing yet. His fingers kept twitching toward the trigger bar but not quite touching it.

What were all these dried plants hanging from the ceiling? And there, behind the woman-Ticker—were those shelves full of glass jars and phials?

He found his Leveler dipping.

And that's when the Ticker dove headfirst through the window.

CHAPTER 22

Lochled exploded back out the door, spewing curses. He felt shocked, but didn't know if it was because the Ticker had sprung so lightly through the window or because he hadn't pulled the trigger bar.

Round the corner of the building, just in time to see the woman-Ticker's heels disappear to the right. He ran after, a dog simply giving chase because something was fleeing from it.

This wasn't the one that had killed Trut, was it? No, he was almost positive the other one had been a male.

The woman-Ticker spared a panicked glance over its shoulder, satchel still waving around in its hands as it ran, the sound of glass shifting on glass suddenly very audible to Lochled.

Glass phial? Yellow powder?

Could it be so easy?

She ducked into an alley, this one covered with woven shades. Thickets of plants to either side of it that smelled sweet and heady when Lochled brushed against them.

When he burst through the skein of plants, he nearly ran headlong into the Ticker. It had stopped, right there in the middle of what looked like the dead end of an alley, or maybe a strange little courtyard between three buildings—those same sweet-smelling plants surrounding it.

"Don't you fucking move!" Lochled gasped as he skidded to a halt, his Leveler maybe only two strides distant from the woman-Ticker's heaving chest. His fingers still twitched all around the trigger bar—why hadn't he just killed the damn thing already?

His command was pointless: the Ticker was already standing there, stock still, its hands upraised in something like surrender, or maybe just the instinct to try to block the load of shotstones that should have been ripping it apart. The satchel still hung in its hand, swinging back and forth.

Lochled's heart pounded, and he wasn't entirely sure whether it was from all the running or the weirdness of standing there and facing one of these things when he really should have been murdering it. He wasn't entirely sure of anything at that moment, but his brain seemed to be catching up, and his eyes were stuck on that satchel, thinking maybe it might contain something that Ord Griman would pay ten golden whales for.

Funny. The gold didn't excite him at all.

Lochled held the Leveler on the Ticker with his right hand, and with his left, he pointed to the satchel. "Gimme that, you fuck!"

The Ticker took a step back, pulling the satchel closer to its body. And as it did, Lochled caught sight of something behind it. Something huddling in all those tufts of scented herbs.

His first thought was that the Ticker had led him into a trap. Damn near triggered his Leveler into the herbs to get at what was hiding inside, but then he realized that the figure in the herbs was small, and it wasn't standing there waiting to spring on him: two small legs stuck out, two dirt-darkened feet. Small. Like children's feet.

"What're you doing?" Lochled hissed. Was that a question for himself or the Ticker? Must've been for himself, since the Ticker had no way to understand him. Why was he even talking to it in the first place?

The woman-Ticker took another step back and started slowly turning its body away from Lochled, as though seeing how far it could get before making him angry. But it couldn't escape now—Lochled had it blocked, and the alley was a dead end.

Lochled moved to his left, trying to get a better view of the smaller Ticker in the herbs. The woman-Ticker kept moving too, both of them almost circling around each other, all caution and tension, as tight as a drumhead.

The woman-Ticker clutched the satchel to its bare breasts with one hand and with the other slowly reached out and pushed the greenery aside, showing Lochled what it concealed. Like it thought that Lochled might be convinced to spare them both, despite all evidence to the contrary.

Why would it have such faith in him? Lochled almost wanted to blow the both of them apart right then, just to prove that he wasn't worthy of it. But he found his fingers farther than ever from the trigger bar, staring at what hid in the greenery.

It was a child-Ticker, that was for certain. Looked like a boy. And it looked bad. The olive skin seemed washed out and waxy, like a candle. Greasy sweat coated its entire body. The eyes were barely open, but the mouth was, and it was breathing hard, breathing rapid.

Cloth wrapped its midsection and was soaked through with scabby brown, centered right there on its gut. Could've been a stab wound, he supposed. But any Ticker that'd gotten close enough to be touched by steel would probably already be dead. More likely, it'd caught a stray shotstone from a Leveler.

Stab wound or shotstone—didn't matter much. Lochled

knew about gut wounds. Knew they corrupted fast—all those bowels and juices getting mixed up inside where they weren't supposed to be. He'd seen men with wounds like that. They'd go sour and sick within a day.

They're from Halun's Landing, Lochled realized. It was the only logical explanation for the thing's sickly look and the scabbed bandages.

You should kill them both.

The woman-Ticker was very still for a moment, staring at Lochled, fear all over its face. Fear so obvious that it seemed more than ever to not be an animal but a person. Because it wasn't an animal's fear of death that he saw in the thing's eyes, like the shock you might see in a deer's eyes when it's bleeding out from an arrow in the chest. In fact, the woman-Ticker didn't look at all like it was scared for itself. There was no way he could've known it for sure—maybe he was only imagining it—but he was somehow overwhelmed with the conviction that it was scared for the child.

What's two Tickers? Lochled struggled with himself. *What's wrong with letting them get away?* Just as Hotsteel had pointed out, there was no way to harvest them anyhow, and even if there were, did this woman-Ticker possess the powers that would make her ash worth anything? If it'd had powers, wouldn't it have tried to kill him instead of run from him?

What would be the point in killing it? It wasn't trying to harm him. He'd gain nothing from it.

"What's in the satchel?" Lochled said, voice low, almost a whisper, as though they might be found out. And he realized he was feeling guilty—guilty for not killing it. Felt like he was betraying Hotsteel somehow. Like he was dangerously close to disobeying orders.

The woman-Ticker moved again, still very slow. It sank low

on its haunches, crouching over the wounded child-Ticker, and slowly drew its hand to the satchel.

Lochled stiffened, baring his teeth. "Slow, now," he hissed. "I will fucking kill you both."

It stayed focused on him. Those oddly round eyes. So much like an Auldlander, now that he had a chance to sit there and trade a stare down, except for the near-green skin, and the nakedness, and the lack of hair anywhere on its body.

That hand kept on moving toward the satchel. Fingers going in. Grasping something.

It held it up, almost as though to show to Lochled that it was nothing that could harm him.

A small glass phial. Filled with a yellow powder.

"Medicine," Lochled croaked.

He could take it. He wouldn't even have to kill the stupid fucks. He could just bop the woman-Ticker on the head if she gave him trouble over it. Maybe she'd just let him snatch it out of her hands. And that would be ten golden whales.

A smarter man would have done it. But Lochled didn't move.

Ten golden whales, and he was watching them slip away. And maybe if he'd been a man who'd come on crusade for riches, he'd have done the deed. But he hadn't come for riches—he'd come to escape the misery of Bransport. And he realized that the gold meant nothing to him. Realized that the child-Ticker meant more.

Slowly, ever so slowly, the woman-Ticker turned its eyes away from him. One hand with the phial in it. The other reaching for the bandage. The child-Ticker twisted about, made a face that should have gone together with a mewl of pain, but there was just silence.

Lochled realized he'd taken a step back. Realized his Leveler had dropped again.

"Go on, then," he whispered. "Save your boy."

Then the world erupted in yellow dust. Lochled watched it happen almost like he was trapped in a dream: the woman-Ticker's arms coming off in a spray; the child-Ticker's head and chest caving in, splattering bright red across the greenery and the white wall behind it.

Something sharp nipped at his cheek. Lochled lurched backward, horror seizing his guts up hard. He felt his back hit the wall behind him, even as the spray of blood came trickling down like a misty rain. Had he triggered his Leveler by mistake?

The child-Ticker was gone—nothing left above the chest.

The woman-Ticker flopped sideways, thrashing and kicking, one stump squirting all over the place.

"It's all right!" a voice came from Lochled's right. "I got 'em for you, hef!"

Eyes goggling, mouth hanging open and sucking in bitter air, tasting sweet herbs and acrid soot on his tongue, Lochled turned toward the man striding confidently down the alley, breaking his own Leveler open, shucking out the spent charge, slipping a fresh one in. Smiling the whole time, like it was all a great joke.

One of Breakwood's men.

"What—" Lochled choked, reaching up to touch his cheek where something had gotten him. A bit of the wall, perhaps? A fragment of a shotstone? "What . . ."

"What am I doing?" the man said, cocking an eyebrow, shifting his Leveler into his left hand while he approached the writhing woman-Ticker and scooped up his axe with the other. "Well, I suppose I'm saving your life." The man stooped over the woman-Ticker and casually swung his axe down on its head, splitting the skull open. "I saw how your—" A grunt as he hacked. "—Leveler got jammed up." Another grunt, another hack. "Good thing I saved you before the bitch-Ticker decided to go and toss you about."

The woman-Ticker was still now. Except for her foot. It kept twitching.

The man straightened up, flicked a bit of gristle from the blade of his axe, and reseated it in his belt. Only then did he turn to Lochled, tilting his head and narrowing his eyes. "Or maybe your Leveler wasn't jammed at all."

Lochled's mouth had gone dry. His throat felt stretched and uncomfortable. His pulse rapid, but weak, like a dying man's. His Leveler in both hands now, held low. His mouth worked, but he couldn't think of anything to say. He felt caught. Terrified. Enraged. Didn't know which feeling was stronger.

The man stood there in front of him, his eyes mocking now. "Maybe it's true, then," he said. "Look at you. Mouth working like a fish. Can't even find words to say." He let out a slow, rasping guffaw. "Oh, how the mighty have fallen. Look at you now. I know who you are."

Lochled blinked. "What . . ." Fuck, but couldn't he find something better to say?

"Redskin," the man said. "Or at least you used to be. Before you got old. Before you got soft." The man shook his head. "I used to want to be just like you. But Breakwood's right. You don't got the sack to fight no more." He sneered. "You're worn out. Past your prime." He sniffed the air, nose curling. "You smell of spoiled meat to me."

Lochled's throat seemed locked up. Mind so consumed with dissonant feelings that he didn't even have language anymore. He'd been rendered as mute as a Ticker. And it made no sense to him, filled him with confusion and frustration.

The man across from him looked pained. "Ah, well. Really thought you'd try something on me. Such a shame. But that's what happens, I suppose." He sighed. "Your childhood heroes always wind up being . . . so disappointing."

The man turned his back on Lochled as though he were a child or a decrepit old man. No threat at all. Nothing to worry about.

"Now," the man huffed. Leaned down. Scooped up the phial that had fallen to the dirt. Held it up. "There we are." Turned back to Lochled. "This here's ten whales, brunny! What kind of a man lets ten whales just flitter away? Swearnsoot, you really have turned into a downright coward. And this here? This ten whales? Goes to me. It's mine now."

He leaned into Lochled, getting close to him now, closer than a man should. A challenge. A statement. Right in his face. Daring Lochled to do something. "Anything?" he asked quietly. "No? Nothing? You've got nothing to say about it? Well, how's about we do this. I'm going to take this to the priest and get my gold, and I don't intend to share it." Gripping the phial in his fist, the man pointed a finger, almost touching Lochled's nose. "And if you say shit about it, you old fucking has-been, then I'll just tell everyone how you got a soft spot for the Tickers now. Can't be trusted to do your job. I'll tell 'em how I found you in this alley, letting a bitch-Ticker waste ten whales of medicine on its worthless fucking spawn." He smiled. Retracted his finger. "Don't think the captain will be quite so friendly with you after that, uh?"

Two men in an alley, splattered with blood—*My Leveler paints it so pretty!* One with his back against the wall. The other looming over him, threatening, young, hard, itching for a fight.

The man sighed again and finally leaned away from Lochled. "Such a disappointment."

He turned and started walking away.

And Lochled spun and triggered his Leveler right into the

man's back, splitting him straight in two in a gout of yellow and red. Upper half simply falling off into the dirt, the lower half staggering forward on drunken legs for two strides before toppling over. Even when the legs hit the ground, they still kept trying to walk. Strangest thing Lochled had ever seen.

Death was like that. Always weird. Always grotesque. Always surprising.

Lochled stepped over and put his boot on the Leveler, sliding it out of the weak grip. He stood over the man, looking down at his face, all agog with shock, skin flushed as though he were embarrassed by the whole turnaround.

Lochled held up his Leveler, still streaming little tendrils of yellow from its maw. He frowned at it, as though it were a great puzzle, then shrugged and looked down at the dying man. "Well, then. Guess I fixed the jam."

Took the man a moment longer to die, but Lochled wasn't hanging around. He scoured the bloody ground around the man's two halves, and found the little phial, shattered, and its yellow powder scattered into the dirt, soaked through with blood.

"Fucking bastard." Lochled bit his lip. Looked to the dead woman-Ticker. Stepped over the dying man's head and walked to where the satchel still lay, near the woman-Ticker's feet. Near the child-Ticker's feet too.

"No point to it," Lochled whispered to himself. "No point to any of it."

He opened the satchel, peered inside.

Three more glass phials. All filled with the same substance.

He straightened, glanced over his shoulder, had the feeling that he was being watched, but there was no one there. Just dirt streets and sweet herbs and white walls. And the dying man, with the two halves of his body still wriggling about. Kind of like a worm after you've chopped it in half to bait a hook.

He took the three phials. Thought about where to hide them and decided to bury them at the bottom of his scaef pouch. Closed it up and cinched it tight.

He didn't even really want the money. Just didn't want anyone else to have it.

He stood there a moment, taking a look at the scene that he'd had a hand in creating. Decided that some covering up of the facts might be the wise thing to do. He didn't have many options, though. So he took the dead man's Leveler—he'd finally stopped twitching—and laid it next to the dead woman-Ticker.

I heard the Leveler go off, Lochled rehearsed his lie. *Came around the corner and saw Breakwood's man, cut in half. Bitch-Ticker behind him with the Leveler—don't know how she got hold of it. Maybe she used her powers to yank it out of his hands? Just guessing. Anyways, I splattered her and her spawn, and that was it. Nothing else to talk about.*

It was a stretch. But it was his word against a dead man's. And a dead man's word doesn't go very far against the living.

CHAPTER 23

The rooftop was empty, Rony realized.

Well, not entirely empty. There was the damned stone-thrower leaning up against the side of the low wall that ran around the edge of the roof. This contraption didn't look quite as large as the one she'd seen in Halun's Landing. And it wasn't bolted in place. Almost like it was meant to be carried, though the Ticker hadn't taken it with him.

"Is he there?" Licker demanded.

"Don't you think I'd've shot him if he was?" Rony snapped.

"Fuck! So he got away?"

Rony didn't bother to answer. Hoisted herself up onto the roof, onto her knees, and then took a moment to cut a full circle while still crouched there. It was obvious why that Ticker had chosen this building—it was the tallest in the whole hamlet. And the only one with a roof that you could even walk on. All the others looked like thatch.

Licker poked his head up. He seemed almost disappointed to confirm that there was nothing there. "Fucker got away. After all that. After Trut. He got away."

Rony rose to her feet. Walked to the edge of the roof, overlooking the rest of the hamlet.

The whole settlement was laid out in a neat little grid, the structures almost perfectly spaced. Reminded her of a beehive. So efficient.

Movement on the streets—Breakwood's squad was half on horse and half on foot, milling about the left side of the hamlet. Hamfist's squad was trooping around in the center, all caution thrown out now as it seemed everyone was relatively certain that there were no more Tickers around. They were poking through the houses, going in hopeful and coming out disappointed.

A clatter of hooves and wagon wheels drew her attention around to the front of the hamlet. The wagon was making its way in. The big boy still on the reins and one of the others beside him, both looking ashen and terrified. Their dead friend was in the back.

Hotsteel, Ord, and Kayna led the way. Hotsteel looked grim and stern. The priest looked as though he found something very confusing. The Seeker looked like she was just enjoying a fine summer ride through the country.

Odd group of people she'd found herself among.

Rony turned again to look back into the hamlet. This time she spotted a familiar face, and she felt a little wash of relief go through her. She cupped her hands over her mouth and hollered: "Sergeant Thatcher!"

Lochled was clear on the other side of the hamlet, but it was small enough that he heard her. He stopped. Turned and looked. He was far enough away that she couldn't exactly tell what his expression was, but even so, what she could see gave her a weird feeling. Made that relief she'd felt sputter out.

He raised a single hand to acknowledge that he'd seen her and then disappeared around another corner.

Rony frowned at the place where he'd just been. Odd people, for sure.

"You see Lochled?" Licker asked, still just a head sticking up out of the roof.

Rony nodded. "Yes. Down on the other side."

Licker shook his head. "Crazy bastard." And then he disappeared inside.

Rony heard the sound of the wagon pulling up out front and considered staying on the roof—didn't particularly care for attention from captain, priest, or Seeker. Especially without Lochled being there. But then, the sun was very hot. And someone needed to round up the horses. Feor knew where they'd run off to.

She stepped back to the ladder and gave a quick scan around the grassy hills on either side. Spotted the horses easily enough: three of them not too far, cropping grass on the hillside near the hamlet. The other two had wandered a little farther.

She swung down the ladder, back into the cool dimness inside.

Licker, Cryer, and Ponts were shuffling around on the inside. It was larger than the other buildings she'd cleared, this one with three separate rooms. An area that sure as hell looked like a kitchen to her, then another with some simple wooden chairs, and a separate room that she hadn't been in just yet.

Hotsteel suddenly loomed into the doorway. "Where's your sergeant?"

Rony couldn't tell where he was looking, as he was just a silhouette against the daylight. She glanced at Cryer, but he was looking at her.

"He's alive," Rony said.

"Well, that's good. But it's not what I asked. Where is he?"

Rony swallowed. "Back in the hamlet, hef. I just saw him. I think he's walking back now."

"Chased the Ticker that got Trut," Cryer announced. "Don't know if he got him, though."

Hotsteel nodded, hands on his hips. A glimmer of teeth led Rony to believe he was grinning. "Damn fine work, men. And cully—you too. Damn fine work." He turned back for the door, calling loudly over his shoulder, "Send Lochled to me if you catch him first."

"Yes, hef," Rony said at his back as he disappeared outside.

Stood there for a moment, Leveler dangling in her grip. Still charged. Probably she should make it safe again. She cracked it open, took the live push charge out and stuck it back in her loop. And only then did she realize her hands weren't shaking at all. She held one up, staring at the fingers splayed out, waiting for the tremors to seize her. Waiting to have some sort of feeling. But there was nothing. And she wasn't quite sure if she was glad about that.

"Oh, hey," Licker announced. "What's this, then?"

Rony and Cryer turned their attention to the Fen on the other side of the room, holding up what looked like some sort of wooden box. Ponts had lost himself in the other room for now.

Licker strode into the center of them, turning the box this way and that.

"Find a good trinket, uh?" Cryer asked, though he sounded a little dubious.

"No idea, really." Licker frowned at the thing. "You ever seen anything like this?"

He proffered it to Cryer, who gave the thing a cursory glance and then shook his head, handing it back. "Looks like a weaving tool or something. Junk."

Rony held out her hand, curious, and Licker handed it to her readily enough. It was lighter than it looked, the wood very thin. About two hands wide, and as many long. Small enough that when she held it in both hands, her thumbs could almost touch.

There was a hole cut into the center of it, and a series of metal tines sticking out over the hole, all different lengths, with the longest in the middle, and then tapering off to either side. Didn't look like any weaving tool she'd ever seen.

Her thumbs were right there, next to the metal tines. She put her thumb on one and gave it a flick, just to see how flexible it was. The tine snapped back into place, the whole thing vibrating in her hand, and singing loudly a single note. She damn near dropped it in surprise, like it'd bit her.

"Oh." Licker scrunched in tighter to her. "You hear that? How'd you do that?"

Rony found a baffled smile coming over her mouth. "Like this. Look." And she flicked that same tine again, stronger and more sure. The note it gave was low and clear, almost like a bell ringing.

"Ah!" Licker looked delighted. "It sings! Cryer, you see this? It's a singing box! You can make it sing!"

Rony tried the center tine—the longest one. The note it made was slightly lower than the first. Then she flicked a few different ones, and felt her heart do a strange thing. It got all light and feathery.

A shadow in the doorway.

Rony looked over, saw Kayna standing there, arms crossed, watching them.

Licker gave the Seeker a glance, but was entirely enamored of the box in Rony's hand. "Make it sing again, Rony."

Rony frowned at it. Flicked this tine and that. Each one carrying a fine, clear note. "You're right, Licker. It's like a little voice inside, singing."

Licker giggled. "I've never seen anything like it."

The shadow in the doorway shifted, Kayna softly chuckling as she approached. "Oh, you Brymics. Such savages you are."

Rony shot her a glance that was probably a little hotter than was wise. "You know what it is, then, uh?"

Kayna stopped about a stride away, her tall form peering over Licker's shoulder at the box. "It appears to be an instrument. Have you never seen an instrument before?"

"An instrument?" Licker's eyes flashed like he'd found pure gold. "What's it do?"

Kayna gave him a bemused smile. "It makes music, my marshland friend."

"A box for making music," Licker marveled. "You saying you've seen things like this before? What? In Drugoth?"

Kayna nodded. "Some wealthy people have things that are . . . similar. With strings. Almost like a bow, but with many strings."

"Oh." Licker nodded. "My brother used to pluck at his bowstring. But it never sounded anything like that."

"Go on, Rony," Kayna nodded at her. "Make it sing a song for us."

"I don't know how."

Kayna shrugged. "Just touch the metal bits until a song comes out. Just like singing, except the box is the voice, and not your throat."

"Oh." Rony stared down at it. Heart still thumping with the strange, excited feeling. How had she not heard about things like this? And how did Tickers have them, but the Brymics not? She plucked at the tines, hesitant at first, but then gaining speed. She was thinking of a song, a simple melody. Flicked the tines until she found the first note. Remembered which tine that was. Then kept flicking until she found the second note.

Ponts had emerged from the other room, plodding slowly toward them as though mesmerized by the sound, even though it carried no melody yet. Even Cryer had given up searching and was watching the box, and then watching her, back and forth.

She got the third note. Then played all three. Realized she was grinning all across her face. Glanced shyly at Kayna, and found the woman smiling back at her. The fourth note, and then the fifth. The sixth was a pesky fucker to find, but find it she did and felt an immense satisfaction. Then she played all six notes in succession and felt like she'd found something she'd been looking for her whole life.

"I know that song," Ponts said. "Don't I know that song?"

"Likely you do," Rony said, unable to stop smiling now.

"Will you sing it, then?" Ponts asked, shuffling closer. "Can you sing it and play the box at the same time?"

Licker looked at him like he was daft. "Sing it and play the box at the same time? What's the point in doing both?"

"People do," Kayna put in.

"Really?" Licker seemed utterly confused. "Seems like a waste."

"Go ahead, Rony," Kayna nodded at her.

Rony flicked through the melody a few more times, getting the feel of it now, getting the rhythm of it right, thinking of how she'd match the words to it. It was a simple song, and an easy melody. Shouldn't be too hard to put them together.

Even so, she started a bit slow and halting. But she rapidly got smoother as she went.

I'll dance with you
You rangy lads
With wild eyes and tender hearts
I'll put sweet flowers in my hair
For you, my lads, for you.

I'll spin with you
You brawny men

With hardened hearts and ready hands
I'll put a fine sash on my waist
For you, my men, for you.

I'll walk with you
You wise graybeards
With tired bones and tales to tell
I'll put my best dress on tonight
For you, graybeards, for you.

But if you find
Him who's all three
With a tender heart and ready hands
And tales to tell, well . . .

And here, she looked up and gave the men a mischievous glance.

I might forget to dress at all
For him, that man, for him!

Ponts immediately erupted in applause. Maybe the fastest she'd ever seen him do anything. Cryer was smiling warmly at her, Licker looking gobsmacked. Kayna gave her an approving nod and a light little clap, one hand on the back of the other, very ladylike.

"You were right!" Licker exclaimed. "It's like having two singers in one!"

"Well, look at that," Kayna said, giving the Fen a wink. "You've just witnessed the height of Drugothan culture. That makes you cultured now too."

Licker looked pleased with himself. Stuck his chest out. "Well, fancy that. Wetfoot like me, cultured. Can't wait to tell my ma."

"So." Cryer reached out a hesitant finger and ran it across the soft wood box. "Question is, Is it worth anything?"

Rony felt that pleasure in her heart wilt a bit. She glanced at Kayna, then at Licker. The Fen's face had fallen into a possessive frown.

"Well," he said. "I found it."

"But Rony can play it," Ponts pointed out.

Licker grabbed the little box from Rony. "I can play the damn thing too." He tumbled his thumbs clumsily over the tines, and it didn't sound bad, but it sure wasn't music. It wasn't singing like it had in Rony's hands. Licker got frustrated rather quickly. "Well, it don't matter whether I can play it. Only matters if the Church'll buy it."

Cryer folded his arms over his big chest. "You know, Rony found the stone-thrower first. And that'll be worth something, for sure—the priest said so."

Licker glanced at him, a little defensive. "Yes? So?"

"So Rony found the stone-thrower first and split it with all of us," Cryer replied, calmly.

Licker made a face. "I suppose." He glanced at Rony. "Suppose we could split it."

Kayna cleared her throat lightly, looking at the box. "Actually, I don't think this particular trinket will be worth much."

"Really?" Licker looked downcast. "Not worth much? But it's . . . it's a singing box!"

"Yes," Kayna nodded, giving Rony a meaningful sidelong glance. "But even so . . . it has no real practical use. I doubt the Church would give much, if anything, for it." She shrugged and leaned away from them. "It's just an amusement. Nothing more."

"Oh." Licker stood there, chewing his lip, looking at the box in his hands as though he thought he could turn it to gold with enough wishful thinking. "Just an amusement. Well." He hefted the thing in his hands—"Fuck it then"—and he made to throw it at a wall.

"Wait!" Rony nearly snatched it out of his hand as he reared back.

Licker paused. "What?"

Rony found her hands moving out toward the box. "You don't need to break it."

"It's junk. Seeker just said so."

"Yes, but . . ." Rony struggled with words. Inched her hands a little closer to the box. Almost touching it now. "But I can make it sing."

"You can sing without it."

"But didn't it sound good with both?"

Licker slowly lowered his upraised arm. Looked at the box. Looked at Rony. Then shrugged. "Doesn't matter to me, I suppose. You want to carry it around, I suppose that's up to you." He handed it to her.

She felt relief when her hands closed around it again. "Yes. I'll just . . . carry it with me. Maybe I can sing for you boys at night."

The others seemed to have lost interest. Except Ponts, who still stood there, watching Rony with this odd look on his face. "I'd like that," he said. Then turned away, almost embarrassed.

Rony pulled the box in close to her. Tried not to look like she was clutching covetously to it. But she couldn't believe Licker had wanted to destroy it. For no reason. Couldn't something be worthwhile just for bringing a sweet sound to your ears? Couldn't something have worth even if it didn't bring you gold?

She realized Kayna was still standing there and glanced at her sheepishly.

But the Seeker was still smiling, like she always was, like she knew something nobody else knew. And she gave Rony a wink. And Rony found herself smiling too and winking back.

CHAPTER 24

The first inkling Lochled had that something was off was when he stopped in the middle of one of those little alleys and stared at another white wall with herbs and flowers growing up all along it and was certain that he'd just passed the same damn wall only minutes before.

He was going in fucking circles. This place. There was something off about this place. Or maybe it was him—maybe he'd caught a nick or a hole somewhere and didn't know it. He wouldn't be the first man it'd happened to.

Swearing softly to himself, he looked his body over as best he could. Looked for the telltale blotch of darkness on his breeches, or on his tunic. But the only wetness was sweat.

It was pouring out of him. Pouring out of him, even though he didn't feel hot. He felt downright cold, in fact, even in the baking sun—wait, no . . . there. Now he felt hot. Really fucking hot.

You got shot in the head.

Lochled reached up, not liking how he felt his lips quiver, and ran his hand across his scalp. Felt warmth and wet and his heart plummeted, but when he brought his hand around, expecting it to be covered in red, it wasn't. He'd felt his own sweat, that was all.

Still, he stood there, staring at his hand. It was shaking bad. Almost like he was doing it himself, but when he tried to make it sit still, it wouldn't. Just kept on going, flopping about all on its own.

What the hell was wrong with him?

He clenched his hand into a fist. Ground his teeth together. Tried to focus on the alleyway ahead of him. Was he really running in circles? Or was it just that this wall looked like all the others? Surely he wasn't so daft he'd get himself lost in a little hamlet like this. Surely.

White walls. Green plants. Red flowers.

The splash of blood. The way that little child-Ticker's head had just disappeared in a spray.

"Fah," Lochled grunted, stumbling to a stop and jamming his thumbs in his eyes. To wipe away the sweat. Or to wipe away the image. Though it barely worked on the one, and not at all on the other.

And what was an image to him anyway? One among many. Thousands, even. Thousands of snippets of time, all across the breadth of his life, and each of them drew a portrait of callous cruelty and bloodshed. What was one more?

Redskin. They called me Redskin once.

But who the fuck was that? That was a dream. A short, bloody dream that he'd awakened from years and years ago. Awakened from it to discover himself covered from head to foot in other people's blood. Except, unlike a dream, he remembered it all with perfect clarity—remembered how he'd gotten that way.

No.

He tried to push on. Had to push on. Had to find his squad. Or Hotsteel. Report back. But his breath was getting weird now. Seemed he couldn't get enough air in his lungs, kept sucking it in and wheezing it out, and every time he did, it seemed that a rope around his chest got a little tighter, a little tighter, until he couldn't get a breath in at all.

"Oh, fuck," he whispered, feeling himself getting small, so small, and the world seeming to get bigger and bigger, more threatening, the distances between where he was and any sense of home stretching out so that it felt he would never get back to where he was supposed to be. "Oh, fuck; oh, fuck; oh, fuck."

Splatter.

How many times? How many times had he seen it? And how many times had he *done* it?

Splatter—Oh, my Leveler paints it so pretty!

He tried to smile, tried to be the savage he needed to be. "My Leveler . . ." he was trying to sing but his voice was broken and lost. "My Leveler . . ." cracking and choking and thready and weak. "Fuck!" He hated that song anyway. Started rocking back and forth, clutching the bastard weapon in his hands.

When had he sat down? He didn't remember sitting down.

Was this even real? Was he dreaming? Or maybe dead? Was he a ghost? How long had he been a ghost? Had he been a ghost all along?

Splatter.

A little boy's head, gone to mush.

"No, a *Ticker*," he wheezed.

No. A child.

Just like his Libby . . .

"Don't even fucking think it." Almost like he was begging himself, rather than commanding himself. No, no, no, it was a terrible idea to think those thoughts. Those thoughts were like giant chasms to either side of him, and he was trying desperately to walk the crumbling ridge between.

But that's the funny thing about thoughts—you can't *stop* thinking about something without first thinking about it. And once it roots, it's a damn hard weed to dig out.

Libby.

Libby laughing. And then Libby screaming.

She hadn't screamed at first. Lochled remembered the strange silence that seemed to hum in his ears as he stood in their tiny home, he and Marna simply watching, dumbfounded, as the Seeker rose with Libby's hand still in his.

The Seeker's words, dim through the humming in Lochled's ears: "It is our duty to free the light of Feor from the daemons of the flesh. That is our duty to Feor." And then he'd looked right at Lochled. "But we also have a duty as servants of the empire. It is a good and wonderful thing to die for the empire, yes? Surely you, as a man who has bled for the empire, understands the truth of that."

"But she's not a draeid," Lochled said, his voice catching in his throat.

The Seeker only offered a wan smile. "I know this will be painful for you. But sometimes we must endure pain in order to fulfill our duties. Both to Feor, and to the empire. Your sacrifice will bring life to others." His hand upon Libby's shoulder. "As will hers."

It wasn't Libby that started screaming first. It was Marna.

As the Seeker turned toward the door, Libby looked back at them, her feet following the man who had her by the shoulders, but her face confused. "Papa? Mama? Where is he taking me?"

And that was when Marna launched herself forward, screaming as though someone had stuck her with hot irons. Lochled barely had time to reach out and seize one of his wife's arms before her clawed hands latched onto the Seeker's face.

He'd stopped her. For fear that the Seeker might kill her. For fear that they might all be executed. For fear that if he rebelled, he would not be a *good man*. Oh, but how he had been consumed by fear in that moment. Sinking into a morass of it. Fear that made no sense and robbed him of reason and paralyzed his thoughts.

The Seeker simply pulled Libby along by the crook of her arm as she began to fall into a panic. It was all screaming and yelling, and Lochled remembered looking again and again at the steels hanging on their pegs, at the rapidly retreating figure in black robes, and at his daughter, his own flesh and blood, who was vanishing through the door, vanishing into the darkness beyond.

Not knowing what he should do. Not knowing what he *could* do. And in that not knowing, he found himself doing what he'd always done: obeying his superiors.

Marna struggled to get free of him, but he kept holding onto her, because he had to hold onto something, or everything would fly off into oblivion. She kept at it right until the moment when Libby's face disappeared into the inky blackness of the Bransport night.

And then she'd turned on him. Beat at him. Clawed at him.

Screamed at him.

Do something, Lochled! Do something, you fucking coward!

The memories came so strong he could feel Marna's fingers clawing at him. And then he realized it was his own hands. His own fingers. Raking his scalp.

"Oh, fuck . . ." Lochled whined, huddled in an alley somewhere far from his home. Looked skyward, but there was no reprieve in the heavens—just white hot light, glaring down, burning him. Made him wonder how much hotter a fire is when it touches your skin. And that made him sick with panic.

What the hell was he even doing here? Why had he even left Bransport in the first place? Why had he even let Marna leave him?

And weren't all of those a thousandstride from the fucking point?

Why didn't you fucking save your daughter? Why didn't you kill that Seeker, right there on your doorstep, and run away with her?

Because orders is orders.

That woman-Ticker—she'd only been trying to save her child. She'd only been trying to do what Lochled *should* have done.

That woman-Ticker was better than he was. Better by a long shot.

And what had she gotten for it?

Splatter.

Lochled slumped back against the wall, mouth hanging open, trying to catch his breath, trying to still his heart, covered with a growing certainty that he was about to die, and not all that upset about it. Only upset because he'd never had a chance to fix it. Never had a chance to prove that he could be a good man.

It was a fucking lost cause anyway.

He looked at the white wall across from him and had the feeling it was teetering over him, and he wished it would topple, wished it would bury him, cover him, so that no one could ever find him.

Movement caught his eye, off to the left. He dragged his eyes that way and saw Libby running toward him. His heart spasmed, lungs locked down, his whole stomach seizing up. He tried to speak, but nothing came out. Tried to say he was sorry but only issued a strange little creak.

Libby slid down onto her knees in front of him, concern all over her face, hands grabbing at him. "Hef? You all right?"

"Libby?" Lochled frowned at her face. Realized it wasn't Libby at all.

Tousled hair with the sun behind it, casting it into a bright halo. That little Fen girl, the one from the House of Draeids.

Lochled coughed, tried to focus on the face but was losing it. "What . . . what are you doing all the way out here?"

A hard slap across the face. Stars in his eyes. Senses shocked back into reality.

And when they cleared, he was looking at Rony, and she was jamming his flask into his mouth. "Take some drips," she said. "That'll set you right."

Set him right? Nothing could set him right now.

But he swallowed anyway.

He still wasn't feeling quite right but did his best to make a good show of it as he stalked up to the wagon. Rony was still hovering along beside him. Kept giving him looks like he might keel over at any second.

"I'm fine, damn it," he grouched at her. "Just the sun. Too much sun and not enough water."

Rony rounded the back of the wagon to the water barrel. Ord stood there with the ladle to his lips, looking at Lochled with some concern in his eyes.

"What's wrong with Lochled?"

"I'm fine, damn it," Lochled said again as he followed Rony up to the barrel. "Just need some water."

Ord offered him the dripping ladle. "You look terrible."

Lochled glared at him as he tipped the ladle back, drained it. Went in for more. "So do you," he remarked, "Theynen."

Ord indeed looked terrible—maybe as terrible as Lochled. Pale skin about as flushed in the cheeks as his vermilion tunic—or was that sunburn? It certainly looked like it was beginning to peel across the nose. As for the tunic, it was hardly vermilion anymore. Soaked through with sweat and powdered with a fine layer of dust.

The two of them held an awkward amount of eye contact while Lochled repeatedly drank from the water. It didn't really make him feel any better, but then, he'd already claimed it was the sun and the heat.

Finally, Lochled handed the ladle back to Ord, grunting and coughing as one does when they've taken a lot of water and not a lot of air in between. He glanced around them. Saw the bodies sitting in the back of the wagon. Flies already gleefully buzzing around their dead flesh. One of them was the boy who'd taken a shotstone to the chest. The other was Trut, facedown. Lochled didn't care to inspect any further.

"Rony, where's our horses?" Lochled asked.

"Over on the hill," she said, pointing.

Lochled jerked his head. "Go fetch 'em up."

Rony glanced back and forth between Lochled and Ord, seeming to gather that Lochled wanted privacy with the priest. "Yes, hef."

Ord dipped the ladle for himself, kept on watching Lochled as he did. Brought it to his mouth. Slurped it up, long and slow, like you might a hot cup of broth.

Lochled's hands weren't so shaky now. The feeling of everything being wrong had left him, but in its wake there was an odd emptiness. The world was normal again, not so downright evil as it had seemed only moments ago. And yet, he couldn't quite forget how he'd seen the world in those moments. Couldn't shake the feeling that he'd fallen over into one of those chasms he tried so mightily to avoid. Couldn't shake the feeling he'd never be able to see things the same way again.

Some part of his mind had been forced to open its eyes, and he was trying to close them again, even now, but once you see things a certain way, you'll never be able to fully go back to the way you saw them before.

Ord hung the ladle back on the side of the barrel. Gave a furtive glance around them. "What happened?"

Lochled didn't immediately answer. He touched his scaef pouch, thinking of those three little phials hiding at the bottom. Ten golden whales. Apiece? Or all together? He wasn't sure. And didn't really care. He still didn't want the money.

And should he even tell the priest about it?

His hand slipped into the pouch, quested down through the scaef, touched glass. Then at the last second, before pulling it out, he grabbed a pinch of scaef instead and crammed it into his lip. It burned slightly. Pleasantly. The older you get, the more your pleasures seem to come with a bit of pain. You begin with a taste for the sweet and mild. And you end with a taste for the bitter and hot.

"Lochled," Ord pressed, quietly.

"There were two of them," Lochled suddenly said, keeping his voice down. Leaning into the priest, and the priest leaning into him, like two conspirators plotting.

"Two what? Tickers?"

Lochled chewed the scaef absently. Spit between his feet. Well, now he'd gone and brought up the two Tickers. Where was he going to go with it now unless he admitted that he'd found the medicine?

"Yes. Tickers," he found himself saying. "A woman. And a little boy."

Ord's eyes narrowed. "A woman and a little boy."

Lochled realized he'd described them like people. But that was one of those things that he'd seen and couldn't unsee. So he nodded. "Yes."

Ord raised his eyebrows expectantly, but Lochled still hadn't decided what all to say. He didn't really have anything *to* say, did he? Why was he even talking to the priest at this point, if not to show him the phials?

"Did you kill them?" Ord asked.

"No." Lochled was staring at a fat, blue-bellied fly meandering over Trut's blood-encrusted hand in the back of the wagon. That feeling was rising in him again. Like it had to be let out or it would claim him once more, drag him down to the depths, and he couldn't let that happen. "I can't go on like this. I can't keep killing them."

"You're feeling guilty?" Ord frowned. "For *not* killing them?"

"They're fucking people!" Lochled suddenly hissed. A pot boiled over. Couldn't put it back now. "We've no right to harvest them like cattle! I don't give a fuck what the doctrine says—it idn't true, and I've seen it with my own fucking eyes!"

"Seen what, man?" Ord rolled his eyes. "Stone-throwing contraptions? We've been over this. Over and over."

Lochled slapped a hand on the back of the wagon, but couldn't quite get himself to mention the medicine. He bandied about for some way to defend the strength of his conviction without mentioning the phials. "Wattle and daub!" he suddenly said, thrusting a hand out at the cluster of buildings. "Wattle and daub, you see!"

Ord looked doubly confused.

"Wattle and daub don't last forever," Lochled tried to explain, and felt it all falling just a hair short. "You want to tell me Halun's Landing was built by the Old Ones—some imaginary race of people we've never seen—fine. I'll accept that, because it's stone and it stands for centuries. Wattle and daub? It don't last more than a decade, if that. Which means they know how to make wattle and daub. Just like we make it in Bransport."

Ord sighed heavily, one hand coming up and rubbing at his flushed and burned forehead. Eyes wide, like he couldn't believe he was having this conversation again. But wasn't that evidence enough? The way they'd built their houses?

"The thatch!" Lochled tried, desperate now. "The thatch roofs! I was a fucking thatcher, Theynen. Thatching roofs idn't . . . it's not . . ."

"What?" Ord hissed at him. "Low minds can't figure out how to thatch a fucking roof?" He thrust a hand out. "Birds make nests! It's not alchemy, Lochled! It doesn't require a mind like a man's to be able to work it out!"

"The medicine," Lochled said—had to say it, was compelled to say it—and immediately regretted it, but he couldn't put the words back in his throat.

Ord stiffened. Looked suspicious and excited all at once. "Did you find it?"

Lochled gave another glance over his shoulder, but the coast was still clear. "The woman-Ticker. She had a phial, just like you described. Yellow powder on the inside. And you know what she was doing with it?"

Ord stared, lips parted like he might start breathing heavily.

"She was taking it to her little boy." Voice almost cracked there. Throat getting thick again. Had to clear it and spit some red juice. "Boy had been gutshot, I think. He was wounded in the stomach. You know as well as I do how quickly that corrupts."

Ord was frowning again, but didn't seem to have anything to say. Maybe he'd run out of all his reasons to hold to the doctrine of Tickers being little more than animals.

"She knew, Ord," Lochled said, voice breathy and urgent. "She knew what the fucking medicine was for. She knew it could help her little boy. Which means she knew that a gutshot sours fast. How'd she know that if she was so low minded, Ord? You fucking tell me. You got any more excuses for that? You want to tell me about dogs or cattle or cats or sheep knowing how a wound corrupts and how to fix it?"

For the first time, Lochled watched his words strike home with Ord instead of bouncing off his bulwark of faith and doctrine. They cut Ord right down off that pedestal, and Lochled could see it in his eyes, the way they started flicking about, started piecing things together. Maybe trying to come up with one of those brownspill excuses he had, but obviously coming up empty handed.

"Are you sure?" Ord whispered dumbly.

"No," Lochled said, knowing that he was lying, and it tasted like gall on his tongue. He spat. "Yes, damn it. Yes. I'm sure."

"Do you have the medicine?"

Weird, but his scaef pouch suddenly seemed to weigh ten stone.

"No," Lochled lied again, but this one didn't taste so bad. "No, it shattered when they were shot. Someone shot them. Another man—"

"His name"—a new voice rose behind them, making Lochled and Ord spin around, Lochled's skin prickling with surprise and dismay—"was Knot." Breakwood stood there, just as casual as you please, his tiny mouth forming the world's tiniest frown. His eyes sharp and greedy. Lochled knew that look.

How long had he been standing there? How much had he heard?

And how'd he know about the man I killed?

Lochled remembered feeling like he was being watched. But maybe Breakwood was just fishing. Maybe he hadn't seen shit at all.

That notion got burned to the ground with a few hard words.

"Saw what you did, Lochled," Breakwood said, striding toward them, hips all loose and swaggering. Confident. Satisfied. Like a trapper with a rabbit in the snare. "Saw you blow my man in two."

Shit.

A deep, heavy dread pulled all the blood from his head and his hands and his feet, left him feeling cold again, clammy, and about to pass out.

You murdered one of your own. What will Hotsteel think of that?

Hotsteel wouldn't think about it at all. He'd just execute him. That's what was called for, and he, much like Lochled, was a man that followed orders. He'd do his duty, old histories or no.

Breakwood stopped right between Ord and Lochled. "Nasty thing you did, Lochled. And in the back, no less. Didn't even have the sack to fight him when he was facing you. Tsk tsk." He reached around Ord, took the ladle, helped himself to some water.

Lochled couldn't find anything to say. Seemed neither could Ord.

Breakwood finished his gulp of water. Sighed with satisfaction. Put the ladle back. Leaned on the wagon, looking off into the waves of grass all around them. "What's in your scaef pouch, Lochled? What did you pull out of the bitch-Ticker's satchel, uh?"

Lochled glanced at Ord, found the priest giving him a hard stare.

"Nothing," Lochled croaked out.

"Oh, nothing. Well, then. You mind if a comrade gets a pinch of scaef from your pouch? I seem to be all out."

"Fuck yourself. Get your own."

Breakwood snickered. Leaned on an elbow so he was facing Lochled, his back to Ord, but when he spoke, it was obviously directed at the priest. "He found the medicine, you know. That's what he done squirreled away in his scaef pouch. Idn't it, brunny?"

The only words Lochled could think of were curses. And that didn't do him much good at this point. And like the bastard killer that he was, he thought about grabbing Breakwood by the neck and bending him over the side of the wagon until his back snapped in two. Wouldn't that be something like poetry? Breakwood and his man Knot, both broke in half by the same man.

"Tell you what," Breakwood said, pushing off the wagon. "There's a way we all win in this scenario. And that's always what I'm about—making sure everyone wins." He pointed to

Lochled's scaef pouch. "You give me what you got hidden in there, and maybe I forget about what I saw. Maybe I forget about the fact that you shot my boy in the back like a fucking coward. Maybe you get away with it and don't have to end this day by swinging from a rope, uh? How's that sound?"

"Lochled?" Ord said, voice a bit high. "Do you have the medicine?"

A bout of laughter reached them, coming from a nearby alleyway. The sound of tramping footsteps.

"That'll be the rest of my men," Breakwood said. He flicked his fingers in a *gimme* gesture. "Hand it over before this goes a way you don't want it to go. Because once my squad is here, my offer's gone. I'll tell 'em what you did, and I'll tell Hotsteel too, and I'll swear on it by soot, fire, and child, and that'll be the end of you."

"Lochled!" Ord snapped, cinching in. "Do you have the medicine or not?"

Footsteps, getting closer.

"Come on, brunny," Breakwood hissed. "Make a good decision for yourself. Hand it over."

Lochled realized with a flash of clarity exactly why Breakwood didn't want his squad to see Lochled hand over the phials to him: because then they'd want a cut of it. And Breakwood intended to keep all ten whales for himself.

"Now, Lochled. Now or never."

"Fuck." Lochled dove his hand into his pouch. Gripped the three phials, then left one and removed the other two. Shoved them into Breakwood's waiting hand.

Breakwood immediately stowed them in his own scaef pouch and straightened up with a smile. "Good man." He turned and grinned—as much as he could with that tiny little mouth. "There's my boys!"

Breakwood's crew came trooping up, all sweat-lathered and dusty. "Cut a few of those fuckers down as they were running," one of them announced. "Can't harvest 'em, but why let them get away? Seemed like the right thing to do." A round of laughter at that.

Breakwood leaned back and spoke under his voice: "Theynen, I'll expect discreet payment once this fucking travesty of a mission is over."

CHAPTER 25

When Rony returned, she found everything had gone strange. She wasn't exactly sure what it was, but as she led the train of horses back, all lashed together by the reins, she stopped just outside where the three squads had gathered. They were all positioned right there, in between the wagon and the building where the Ticker had shot at them.

She frowned, trying to figure out why her shoulders got all tense. Maybe there was something in the air. Hamfist's squad was there, and they appeared jovial enough. Her own squad was there as well, what was left of them anyway—Cryer, Licker, and Ponts.

And Lochled, of course. Standing stiffly against the wagon near Ord Griman. Maybe the feeling she was getting was due to how still the two of them were. Or maybe it was the expressions on their faces—both of them a little slack, but eyes sharp and focused and flitting back and forth across the gathering.

Lochled made eye contact with her for the briefest of moments and then looked away again.

What the hell had happened when she'd left? What had been said?

Breakwood was standing there with his own cluster of men.

His squad seemed normal enough too, but there was something off about him as well. Or, at least more than usual. He had a hard, predatory look in his eyes. Kept looking over his shoulder toward Lochled and Ord.

The horse she had the reins of gave a nicker and tossed its head, as though to remind her that it was still there. She blinked a few times, kept watching the crowd of soldiers out of the corner of her eye as she went down the line of horses, unleashing them.

"Lochled!" Hotsteel's big voice boomed as he strode out of an alley. At first, it sounded like he was furious about something, but then she caught sight of him and saw the big grin stretched across his face.

She looked to Lochled. Her sergeant hadn't moved, was just watching the captain approach him. Had the look about him of a man who's just woken up from a dream and isn't sure where he is or what he is supposed to be doing.

Hotsteel reached Lochled and grabbed him by the shoulders. "Lochled Thatcher!" The captain turned, looping his arm over Lochled's back and giving him a rough but affectionate shake. "You did good!"

Lochled stared at his captain like he didn't understand the words. "I did good?"

"Yes!" Hotsteel boomed.

Rony glanced at Breakwood, knowing how little he liked Lochled and wondering how he'd feel about their captain's praise of him. Predictably, his little mouth was poised in a sneer.

"If it wasn't for you," Hotsteel went on. "We might've lost more men to that bastard with the stone-thrower. You thought quick, you realized what was happening, and you sounded the alarm before anyone else." He roughed him by the neck again. "A good man, you are, Sergeant Thatcher. Good man!"

Everything about Lochled was off in that moment. He should've been pleased with the praise—any man would be pleased to have their captain say such things about them. But Lochled didn't look happy.

Rony wasn't sure she wanted to be anywhere near what was happening, but she found herself moving toward the group anyway, angling for the spot between Cryer and Licker. She could only see their backs. Was curious if they were as put off as she was or if she were only imagining things.

Maybe Lochled was just recovering from his little bout of heat sickness. Maybe he hadn't quite cleared his head yet.

She squeezed into the gap between the two, glanced sidelong at both of them in turn. "What the fuck's happening?"

Cryer was staring at Lochled, almost suspicious. "I've no idea. Lochled don't seem himself."

Licker had his lips pursed, brow cinched down, as though trying to puzzle something out. "He seems off. What happened?"

"Heat sickness," Rony offered, but it felt flat and untrue. Not enough to explain what she was feeling. And it wasn't just her, apparently. Cryer and Licker both seemed like they were picking up the oddness as well.

"Heat sickness?" Cryer chuffed, quietly. "I was in the Pan with Lochled. Never seen him get heat sick before, and this idn't near as hot."

Licker tilted his head. "Well. Men grow older."

"Weaker, you mean?" Cryer asked, as though it were a betrayal of Lochled to say such a thing.

Licker shrugged. "Older," he reiterated. "Happens to the best of us."

"Fah," was Cryer's only response to that.

On the other side of Licker, Ponts was shaking his head. "Weren't the heat," he intoned, voice low, barely even audible over Hotsteel. "Sergeant's torn up about something. You can see it in his eyes."

"Torn up about what?" Cryer scoffed. "Lochled's not a man to get torn up."

Rony thought of when she'd found him, collapsed against a wall. That look in his eyes, not the wavering lack of focus from someone succumbing to heat. His eyes had been haunted.

"He called me Libby," Rony said.

Cryer looked at her sharply. Then at Lochled again. "Shit."

"What? Who's Libby?" Rony asked.

Cryer shook his head. "Libby was his daughter."

Her eyes shot back to her sergeant, and this time didn't look at his face but looked at his hands. They were sitting there, thumbs hooked into his dirty sash, but not relaxed at all, Anyone with eyes could see. He had his fingers curled around the haft of his axe, the grip of his long-knife.

Breakwood was speaking now. The words seemed to be for everyone, and yet he only had eyes for Lochled. "Sent half my crew on horse after the fuckers that ran out the back. Cut 'em down like the animals they are. Dumb bastards never even put up a fight. It's so easy it almost makes a man feel bad. Don't it, Lochled?"

"We need to get him out of there," Rony said, already moving forward.

Her eyes were fixed on Lochled's hands, willing them to stay where they were. Willing him not to start a bloodbath.

Breakwood swaggered forward a few steps, and a very clear area was being cleared, as though everyone could sense the violence in the air, like a thunderhead forming. Hotsteel still wore his smile on his lips, but it had completely melted from his eyes.

"Does it make you feel bad, Lochled?" Breakwood asked. "Does it make you feel guilty, all those little bitch-Tickers getting cut down like wheat under a scythe?"

"What are you on about, Breakwood?" Hotsteel growled. "Lochled's harvested as many Tickers as any man in Brytan Company."

"Oh, yes, perhaps," Breakwood nodded, edging closer still, now standing in the middle of the empty circle that everyone had drawn back from. Except for Rony, who was marching right across it. Breakwood paid her no mind. Kept squinting at Lochled. "But then again, maybe he's had some opportunities to harvest a few and chose not to."

Rony swept up to the other side of Lochled from Hotsteel, put a hand on his knife arm. "Don't, hef," she whispered.

It was like he hadn't heard her. Had a look about him like a dog being pushed into a fighting pit.

Breakwood's pucker of a mouth turned up at the edges. "Have you let a few slip by you, old timer? Maybe you don't have the sack for it anymore, these crusades. Maybe the poor little bitch-Tickers remind you of some cully back home. Is that it?"

Rony felt Lochled's muscles writhe beneath her grip, turning hard as rock. She tightened her grip on him, for what good it would do. She had no illusion that he couldn't toss her off him if he chose to. She just had to keep him from choosing to.

"He's goading you," she murmured in his ear.

"What that, cully?" Breakwood inclined his ears. "You whispering sweet nothings in your sergeant's ear?"

"That'll be enough of that," Hotsteel said, low and dangerous.

"Of course, hef," Breakwood held up his empty hands. "I'm only curious why Lochled's found a soft spot for the Tickers is all. You can ask him yourself. He's turned downright merciful for woman-Tickers." Breakwood smirked back at his squad. "Then again, maybe he wants to fuck 'em. Gets lonely out here on crusade. But I'd assumed you were being properly serviced already—why else would you have a cully on your squad?"

One brave—or dense—individual from Breakwood's squad gave a loud guffaw, but immediately silenced himself when he discovered that the rest of his compatriots weren't finding the situation too humorous.

Hotsteel removed his hand from Lochled's shoulders. Gave him a long, suspicious look. "Any truth to it, Lochled? You been sparing some on the sly?"

A shadow of fear crossed over Lochled's face. He blinked a few times, and it was gone. "I have, hef. No point in harvesting what can't be burned, is there?"

Hotsteel's eyes narrowed a pinch more, but then he shrugged. "Well, you have the right of it. Not like we can burn 'em for ashes, now, can we?"

Breakwood rolled his eyes. "Oh, of course, of course. But the rest of us are doing our jobs. I'm just curious why Lochled's not."

Lochled took a step forward, arm jerking out of Rony's grasp. "Some of 'em fight us. Them I'll kill. But some of 'em don't. And I don't see the purpose in killing folk that don't need killing."

"Folk?" Breakwood feigned shock. "Ah, I think I see the problem. Lochled thinks they're *folk* now, is that it? You think they're people?"

"More than you," Lochled spat.

Breakwood laughed bitterly in his face. Shit—when had they gotten that close? Rony wanted to jump in and grab Lochled again, but knew it would go poorly for her. A glance up at Cryer confirmed her fears: he was shaking his head sternly at her, telling her to stay out of it.

"People, then, uh?" Breakwood almost shouted. "No, Lochled. You've got it all twisted. See, *people* was my boy

Knot—and Pully before that, who your skelpie wounded for no fucking reason! People was Hamfist's man, crushed underneath his horse, and that boy in the back of the wagon, shot through the chest! For fuck's sake, people was your own man, Trut, shot in the fucking neck! Those were people! You value the fucking Tickers more than you do your own comrades?"

Lochled ripped his knife from his belt. "Are you trying to have a big fucking mouth, Breakwood? Come here and I'll carve it a little wider for you."

"I said, that'll be enough!" Hotsteel roared, swooping in to cut Lochled off, slapping his knife hand down. "Stand down!"

"This fuck's had it in for me since the boat!" The words frothed from between Lochled's clenched teeth, spittle red from scaef juice. Made him look like a wolf fighting over a kill.

Hotsteel grabbed him by the front of his tunic, their noses almost touching. "Stand. Down."

Breakwood let out a biting snicker. "Sorry, hef. Just trying to make sense of how the great and formidable Redskin went so fucking soft."

Hotsteel spun so fast that Rony didn't even know what had happened until she saw Breakwood's head rock, heard the hard thud of a fist across a jaw, and Breakwood went tumbling down like all the bones in his body had up and disappeared.

A strange little cry of dismay went up from Breakwood's squad as they watched their sergeant hit the dirt and roll, gasping and spitting blood, along with a single tooth. His eyes rolled around in his head, sightless for a moment, seemed to be pointing two different directions.

Hotsteel stamped up and stood over the fallen sergeant, an open cut across his knuckles welling up and dribbling blood. Hotsteel didn't seem to notice. Bent at the waist and screamed at the barely conscious man on the ground: "When I said, 'Stand down,' I said it to the both of you!"

Lochled had taken a step back, his knife already back in his belt, his narrowed eyes fixed on Breakwood's unfocused ones. He didn't look happy. Didn't look pleased. Only looked like a chance to satisfy a strong appetite for murder had been denied him, and now he was downright starving.

Breakwood swam unsteadily to his feet, heaving air. Hotsteel grabbed him by the front of his tunic, much like he had to Lochled, and stood him up. Rony couldn't tell if he was trying to help the man he'd just knocked down or if he was getting ready to throttle him something worse.

A searing, heavy silence seemed to have taken everyone's breath away but for Hotsteel and Breakwood, the two of them standing there, huffing into each other's faces like a pair of bulls. Neither of them moved for what seemed like an inordinate amount of time. Perhaps Hotsteel was waiting for Breakwood's senses to come back to him, which took a moment. His knees buckled, but Hotsteel held him up again, kept him from toppling until he seemed able to stand on his own. Eyes got focused again

Finally, Hotsteel gave Breakwood a small shove. The man staggered back, but kept his feet. Hotsteel pointed a finger in his face, all streaked with running blood from his cut knuckle. "You can dig the graves of all those *people* you mentioned. Dig 'em deep and set the bodies right." He turned that bloody finger on Hamfist. "And you watch him. Make sure he don't do nothing spiteful."

Hotsteel then spun, as though just realizing there were three squads of men around him. He blinked at them, then seemed to get angry all over again. "Anyone else gonna have trouble following orders today, uh? You've got a mind to think for yourself, go ahead and step forward. I'll handle that misconception right now." He glared. Spinning in a slow circle. Looking at each and every one of them, including Rony, who felt her guts get a little weak under that stare. "No? No one? All the rest of you are good soldiers, then, uh? Fantastic! Now carry on!"

Rony thought they were done. Started to try to squeeze her way out of the situation, find something to do, maybe hobble their horses . . .

She pulled up short as Hotsteel crossed right in front of her, and for a terrifying second, she thought he was aiming his ire at her, but instead he pressed himself close to Lochled, and she froze there, not sure if she should turn and escape the other way or lay still, like a rabbit trying not to be noticed.

"And you," Hotsteel whispered out, inches from Lochled's face. The sergeant averted his gaze, wincing like he had a pain in his guts. "Enough, Lochled. Fucking *enough*. I don't care what you believe. I don't care what you think you've seen or even if it's true. I only care that you do what you're told. And I'm telling you right now: you're on a fucking crusade, Lochled. And the whole fucking point of a crusade is to harvest Leftlanders, whether they're people or not. Do you understand that?"

"Yes, hef," Lochled murmured.

Hotsteel held him there for a few beats more, as though maybe he didn't like how dismissively Lochled had said it. But finally, he just let a snarl work its way across his face, shook his head, and turned away.

CHAPTER 26

Ord stood there, not quite sure what the hell had just happened. It had all come at him so quickly, one thing after another, and before he knew it, he owed one of these ruffians ten golden whales. Then, before he'd even wrapped his mind around that little problem, everything had gone all cockeyed, and Ord was left plastered to the wagon and watching a handful of madmen bandy about the idea of killing each other.

Violence, violence, and more violence. Seemed all these people were stuck, treading the same worn circle over and over. It was their answer to everything. It was the way they solved their problems, but in the solving, only managed to create new ones. And he was the only one that had his head above water on that count, could watch them and think about how ridiculous it all was, even as it scared the shit out of him.

He'd never felt so incredibly alone as he did in that moment. Never felt so far from home. So far from anything that made sense. And he desperately *needed* things to make sense. He needed for things to add up properly, like the columns of numbers in his ledger.

Everything he'd ever believed was now turned up and over, like stones with perfect, clean faces, but underneath it's all mud and crawling things. He'd much preferred the look of all those stones when they were in their proper places, but you can't unsee what lies beneath them.

He kept picturing what Lochled had described—a woman-Ticker trying to give medicine to her son. Feor help him—now *he* was thinking of them as people.

Damn you, Lochled. The Elder that he'd mentored under had told him to be wary of just this thing: how the doubts of others can whittle away at your faith, and before you know it, you have doubts of your own.

But hadn't he already had doubts of his own? Squashed and pummeled and beaten into submission and hidden in dark corners, yes. But doubts just the same.

But what about evidence? What about the ugly underside of those stones that he'd loved so faithfully? And just like an overturned stone, you can never quite get it back in its place. It never sits quite the same as it did. Always off by a bit. Always leaving that little edge of darkness around it, to remind you of what you'd seen underneath.

More and more, the evidence seemed to show that the Church *had* been mistaken.

And in that moment, a new and terrible thought occurred to him: Was the Church's mistake simply ignorance—or was it deception?

"Theynen."

Ord jerked, realized he'd lost himself in his thoughts, still hanging on the side of the wagon. Hotsteel was standing in front of him now. Shit. Was he in trouble too? He couldn't imagine what for, but after everything that had just happened, there was still a sense in the air that they were *all* in trouble for *something.*

"Yes, captain?" Ord managed to sound like he wasn't a terrified child, even if that's what he was feeling.

"Need to take a look at those maps," Hotsteel said, already turning away and heading for the big structure beside them. The one with the roof that the Ticker had shot at them from.

Ord hesitated, then realized he must be expected to follow. "Right." He spun about, searching for his maps, then realized they were still in his saddle bags. Where the fuck was his horse? "I'll be there momentarily."

So many of these damn horses looked exactly like each other. He remembered his mare was chestnut, but there must've been a dozen chestnut horses, all cropping grass without a care in the world, completely ignoring the drama of man unfolding at their backs. He supposed war horses had to do that or they'd go mad.

Shit. Now he was thinking of *every* animal like it was a person.

He identified his horse by the baleful stare she gave him. What horse would look at him that way but the one that had ill tolerated his hapless presence on her back? That, and he could see his cloak sticking out of one saddle bag.

The horse at least had the good grace to stand still while he approached and shuffled about for his collection of old maps. He was always concerned she'd run or rear on him. He just couldn't make sense of what was going on behind the creature's eyes. Couldn't tell the difference between a happy horse and an angry one, or one that was considering trampling him to death.

"Good girl," he tried, as he bundled the maps under his arm and closed the flap of the saddle bag. The mare gave him a single snort. Sounded almost derogatory. "Yes, well, I'm no fan of you either," he commented. "But we can at least be civil for the remainder of the journey, can't we?"

She went back to cropping grass. Turned her big round hind end on him, somewhat dismissively.

Ord hurried on to the building, taking care to choose that path which kept him furthest from all of those heavily armed and quite volatile men. Ducked his way into the dim interior of the building and blinked the sunshine out of his eyes until he could see.

Hotsteel was waiting at a small wooden table in what appeared to be some sort of kitchen. Waiting was a generous word, Ord thought. It was more that he was stewing. Hands planted on the tabletop, face glowering.

Ord licked his lips. How had they gotten so dry again? He'd just been at the water barrel. He proceeded into the room and approached Hotsteel with the same reticence he had shown with his troublesome mare. "Well. That went well."

Hotsteel snorted. Shook his head. "Savages. But that's what you get on crusade, I suppose."

Ord gently laid the rolls of parchment on the table. They weren't exactly ancient, but the edges were dried and cracking, and the information on them was valuable enough to handle them with care. "It's a difficult role you have to fill," he observed. "Are you concerned at all?"

"Concerned?" Hotsteel frowned at him. "I'm concerned about everything. You'll have to be more specific."

Ord chose his words as carefully as he'd handled the brittle maps. "We're somewhat removed from the control of usual martial rules. Savages that already have trouble following the rules might be inclined to . . ." He cringed at himself, then decided it was best to have out with it. "Are you sure beating Breakwood was the best option?"

Hotsteel squinted at him. "It's *because* they're savages that I think beating Breakwood was the best option. Men of violence only understand violence."

"Funny, I was just thinking the same thing."

"Trouble between Breakwood and Lochled can't be left to simmer," Hotsteel said. "Captain's job, amongst many other things, is to keep his men united. Sometimes the men need to be united by their common dislike of their superior. I'd rather have them sore at me than sore at each other. Sore at me? I can handle that. Sore at each other? Well, that tends to lead to mornings where you find some men's throats have had midnight meetings with knives."

Ord considered that for a lengthy moment of silence. "Intriguing theory," was what he ended up with. Which was the nicest way he could tell the captain that he thought it was a dangerous game he was playing.

"Priests need not worry about the details of soldiering," Hotsteel grunted. "You be the theynen, I'll be the captain."

"Of course," Ord said. "But I must ask, Is there anything a priest can do to help you . . . maintain order?"

Hotsteel sighed. "If you want to be useful, get Lochled to stop worrying about the Tickers."

Ord couldn't tell if Hotsteel was serious or not. "I'm not sure there's anything I can say at this point to change his mind." *Fact is, the opposite might be happening.* The woman-Ticker and her son. Doctrine versus evidence. How do you explain that conundrum? "Although," Ord continued cautiously, "there might be *some* veracity to his claims."

Hotsteel's eyes widened. "What?"

Ord immediately felt the need to retreat from that stance. Sometimes you plant your flag on a hill, then realize it's not the hill you want to die on. "Well. You know. Nothing is *proven* yet. But . . . there may have been . . . things. That Lochled witnessed. And maybe me. That might lead one to believe . . ." he trailed off. Feor help him, what the hell was he trying to say?

Hotsteel raked a hand down his face. "You must be joking. He's gotten you all twisted up about it too?"

"No," Ord lied. Didn't even realize he was lying until it came out of his mouth. "Well . . ." trying to tell the truth now, but in a way that might stand up to the scrutiny on Hotsteel's face. "I wouldn't characterize myself as being twisted up about it. Let's just say that I have some scientific interest, perhaps. And Lochled has raised some very interesting points. Some, uh, observations, you might say, that lead me to believe there might be some . . . shred of thought? Inside the Ticker's minds? Perhaps?"

He sounded like an imbecile. Hotsteel clearly thought so. The captain leaned on the table, staring at him. "Theynen. You are a representative of the Church of Alchemy. You can't be the priest and the philosopher at the same time. Not when the philosophies are in direct opposition to Church doctrine. Now, I'm not a man as learned in the scrolls as you are, but I myself hold to the Church's doctrines, and to try to prove that the Tickers are people is to call the Church a liar."

The captain looked almost concerned for Ord. Like he was worried about his soul. It was not a look priests like to have directed at them. Usually they're the ones directing it at others.

Ord found himself slightly defensive. Because he hadn't quite abandoned that hilltop, now, had he? Just couldn't quite let it go now that those images were in his brain. Images of slaughter, which hadn't been quite so distressing when the slaughter had only been animals. Harder now that they might be people.

"Yes, I'm well aware of the doctrines," Ord snipped. "It's just—"

"Theynen." Hotsteel's voice was softer, now. "You can't let the doubts lead you astray. Thinking is one thing—all men think. But doing is another. If your actions are opposed to the Church, then . . . what exactly are you?"

"My actions have not opposed the Church."

"Not yet, perhaps. But if you go down this road with Lochled?" Hotsteel reached out and laid a friendly hand on Ord's shoulder. "We must have faith, Ord. The Church has already studied the Tickers. They've already concluded that they have no mind. To question that is to question . . . everything."

Ord felt his cheeks burning. Turned away from Hotsteel so that he couldn't see the obvious flush on his pale skin. Nothing quite so humbling for a priest as to be rebuked in his faith by a man as rough as Captain Hotsteel.

And what would Hotsteel think if he knew the truth about Ord's obsession with the plague and the medicine? What if he knew that Ord's sense of truth was already in opposition to the Church? What if he knew that only a few moments ago, Ord had wondered if the mistake in doctrine was ignorance or a direct attempt to deceive?

Feor forgive him, he was a poor excuse for a priest.

"Of course," Ord croaked. "We all have our challenges of faith. That is why the Church has doctrines in the first place, uh? To help us to the truth." He cleared his throat roughly and gestured to the maps, eager to disengage from this perilous topic. "What was it you wanted to see?"

Hotsteel watched him for a moment, like he could see right through him, see that base of faith that had held up the structure of Ord's life slowly crumbling to dust and ruin. Finally, he released Ord's shoulder and looked to the parchments on the table. "Maps from the Second, if you please."

Ord pushed two of the three rolls off to the side, unrolled the third. It was a large piece of parchment, took up most of the table top. In an effort to justify his existence, whoever had drawn the map during the Second Crusade had taken some artistic license with the bulk of it. The coastline was well mapped, but the rest of Leftland, which took up the majority of the map, was simply the artist's imagination. Which seemed to manifest itself in collections of beautifully rendered trees, hills, and strange little figures in clumps that Ord took to be Leftlanders. As though the artist had thought to himself, *Well, it's Leftland, so I'll toss a few Leftlanders in—they must be out there somewhere.*

Hotsteel hunched over the map, placed his finger lightly on the diagram of Halun's Landing, then traced his way inland from there. "We're about here, yes?"

Ord tilted his head. "Best I can determine, yes."

Hotsteel's finger ranged around the artist's rendered imagination, and settled on a clump of squat squares with what appeared to be thatched roofs. "Quite possible this is us right here."

VILLAGE, was all the map said.

Ord nodded. "It's the right direction. About the right distance, I'd say."

Hotsteel went a bit further. Stopped at what might be a day's ride from them. There, a set of larger buildings had been sketched, something more like what they'd seen in Halun's Landing. It had no name, not even the throwaway effort that the artist had given *VILLAGE*.

"It's not named," Hotsteel pointed out. "So is it an actual place, or just a drawing?"

Ord took a measurement with his thumbs, from the shoreline of Leftland all the way to the depicted city. "Furthest inland the Second ever went was two day's ride. That's roughly three. Possible it was reported by scouts, but the main body of the Second never got that far."

Hotsteel rubbed his stubbled cheeks, making a rasping sound. "They drew it large."

"The accuracy and scale is . . . dubious."

"Even so. We'll want to go around it, I think. And I don't

want to camp within sight of it if they got watch towers." Hotsteel blew a breath that flapped his lips. "Which means it'll take a full day's ride and then some to get around it and camp. Best if we stay here, then, uh?"

Ord flashed a small grimace. "Our timeline is unforgiving. I'd hate to waste half a day. But I see your point. I suppose, in the grand scheme of a month's time, half a day won't make a difference."

"Likely not." Hotsteel didn't seem entirely decided, though. Cast a look at the daylight pouring in from the bashed-open door. "I'd prefer to keep the men busy and out of trouble, but I'd prefer even more not to have them killed by some ambitious Tickers, if that city is standing there."

Ord nodded. "Nothing to be done for it, then. We camp and continue in the morning."

Hotsteel glanced around the room. "Suppose it might be nice to have a roof over our heads, but sleeping in these places gives me the jitters. Ah well. That's soldiering for you." A smile and a wink at Ord. "Which you're learning all too quickly."

CHAPTER 27

"Ah! Careful with that!" Lochled winced, but tried not to pull away.

Rony sighed irritably at him. "Calm down, you old sourslit. Longer you moan, the longer it'll take."

Lochled's eyes were ratcheted as far to the right as he could, barely able to make out her fingers with the needle and thread. "Hard to calm down with that needle so close to my eye."

Rony leaned back and raised her eyebrows. "You can always do it yourself if you prefer."

It was a temptation, but Feor help him if he actually did it. He was not known for his prowess in stitching cuts closed. "Fine, then."

"Steady on?" Rony asked.

"Steady on," Lochled grumped, forcing himself to relax. Wasn't so much the pain of the needle going through his skin as it was Rony's trembly fingers with that little shiv of steel. But his fingers would have been no better. Cryer's paws probably couldn't even grasp something as tiny as a needle, and Ponts likely wouldn't be any better. And Licker . . . well, Licker was a Fen, and they did strange things for healing. Lochled trusted him with an axe and a knife, but not with a wound.

Looking about didn't help him relax much. They were squatting in one of the buildings, each of the squads having laid claim to their own. And he felt like a trespasser doing it. These places weren't old abandoned ruins. They had the smell of being lived in. A smell not at all unlike people.

People that they'd killed.

It was still daylight outside, sun pouring in through the windows, heavily slanted and bright yellow, but the mood was anything but cheery. It wasn't just Lochled's run-in with Breakwood that had dampened their spirits. It was also the absence of Trut. Just a little more quiet in that single-room building than it should have been. Just a little more empty.

Ponts, Licker, and Cryer were seated on the floor, picking through Trut's meager belongings and divvying them up. They managed to keep a steady conversation going among themselves, soldiers being a rare breed of people that could amuse themselves by running their mouths incessantly, but even that had a washed-out feel to it. Trut's sharp comments were missing. Like a stew without any salt.

Lochled didn't like getting maudlin about comrades lost. He'd lost too many to grieve over each one. But even he found himself a bit sullen. Mind going back and forth between unpleasant things: Trut's choking and the boy-Ticker's head getting splattered on a wall. The wash of blood down Trut's neck and chest and the pleading look in the woman-Ticker's eyes.

No point to any of it.

He felt Rony's needle slide into his skin and hit something. He hissed through clenched teeth. "You stabbing my bones, Rony?"

Rony frowned at the wound. "No. But it hit something. Hold still."

He felt her fingers prize the wound open. Felt sharp little jabs of pain as she tried to fish something out with the tip of the needle. The sensation of something being pulled from his flesh. Rony inspected it for a moment, then held it up in front of Lochled's face between pinched fingers.

A little, triangular piece of white, all smeared with red.

"What is it?" She asked, curious. "Bit of wall exploded in your face?"

Lochled took it from her fingers. Rubbed his own blood from it. Stared at it sitting in his palm. "Bit of skull, actually." *Exploded in my face*, he thought, but didn't say.

He turned his hand over until the piece tipped out and fell to the floor. Rubbed his hands together as though to clean them. But they still felt dirty. Everything on him felt dirty, but his hands most of all.

Maybe he *had* gone soft.

"The dice," Licker said from across the room, holding them up in his palms. He looked at them for a moment. Then at the rest of the squad. "Anyone want them?"

Ponts slowly shook his head.

"Wouldn't feel right," Cryer murmured. "Tossing dice without Trut."

Lochled summoned his most coldhearted side. The armored side of him. "What's that, then, uh?" He glared at Cryer. "You never going to toss dice again? We're not allowed to play the game 'cause it was Trut and Wen's favorite?"

Cryer only shrugged. "Wouldn't feel right," he repeated.

Licker held them out toward Lochled. "You want them, then?"

Lochled wanted the fucking things about as much as he wanted the shard of the child-Ticker's skull. "Fah. We'll put 'em on his grave. Say a few words."

Licker nodded and set them off to the side. He and Ponts

and Cryer went back to muddling over the items. Licker laid claim to the hand axe, as his own had a large notch in the center of it. Ponts took the long-knife, as his own was getting loose at the hilt. Cryer took his scaef and flask.

On and on it went. Always the same. Man dies, and his belongings get distributed. Like a tree falling in the forest, its body turned to homes for beetles, its rot giving nutrients to the other plants around it. Man dies and opens up a hole in the squad to be filled by another man sometime in the future. Like the saplings reach for the sunlight opened up in the canopy by that fallen tree.

A circle. A never-ending circle.

"Tell me about the Pan," Rony said quietly as she passed the needle and thread through his skin, around and around.

Lochled's ears gave an unpleasant little hum. Heart gave an unpleasant little lurch. "The fuck you want to know about the Pan for?"

A minimal shrug in response. "Just want to know how you became you."

"How I became me?" He stretched his eyes sidelong at her. Only caught a flash of hers connecting with his. "I was always me. If anything, the Pan made me *not* me."

Rony didn't reply. Just kept stitching. Like she knew the silence would weigh on Lochled. Knew he'd be compelled to explain himself better. And he was irritated that she was right.

"Wasn't the Pan did shit," he mumbled. "The Pan's just a place, nothing more. It was the people in it that did the shit. Myself included."

More silence. The pinch of the needle, almost numb now. Barely even hurt anymore.

"Hot. Dry. Flat. Wounded men died quick. They'd pass out and cook alive if they didn't have shade to rest under. And there weren't much. Had to choose between roasting in your clothes or burning your skin. Wasn't a good place for Fens, I can tell you that. They'd turn as red as lobsters in a boil if they didn't have the sense to keep every inch of 'em covered. Then if they did, they'd pass out from too much heat. Lot of 'em just died from that alone, never even saw steel drawn in anger. Squad could go through a barrel of water a day and still be parched."

"Fuck the Pan," Cryer murmured.

Lochled nodded. "Fuck the Pan. And fuck Medeland. They ever revolt again, I say we just let 'em have their patch of scorched rock. Better off if the empire never went there in the first place."

"Ah, but you can't have alchemy without whatever they mine in Medeland and Fareach," Cryer pointed out with substantial bitterness.

"Fuck alchemy," Lochled said, matching the bitterness. "Church and Brannen can make pretty speeches about progress. But all alchemy has really ever given us is weakness. Dependence. Whole generations growing up, all packed into these cities with their running water and their alchemic lanterns and their heat pumps. Young men not knowing how to make a fucking fire for themselves. Young women who've forgotten how to make bread. Easier just to go stand in a line and let the Church hand it to them. Everything just so fucking easy these days, and everyone's fucking mad with it. Demanding more. More draeids burned. More Leftlanders harvested. And the Church and the Brannen all too willing to provide it." Lochled scoffed. "Alchemy's just a big, milky fucking tit, and it's turned a hard race of people into suckling babes."

"Didn't you live in the city?" Licker asked, quirking an eyebrow. "Suckling the Bransport tit?"

"Not out of choice," Lochled shot back, a bit more defensive than was called for, maybe. He frowned. Stewed for a bit.

"What made you move to the city?" Rony asked, cinching his cut closed with a final stitch.

Lochled almost didn't answer. But the damned skelpie had reeled him in, hadn't she? Naive as a fish on a hook. He worked his jaw, like he was chewing on the thought. Chewing on the words. "Bad times a few years back. Lived out in the flats, nyhtside of the Cursflow. Just me and Marna and my little girl, Libby." His hand crept up to his jaw, rubbed slowly at his beard. "Lot of bloodriders. Men with nothing better to do after coming back from the Pan but to use their killing skills to take what they could from whoever they could take it from. Men who claimed to live by the Old Laws. But they didn't have no laws at all."

Lochled bared his teeth for a flash. "They came through a village. Name of Crannock. It weren't my village, but it was the one I went to most often. Knew everyone there." He shook his head. "Don't even know who lived and who died. I wanted to go see if there were survivors or if any of those damnfuck bastards was still hanging around. But Marna was all in a fright. Didn't want me to leave her."

No one else spoke. Just stared at the leftovers of Trut's things. Rony, not moving beside him. Just watching and listening.

"Marna wanted to move to Bransport after that. Thought we'd be safer there. And I didn't know any better. Never lived in a city myself. So I gave in." He shook his head slowly. "She would tell me, 'The ocean heals all wounds.' That's why she wanted to live in Bransport—had this fanciful notion of a beautiful oceanside city. But it weren't beautiful at all. Weren't there for two weeks before the Seeker came for Libby. I'd never known she had the powers. She'd never done anything to make me suspect. But *they* knew. Somehow, they knew."

He'd lost everything in less than a month. First Crannock.

Then the little homestead he'd slaved over for so many years, left abandoned. And then his sweet Libby.

And when did he lose Marna? A year after. At least, that's when she finally left. Couldn't look at him anymore, and he didn't know if it was because he'd been a coward and let them take his daughter or if it was because she just didn't want to think of all they'd had and how fast it got taken from them. Fact is, he'd probably lost her the second Libby was dragged out of their sight—it just took her some time to realize it herself.

"If I make it back, I won't live in Bransport," Lochled croaked out. "Won't live in no city. I don't want to watch the sootfall every evening and pretend I don't hear children screaming. I don't want anything that the Church gives. Fact is . . ." he reached up a finger and ran it along the rough stitches on the side of his face. "Not even sure I want to live in Brymsland anymore. Not even sure I want to live in any place run by the Church."

"Church runs the whole of Eormun," Cryer pointed out. "Don't leave a lot of options."

"They don't run Haeda," Lochled said, thinking of how he should've taken Libby and run for Haeda. Even if it was hotter than the Pan. He'd survived it once. Could've survived it again. Could survive anything if it meant having her back.

"Or Fenland," Licker put in with a touch of pride. "Well, Seekers still come around, that's for sure. But other than that they leave us alone." He frowned at nothing in particular. "Suppose draeids is all they want from the Big Black Mud."

That little girl in the House of Draeids. A young Fen. When had she been taken from her wic? As a babe or older? Did she even remember it?

Was there even a place in the world that the Seekers wouldn't go?

"So," Rony said, her voice quiet as she put away her needle and thread. "You came on crusade to escape."

"War's an escape," Lochled nodded. "There's many a man has gone to war to escape one thing or another. And maybe I did want to escape. Or maybe I thought there just wasn't shit else I was good for."

"High price to pay to feel worthwhile," Cryer agreed solemnly. "And yet, here we are."

"Here we are," Lochled nodded. He reached to his belt and took up his flask. Then held it there in front of him, still corked. Glanced sideways at Rony, now sitting there beside him, watching him. Curious. Concerned. Maybe fascinated. "There's men will tell you war is hell. But that's not all it is. If that were all it is, men wouldn't take to it so much. No man wants hell for himself. And yet we keep coming back to it."

Rony's brow creased in the middle. "Why would you ever come back to this if you didn't have to?"

Lochled chuckled humorlessly. Uncorked his flask, but still didn't drink from it. "War's like drips, cully. First taste is bitter and hot. But . . . there's just something about it makes you want another taste. And every taste gets a little easier. Eventually, it shows you things you would never see on your own. Beautiful things. Oh, yes," he nodded at her, eyes wide. "There's beauty in war. It's got its hellish parts, but it's got its wonderful parts too. Man's never been to war don't know how good a crust of bread can taste. Don't know how wonderful a comrade's laugh can be around a fire. Don't know the feeling of just having survived to get the sun on your skin for one more day. Beautiful things. Wonderful things. Things you can't have outside of war. But, just like drips, you'll eventually drink yourself sick. And you'll swear the next morning that you'll never drink again. But that sickness passes. It always passes. And then you'll come back for more."

Lochled raised the flask to his lips. Sighed as it went burning down his throat. "You drink enough from that cup, you start to believe you can't live without it. And that's when it rots you from the inside." He corked the flask. Turned to Rony and laid a hand on her knee. "You've had your taste of it now, cully. You've seen the beauty and the hell of it. But you're not so far gone as you might think. Remember the beautiful parts and bury the hellish ones. And once you get free of it, don't ever come back. There's still beauty in the regular world. You'll just have to work a little harder to see it."

A knock came from the front of the building.

Lochled turned, expecting Hotsteel, but it was Kayna Redstone who pushed the curtains back. He stared at her numbly as she stood there in the entryway, not coming in. Maybe he was waiting to feel that old hatred for Seekers. And it was still there, but it was like a fire that'd gone too low to cook with.

"Lochled," she said with that silky voice of hers. "Can you spare a few moments to walk with me?"

He thought about telling her no. But looked around the little place they'd shacked up in. Thought about how he was a trespasser. Thought about how it was too quiet without Trut there, all his belongings on the floor, like a scattering of old bones that was supposed to reveal some sort of meaning, but in the end had nothing to say.

Getting free of the place—even for only a few minutes, even with Kayna as company—didn't seem so bad.

"Yes," he grunted, standing. "I can spare a few."

"What's on your mind," Lochled asked, as he let the curtain fall behind him. The sun just hitting the tops of the mountains in the distance, behind which Halun's Landing stood. Glimmering across the fields of grass and lighting them up so that it seemed a sea of glowing green.

Beautiful. If you could ignore what they'd come for.

Kayna cast a glance behind her. They were walking away from the wagon and the handful of buildings that now housed their detachment of soldiers. Hobbled horses muddling their way back toward the wagon as the big boy stood in the back and shook a bag of grain for them.

"We'll go a bit further," Kayna said. "If you've the patience."

"Don't got anywhere else to be."

"Does my company not disturb you as much now?"

"You ever done any seeking?"

She looked at him for a few quiet paces. "You mean seeking draeids?"

He nodded.

She sighed. "Would you believe me if I said that I haven't?"

He shrugged. "You've never given me reason to believe you're a liar."

She smiled that big, bright white smile. "Oh, but we're all liars in some way, aren't we?"

Lochled glowered forward. "Perhaps. And also very good at deflecting questions."

"A canny observation." A few more strides of silence. They were nearing the corner of the last building. "I've taken three draeids, before," she said with a voice that held no emotion, like she was reading it from a parchment of history. "The first was a boy of ten, who had gone unnoticed by virtue of living in the hinterlands of the Saydlith. But his family . . . they were . . . so proud."

Lochled grunted. "Fucking fools."

"Perhaps. The second was a girl. Just an infant. I took her

when she was weaned. The father stormed off, and the mother wept but said she understood. Said it was the patriotic thing to do. More fools, by your measure, uh?"

Lochled pursed his lips. His heart was beating heavy, like it wanted to get mad but couldn't quite summon the energy. "People are easy to manipulate. Men with big hats and fine sashes tell them something, they're likely to believe it." *Not so different from myself.*

"The third I never actually took. Or at least not far. Another girl, a Fen this time. Sold by some slavers in Barton's Hyth after they'd raided her wic. But they didn't do as good a job as they'd claimed, and her father and her uncle came for her while we were on the road."

Lochled frowned sideways at the Seeker. "And you gave her up? Just like that?"

Kayna shrugged. "Black robes speak volumes to most. Others care less. Her father and her uncle didn't care at all. Which was a tragedy, in a way, because they were all slaughtered by Brockton Deorfend's men the very next day." She looked thoughtful. "Steadman by the name of Clapper. Are you familiar?"

"No." They rounded the corner, and Lochled stopped. "There. We're out of sight. You can come out with whatever secret shit you've got on your mind."

"How do you know it's secret?"

"Couldn't even say it in hearing of the boy in the wagon. Figured it must be quite sensitive."

She gave him a respectful nod. "Again, canny."

"I pay attention."

"And have you paid attention to the Brannic Empire?"

Lochled coughed out a laugh. "Well, I've lived there and fought for them all my life. Does that count?"

Kayna gestured forward. "Let's keep walking."

Lochled let out an ornery grumble, but walked on. Always so fucking shifty, these Seekers. Must be a requirement that you be a shady bastard before they give you black robes.

"These are strange times, Lochled. Progress, some say. But the trouble with progress is that it hurtles everyone into new territory every day. Every step is a frontier. And frontiers are known to be . . . dicey."

"Uh."

"Most see the Church and the Brannen as a united front. After all, they stand on the same rostra together. Say the same speeches. Why would anyone think different?"

Lochled frowned. Strange, but he hadn't thought different himself. Now he got the sensation that he might end this conversation feeling a bit of a rube. All that bluster about fools taken in by the propaganda of Church and Brannen, only to discover that maybe he was a victim of it himself.

"The Church is wealthy and powerful. They are the keepers of alchemy, and every bit of our so-called progress depends upon that. Without the Church, Curn the Conqueror would never have conquered, and the Brannic Empire would never be. Without alchemy, the Brannic Empire would cease to exist. Which leaves the chiefs and the Brannen in a bit of a dilemma. They derive their power from the alchemy afforded them by the Church. But they cannot control the Church. The Church possesses the secrets of alchemy, but they have no army."

Lochled stopped again. "The fuck would the Church need an army for?"

Kayna gave him a strange look. "Why, to fight a war, of course."

Lochled blinked a few times. Shifted his weight. Suddenly felt that they were getting close to some sort of treasonous talk.

He glanced around them, but there was no one about, as he knew there wouldn't be.

"What's your point, then, uh?" he said gruffly. "What do you want from me?"

"I want nothing from you, Lochled. Simply consider me a messenger bearing a word of warning. There is a war coming. It cannot be stopped. Its wheels are already turning. Things are already set in motion that can never be taken back. It will come for the Brannic Empire, and it will engulf the whole of Eormun in fire and blood."

"Eormun's engulfed in fire and blood every five years by my reckoning." He wanted it to sound dismissive, but it rang flat in his own ears. A war here, a war there, those were the constants—always far-flung corners of the empire. But Brymsland itself hadn't been a battlefield since the Red Rains more than a hundred years before Lochled had even been a thought.

Lochled lowered his voice—seemed appropriate for the type of conversation this was. "What makes you think there's a war brewing? And a war between who? The Church and the Brannen?" He chuffed. "The new Brannen owes them everything. He'd still be a chief in Lefbyrne if it weren't for them."

Kayna allowed it with a nod. "Morric Fyrngelt is every bit a Church man as there ever has been. But his predecessor was not."

"What? The Mad Queen?" Lochled shook his head. "Annistis is locked away in Bransport."

Kayna lifted an eyebrow. "Is she?"

Lochled felt his throat get a little hot. "Idn't she?"

Kayna waved it away. "She is not the only player in this game, Lochled. For generations, tensions between the Church and the Brannen and the chiefs have been like a field of grass, drying in a drought. Annistis Fyrngelt is simply the spark that is going to set it alight." She reached out a hand toward him, and he almost jerked away from it but stilled himself, and she laid it gently on his shoulder. "You've spared no words in how you feel about Church doctrine. And I am not here to argue any of that with you. Only to tell you that sides will be taken, and soon. A wise man will remain silent until he knows which side he wishes to take."

Then she gave him a little squeeze, turned, and began walking back.

"That's it?" he asked, somewhat incredulous.

"That's it, Lochled," she tossed over her shoulder. "Be wise."

CHAPTER 28

The five left of Lochled's squad stood in the last of the gray-lit hours, looking down pensively at a great mound of freshly turned earth.

"Fuck," Cryer spat. "Which one's Trut?"

"They buried them all together," Licker observed.

Lochled shook his head. Didn't it figure that Breakwood would toss them all in on top of each other, the lazy fuck, rather than give each man their own place to rot for eternity. Is this what waited for him? This destiny that he'd seen so many others receive? An unmarked grave in a foreign land, piled in on top of a bunch of other unlucky bastards?

"No time for individual graves," Lochled conceded. It was reasonable, but he still resented it. Anything Breakwood did was contemptible to Lochled, but if he were being honest with himself, he'd have done the same. Soldiers often filled the role of gravedigger, but they lacked a sense of professional pride in the finished product.

"You still want to leave the dice?" Rony asked.

Cryer glowered over the pile of dirt. "I suppose so. Don't matter anyhow, does it?"

"Nothing matters to the dead," Lochled sighed. "This, we do for us."

Cryer heaved out a breath of acceptance. "Fuck it, then. If Trut's watching from some high heavenly perch, I'm sure he's laughing at us."

Licker nodded solemnly. "Laughing at us was his favorite pastime."

"A man who truly knew how ridiculous it all is," Lochled agreed. "Who'll give us that perspective now?"

Licker raised his hand. "I can fill that role." He cleared his throat, looked thoughtfully at the sky. "Ten hard-hearted bastards on a boat becomes five idiot bastards on horseback, riding for who knows where, accomplishing who knows what."

"Well said," Cryer grunted. "I'm sure Trut would agree."

"He weren't a good man," Licker went on. "But that's fine to say, because I don't think he ever cared to be. Or tried. He played his part with a cockabout smirk the whole way. Trut, you were a savage amongst savages. We're weaker without you and probably more prone to angsty thoughts about the meaning of it all. I'll do my damnedest to not let our poor, angsty sergeant get too carried away by his search for meaning in the utterly pointless."

Lochled rolled his eyes. "I'll try to be more careless. It's what Trut would've wanted."

Cryer held up the dice. "In your honor, then, Trut, fuck it all. You rolled the dice many a time, but this time you came up six-count. Happens to everyone who plays the game long enough." He knelt his big frame down over the dirt, carved out a little hollow with his hand, placed the dice in it, then filled it up again and stood, patting the soil from his hands. "There's your dice, friend."

"You can play with Wen again," Lochled said, surprised

that his voice gummed up in his throat as he said it. Thinking about that hole in Trut's throat. Thinking about laying there on him in the forest not too far away and telling him he'd be with Wen again.

That's about all you get out of the soldiering life: the promise of being with all your dead friends at the end of it.

Cryer glanced sidelong at Rony. Didn't say anything to her, but she took his look and appeared a little at a loss. Shuffled her feet around a few times. Hands wringing at each other. "Trut, you were the one hated me the most when I first got here, and loved me the most before you took a shotstone to the throat. I hope you find yourself on a Ceapsland hill, where war has never been."

"Well said," Cryer approved with a nod.

Lochled sniffed, swallowed. Waited for his throat to feel normal again so he could speak without sounding weak. "Right, then. Light unto light, and all that shit." He turned his back on the grave. Didn't care to look at the dirt anymore. "Rony, you take first watch."

Rony had extremely little experience in sentry duty, but even she could see the hazard of standing stationary when the enemy had stone-throwing contraptions that could hit you from a thousandstride off.

Seemed the other sentries shared her conviction, and they seemed to all silently agree that a foot patrol was called for, specifically *behind* the first line of buildings so at least there was some protection from any Ticker bastard with a stone-thrower that might be lurking in the tall grasses around them.

Rony also lacked the experience in sentry duty to know that

it was mostly hours of crushing boredom. So she went into it all tense and vigilant at first. But as the graylit hours gave way to full dark, vigilance gave way to the excruciating dullness of repetition: Walk, walk, walk. Stop. Stare off into the dark, as though anything farther away than the nearest white-walled building could be seen. Then more walking.

Why were they standing guard anyway? The Tickers had never even bothered to attack them, only to defend themselves when attacked.

The Church claimed they were daemonic and low minded, but how the hell had they come to *that* conclusion? Rony didn't care to take on Lochled's argument, but there was something to be said for the evidence of her own eyes. And all of it together, combined with the fact that the Tickers had never really attacked them, gave her the impression of a race of beings that were, at their core . . . gentle.

But then again, gentleness and low-mindedness seemed to go hand in hand, now didn't they?

She'd known a big, soft lad by the name of Kort. Lived on a neighboring farm. Soft in the body and soft in the head. Gentlest creature she'd ever met. Cried when slaughtering time came 'cause he'd made friends with every fucking four-legged animal their family raised. But she'd never accuse Kort of having more than the dimmest glimmer of intelligence.

But then again, just because Kort was soft in the head, didn't mean she thought it her right to take his life whenever she pleased.

She stopped once again, staring down an alley at the blackness beyond. Seemed the scent of the herbs and flowers that grew everywhere got more intense at night. Sweet and gentle. Filling every breath. And all of the wonderful little creatures that had tended to it now dead or evicted.

She needed a drink. Leaned up against the nearest wall with a grumble and unhooked her flask from her belt. Yes, Lochled had been right about one thing: You always swear off drips when your head's burning with them in the morning. But by nightfall you always wind up craving more.

She uncorked it and took a long sip, thinking maybe she'd rest here for a while.

A murmur of voices from frighteningly close by made her jump, guiltily slap the cork back into her flask, and stand up straight and attentive, fearing Hotsteel might come striding around a corner right then.

"What, then, uh?" one voice said, little more than a whisper. They must've been very near. "We keep on trooping through Leftland, not even knowing where we're going?"

Rony slipped quickly along the wall to where a patch of those sweet-smelling herbs stood and sank in behind it. Feeling a bit foolish as she did. Hiding in an herb patch like a child playing.

"It's what the priest wants," a second voice replied, this one lower and more rumbly. "It's what the *Church* wants."

Rony frowned through the thicket of plants, leaves tickling her face, the smell of them enveloping her. She knew that second voice: Hamfist.

"Oh, yes. It's what the Church wants, for sure and for certain." Wait. She knew that voice too, only it was slightly harder to identify on account of it being so breathy. But she was almost certain it was Breakwood. "But what do *you* want? What do your *boys* want?"

Hamfist gave a great huff of a sigh. "Trinkets. A chance at riches."

"A chance to make all of this worth it, uh?"

"Does seem a lot of effort for nothing."

"Precisely so. And do you see any chances at riches around here? Just a collection of fucking hovels. Pots and pans won't make a man rich when he gets back to Bransport."

The two figures rounded the corner, just a few strides from where Rony had been standing a moment before. They stopped there, looking about. Not much to see in the darkness but the starlight glimmering in their eyes. But she was certain it was Breakwood and Hamfist.

She sunk a little lower behind the plants, peering at them from between the leaves and stems and flowers. Couldn't very well get up now. Silly that she'd hid herself, but it'd be sillier still to come emerging from a thicket of herbs. She'd look a complete fool.

"It's a dangerous proposition," Hamfist said, one big, meaty hand rubbing at his face.

"Crusades are always dangerous propositions," Breakwood replied. "But what's worse? To risk your life for a chance to be rich? Or to risk your life for nothing? For some fucking expedition for the Church?" Breakwood shook his head. "Would've been easier to accept if they gave us special-duty pay, but they didn't even offer that, now did they?"

"No, they didn't."

"So we just have to take it in the hindshole like good little whores? Fah. We were chosen for this duty because we all did a fine job of taking the beach. And this is how we get repaid for our bravery? For our men's cunning? Doesn't seem right to me. Does it seem right to you?"

"No. But . . ."

"But what?" Breakwood snapped. "What's right is right. And this is wrong. Treating our men like fucking slaves, not even giving them the chance to get what they came to get. Wrong all over."

"What about the Seeker, then?" Hamfist grumbled. "Did you think of that?"

"Of course I thought of that."

"And what's your plan for her, uh? I don't know how the Seekers communicate, but it's a risk, seeing as how she can just . . . send a message to the others. Or however it works. Mysterious bastards."

"Well, we'll just have to deal with her first. Straightaway. Before anything else."

"Ah, now. That don't feel right. She's been as kind a Seeker as I've met."

"Oh, fuck her kindness. You'll get all twisted up over one pitch-skinned Haedan skelpie? Come now, Hamfist. You were in the Pan. You fought the burned men. She's only one step away from that, I tell you. Church and Brannen can hang fucking black robes on who they please, but that don't change who they are inside. Haedans is treacherous. You can't trust her as it is, and you certainly shouldn't feel anything for her."

"Didn't say I *felt* for her. Only . . ."

"Then you let me handle it, uh? How's that?"

Silence.

What the hell were they talking about? Rony felt her stomach getting all tight and worried. All of a sudden, hiding in the herb patch didn't seem such a foolish thing. All of a sudden the two men didn't feel so much like comrades.

It had the feel of something bad, all the words pointing in a single direction, but what had she really seen besides two men complaining?

But men complaining don't fear a Seeker sending messages, do they? Men complaining don't need to "deal with" anyone. At least not in the way Breakwood had said those words. Those words seemed to have only one import: murder.

Something tickled at her neck, and she restrained the urge to slap at it, telling herself it was just a leaf. But then it kept at it. Not just the brush of a leaf, but something crawling down under her collar.

She let out the tiniest hiss and slipped a finger into her collar, catching a little nugget of a bug just as it bit her skin.

Never took her eyes off the men, though, and watched them wheel around in her direction. Neither said anything. Just stood there staring at the patch of herbs.

Rony's heart tripled its efforts, setting her head buzzing and her vision sparkling with panic.

Shit, shit, shit . . .

She didn't move. Couldn't move. Just crouching there, with the little bastard bug pinched between her fingers. She could still feel its legs squirming. A hard-carapaced beetle. She pressed harder until she felt it crack and squish. Struggled to remain still as a shudder worked down her spine, now every single leaf, every breath of wind on the tiny hairs across her body felt like crawling things, but none of them so threatening as the two things staring right at her.

Don't breathe, Rony. You've gotten yourself into it now.

Into what, though?

Breakwood straightened a bit. Gave Hamfist a gentle backhand to the shoulder. "Right, then. Let's carry on our patrol. Make sure our sentries are doing their jobs."

Hamfist looked at Breakwood, and finally gave a nod. "Right. On we go."

The two turned, somewhat stiffly, and walked away with just a bit more haste than seemed natural.

Rony still didn't move. Kept waiting for their voices to pipe up again, continuing their conversation, but they never did. Which only made what they'd said seem darker. Men just complaining don't silence themselves because of a rustle in the weeds. Men on patrol don't simply walk away from a rustle in the weeds either. Not unless they feel they have something to hide.

Was she simply making something out of nothing? Again she went over their words in her mind, and then over them again, wondering if she'd heard it right. What was it that she could say about what she'd heard? Everything was left to her interpretation. Small, intangible things that cast it black and deadly: Their low whispers—could've just been trying not to wake the others. The words "deal with"—could've just meant that they needed to talk to her about something. The fact that they'd scuttled away like a pair of thieves—could've just been spooked.

Everything that she could articulate had a reasonable answer, and she knew what that would wind up making her look like: Little Roan got all panicky when some big scary men surprised her in the dark.

She sucked in a slow, silent breath. Let it out just as quiet. She needed to get out of there. Looked to the outer edge of the hamlet and considered running into the grasses, or running anywhere, really. But running would only make her look scared, and if you're a man wondering who might've been listening to you in the darkness, it's awfully easy to pick out the most frightened-looking person you see.

So it seemed she had only one option.

Just walk. Saunter. Calm as you please. As bored as she could make herself appear, and therefore, completely innocent—just another sentry out wiling away the hours until the change of guards.

She eased out from the patch of herbs, slowly at first, and then, when she knew she wasn't hidden anymore, she jumped out of them, trying to transition to calm, complacent innocence as fast as possible. Though she did keep a hard grip on her Leveler, and her finger just shy of the trigger bar.

Started walking. Took nearly all her self-control to do it slow.

And where was she going? Well, there was, perhaps, one person that might not dismiss her as a scared girl: the only other woman in the bunch. And something told Rony that Kayna might pay a bit more attention to what she had to report, seeing as how she was the subject of something needing to be "dealt with."

CHAPTER 29

Rony almost barged right into the building that Kayna had set up as her own—Seekers seemed to relish their privacy. But she pulled up short at the sound of a low sigh from inside. No reason that the noise should have made her stop. Except that it sounded . . . well, there's just a way that women sound when they're . . . involved.

So Rony stopped just to the side of the doorway. The damn bite on her neck was stinging and itching something mad, alternately throbbing and sending chills down her back. She reached up absently and touched it. Almost yelped when she felt the swelling—like someone had slipped a hen's egg under her skin.

Bastard fucking beetle. She rubbed at it, but that only made the pain worse.

The glow of an alchemic lantern shone from inside, casting a long sliver of amber light across the ground as it leaked past the closed curtain. She listened for a time, wondering who might be in there with Kayna. Just her luck to be all sweaty and scared, brimming with troublesome news, only to find the one person who might listen deeply involved in something that most people would consider quite rude to interrupt.

Did she care about manners at this point? Well. She supposed that depended on how seriously she was taken. It might be considered fully justified.

But she hadn't heard another sound. Which made her doubt what she thought she'd heard in the first place.

Maybe just a quick peek, then. Just to see what she was getting herself into.

Oddly enough, she pictured Cryer, stripped and sweating, muscles clenching atop the Haedan woman. Surprisingly, it gave her a sharp pang of jealousy. That, maybe more than any other consideration, spurred her on.

She twisted so that she was facing the wall, then slowly slid over until one eye was peering around the corner of the doorway. The curtain was shut, but there was a gap, and Rony could see through into the dimly lit room beyond. Felt her breath catch in her chest. A frown forming on her brow.

Kayna Redstone sat cross-legged in the middle of the room, not a scrap of clothing on her. She was facing the door, but her eyes were closed, mouth hanging slightly open, a twinge of a smile at the corners. She swayed gently back and forth, like sea grass moves slowly in the underwater currents. Every inch of her was covered in sweat, which seemed odd, as it had turned into a rather cool night, and everyone knew how tolerant Haedans were to ghastly levels of heat. Yet she was as sodden as a smith working a forge.

But there was no one else.

Rony thought that Kayna might be taking things into her own hands, but if that were the case, she must not need fingers to do it. Kayna's hands were resting on her knees, the left hand holding a tiny jar in loose fingers. A single drop of some clear liquid shimmered like a diamond at the lip of the jar, then slipped to the floor.

So she'd taken something, then? Rony couldn't even begin to guess what it was. Only a tiny note of fascinated envy as she saw the sweaty, ecstatic calm that had taken Kayna.

Well, shit. What to do now? Just knock? Was Kayna even capable of listening at this point?

"Rony."

Rony jumped at the sound of her own name, realized that Kayna had a single eye cracked open, looking right at her. She had the urge to run or to leap back and pretend that she hadn't been staring at another woman naked. But it was a bit late for pretense, now wasn't it?

The startle worked through her like pins all across her skin, and when it settled, it left her feeling woozy. She averted her eyes and was disturbed to see everything sway and drag in her vision. "S'ry, Seeker . . ." The words like mud bubbling out of her mouth.

The sound of movement. The voice, soft and sweet: "Rony?"

Rony blinked at the ground where her gaze had fallen. Frowned at it. Was she imagining it, or was the ground moving like water? Seemed to be flowing into one spot, right at the center of her vision. She dragged her eyes back up to Kayna and saw that Kayna had stood up.

The Seeker had both eyes open now. And what was this expression on her face? Rony had never seen anything like it before. Like Kayna saw everything, knew everything, had transcended petty human concerns. But also a hunger. A humid, hot desire.

Kayna made no effort to cover herself. Simply started walking toward Rony—so slowly. Oozing, like honey made shadow. The walls and the ground seemed to be retreating, while Kayna was getting closer. Rony had the sensation that she was moving too, but when she glanced down, she saw that her feet were still stuck in the same spot.

A harsh shiver worked through her. Made her wish she could be as warm and lovely as Kayna.

She opened her mouth to speak, but forgot what she'd had to say. "There was . . . I was . . ." What the hell had she come for anyway? Something about shadows. Something about patches of herbs. And a damn beetle.

Kayna kept moving toward her, and Rony was suddenly terrified by the look in her eyes. They were dark, so dark, darker than black, so they seemed to swallow all the light in the room. How long had she been moving toward Rony? It was such a small room, but she'd been approaching, unstoppable, inexorable, for so long that Rony's feet were starting to throb from standing there.

Hands. Her hands were coming up. Smiling. Gentle. Starving.

What the fuck's happening to me?

"Calm," Kayna said again, voice low and throaty.

Rony's stomach pitched, and all of a sudden, everything felt nightmarish.

"There's summing wrong," Rony burbled out, trying to move her feet but finding that the ground seemed to have a solid hold on them. That or they weighed a hundred stone each. Her heart was beating so hard. Her breath was coming fast too, but for all the huffing, she didn't seem to be getting enough air.

"Calm," Kayna whispered again. Hands reaching out, sliding across Rony's face, slick with sweat, warm, firm. Grasping her now. Kayna's face so close to hers, her breath sweet as nectar but with a tinge of something sooty in it.

"Wha . . ." Rony wanted to move, but she didn't know which way. Forward, right into Kayna's arms? Or away from them? Away from that terrifying embrace.

Kayna pulled her close. She felt her feet stumble, barely staying on them. Felt the Seeker's breasts against her own, lips so close to hers that she could almost taste her breath . . .

And then Kayna stopped. Frowned. Something like mindfulness coming back to her eyes. She twisted Rony's head gently and looked at her neck. "Oh, my dear cully. What's happened to you?"

The ground was moving up at Rony, and she tried to right herself but then had the overpowering sensation that she was pitching backward and tried to correct that too. Wound up sliding into Kayna's arms, her own hands flapping uselessly about Kayna's bare hips.

"Fuckdamnedbeetle," Rony managed, before the ground sucked her into it.

She didn't sleep, so you couldn't exactly say she woke up. Her mind thrashed through a feverish wakefulness filled with crawling beetles and sneering faces and Breakwood's hard, callused hands around her throat, choking her, choking her, and then Kayna, with her sooty-sweet breath, speaking words that made no sense.

Throughout it all, she was aware enough to know that she wasn't in her right mind. At first, she was convinced that she'd somehow been poisoned, so at mostly conscious intervals when she knew she was in the room with Kayna, she felt terrified and wanted to flee, but her body seemed incapable of responding to anything but an occasional seizure of rolling about on the floor.

The light in the room changed—sometimes brighter, sometimes darker.

Lochled was there. And Hotsteel too. Faces sleep bedraggled. Asking what had happened to her, what went wrong.

Poisoned! she wanted to scream, but only wound up gurgling.

Kayna, standing over her, gently pushing her head to the side, exposing her neck, and Rony was suddenly convinced she meant to bite it. But Kayna simply said, "She was bitten by something."

Oh. Yes. The beetle.

She'd somehow forgotten about that in all the confusion. It hadn't been poison at all—at least not poison from Kayna.

A beetle. Was she going to die from a beetle? After everything she'd already survived?

Fuckdamned beetle.

With a new reality to worry over, she forgot how terrified she'd been of Kayna. In her mostly conscious moments, she was aware of the Seeker beside her—clothed, this time—softly murmuring comforting words and pressing something cool to the side of her neck that felt refreshing, and then stung like hell.

She tried to resist it, but Kayna shooshed her, soothed her, all softly spoken words that Rony couldn't hold onto but relaxed into nonetheless.

When she finally came to, it was like she'd been hunkered down while a storm raged in her body, and then it suddenly lifted, and she came upright, blinking.

"The fuck happened?" she murmured, words still a little loose on her tongue. Her body felt like it had broken a fever—washes of trembling relief all through her limbs. She looked down at her tunic and found it so sodden she thought someone had dumped a bucket of water on her. But her forehead was slick with cold sweat.

"Here." Kayna's voice, off to the side.

Rony jerked. Head swimming a little, but eyes able to focus enough through it and see Kayna kneeling there at her side, offering a little tin cup of something that steamed and smelled like dirty feet. Quite reasonably, she recoiled.

Kayna only smiled, but it had a sad aspect to it. "It tastes foul, but it'll get you back on your feet. And you need to get back on your feet." She nodded to the doorway, and Rony saw bright, clear daylight beyond.

"Sootydamned hell," Rony murmured. "When did it become day again?"

"After approximately eight hours of night, and two hours of graylight," Kayna replied, good-humoredly. "As per usual. Here. Drink it."

Rony looked at the cup. Looked suspiciously at Kayna. But then reached out and took it. Kayna gently guided the cup to her mouth, encouraged her to tip it up.

The smell was ghastly, but the taste was mild. She held her breath and gulped it down.

"You were bitten by something, if you recall," Kayna said, as Rony gasped for air and handed the empty cup back. "A beetle, I believe you said."

Yes, the beetle. Which had bitten her when she'd been hiding in the patch of herbs. Which she'd hidden in because . . .

Breakwood and Hamfist. Shit!

"Kayna . . . I . . ." she fought for how to say it. Remembered her doubts as to what she'd actually heard. In the light of dawn, woozy and exhausted, everything seemed muddled, and the line between truth and figment was blurred beyond any real comprehension.

Kayna had risen and strode to one of the windows. "I must apologize first." She turned her head so Rony could see her profile, her dark skin gilded by white light. But she wasn't really looking at Rony; her eyes were downcast as though ashamed. "There is a reason Seekers desire privacy when we're about our . . . special duties. There is a substance that helps me to do my work." A faint smile on her lips. "But it has a tendency to make me . . . uninhibited."

Rony frowned. Remembering it with a flash: Kayna's hands

taking her face like a lover, moving in so close that their lips were almost touching. The memory stirred up a handful of feelings. Part of her gut felt a tingle in it at the thought of Kayna's lips so close to hers. But most of her felt shocked, almost prudishly so. Which almost made her want to laugh.

Kayna turned to her. "Do you accept my apology?"

Rony studied the other woman for a moment, tilting her head to one side. "I should apologize to you. I didn't know . . . you needed your privacy."

Kayna shrugged. "It is not something that is talked about. And I'll thank you to keep it quiet. Your discretion will suffice as an apology. And I hope my care of you will suffice as mine."

Rony nodded. Sure. Bygones and all. Hard to forget, but she could keep a secret if she needed to.

"Now." Kayna took a step forward. "You had things on your mind other than bites to your neck, didn't you?"

Rony felt her face flush with fear as she thought of it again. Fear of Breakwood and Hamfist. And also fear of Kayna, dismissing her outright, not taking her seriously.

"Go on, Rony," Kayna said. "You've nothing to fear from me."

Rony frowned at her. Odd how that her statements were always so straight to the heart of the person she was speaking to.

Rony felt the need to stand up—couldn't make this type of accusation while sitting on the floor as though lame. She scrabbled to her feet, Kayna moving a bit closer with a cautious hand out, as though ready to catch her. But she didn't fall—came damn near close, but managed to steady herself until her heart decided to let her head have some of the blood it seemed to be greedily hoarding in her stomach and chest.

Right, then. Best to have out with it. Dancing around the subject would only make her seem unsure of herself, only render what she had to say more suspect.

"I think you're in danger," she spilled out, standing stiffly with her arms limp at her sides. "I . . ." she glanced around at the open windows, the door with only a curtain over it. Lowered her voice to a whisper. "I overheard Breakwood and Hamfist speaking last night. And I think . . . well . . . I don't know for sure, but I think they're planning something." Voice even lower now, just a shush of breath across tongue and teeth: "I think they're planning to kill you."

The complete absence of reaction on Kayna's face made Rony feel all hot and cold and prickly across her skin. Damn it, she'd known this was going to happen. Known that she wouldn't be taken seriously—especially now that she'd been in a feverish state. They'd dismiss her as having dreamed it all up in the night.

But then Kayna nodded. "That makes perfect sense."

Rony held her breath for a moment. "It makes sense?"

Kayna crossed to Rony and laid a hand on her shoulder. Her lips stretched into a smile that had no humor in it, just sadness. "You need not worry about me, Rony. I've taken care of myself amongst rougher men than these. But your warning is very much appreciated. You did the right thing by coming to me. I will handle it."

"You'll handle it? How?"

A light pat on the shoulder, and then Kayna's hand withdrew. "Well, that remains to be seen. The best we can do at this point is simply . . . wait. And watch. You will know when the time comes for action. And you will know what action you need to take when it is time to take it."

Rony found her eyebrows raised as high as they could go. She couldn't decide if she was being taken seriously or merely humored like a little girl with fanciful notions.

"Now," Kayna said before Rony could articulate any further misgivings. "Some things have happened in the night. I received new orders from Gunnar Thaersh. The men are already packing to go. I'm sure Lochled can fill you in. But you'll need to hurry."

Rony stood there for a few breaths more. Should she press? Or leave it be? But what would pressing get her? She could see that a wall had come up between them. It wasn't hostile, but it wasn't open at the gates either.

She was being dismissed. Just like she knew she would be.

She chuffed softly. Shook her head. "Right, then," she grunted, a little bitterly, and turned toward the door, stopping only long enough to gather her Leveler from the ground where she'd lain—unloaded, she noticed. Probably for everyone's safety.

Just as she reached for the curtain, Kayna stopped her with a word.

"Rony."

She turned at looked at the Seeker.

Her dark eyes were deadly serious. "Watch. And be ready."

Rony frowned. Then nodded and turned away.

But what am I supposed to be ready for?

CHAPTER 30

Lochled hunkered over the back of the wagon. Hotsteel right there in the center of a huddle of bodies, Ord beside him, Breakwood and Hamfist on the other side.

A map laid out on the flat of the wagon's gate. Hotsteel pointing at a little collection of scribbles on the map—crudely drawn buildings that looked like they'd been depicted as derelict. Took Lochled a moment to sound out the letters below.

"Roo-ins," Lochled read aloud, only marginally proud of himself for knowing his letters. "Ruins?"

"Right," Hotsteel grumbled. He seemed in a foul mood this morning, but there had been that whole interruption last night with Rony and the bite on her neck. His face looked haggard, like he hadn't gotten much sleep afterward. "Steadman Thaersh has requested with the utmost urgency, by way of our Seeker, that we divert from our original destination and take and hold these ruins."

Breakwood, cheek bulging with scaef, issued a thin stream of red from his puckered mouth and wiped it with the back of his hand. "What for?"

Hotsteel drew himself up with an irritable sigh. "Last two nights, the army was attacked by a small group of Tickers with stone-throwers. Slaughtered damn near a whole company's worth of soldiers so far. Scouts were able to follow them partway as they retreated, and there is reason to believe that they are using these ruins here as a fallback point."

"Oh." Hamfist's wide face scrunched with consternation. "So the whole fucking army can't handle these Tickers, but three squads will?"

"Two and a half," Breakwood murmured with a stabbing gaze at Lochled.

Made Lochled want to reach across and grab the bastard, scoop that fucking wad of scaef from his gums and jam it into his throat, cram it down and hold it there until Breakwood stopped twitching.

Hotsteel cleared his throat, placing his hands on his hips, next to his steels. "Steadman Thaersh says they seem to travel during the day—tracking the army and attacking at night. His hope is that we can set up an ambush there in the Ruins, while a detachment from the main body of the army pushes this group of Tickers back, squashing them between us. The old hammer and anvil."

Hamfist huffed. "Awful small anvil."

Hotsteel looked at him hard. "Orders is orders. Straight from the Steadman. This is what we're doing. It's not our job to argue about it, it's our job to get it done—no matter what it takes."

"Which will be killing Tickers," Breakwood said, again with that pointed look at Lochled.

Oh, but he was really trying to get murdered today, wasn't he?

Hotsteel didn't even look at the two of them. Simply raised both hands, a finger pointing in each of their faces. "Next bout of words between you two, we'll circle up and let you handle this the Old Way."

Breakwood and Lochled stared at each other like their eyes were siege cannons and their violent thoughts thrown stones. Lochled kept waiting for Breakwood to say it—say that he'd take Lochled on—and he was fucking ready for it. No need for a circle-up. No need for duels. Lochled would just hack him to pieces right there at the back of the wagon. He might not care for the name Redskin, but there was a reason he'd earned it.

But Breakwood simply smirked and nodded. Didn't say a word.

"Right then," Hotsteel waved dismissively at the map, and Ord obediently rolled it up. The priest hadn't said a damned word all morning. Had a sour look about him like he thought this was all a huge misuse of their time but had opted to keep his opinions to himself. Or maybe he'd already had it out with Hotsteel during the night. "To your squads then, sergeants. Breakwood, you'll take the lead, then Hamfist, then Lochled."

Lochled grunted acknowledgment. Being separated like two little kids who couldn't get along . . . but if he were being reasonable, he'd have to admit they hadn't left their captain much choice in the matter.

He spun away from the wagon, hefting his Leveler in his arms, and caught sight of Rony emerging from Kayna's building, blinking blearily at the morning sunlight.

Lochled's first instinct was to gripe at her for being so much fucking trouble last night. But his second was a bit more fatherly—a good sergeant is like a father, after all.

"You all right, cully?" he asked, striding up alongside her and slowing, not sure how quick a pace she could manage.

Rony glanced warily about them. Seemed a little drifty in her stride, like she might still be half-asleep. "Yes, hef. Better than I was last night."

Lochled inclined his head to see her neck. It was still noticeably swollen but nowhere near as terrible as it had been last night. Damn thing had puffed up so bad she'd had trouble breathing, poor girl. Now it was just a little lump under her skin with an ugly pimple head on top. A little dark bruising in a ring around it.

"Looks nasty," he said.

"Feels nasty," she replied.

"Well. Glad it didn't kill you."

"Me too."

They walked over to where Ponts had gathered up the horses and removed their hobbles, Licker at work getting them saddled.

Licker smiled over his shoulder as he cinched a girdle. "Oh, now, look who made it through the night. Good thing you didn't die, cully. We've exciting deeds to do today! For the glory of the empire!"

"Kayna mentioned it," Rony said, glancing at Lochled.

Lochled gave her the briefest rundown he could manage: "Tickers in some ruins daeside of us now. They've been bothering Steadman Thaersh. So we're going to go help kill 'em."

Rony rubbed a hand across her forehead. "All right." Then she surprised Lochled by grabbing his upper arm and pulling him close to her. Grip quite insistent. Strong for someone who'd spent the night nearly dead. "We need to watch Breakwood and Hamfist."

Lochled frowned down at her. "Oh, I'll be watching Breakwood, that bastard. But I've no problem with Hamfist."

Rony's eyes jagged everywhere but his. "They're planning something. The two of them."

"Planning what?"

Rony snorted, let out a laugh that didn't sound very jovial. "Well, I can't really tell you that, hef. Just watch. And be ready."

Lochled considered this for a moment. Narrowed his eyes at her. "Your head all right, Little Roan?"

She finally made eye contact with him. Somehow looked a decade older than she had last night. Tired and worn and not a lot of argument left in her. "Oh, my head's just fine, hef." She grabbed the horn of her saddle and hauled herself up with an exhausted groan of effort. "Clear as fucking mud."

Licker chortled, handed her the reins like she was a chief's daughter. "Least you still have your sense of humor."

"Yes," she said, with her teeth clenched in a grin. "I'm fucking hilarious."

Banished to the rear guard, like a troublesome child stuck in a cobwebbed corner. But really, Lochled didn't mind all that much. The small remains of his squad clopped steadily along at the back of the column as it wound its way over small hills and around larger ones.

For all the fuss of the previous night, it was turning out to be quite a fine day. He'd had just about enough of that sun beating down on him, and Leftland had chosen to capitulate and send him some clouds, and the wind that was blowing at them was just a bit cooler today and smelled of rain.

Good. If you were going to be sodden, it was better from a cool rain than from simmering in your own juices.

Rony was trundling along right behind him. She had a box that she'd found somewhere in the hamlet and was causing it to make all kinds of pleasant noises. Lochled kept frowning back behind him to see how in the hell she did it, but it might as well have been alchemy—she simply flittered her fingers and out came a tune as clear as if it had been sung.

"World needs more progress like that," Lochled said, smiling and turning back around.

"How's that, then?" Cryer asked, glancing back at Rony.

"Little box that sings? Makes beautiful noises? Why idn't *that* worth something?"

"Reckon it's because a little box that sings can't kill nobody," Licker pointed out.

Lochled pointed to the Fen. "And there you have it."

A tiny raindrop tickled the tip of his nose. Lochled squinted into the air and looked around him, found one of those stands of forest to provide a dark backdrop by which he could see the rain. Just a drizzle now.

"Looks like rain," Ponderous Ponts intoned.

"Oh, did you figure that out on your own?" Licker asked, sniggering.

"Fact I did," Ponts said. "Hef, why can't we come to Leftland for nice things?"

Lochled frowned. "What do you mean?"

"I mean what you just said: we only take the trinkets that the Church can use to make weapons."

"Not entirely true," Rony said, not pausing her song. "The Church has made other things besides weapons. They push water through pipes so folk don't have to go to the well. They push heat around the slums so poor folk don't freeze. They make bread for the hungry. It's not all weapons and death."

"Oh." Ponts said. "So, Sergeant Lochled was wrong, then?"

"Banish the thought, Ponderous," Lochled said, feeling good, so he took out his flask. That's the thing with drips—they're good when everything's bad, and they're even better when everything's good. "Our Little Roan is feeling idealistic today. What she neglects to remember is that the Church had push power figured for damn near a hundred years before they ever thought to use it for anything but killing."

Cryer nodded at her. "He's got a point."

Rony chuffed. "Don't you ever get tired of whingeing about the Church, hef?"

Lochled shrugged, drank from his flask. "Yes. In fact, I'm tired of talking about it already. Let's change the subject. Ponderous, congratulations."

Ponts didn't reply until everyone turned around and looked at him. He seemed surprised. "Who? Me?"

"Sooty fucking . . ." Licker gasped out. "Yes, you, you twank!"

"Oh." A slight smile on his lips. "Why congratulations?"

Lochled raised his flask to the man. "You made it to your third day in Leftland."

Ponts frowned at that, confused.

"That's two more than I gave you credit for," Lochled said. "Had you written off to die on the beach, and yet here you are. You too, Rony. Feor's mercy, I didn't even think you'd make it onto the landing craft with us."

"Well." Ponts considered it. "I do have a very large shield."

Everyone twisted to look at him again, primed to laugh if he'd meant it as a joke. But he was simply riding along, as earnest as you please, so everyone settled for a snicker and faced forward again.

The drizzle was growing. Lochled tilted his head back, let it patter across his face. He hadn't done that since . . . no, best not to ruin it by going there. He was doing it *now*. It was pleasant *now*. With the rest of the column ahead of them, and the shushing of the rain in the tall grass, and the cool breeze on his moistening skin . . . well, he could almost imagine he was riding through Ceapsland, and these were his friends instead of soldiers under his care.

"Ponderous," Licker said, looking skyward with great and lofty thoughtfulness. "Why *are* you so ponderous?"

"Well . . ." A long pause from Ponderous Ponts. "I suppose that depends on why you've chosen to call me Ponderous. Is it because of my slow speech or my slow movements?"

Everyone turned in the saddle again. It kept feeling to Lochled that every time he looked at Ponts, he'd see a sly little glint of sharpness in there, hidden under layers of good-naturedness. But once again, he was just bobbing along with the face of a man who'd never learned how to lie—or even the purpose of it.

"I suppose both," Licker said, restraining a laugh.

"Mm." Ponts swayed along gently to the rhythm of his horse, giving it the greatest consideration—as, it seemed, he gave everything.

"My father always told me," Ponts finally said, nodding his head along to his own thoughts, "to let my words pass through three gates. At the first gate, challenge the words with this question: Are you true? If it is, it can proceed to the next gate, where I challenge it again: Are you necessary? And lastly, if it has gotten to the final gate: Are you kind? And only then do I let it out of my mouth."

Lochled stared at him, twisted in his saddle until it started to hurt his neck. Still couldn't quite look away. Still was parsing what he'd just been told. Took a sip of his flask to try to wash down the words. What the fuck was that? He wanted to slap the big bastard upside the head and at the same time tell him to get the fuck back to Bransport, double-quick—he didn't belong on crusade.

"That's . . ." Licker began, but then trailed off. Looked forward again, frowning. Held up a hand and ticked off three fingers, murmuring to himself: "True . . . necessary . . . kind."

Cryer had already faced forward but was shaking his head. "What . . . in the fuck . . . are you doing here?"

Lochled had to face forward again as well, stretching his neck side to side. He didn't see Ponts's face, but he heard the long pause before he spoke—letting the words pass through the gates?

"I am here on crusade."

"Lot of men on crusade," Lochled said, not sure if he was sobered or delighted. "Most of them aren't worth shit. And here you are—a whole squad's worth of humanity jammed into one individual." He snapped around again, briefly irritated, though he wasn't sure by whom. "You know, there's a shortage of good people in the world, Ponderous. And they shouldn't be running off on crusades, or really any war. What in hell were you thinking?"

Ponts nodded along with what Lochled said. Then, a guilty cringe. "Well, hef . . . it's somewhat of a family obligation."

"Family obli—" Lochled furrowed his brows. "Who's your father, then?"

For just a second, barely even perceptible—so quick in fact, that Lochled thought maybe he'd just imagined it because he was looking so hard for it—there was a flash of needle-sharpness in Ponts's eyes.

"Beor," Ponts said, a little quietly, and kind of off to the side, like he was hoping he could just get away with one name, but in the doing, had made it oh-so-obvious that the last name was the more important of the two.

Lochled let out a tiny chuff, blew a spray of rainwater from his lips. "Beor, uh? Well, idn't that interesting. You know"—he wagged a finger at Ponts—"I can see the resemblance."

Ponts didn't bother arguing. He simply sighed.

"Heads high," Lochled said, smiling. "Chest puffed out, boys! We're in the presence of a future chief. Tell us, Ponderous Ponts, when do you expect to take charge of Denesburg, uh?"

"Denesburg?" Cryer goggled at him. "You Beor Fyrngelt's

son? You have to tell me true—that's the first gate! You said it yourself!"

Ponts sighed. "Yes, Beor Fyrngelt's my father. But I won't ever be taking charge of Denesburg." A glance from side to side. "On account of being a whoreson."

They were all quiet for a moment after that.

"Well then," Licker said dismissively. "Fuck being chief, uh? Seems a dreadful, thankless job to me. Whoresons and Fens—now, we're truly free men, 'cause no one expects shit from us."

"Except to go on crusade," Rony said, looking at her singing box. Brushing some rain drops from it. "That's expected, I guess, even if you are a whoreson."

"Well," Cryer said gently. "At least your father took you in. More than can be said for most chiefs."

"Yes," Ponts said, and nothing else.

"So." Licker swiped rain out of his face. "Why do you *move* so ponderous, uh? We haven't gotten to that yet, have we?"

Lochled almost told Licker to leave it be, but for once, Ponts was quick to answer.

"Well, Licker, you know how a whale always looks like it's moving so slowly, but when you're sailing alongside it, it's actually moving quite fast?"

Licker considered this. "Yes."

"Well, it's because a whale is very large, and a man is very small. Things that are small, see things that are big as moving slower than they actually are." And here, Ponts had that rare little glint in his eye as he looked at Licker. "So it's really not at all that I'm so ponderous, but just that you're so damned small." And then, leaning across his saddle so his face nearly reached Licker's. "You fucking ghosty wetfoot twank!"

Lochled spewed drips in a spray, damn near snorted them up his nose. Licker had a look on his face that was some form of terror, fascination, and burgeoning hilarity. Rony and Cryer both let out noises like coughs.

Ponts pulled himself back straight in his saddle. "There you go, you bastards. Gates are all rammed through."

Licker was applauding, face like a man who'd seen a performance so beautiful he'd transcended to the light.

Ponts shook his head, the barest hint of a smile on his lips. Held up a single finger. "Once only. That's all you'll ever get out of me."

"You giant, beautiful, blubbery halfie!" Licker gushed. "How did it feel?"

Ponts sniffed. Flicked his nose. "Don't prefer it." He shrugged. "Simply felt the need to do it on account of you all seeming to believe I was a half-wit."

"I did!" Licker was all grins, nodding exuberantly. "I really did think you were daft!"

The five of them snickered and giggled and outright laughed for a few precious seconds. Licker the loudest, and Ponts the quietest. Lochled, smiling, looked back at them and felt a fullness in the center of him. Rony's eyes squinched up with humor. Licker's enthusiastic guffaw, jiggling him about in his seat. Ponts's vindicated, satisfied smirk. Cryer's great big grin and his rumbling chuckle.

This is one of the beautiful ones. One of the moments you keep.

Cryer waved a hand at Lochled, as though he'd have given him an amiable slap if they'd been closer. "You remember Froneg, hef? Now *there* was a half-wit."

"Oh, I remember him," Lochled said, wiping at his eyes, laughs turning to wheezes in his chest. "Old Brownspill himself."

"Brownspill?" Rony said, still snickering, nose wrinkling. "That a byname?"

"Oof," Lochled shook his head. "It was a byname for sure, poor bastard."

Cryer broke into raspy giggles, big shoulders bouncing up and down. "The poor, stupid flopfin. Don't know what captain put a fucking pike in his hand, but he didn't know gold from gullspit."

Rony shook her head, still smiling but her laughter trailing off a bit. "Shame to let a soft-headed boy go off to war."

"Shit his pants before every engagement," Cryer eked out in gasps. "Every. Fucking. Time."

Lochled's belly kept on bumping with laughter for a few seconds after he didn't feel it anymore. Still smiling, still glowing a bit on the inside, but with a cool whiff of melancholy now. Memories could be like that sometimes. Hilarity and tragedy all mixed together. Maybe tragedy was always hilarious in a way. Just not to the people that cared.

He turned away from the others because he didn't want Cryer to see his face, the big man still laughing so hard. Lochled forced a few more chuckles out for solidarity's sake. "Poor, stupid boy."

"Oh. Ah." Cryer was getting ahold of himself again. "But damn! Could he march! Could carry his pack and half the squad's on his back and keep up a pace'd leave us gasping. Good marcher, that boy was."

Lochled nodded, keeping his smile, though it no longer fit him. "That he was. Good marcher."

"Would've made a fantastic peacetime soldier," Cryer offered up, as though feeling the need to compensate for his mockery. "Poor Froneg. Took a spear right through the head, so at least it was quick for him."

Lochled sniffed. Mouth fallen somewhere in the graylit area between smile and grimace. "Poor Froneg."

"Never had a chance."

Thud-thud, went the horse's hooves. *Thud-thud*, and the rain whispering all around them, steady and even. Wet squelches as the riders swayed in their saddles. Grass shimmering with wet, twitching and shaking as rain dropped steadily from their bowed tips.

Lochled took another sip from his flask. Wished he could have that shining moment back again, only just a handful of breaths before. But that wasn't how things worked. The good moments, they come and go like flashes, and you have to be ready to swipe them up when they're close, like children catching glow-flies. Have to be ready when those rare opportunities come, so that you can tell yourself, *Remember this. Remember everything about it. The rain. The drips. The laughter. The feeling that everything might just work out all right. Remember it and save it for later, save it for a dark night when you've nothing left, so you can pull it out like the last gold coin in a miser's purse and touch it and know that there'll be another beautiful moment sometime in the future. You just have to be ready for it.*

The air warbled and Lochled looked up, seeing the black spot in all those gray clouds getting bigger and bigger, the noise of it hurtling through the air, getting louder and louder—a big stone, a low trajectory.

He almost laughed at the silliness of it all, but there wasn't time.

"Well, shit—" Lochled murmured, but he was cut off by the impact.

CHAPTER 31

Rony couldn't tear her eyes from it, it was almost a marvel. A marvel how quick things turn—serenity to panic, laughter to screams, falling rain to falling stones. Of course, none of that was articulated in her head, it was only a feeling, shock and terror and awe, like you might feel for an instant when you trip on a stone and know you're going to fall all the way to the—

BOOM!

The massive stone—half the size of their wagon—struck just to the right of the very front of the column, sending up a great black spray of dirt while horses reared and screamed and their riders cringed away from the impact—

Oh, Feor's mercy, it wasn't done. She saw the great bulk of the stone emerge from its cloud of dirt, still roaring onward, angling toward Hamfist's squad in the very center, but they only had time to see it coming, not enough to get out of the way.

Rony watched it with a gaping mouth, even as she instinctively hauled on the reins and spurred the horse to the right. The stone caught one man and his horse and seemed to absorb them on its way to a second and then a third, rolling and bouncing and, as it did, spitting out mangled human and horseflesh behind it so that rider and beast were all mixed together.

One of Hamfist's men, clinging to his rearing horse, managed to turn his terrified face to them, eyes wide and mouth stretched, screaming, "Stones!" as though they couldn't see the carnage for their own damn selves.

The stone ground to a halt in the grass, and all that frozen, tar-slow time up and started thrashing like white water, everything, all at once, happening too fast to keep track of.

Rony's horse was galloping under her, hooves sending mud and water into her face and sides. Sprays of rain, sprays of water off the grass. Shouting to the sides and in front of her. Hotsteel's voice like a belching cannon: "To me! To me!"

She caught a jittering glance of him near the top of the hill, waving his axe wildly at them, the picture of a battlefield commander—oh, so heroic—and all Rony could think was, *Get down you fucking fool!*

Someone screamed something, and it might've been Hotsteel or might've been someone else, but it didn't seem to matter, because then everyone was screaming, so damned loud that Rony almost didn't hear the warbling of the next incoming stone until it was nearly on top of them.

"Ah!" she yelped, as the thing swelled in her vision, hurtling out of the gray wash of clouds and rain. Barely got her horse turned to the right before the thing went roaring by so close that she felt a great buffet of wind that nearly pulled her from her horse. She followed it with her eyes, thinking that it was heading right for Ponts.

When she turned, it was just a gout of mud, the piebald color of Ponts's horse vanishing in the spray, and she thought, *I only just met him.* But then piebald horse and big, scrunch-faced rider came shooting out, the horse's back end tucked like that of a dog with something on its tail. The whole right side of Ponts's face was black with mud, but he seemed not one bit perturbed, was focused on the hilltop where Hotsteel had called them, and charged on.

She was the last in the pack now, and everyone was surging for the hilltop. Hotsteel and Breakwood's squad had already disappeared over the edge, and the remnants of Hamfist's followed after.

She got in behind Ponts as they hurtled toward the top of the hill, Hamfist's men now disappearing over the other side. Too much muck spraying in her face. She coughed, spat dirt, blinked it out of her eyes again, and adjusted her horse to the side, hunched low in the saddle.

Up, up, up the hill, just gray sky and lashing rain, like she'd gallop right off the face of the earth and go sailing into the slate skies. Up and up, and then level. There was a horizon in the distance, washed out by curtains of rain, and then she was going down, down the hill on the other side. Saw all the squads in one big bunch, hauling down the slope, the wagon clattering after, looking like it was one gopher hole away from coming apart, the boy on the bench flying around helplessly, as though the only thing keeping him tethered to the wagon was his grip on the reins.

Stones. Where were they coming from?

Eyes up. She peered through the gloom and saw dark outlines ahead, jagged structures lifting out of the ground, seeming to spear at the sky, higher and higher the lower she made it down the hill.

The Ruins.

Had to be where the stones had come from. Some bastard Ticker was tossing pieces of the Ruins at them.

Where was the fucking Ticker? Rony's eyes scoured the edges

of the Ruins, looking for that flash of bare olive skin somewhere in there. And she realized, almost as an afterthought, that she *wanted* to spot the fucker—wanted to be the first one to him so she could scatter his bits. Had one hand already pulling the Leveler from where it was stuck in her saddle packs.

She didn't spot the Ticker, but she did see the stone this time. The top of a derelict tower simply exploded off and went sailing into the air—not high, but coming straight at them, just like the others.

Not a fucking chance she was letting that thing hit her. The bastard Ticker might've got a few kills by tossing stones when the hill was between them, but now that she could see where the stones started, it wasn't hard to spot where it was going. She guided her horse to the right, watching that big, dark shape come at them. The column of horses and riders split right down the middle, and the stone slammed into the dirt right where they'd been, then skipped, and ripped the wagon to shreds. The poor boy on the driver's bench couldn't get out of the way, and then it was just pieces of gray wood flying in all directions while the heartless stone rolled to a stop. The horses were free, cutting a wide angle to the left, not interested at all in getting involved in men's affairs, but the wagon, and anything and anyone on it, was simply gone.

That poor boy never had a fucking chance.

A glimmer of color caught her eye to her right. She couldn't help but glance at it and, for a bare second, saw that face, that round-eyed, greenish-skinned face, peering at her just above the tall grass on the side of the hill. And then it ducked and disappeared.

"Bastard!" Rony snarled it out, heels down, reins back, pulling her horse nearly to a stop as she guided it to the right and spurred it on again. Grabbing her Leveler. Breaking it open with one hand, like she'd been born with the damn thing in her grip—it felt that natural.

The Ticker seemed to realize his attempt to hide wasn't sufficient and burst from concealment like a bird out of a bush.

That's how it was, then, uh? Was he the one throwing those fucking stones? Or just watching while it happened? Rony didn't know how their powers worked, and she didn't care. It was one of them.

And that poor boy. He'd never even fought the Tickers! Never even raised a hand against them, and still they squashed him flat!

The Ticker was running, but Rony wasn't even the least bit concerned. She had a horse, and she was good on it. You could be the fleetest foot in all the world, but you still couldn't outrun a horse.

She was halfway to getting a charge pulled from her loop, but she was gaining ground on the Ticker too fast. Made a quick decision, and it felt, oh, so right. She snapped the thing closed, spun it in her grip, surprising herself with how fluid it all was, but that seemed to be what rage and killing did for you—you went in normal, and you came out the other side a beast, but one that knew damn well how to handle themselves.

Gripping the Leveler by the thick bore, she reared back as far as her shoulder would allow, leaning in the saddle, waiting for just the right moment as she brought her galloping horse alongside the Ticker. It spotted the horse huffing in its ear and tried to veer away from it, but it was too late at that point. Rony swung the Leveler with everything she had, with every bit of rage, with every bit of fear, all the blackness that had curdled in her soul—it all came out in one big push of breath, and the heavy wooden butt of the Leveler cracked loudly across the back of the Ticker's skull, sending it wheeling, head over heels.

She pulled her horse to a stop before the Ticker had even

come to a rest. Was lurching out of the saddle even as it slid a stride or two in the wet grass and came to a stop, hands up, still waving about.

Rony's feet squelched in the rain-soaked field. She pressed her way through the tall grass. Couldn't see the Ticker for a second, the grass was so high, but then she spotted its writhing hands, waving arms, and then all of it, doing a little jig on the ground like it wanted to get up and keep running but couldn't figure out how.

"Bastard!" she shouted at it again, emerging from the long grass into a path of it laid flat by the Ticker's slide. "You didn't have to do that! You didn't have to kill the boy! The boy never done anything to you!"

Dark eyes, staring at her, tears in them. Blood soaking the back of its skull. Hands up. Legs kicking. Pintel wagging. Not going fucking anywhere. Oh, no. This Ticker owed her, and she intended to collect.

She stopped, right there over the top of it. Had the charge in one hand, Leveler in the other, steels in her belt. Rain streaming down her face. Dribbling off of nose and lips and chin.

She had it. The Ticker was at her mercy.

Rony wasn't a merciless woman. But she wasn't quite herself in that moment. One never is when the killing starts. That's when the daemons in your flesh come out to dance.

"You fuck!" Rony gasped out. Leaning forward so her spittle mixed with the rain and speckled the thing's face. "You didn't have to do that!"

She charged the Leveler, snapped it closed. Stood over the thing, staring at it, right down the length of that weapon, finger on the trigger bar.

Do you really need to do this?

She sucked in a breath. Rain tasted of salt after running down her skin, and she spat it out.

"Ah well," she said to the Ticker. "You're probably nearly dead anyways. Some might consider this a mercy." She leaned closer and put the maw of the Leveler against its chest. "But it's not."

As she walked back to her horse, breathing heavy, face spattered with mud and gore, a mess of strewn parts behind her, still surrounded by a mist of yellow smoke, she was surprised to find that she felt good.

Then she wondered if it would last or if she'd have to keep killing.

Maybe it really was like drips. Maybe she'd regret it in the morning. But not now. Now it was the rightest thing in the world.

CHAPTER 32

It was the strangest thing Lochled had ever seen. This whole time, he'd assumed Tickers could toss stones from and to wherever they pleased, but for the first time, he was actually watching a Ticker throw stones, and that wasn't how they did it at all.

"Hold!" Hotsteel was bellowing. "Hold, hold!"

Lochled pulled on his reins, only slightly distracted by the thought of why Hotsteel was calling for them to hold when they were still several hundred strides from the Ruins. But most of his focus was on that Ticker.

Apparently they couldn't just throw them from wherever they pleased—they had to be right on them, as the Ticker was in the tower, dismantling it as it went. He'd get right close to the stone, heave it up into the air, and then launch it after them, all in one motion.

But his throws were getting weak. At first Lochled thought they were falling short because the Ticker was trying to range them as they approached, but now that the squads were pulling to a stop, milling about in a confused line, he realized the Ticker's throws were falling shorter and shorter.

"Lookit that!" Breakwood called out. "It's wearing out!"

"Let's fucking get him while he's weakest!" someone called out.

"Could be a ruse to get us closer." Hotsteel was cantering back and forth, keeping the same distance but apparently needing to stay moving. His face was clouded and scrunched.

"Fah!" Breakwood spun his horse in an angry circle—or maybe the horse spun him. "Look at him! He's fucking tiring out!"

Hotsteel flashed teeth like a badger. "Then let him tire out!"

Lochled was only half paying attention at this point. He'd taken his Leveler out but not charged it yet. Had it laid across his lap as he let his horse trot this way for a few lengths then the other, always with his eyes on the tower, watching the Ticker up there.

If it was acting tired, it was an incredible performance. The thing was standing there at the edge, staring at them, and even from this distance, Lochled could see the shoulders moving, the chest heaving. Its mouth was hanging open as though gulping air.

For some reason he'd always assumed they could keep at it all day—that the use of their powers didn't cost them a thing. But that's never how it is. Everything has a cost.

He thought about the beach again, the shield wall, and listening to the gradually slowing rate of shotstones being thrown at them. He'd thought it was low ammunition, or maybe strategy, but now he wondered if it wasn't just because they'd worn themselves out.

"Come on down, Ticker!" someone shouted, but it was likely too far to hear, especially over the rain.

It was almost as though the Ticker *did* hear, though. It lurched straight, swung its arms behind it as though to grab something, and up came a stone, the grinding and cracking of it as it was torn from its mortar, and then it started accelerating toward them.

A worried ripple through the men on horse.

But then the stone drooped, knocked another stone still attached to the tower, and toppled over, kind of drifting to the ground in a highly unnatural manner. It barely even got to the edge of the Ruins before thudding into the dirt and not moving again.

Someone laughed—a nasty, jeering laugh—and some other hindshole felt the need to join in.

Lochled had no pity for the Ticker. No, he might wonder if they thought like men thought, but like he'd said to Breakwood yesterday, he'd run all out of pity for things that tried to kill him.

Lochled tilted his head. Judging the distance. No, it was way too far. But even though Levelers weren't meant for distance, Lochled needed only one stone to land. And they couldn't just stamp around outside the Ruins all day waiting for the fuck Ticker in the tower to get so tired that it fell asleep—or worse, got its energy back.

Lochled clicked his tongue, nudging his horse forward a bit, while he drew a charge from his loop.

"Lochled!" Hotsteel roared. "Back in line!"

Lochled stopped. Looked over his shoulder. "Just me, hef. Just let me get a little closer."

Hotsteel glared at him, his brows so low against the rain that Lochled couldn't even see his eyes, just dark shadows, like unseen things lurking in dim caves. He waved a hand. Seemed dismissive enough to Lochled, so he turned back around.

Charged his Leveler as his horse clopped forward a few more paces.

The Ticker stood on the tower, still heaving, and watching him come.

"There you are," Lochled whispered. "You see me. I see you. You want to kill me, and I want to kill you. Like it's supposed to be. Like the Old Ways." He snapped the Leveler shut. Raised it slowly.

"Can't hit it from there, you twank!" Sounded like Breakwood.

Lochled aimed high, then slowly pulled the trigger bar until he felt it pop inside, and then *FWOOM*—yellow dust in a great, blinding brocade.

The laughter from Breakwood's squad told him he'd missed before the smoke even cleared and he could see for himself. But the Ticker was hunched down now. Seemed to work at dredging itself up. Lochled's eyes never left it. The two of them, staring right at each other, neither willing to look away.

Lochled went for another charge, and the Ticker stooped for a moment, then came up with what looked like a smaller stone, about the size of a head.

"Smart," Lochled said, wondering what Ord and Hotsteel would think of *that*. He held the Leveler and push charge in one hand and the reins in the other, ready to move fast to one side or the other.

The Ticker held the stone in front of it with both hands, and then it rocketed forward.

But not fast enough. Lochled saw it coming and nudged the horse sideways. Even so, it struck awful close. If Lochled kept on creeping closer to the Ruins, he'd need to be more agile. So he chose to dismount.

Lot of gobbledygook coming from the squads behind, but even so, it sounded like maybe a handful of men—probably Breakwood's—that had it in for him. The rest were likely just watching, curious how this was going to shake out.

Lochled strode forward a few steps, plucking the old charge out, and seating a new one. Closed it. Raised it high. Fired it off and immediately side-stepped so he could see around the plume of yellow smoke to where his shotstones hit.

The Ticker lurched, blood spurting from its shoulders.

"He hit him!" Sounded like Licker. "Did you see that?"

No more jeering now.

The Ticker sagged against the stone. Lochled recharged his weapon, moving faster now. Both beings locked on each other. He raised his Leveler at the same time that the Ticker stooped and swung up, all in one movement, hurling another stone but damn near also hurling himself off the tower with the effort.

Lochled dove to the side, sliding down on one knee and gliding like a ghost through the wet grass, Leveler already coming up, while the stone smacked into the mud right where he'd just been. Didn't matter now. Lochled knew this for what it was. Knew he wouldn't have to fire another shot after this one.

Yellow dust, a kick to the shoulder, and the Ticker staggered, clawing at its neck. Just like Trut had. Staggered to one side of the tower. Then to the other. Then tried to catch itself but wound up slipping right through a gap—a gap made by the absence of one of those stones he'd thrown. Lochled sincerely hoped that the missing stone was the one that had killed the boy in the wagon.

Lochled rose as the Ticker plummeted to the ground. He never heard the impact—there was too much rain, too much distance.

"Right then!" Hotsteel screamed at them. "Clear it out!" He fixed on Lochled as he turned, recharging his Leveler. "And kill *any* Ticker you find!"

Whoops and hollers rose up from the men as they kicked their horses and galloped on toward the Ruins. Lochled stood there soaked, wetness seeping in through his boots. His heart was steady. Hands steady. Breathing even.

He turned back to his horse in time to see Breakwood trotting past.

"Oh, quite heroic hitting something from three hundred strides off," Breakwood growled at him. "Wonder how you are with your steels."

Lochled blinked rain out of his eyes and watched him pass, heeling his horse into a gallop. He almost laughed at his back, the stupid fuck. What type of a man makes spurious challenges while trotting past with no inclination to stop and make good on them?

"Fine shot!" Hotsteel called to him as he charged in the other direction.

Yes. It was a fine shot. And Lochled felt proud.

He hoisted himself back into the saddle, eyes on Hotsteel as he sped past Breakwood. Why was Breakwood all of a sudden slowing? Lochled held his Leveler in the crook of one arm and touched the grip of his long-knife with the other hand, wondering if Breakwood had perhaps decided to back up his words.

His gut tightened, but not in a particularly unpleasant way. Breakwood had been angling for an axe between his eyes for several days now, and Lochled had no qualms about offering him what he clearly so strongly desired.

Breakwood turned his horse around, and Lochled clenched his fist around his long-knife, half drew it out, until he realized that Breakwood wasn't even facing him. The other sergeant gave him a cursory glance, but apparently he wasn't planning on getting himself killed today after all—Breakwood heeled his horse and went galloping away from the Ruins, back toward the hill from where they'd come.

Lochled watched him, sitting there on his horse, not quite sure what was happening. As he looked to where Breakwood was heading, he spotted the lonely figures of Ord and Kayna, still on horseback, but stopped at the crest of the hill.

Odd, he thought. But then, perhaps Breakwood meant to escort them in.

Fucking twank. After all that bloodthirsty talk, he decided to let the others clear the Ruins and set himself to tending the priest and the Seeker.

Given the fact that neither Ord nor Kayna had a weapon, they'd very sensibly chosen to remain behind while the men with the steel did their work in the Ruins.

Even now, Ord watched them, squinting through the rain as the wave of men on horseback charged into the Ruins and disappeared behind the jagged stone remnants, Levelers out and axes waving.

Ord wasn't entirely sure there were any Tickers left in the place, but that wasn't for him to decide. He squirmed in the saddle, his sodden robes sticking to all kinds of uncomfortable places and making him grimace. Yet another mark against going to war—very little shelter from the elements.

He sighed and looked at Kayna. "Well, then. Shall we proceed?"

But Kayna was staring straight ahead, and any semblance of that usually calm demeanor had fled her face. Her dark eyes were pinched in the corners, as though she were suddenly in pain, and the skin around her mouth had gone a strange, ashen color.

He frowned at her, then followed her gaze and spotted a lone rider heading back for them. Looked like Breakwood. Returning to give them an escort, then? Well, the man was an absolute cockabout, but Ord found himself somewhat cheered that the sergeant would care enough to come back for them.

"Ord," Kayna said, her voice thin and tense, eyes still on Breakwood. "This won't make any sense to you, but the time has come for me to leave you. And you need to run."

Ord drew his head back. Let out a confused cough of laughter. "Run? Where?"

Kayna finally tore her eyes from Breakwood and fixed them on Ord. And in those eyes was a depth of knowledge that couldn't be articulated but which suddenly made Ord's guts twist up tight.

"Ord, I know you don't trust me," Kayna said, her breathing coming out strong and rapid, her words like shotstones. "But if you want to live, you need to run!"

Almost by reflex, Ord clumsily pulled his reins to the side, and the horse beneath him danced a little jig, confused, perhaps sensing her rider's burgeoning panic. "I don't understand."

Kayna's eyes flicked to Breakwood again, now just a hundred strides or so from them and closing fast. When they went back to Ord, they were wide and terrified. "He's going to kill us both! Go!"

Ord's jaw dropped, horse nickering, prancing. Kayna's mouth worked with a few unsaid words, and then she bared her bright white teeth and yanked her reins, cutting behind Ord and spurring her horse down the hill at an angle.

"Lochled!" Kayna screamed as she tore past Ord.

Why on earth was she yelling for Lochled?

Ord's head whipped this way and that, trying to piece things together so that it made sense, but they just didn't seem to want to fit. Had the Seeker gone mad?

Then he saw Breakwood turn, angling his horse to intercept Kayna. And his face was all coldhearted violence and clenched teeth. Not the face of a man sent to escort unarmed people.

"Feor, have mercy," Ord breathed out.

No. It couldn't be. And yet he was watching it happen. Watching it happen, and he couldn't move, found himself paralyzed in the saddle, the horse stamping out a nervous circle so the whole world turned around and around in Ord's vision—ruins, running men, rain-lashed fields, Breakwood galloping hard after Kayna, and Kayna trying to get away, stealing terrified glances behind her.

"Whoa," Ord rasped at the horse, then the shock and fear cleared just long enough for him to lean forward in the saddle and bolt for the Ruins.

"It's fucking happening!" Rony yelped, right in Lochled's ear, but it barely made him twitch. Where had she come from anyway?

He stood in his saddle, blood humming, every pulse seeming to carry with it some substance other than blood. Something fiery hot and ill-controlled. He was watching Breakwood chase after Kayna's horse, and there was nothing in it that looked friendly.

"I told you—" Rony gasped.

Lochled jerked his head at a sudden smattering of Leveler reports from the Ruins, followed by the screaming of men. He felt not an ounce of panic. Just that tingling heat growing out of the center of him, rooting through his arms and legs, making his scalp feel warm and his head like it was rushing.

"It's a fucking mutiny," Lochled seethed, half-enraged, and half-overjoyed. He hadn't heard that tone come from his voice in so long that he almost didn't recognize it. He hadn't succumbed to this reckless, all-consuming sense of violence since . . .

Lochled thrust a hand to the Ruins. "Rony. Find Hotsteel." He snapped his eyes to her, and Rony pulled back from him like he'd become a complete stranger. "Don't let them kill Hotsteel."

He grabbed the pommel of his saddle and swung into it, heeling the horse and working it into a gallop before his hind end ever touched leather. Breakwood was closing the distance with Kayna's horse as she fled hard aleft, and it didn't look to Lochled like she was going to get away from him—she rode well, but Breakwood was a horseman from hell.

But it wasn't about her.

All he had eyes for was Breakwood.

All he could feel was his blood singing a war song in his veins.

Rain coming down in sheets. Cold on his skin. Seemed like it should've been steaming, he felt so hot inside. Screams from the Ruins—men's screams, wounded men—and more Levelers going off, and now the clash of steel, all mixed with the thunder of his own horse's hooves.

Breakwood might have started off a hundred strides distant from Kayna, but his fierce riding had closed that gap to arm lengths. He was coming in on her right side now, leaning hard in the saddle, looked like he had his reins in his teeth and his steels in his hands, and intended to take Kayna's back at a full gallop.

Lochled, calm in the saddle, seemed to hover over his horse while it surged on fast, so fast, but never fast enough to cross the few hundred strides between him and Kayna before Breakwood's steel would start falling.

Kayna cast more rapid glances behind her as Breakwood reached out toward her with a long-knife.

Breakwood's right foot slipped from the stirrup, and Lochled knew he was about to jump—and when he jumped, he was going to land with his knife in Kayna's back and his axe-head under her throat.

But just as Breakwood launched himself across the narrow gap between the horses, there was a swirl of black robes, midnight cloth billowing like a cloud of soot. With one foot still in the stirrup, Kayna swung all the way down until her free leg skipped off the ground beneath her, her back smashed flat to the horse's left flank, while Breakwood soared through empty air.

Lochled couldn't even see Breakwood as he fell, the grass was so tall. Just a flailing boot, an arcing bit of weaponry, and a shimmer and rustle of the sodden grasses as he went tumbling through it all.

All that time, Lochled never took his eyes off of where Breakwood was—didn't even bother to glance at Kayna, though he detected her swinging back into the saddle out of the corner of his eye. And it didn't look like she had any intention of stopping now. She was still riding hard aleft, as though she were going to find the ocean on the other side and run straight through that too.

Lochled, however, slowed.

He soothed his horse with a gentle word and pulled back on the reins, standing tall in the saddle and looking down into tall grass, maybe fifty strides distant from him now, where Breakwood had taken his fall. Lochled took up his Leveler then thrust it securely between his saddle bags. He wouldn't be needing it.

For a moment, nothing moved in those grasses, and Lochled had the thought that maybe Breakwood had gone breakneck, and that thought was oddly sad to him, like being promised a sweet apple but receiving only the worm inside.

But then up Breakwood came, breaching the tops of the grass and thrashing like a blackfish caught between two harpoons. Lochled was a bit shocked to see Breakwood come upright appearing whole and unbroken by his crash to the ground. He'd expected at least an out-of-socket shoulder or some such, but all Breakwood looked was pissed.

Breakwood craned his neck aleft for a moment, watching the retreating figure of Seeker Kayna Redstone cresting a hill a ways away and slipping out of sight, seemingly forever. Then

Breakwood glanced back and spotted Lochled. The man's slim face slipped into a snarl, tiny mouth moving rapidly with words that Lochled couldn't hear and didn't care to. He fixated on that mouth of Breakwood's, that mouth that Lochled hated so fucking much. Thinking of cutting it a little wider—ear to ear, in fact—just made the head rush come on stronger.

Feor help him, he'd fought so long not to give in to this feeling, not to lose his hard-won control over the daemons of his flesh. But he needed those daemons now. Everything had gone to shit, and in the shit pile is where the daemons danced best.

"So you want to be next, uh?" Breakwood roared at him.

Lochled stopped his horse. It smelled the terror. Smelled the fury. Shook its head and let out a worried snort.

Breakwood stooped. Came up again, this time with steels in hand. "That it, then? That as close as you're willing to come to me, you old fuck?"

Lochled swung one leg up and over, then hopped down. Grass and mud and wetness. Rain coming down in more of a drizzle now. Thick mist starting to rise up from the grasses. He started walking. Unrushed. Unruffled. Steady on.

Breakwood's puckered little mouth tried out a savage grin. "You don't got Hotsteel here to protect you anymore, Lochled. Or should I say Redskin? That what you're trying to be right now? Relive those glory days, uh?" Axe and knife, held ready. "You think you still got the sack for it? I don't think you do."

Lochled kept striding forward. Wading through the grass like hip-high water.

"Draw your steels then!" Breakwood screeched, feet dancing. "Let's solve this once and for all! You're nothing, Lochled! Fucking nothing! You're not Redskin anymore! You're just a sad old man whose glory days are far behind him. What do you think you're going to accomplish here, uh?"

Breakwood had his steels gripped right and proper—ready for fighting. And he was no slouch. Lochled would never accuse him of being a worthless fighter. Just a worthless human being. But weren't they all?

"You're right, you know," Lochled said, finding that with each word, with each pulse of his singing blood, his reality was changing. It was like he didn't really see with his eyes anymore. He was seeing with his heart, and his heart felt like a lump of metal that'd been heated up to running red. Everything the color of fire. "I'm a fucking relic. Times have changed." Lochled stopped and shook his head. Looked skyward, a touch wistful. "There's no pitched battles anymore. Can't just go mad in the middle of a field like we used to. Now it's all hiding round corners and triggering Levelers."

Breakwood spat. "A fucking coward's weapon, some say. Your favorite one too."

Lochled shrugged. "I don't have it now."

"Draw your fucking steels then!" Breakwood snarled again. "Let's see how you earned the name Redskin!"

Lochled still didn't draw his weapons. Had his hands on them, though. Ready. Feet planted. Steady. Body balanced, tense and loose all at once. And so hot, all throughout him. So ready to *release.* Those damned daemons were pulling at their chains, and Lochled was slowly letting them slip through his fingers, link by link.

"It was a little village, actually," Lochled said. "Name of Flat Rock."

Breakwood looked confused, like he was trying to decide how pertinent this was. For just a moment, his dancing feet slowed.

Lochled chuffed, humorlessly. Shook his head. "Weren't even soldiers I killed. Just people. Farmers and wives and children—all of them. We were just so angry, and I let my daemons dance, and it felt so *right* in the moment. But after it was done, all I felt was shame." He looked down at the ground. "And men called me Redskin and slapped my back and made up songs, like I'd actually fought. But I hadn't. I'd just let myself go mad and killed a score of weaponless people. Wasn't even that hard to do. Like scything wheat."

Breakwood stared at him. Then tilted his head back and let out a great big, hilarious guffaw, right from the belly. "This whole time! This whole time I thought the songs might have some tiny shred of truth to them! But you didn't even do anything brave!"

Lochled nodded. Can't deny the truth, after all. "Nothing brave about it at all. I just . . . went mad." And he started walking toward Breakwood, slow, measured. "It's just been . . . so long . . . since I let myself go." A great, shuddering breath in his chest, and then, barely more than a whisper: "Since I let them run."

Breakwood's tiny mouth sank into a frown, even as Lochled's twitched up, feeling that mad rush of glee as the daemons started to run, and he let them go, gave them freedom to do their dark deeds.

He was smiling as he drew his steels.

CHAPTER 33

There were many prayers to Feor for self-preservation, but all Rony's mouth could work out was "Shit."

She dropped from her horse, heels scuffing off slick wet stone, nearly toppling her. Got her balance back, Leveler in her hands already open and a charge going in. Her eyes up, in those brief few seconds where her Leveler wasn't ready, expecting some madman with an axe to come hurtling from around every stone.

Levelers burst further off in the Ruins.

Someone yelled something brave and commanding, but Rony couldn't tell what. Probably the usual shit that men say when they're pissing their pants but can't admit it. Usually comes out as telling everyone else how to be brave.

Rony snapped the weapon closed, moving forward through drizzle and a mist that seemed to have sprung up from the stones themselves. Everything was just jagged shapes and leering figures. She heard Hotsteel's voice bellowing, but couldn't really pinpoint where it was. Somewhere ahead, maybe to the right, but the Ruins echoed treacherously.

"Shit. Shit." She was trying to move fast, trying to get to

Hotsteel like Lochled had ordered her, but there were just so many angles, so many places where a man could hide and then plant his steel in her head and hack her down.

I tried to tell them. I tried . . .

But she realized it was a lie. She'd done the very thing that she'd been so afraid of everyone doing to her: she'd doubted herself.

"Shit."

No more.

She threw herself around a corner, finding nothing but some shadows moving through the mist—too far to see if they were friendly or not. And who the hell was friendly at this point? Had Breakwood convinced Hamfist to mutiny? Was it Hamfist's whole squad or just him and a few of his boys?

Never again.

A breathless whisper came from her right. She jerked and didn't hesitate—couldn't hesitate, because hesitation was death, and she had to attack. That was the only way she could foresee living through this: being meaner, nastier, and quicker than everyone else in this tumbledown pile of rocks.

She burst through a breach in a wall, came skidding to a stop, Leveler up . . .

No roof. Four stone walls. All of them painted with running red and squiggly lines of white—tendon, gristle, or guts, she couldn't tell. Pieces of a man, some of them still moving. He had most of his chest and one arm still attached. Oh, and his head too. Trying to speak, but it was just a fruitless, gagging whisper.

Who was he? She didn't even recognize him. His face was covered in gore and seemed melted on one side and agonized on the other.

"Shit." She moved past him. She couldn't help him. Didn't

know who the hell he was, but he wasn't one of Rony's, and they were the only people she cared about.

Someone screamed, high pitched: "I'll fucking bash your head in, you—" then the same voice started screaming, right along with a nasty, wet thwacking sound.

Rony scrambled over a crumbled wall, slipping and sliding across moss on the other side. Found herself in something of an alley. More unidentifiable shapes in the mist, but this time she didn't shy from them. She plunged toward them, finger on her trigger bar, hoping to see Cryer, or Licker, or Ponts . . .

The shape suddenly sped toward her. Face emerging out of the gloom. Knife in one hand, axe in the other. Maybe one of Hamfist's men. He came skidding to a halt when he saw that Leveler trained on him, face going from gleeful malice to child-like terror in an instant.

He tried to backpedal. "No, wait, don't—"

Rony triggered her Leveler. Sent his lower half skipping out from under him. She had to. She didn't know whose side he was on. And she wasn't going to take that kind of chance. She had to be the maddest and the quickest.

She tried to move past the halved man, breath roaring in her ears, in her throat—sounded like a storm on the ocean. The body thrashed, head coming up, pouring blood from the mouth and squealing something terrible, which cut off in a bloody gurgle.

"Shit!" She kicked the face as hard as she could, snarling while she did. Then stomped it simply because that seemed like the thing to do to get the fucker dead. And after that, he was.

Gasping, careening off derelict stone walls, taking a turn here, trying to follow the sound of Levelers, then registering that she wasn't hearing them anymore—she was hearing the keening notes of steel on steel.

It was only then that she looked down at her loop and realized she only had a few push charges left.

"Shit, shit, shit!" She fumbled a fresh charge into her weapon, feet still moving.

Gloomy and gray and bleak and drizzling. Stones and mist.

Another shape coming toward her, seeming to materialize, and she didn't stop moving toward it, but she held back, waited to see that face, to see if it was someone she recognized—

"Aaagh!" Licker came swimming through the mist at her, and she damn near cut him down, only managed to hold off at the last second.

Licker raised his axe toward her, eyes wild, teeth bloody, but held up and then slumped to the side. "Rony," he whimpered. "Rony, help me!"

She realized his other hand—still gripping his knife—was pressed to his stomach. Hands coated in red and, behind them, squirming, pulsing organ flesh trying to escape through a great slash across his belly.

"Shit!" Rony leapt forward, grabbed him under the armpits, and he melted into her. Even a small man is fucking heavy, though, and Rony staggered under the weight of him.

"Behind us," he whined.

Rony snapped a glance behind, saw two shapes, and heard the pounding of footsteps. Couldn't really put her finger on why, but she was suddenly enraged by it. Held the Leveler with one hand, the other still clutching Licker's body to her.

"I'm helping my friend!" she shrieked at the shapes.

Faces. Not the ones that mattered.

FWOOM!

Right through the middle of them, but each of them catching a few shotstones that sent them spinning and howling, and one of them almost sounded like he was singing, the way his voice yodeled up into an almost pretty pitch.

"Fuck! Bastards!" Rony couldn't recharge her weapon while holding Licker at the same time, and she desperately needed something sharp in her hands, so she tossed the Leveler and snatched her long-knife out. "Where's Hotsteel?"

"Oh, Rony!" Licker burbled. "Help me, oh, no, help me!"

"I'm fucking trying!" She shouted in his blood-speckled ear. "Shut up! Shut up!"

"Rony!" A new voice—blessedly familiar.

A massive, brown-skinned shape hurtled out of the gloom, but she'd already recognized the voice and tilted her blade away from it. Cryer's face, all fearsome concern, a great nasty gash across his jaw with the muscles bulging out.

He snatched her by the shoulder and hauled. "Get in here!"

She stumbled, nearly dropped Licker, then just held on to him and let Cryer carry them both, dragging them over the remnants of a wall into another room with no roof, the walls only about chest high, save for a little corner of it where Hotsteel had himself backed in, someone's Leveler in his grip.

Licker howled, and as though it needed stating, Rony gasped out, "Licker's hurt!"

Hotsteel damn near stabbed her with the flint of his eyes. "Where's your fucking Leveler?"

Rony gawped at him, the question seeming inconsequential given Licker's guts hanging out. "Dropped it."

"Damn it, woman!" He was stomping toward her now. She found Licker wasn't in her arms anymore and glimpsed Cryer easing him down to the ground, shushing him. Hotsteel's Leveler hit her in the chest, and she realized, somewhat belatedly, that she was supposed to take it.

"Here!" Hotsteel barked, even as her tingling fingers closed around the wet wood. He shucked a loop of charges from around his neck and slung it onto Rony's. Only two charges left on that one. Plus the three in Rony's loop. "That's all we got! Now get on a fucking corner and turn everything that moves into meat!"

"Yes, hef," she choked out, feet moving while her mind caught up. She registered Ponts holding a low bit of wall with his greatshield posted on top.

Ponts jerked his head. "Here, Rony!"

Voices started going off all around her, muffled and bouncing in the mist and stones, so that Rony could hardly tell where they were coming from.

"We got no quarrel with you, Cryer and Ponts and Licker!" a voice shot through the mist—no voice that she recognized.

"Shh, shh," Cryer gently shushed Licker.

"They opened me up!" Licker was squealing. "Aw, no, they opened me up!"

"Just toss us the captain's head, and we can all figure out a way through this!"

Rony wondered why they hadn't included her in the offer. Just Cryer, Ponts, and Licker.

"Rony!" Ponts's hissing voice. "Come here!"

"You'll have to come take it yourself!" Hotsteel screamed into the mist. "You traitorous fucks!"

"Put it back inside me!" Licker begged. "Please! Put it back! It's not supposed to be outside of me!"

"Rony!" Ponts's hand yanked her into the cover of his greatshield. His eyes were fixed out into the mist. "I think that's one of them! You see that shadow there?"

Rony raised her Leveler to her shoulder. She knew Lochled had told her not to fire it like that unless she wanted her shoulder popped out of socket, but it was too hard to aim from the hip, and she didn't have charges to spare.

"I don't see anything!" she whispered.

"It's just there!" Ponts's finger pointed, but frustratingly, didn't point to anything but mist. What the hell was he seeing out there? Should she just shoot the mist?

"Where's the priest?" Hotsteel's voice jabbed at the back of her neck, making her spin around to face him.

"I don't know," she snapped.

"What about the Seeker?"

"Breakwood tried to kill her, but she ran off."

"Fucking animals. It's a fucking mutiny!"

Rony stared at him for a brief moment. *You don't fucking say.*

"It's moving again!" Ponts said.

Rony whirled around, and this time caught the tail end of what Ponts saw: a shape, oozing its way over a pile of rocks like a man on all fours trying to sneak up on them.

Rony pulled the trigger bar. Yellow dust erupted, combining with the mist. The clattering of shotstones. "Oh, unholy fuck!" she gasped. The kick of the thing was something like what she imagined taking a full punch from Cryer might feel like.

"Did you get it?" Ponts asked.

"I don't know." She sank, trying to get some feeling back in her hand while she recharged the Leveler, fingers clumsy and numb and tingling like she'd fallen asleep on her arm.

The stones in front of their faces shattered just a slim second before the report of a Leveler reached them. Rony yipped like a dog and dropped below the wall.

"Ah!" Ponts reared back, but maintained his grip on the shield. "Fucking bastard!" One hand keeping the greatshield in place, the other trembling as it went up to a ruin of flesh on the left side of his face. Pocked and puckered all along the jaw and cheek and up into the eye, blood running, eye gone all red and visibly swelling by the second.

Rony reached out and touched his leg. "You still with me?"

"Ah." Ponts's breath hissing in and out. "Ah, fuck. Ah." He tried to touch near his eyes but jerked his hand away. "I can't see out that eye. My eye's ruined." He sounded unnaturally calm about the whole thing.

"Give it back to 'em!" Hotsteel barked in Rony's face. She realized he'd ducked into cover with her, and the two of them were now all smashed up, back to chest, like a pair of lovers.

Rony gritted her teeth, came up—not wanting to feel that punch to her shoulder again, but wanting to die even less—and triggered the Leveler. The shotstones went punching off into the misty dampness. Someone swore, but no one screamed.

Rony eased back down again, breathing hard through her clenched teeth, her shoulder throbbing like the bones were on the verge of cracking, her arm barely able to move. "I can't do that again!"

Hotsteel growled, thrashing to his knees and snatching the Leveler out of her arms. "Hope you're better with your steels, then!"

"Cryer," Licker's voice, much quieter now, and shaky. "Cryer?"

"Shh. Steady on, Licker."

"Cryer? I'm sinking, my friend. Don't let me sink."

"You're not sinking. You're right here with me."

"It's swallowing me up," Licker whimpered. "Swallowing me up like the Big Black Mud."

"Captain Hotsteel!" Was that Hamfist's voice? "There's no point in dragging this shit out! We've got you surrounded anyways. Do the honorable thing and come out so we don't have to fight it down to the death! Been enough killing already!"

Hotsteel writhed around, keeping his body low, then came up right alongside Ponts. "Lemme see your eye."

Rony realized she still hadn't replaced the Leveler Hotsteel had taken from her. Scooped up her knife and axe and lay there, leaning up against old, wet stone, staring at old, wet steel. She'd yet to fight with them. All this time they'd been dangling from her belt, and she'd never thought to ask Cryer or Lochled—or any of them, really—how you were supposed to fight with the damned things.

All she could do was mimic what she'd seen the others do and hope for the best. So she gripped the knife underhanded in her left so the blade ran along her forearm. Gripped the axe close to the head. Mostly it was slashing, she thought. But then sometimes stabbing and hacking.

Simple enough, really.

"Captain!" Hamfist yelled again. "This is your last chance to end this peacefully!"

"Peacefully with my head off," Hotsteel remarked, ripping a piece of cloth from his own tunic to bandage Ponts's eye.

"Don't make us— Wha—!" A brief silence, wherein Rony's widened eyes clicked this way and that, wondering what the hell was happening out there in the mist. Then came a scream. The type of scream that only meant one thing. The type of scream that Licker'd probably made when he'd been opened up.

And then silence again.

Everyone in their little redoubt had stilled. Hotsteel with the bandage half wrapped around Ponts's face. Cryer, hovering over Licker. Even Licker had quieted, though his breathing was coming in short, sharp gasps.

"Hamfist?" someone called out from the mists. "You all right?"

More deathly stillness. So quiet you could hear a raindrop on moss. But mostly it was just their breaths, all of them, heaving in and out. Ears straining for the slightest sound.

Then came a clash of steel all at once, slick and slashing,

singing, crashing, so rapid and sharp you couldn't even hear the voices that screeched between the blows; they just kind of melded in with the rest.

Someone over to the left side of their redoubt started shouting. "They're on our flank! Attack! Attack!"

A shout rose up—hair-raisingly close. They must've been only a handful of strides from where Rony and the others were hiding. Rony had no choice but to lurch to her feet, brandishing her weapons, gut in knots, knowing that all she had now was ferocity. No skill. Only sheer meanness.

"Cryer!" Hotsteel screamed. "Leave him!"

Cryer didn't leave Licker, but he stood up, straddled the half-dead man, and drew his own steels, whirling the axe in his hand like a child with a toy and just as casual. Rony moved to Cryer's side and had barely set her feet when a man came hurtling over the stone wall to Cryer's left, already hacking and slashing before he was anywhere within range.

Cryer didn't give up his position over Licker. He pivoted, caught one downward axe blow with his knife, deflecting the attack, then cleft half the man's head off with his axe.

Rony spotted another coming and screamed, because that's what you do when people are running at you with sharp objects. The other guy was screaming too. Cryer turned, swinging his axe, but the man ducked under it and came up, face-to-face with Rony. He looked downright shocked about it, and then Rony realized that she'd stuck him in the belly with her knife.

He grabbed her hair, almost reflexively. Pain lanced through her scalp, her head twisting to one side as he started to fall and drag her down with him. He gasped and hiccuped, the edge of his axe blade trembling at her throat. Wound up getting his hand right on her chin, so she sank her teeth into it until she felt tendons pop between them and blood boil up in her mouth.

He wailed as though the bite had hurt his feelings more than his hand, but he let go of her hair, and at that point she was fucking furious. Had the taste of the man's blood in her mouth, and it was something between disgust and a strange, loathsome excitement that she felt when she reared back, spitting the man's own blood in his face. She started stabbing at his belly with that knife again as they went all the way to the ground, her on top of him, squeezing him tight with her thighs, grip on the knife getting slick as she plunged, plunged, plunged, then used the axe. Now going back and forth: stabbing him and hacking him and . . .

"Look out!"

Cryer had the haft of a man's axe in his hand, the blade just a few inches from having split Rony's head like a gourd. He heaved the man backward, but was then caught by a handful of his comrades. Rony jolted to her feet, taking a glance around and wondering how the hell so many of them had gotten in.

FWOOM!

Parts went flying. Attention shifted to the side. Hotsteel, crouched behind the edge of Ponts's shield with the Leveler, but whatever he'd just spent must've been his last, because he threw the Leveler at the face of the first man who jumped toward him, then drew his steels.

It was really only by pure chance that Rony saw it all, because it happened so quick. Like a lightning bolt—you just have to be looking in the right place at the right time.

One more shape came careening over the stone walls, just like all the others except . . . not. Where the others had scrambled clumsily, this one flew. Where the others had snarled and shouted, this one was silent. Where the others had brandished their weapons and waved them about as they closed the distance, this one wasted no movement. Every blow was a killing blow.

Rony found herself backpedaling, even though it was killing the people that were trying to kill her. Something told her it might not stop when it'd finished with them. Might just keep on going until it'd shredded the whole world to bloody tatters.

A man raised an axe, face all fearsome, like he could see the victory before it happened. Then his upraised hand simply fell off at the elbow, and he stumbled into the shadowy figure, just to be rebuffed like he weighed nothing at all, flying back with dismay all over his face.

Another tried to juke around to the back of the shadow, but he slipped in all the wet, went down and caught a hard boot that smeared his nose all across his face and turned his mouth into a toothless red hole.

Three came on at once, and the shadow was buried. Axes rose. Knives fell.

Cryer lurched forward, and Rony almost stopped him, wondering what the hell he was thinking getting closer to that thing, until she heard him shout: "Lochled!"

Ponts and Hotsteel screamed, charging forward along with Cryer, so that the greatshield slammed into the backs of men too distracted or terrified by their new attacker to react and were now being pushed inexorably closer, into the flashing machinery of pointy tips and sharp edges.

Rony blinked, brandished her steel, and forced her feet to start moving her *forward*.

A man's leg went out from under him. He gave a whoop, landed on his back, and tried to roll and crawl away. Then his whole body stiffened, back arching, face scrunching up. Down in the darkness, under all those bodies, something fearsome writhed into the light. And if Cryer hadn't named him only seconds before, Rony didn't think she would've recognized him.

He clawed his way up the downed man's body with his knife

and axe as aids. One final thrust of the knife, right into the base of the man's back, and then the stranger rolled and slashed another's hamstrings with his axe, causing him to drop to a knee. Jammed the blade into another man's groin, even as he hooked the first around the neck with his axe and ripped his throat out in one quick yank.

The jumble of bodies seemed to realize that they didn't even have a target for all their hacking and stabbing and started to right themselves, heads coming up, but bodies still tangled together.

Ponts and Hotsteel pressing the greatshield into one side of the scrum, Cryer hacking his way into the other side, Rony right behind him. And it was Lochled himself between them—no, not Lochled, because this man had no soul in his eyes, and if ever there was a picture of what a man looked like when he'd released all control to the daemons of his flesh, this was it.

This was Redskin.

Rony had a man's back and almost distractedly decided to stab it. Felt the blade nick the bones, slide roughly between the ribs. The man spasmed and tried to fight her, but she couldn't quite take her eyes off the bloody figure to her right—kept thinking he might start swinging at her just because she was there and had a beating heart.

The man she'd stabbed wrenched around, snarling and gnashing his teeth, and Rony's knife slipped out of her grip. The man seized her by the throat, brought his axe up, but then stiffened, eyes wide. A pair of weaponless, red hands snaked around his head, fingers sinking into the eyeballs, something squirting out the corners that made Rony think of her mother's berry mash.

The man squealed, then was tossed to the side like so much trash, those red hands deftly plucking knife and axe from where they'd been buried in his shoulder blades, like they'd been stored there for safe keeping.

Rony realized that the rest of her squad wasn't even striking out anymore. They were pressing and pushing and cramming the last half-dozen men into that corner of stone. The war cries of their attackers were turning to bleats and begging. Strange how men just forgot and expected some sort of mercy when they'd intended to give none themselves.

Well, they were getting none now.

It wasn't even a fight anymore, it was just slaughter. Murder.

The thing she'd known as Lochled didn't seem to mind. Axe into the top of a skull, knife through the jaw. Ripping them out. Slashing sideways in the same motion, catching two others, on either side, who gazed into the misty, drizzling heavens with a sort of abandoned look on their faces. But the thing known as Redskin didn't care. It only saw unprotected throats and slashed both of them at once, then hooked them behind the necks and hauled them out of the way, like a reaper tossing wheat into windrows.

"Mercy!" someone was screaming. "Mercy!"

Someone tried to grab at Rony, and she almost sliced him up, but saw his desperate face—one of Hamfists's men, she was pretty sure—and held back, just for an instant.

"I didn't want to—" were his last four words before an axe hooked his throat, tilted him to the side, and a knife flashed three times right into his heart as he went down.

I didn't want to either.

"Lochled!" Hotsteel screamed. "Spare the rest!"

The rest? There were only two more, Rony realized, and she wasn't even pushing on them anymore. Neither was Cryer or Ponts, and Hotsteel seemed to just be trying to get Lochled to stop swinging. And was failing utterly failing.

"Please, for the mercy of Feor!" one of the men begged, even dropping to his knees, but that only made it easier for Lochled to kick him straight in the chest. He dropped backward, tangled up with the second survivor.

"Spare the rest, Lochled!" Hotsteel tried to say again. "We can't hold the Ruins with just—"

Lochled might have listened. But Redskin sure didn't.

He actually turned and looked at Hotsteel, and a flash of fear came over the captain's eyes, like he'd realized for the first time he wasn't in control anymore. Redskin, or Lochled, or both, or nobody, they just kept staring at Hotsteel as they grabbed one man by the hair—not even a man, a boy not more than sixteen rains—and slid the knife, terribly slow, right through his neck. Then a quick flick, and the knife slashed through the front, and the body dropped right at Hotsteel's feet.

"Whassat, hef?" a voice rasped. Rony knew it was Lochled, but it didn't sound anything like him. And he said it at the same time he was grappling with the last survivor, trying to pin his flailing arms down while he straddled him.

"I said," Hotsteel began, but the last survivor hollered something fierce right at that moment, and by the time he fell silent, Lochled had already gotten his knife right up under his chin and was pressing it in. "No, I said . . . !" But the knife kept going in, and Hotsteel's face fell with disappointment and exasperation, like he'd finally figured that trying to save the one just wasn't worth the effort. "Fuck it, never mind."

"No!" the man said, his voice strange and clenched with the knife sliding into him. "Prease hehrp—uh—guh . . ."

All the way to the hilt. And Lochled's blood-slicked hand crawling over the man's cheek to fasten itself over his mouth, strong and sturdy. Lochled leaning on the man's face, body quaking as though with unspent energy. Muscles in his arms jolting and jumping as he pressed, pressed, pressed against the man's face until there was nothing left but flesh and slow, oozing blood.

CHAPTER 34

"Sorry, hef," Lochled's mouth said, while his eyes darted around, searching for another target, and finding themselves disappointed. He'd just up and got started, and now they were all taken apart. Made him feel like a child whose new toy had broken to pieces right after he'd gotten it.

His blood was singing a song of insanity and chaos—because that's all war ever is. Made all the parts of his body hum. The taste of blood in the air as he heaved for breath. The stink of spent push charges. Every inch of his body slick with sweat and rain and blood. It clung to his eyelashes and gave the world a reddish tint, and Lochled found it beautiful.

There's beauty in horror sometimes. If you're doing the horrors. That beauty is release. Not caring. Not having to worry about morals or whether someone should die or be spared. Such clunky, awkward thoughts, but when you removed the restraints, well, then things flowed so nice and easy.

But as he looked for more to kill, and found none, the rush of hatred and madness began to wane. Left him feeling wrung out and queasy and jittery, like he'd feel after a night of too much drips and too much scaef. Like he'd felt the morning he'd left Bransport.

"Did I get 'em all?" Lochled croaked out, spinning in a slow circle, axe and knife drooping lower and lower in his hands, dejected.

Someone was saying something to him, but it was muffled and confusing, especially on his right side. He reached a hand up, fingers sticky on the haft of his axe, and probed the right side of his head, realizing only then that his right ear was simply gone. Big slash through the side of his face. That might be contributing to his lack of hearing.

He turned to face Hotsteel, and for a bare second, saw just another live one, like a problem that needed correcting. But Hotsteel was beaming at him like a proud nephew meeting a beloved uncle, and that calmed Lochled's bloodlust even more.

"Can't hear too good," Lochled interrupted his captain, motioning to his face. "On account of my ear gone missing."

Hotsteel leaned in, grabbed him by his shoulders, and raised his voice: "Redskin, you fucking mad bastard! You got every last one of those mutinous fucks! I knew it was the right call pulling you onto this crusade! I knew you'd come through for me in the end, you legendary madman!"

Redskin.

Madman.

That head rush of hatred and aggression, now simmering down to a warm feeling of acceptance, and this time, there wasn't any shame to it. Lochled had done the right thing, hadn't he? Killed the fucking mutineers—it doesn't get more right than that. No, there was nothing to be ashamed of at all. Not this time.

"Good fucking man!" Hotsteel shook him, then looked down. "Shit, Lochled, you're wounded something fierce!"

Lochled frowned down at himself. His gray sergeant's tunic wasn't so much a tunic anymore. Wasn't so gray anymore either. And it wasn't just one wound—it was a handful of them, all across his torso and arms. Slashes mostly, it looked like. Blood coming out strong in a few places where he could see muscle trying to push its way out. One in particular, right in his side, seemed to be making it hard for Lochled to stay standing. So that was odd.

"So I am," Lochled husked.

"Oh, thank Feor it's you!" Ord's voice made every last one of them jump and raise their weapons again. The priest tumbled clumsily over the low point of the wall, not seeming to care two shits for everyone's steels, he seemed so relieved. "I only heard voices, and I prayed, I hoped that it was you!" He looked aghast at the carpet of bodies. Looked even paler than normal, except for two red rosettes on his cheeks. "It was a mutiny! Did you get them all?"

Hotsteel shook Lochled's shoulders again, sending stabbing pains through . . . well, pretty much everywhere. "Old Redskin here certainly did! Now, we all had a hand in giving those fucks their just wages, but he did the heavy lifting, that's for sure and certain, and I don't believe it's too much to say that we might all be dead if it weren't for him. You just remember that, Theynen—you remember that for when you report back to the Church!"

Rony took an aggressive step toward the priest, using her knife to point at him. "Where'd you go, uh? Kayna got chased, and you just ran the opposite way."

Ord looked flummoxed. "I didn't have a weapon."

"Ord did the smart thing," Lochled grunted at Rony. "No offense, Theynen, but you couldn't have taken Breakwood."

Ord apparently had no shame in admitting it. He nodded hastily. "But you . . . did you . . . ?"

A raised eyebrow. "Did I kill him?"

Ord was silent, waiting for the response. Seemed everyone was.

"Yes," he said. What a stupid question. Of course he had.

"Swearnsoot," Hotsteel exclaimed. "You are a fucking savage. But we still have an ambush to plan. Rony, get some bandages for our man here!"

Rony still had her knife pointed at Ord. "Gimme that tunic . . . Theynen." The last part added begrudgingly.

Ord touched the fine, vermilion tunic. "Why mine?"

Rony's eyes narrowed at him. "'Cause it's the only cloth within sight that isn't covered in blood and filth. That's why."

"Oh." Ord looked sadly down at it, but acquiesced and pulled it off. Just an undyed shirt beneath, clinging wetly to Ord's skin.

Rony took it from him with a little snap of her wrist and a glare, and set to knifing it to usable tatters, which did seem to cheer her up, even as it depressed Ord.

"Captain," Cryer said, wiping blood from his steels. "There's only the five of us."

Five? Lochled frowned, and glanced around for the sixth that should've been there, then spotted Licker's face, half buried under a blanket of limbs. Eyes open, but not there—Lochled could tell.

"They killed Licker," Lochled said dully.

"Sit down," Rony said, pulling him toward a sizable chunk of stone with a flat top.

Lochled obediently sat down, still looking at Licker. Realized he still had his steels in his hands, but didn't want to let them go.

"Don't have a choice in it," Hotsteel replied. He said it like it pained him to admit it, but the glint in his eyes said different.

"Our Seeker is gone. We've no way to communicate and change the plans. Steadman Thaersh is likely already pushing the Tickers our way, and expecting us to hold these ruins."

"Five's enough," Lochled said as Rony took a wide strip of Ord's tunic and wrapped it tight around the worst of his belly wounds.

"Damned right," Hotsteel declared. "We hold these ruins, to the death if we have to!"

Well. That sounded just fine to Lochled. Wasn't like he had anyone to return to. Marna gone. Libby gone. Any hope at a normal life—gone. Ashes, all of it.

"Ord," Hotsteel was saying, his voice urgent and heated, really feeling the heroism, Lochled thought. "You'll need to help us. Go climb that tower to the top and keep a lookout. The second you see *anything*, you come running and tell me." Hotsteel immediately spun to Cryer and Ponts. "Cryer, gather the horses and hide them. Ponts, help me collect weapons—we need all the Levelers and charges we can find."

Oh, Captain Hotsteel was feeling it for sure. Death-defying captain, courageous in the face of insurmountable odds. Just like his father, Othis. Lochled remembered Othis being like that in the Pan. Remembered how fired up he was. How fired up he got Lochled, just before Flat Rock.

Everyone hurried off.

Lochled blinked, and realized it was just him and Rony. Well . . . them and all the bodies. She glanced up at him as she tied off a bandage around the gash in his shoulder. Pretty little cully with a face all drawn with violence and befouled. Eyes hard but haunted. Almost made him want to say something soft to her.

No softness. Not yet.

She had a weird look to her, though. Kept glancing at him, then looking away.

"What?" Lochled grunted, looking down at himself. "I fucking shit myself or something?"

It was only when he looked down that he saw his vision blur, and he realized there were tears in his eyes. He blinked, a little confused. Brought a finger up and wiped at one eye, but it was all just red, red, red. There was no cleaning him off now. He was soaked in it.

"Huh," he said. Didn't make any sense. He was fine. Completely fine—except for all those cuts and slashes and pokes all over his body. But he didn't feel anything at all that might've turned into tears. It was like he'd been put in another man's body. His mind felt right as sunshine, but his damn eyes wouldn't stop with the briny leakage.

"Don't worry about that," Lochled said, confusedly continuing to wipe his eyes. "Not sure what's . . . got into my eyes. Blood, I guess."

"Thought you didn't let nobody call you Redskin," Rony said as she turned his head and inspected the wound that had taken his ear off.

Swearnsoot, but he just couldn't stop his eyes. Every time he got them clear, they went on and welled right up again. He kept telling himself, *Stop—just stop fucking crying.* But he couldn't. Might as well holler at the wind to stop blowing. Seemed he had no control over this. Had to just wait it out.

Rony had stopped moving and was looking down at his steels. "You want to put those away, hef?"

"What?" Lochled looked down again—and again had to blink through tears to see clearly—and realized his hands were working the grips of his weapons like you might wring a chicken's neck. The point of his knife and the blade of his axe making little, trembling circles, not too far from Rony's chest. "Oh." Lochled slid them, a little mournfully, back into his belt.

He looked at his bloody hands. Didn't know what to do with those two bruised, cut-up appendages. Felt weird just having them lay there. So he decided to busy himself with his flask.

"There you go," Rony commented, cutting more strips from the tunic while Lochled drained his flask in a go. "Get yourself calmed."

Lochled gasped when he finished. Nearly gagged, but held it.

"Ah," he shook his head. "I don't need to fucking calm down." Suddenly mad again, mad at Rony maybe. He wasn't quite sure. But mad. Or at the very least, trying to be. "Who knows how many of those fuck Tickers are going to come crawling right up our hindsholes, uh? Calm's not what we want."

"In control, then?"

"No. Not that either. We don't want any of that. Not yet." All the cuts and jabs and gashes, skinned knees, bent toes, stubbed fingers, bloody knuckles—all the ignoble shit that no one mentions after a fight but are guaranteed to be there—they all started speaking up. But the fight wasn't done yet. Wasn't time to lick wounds and relax. No, he was just getting warmed up.

He grabbed his scaef pouch. Only remembered the little phial in there when he brushed it with his fingertips gathering up a monstrous wad. He was surprised it had survived all the thrashing.

"Why come Hotsteel can call you Redskin, but no one else can?"

Lochled's jammed the scaef into his cheek. "'Cause he's the fucking captain," he growled, tonguing the wad into place. Realizing that wasn't the whole truth. "And his father was there with me."

"Did his father kill a hundred rebels that day too?" Rony was speaking in a preoccupied way, but Lochled could feel she had more interest in it than she was letting on.

He sat there, just his eyes moving, tracking Rony's as she worked. He was waiting to feel some defensiveness about it all—the very reason why he hated it when people called him Redskin, hated it enough that he'd fight to the death about it. But what was he really fighting when he got all mad and drew his steels about it? Just himself. He was battling his own shame, like it was a thing that could be hacked to pieces.

But you know what was funny about the whole thing? He didn't feel the same sense of shame now, after having admitted it to Breakwood. This whole time, keeping it locked away, only he and Othis knowing the truth—well, that had made it worse. Sins are shackles, the priests always said. And confession is the key.

"He didn't kill nobody," Lochled suddenly said. Rony stopped working at binding his head wound and looked at him. "He just pointed me in the right direction." He frowned. "Seems that's the way of things, uh? The captain points, and I kill."

Rony swallowed. "Well. Orders is orders."

"Right." Lochled said, still frowning.

Rony started to wrap his head again.

"Weren't any rebels either," he said, causing her hands to stop again. She leaned back, her eyes a tad narrowed at him. Didn't speak. Didn't ask questions. She was a sharp cully. She could tell Lochled was confessing. And a man confessing simply needs to be given space for those cumbersome words to come out. "Not in the town, anyways. Not like the stories and songs say. Rebels hit us hard, took out a good bit of the company. And that was all that was left of our squad—just me and Othis. We were supposed to track and report back, but we didn't do that. Fact is, we didn't really track. We lost that trail and couldn't find it again. But there was a town not too far from where we lost the track. Flat Rock, it was called. And I guess . . . well, I guess we just figured that's where they had to be."

He chewed on the scaef a few times. Spat to the side. Some of it dribbled down his chin, but he didn't even bother to wipe it away. No point to it now—scaef or blood, could you even tell the difference?

"They weren't," he finally said, eyes looking at the Ruins around them, but his mind seeing something entirely different—that sad little village in the middle of the Pan. Those sad little people. Never had a fucking chance. "But it didn't seem to matter at that point." He sniffed. "Daemons were already running, I suppose. Hard to put 'em back on the chain once you let 'em loose."

Rony swallowed audibly. Then leaned forward, her movements a little quicker. Wrapping the bandage. Tying it off. "You followed your orders. That's all."

Lochled nodded, but didn't say anything. Wasn't it an odd thing that he had more regrets from following orders than disobeying them? That thought gave him pause, and he realized with a bit of a sinking feeling that he couldn't really make that comparison. Because he couldn't think of a single instance where he *hadn't* followed his orders.

Come close a couple times. But he always caved in the end.

And perhaps oddest of all, the ones he'd wound up caving to seemed to be the ones he regretted the most.

"But that's what a good man does," Lochled muttered, not sure if he'd said it to Rony or to himself. Eyes flashed over to hers. "He follows his orders. He does what his betters tell him. Right?"

Rony nodded, lips a little tight. "Far as I can tell, hef. Good soldiers follow orders."

Lochled's brows twitched down. He hadn't said *soldier*, he'd said *man*.

But then the slap of panicked footfalls suddenly grew on them, followed immediately by Ord's voice, shrill and hissing, trying not to shout: "They're coming! They're coming!"

CHAPTER 35

Ord had already established—to himself and everyone else—that he was not in fighting shape. Or running shape. Or, really, a shape good for anything besides reading and pontificating. Yet he still found himself somewhat shocked at how quickly the combination of running and panic will suck the air right out of your lungs.

"They're coming!" he wheezed as his feet landed him back at their redoubt. Barely had the breath to say it again: "They're coming!" He collapsed against the wall, gasping, his vision already sparkling, and he'd only run maybe two hundred strides—including the stairs down the tower.

It took him a moment to realize only Lochled and Rony were present. He frowned, fresh fears colliding in his brain. "Where's Hotsteel?" he hacked out. "Where're the others?"

"We're right here!" Hotsteel's voice hissed out just before he emerged from around a corner with an armload of Levelers, glaring shotstones at Ord. "Keep your fucking voice down!"

No *theynen* attached to the end of it, Ord noticed, somewhat distractedly. Gave him a bad feeling that he wasn't seen as the priest anymore. Which would make him what? Another soldier? Feor help him if that was the case. Feor help them all.

Ponts followed behind his captain, lugging a handful of loops with not that many push charges among them all. The two of them vaulted the low part of the wall, and suddenly Ord felt like he needed to be inside that protective little womb of stone as well. He tried mightily to haul himself over the wall where he was, but he was just so spent already. Face burning with embarrassment, he shambled quickly over to the low point and continued his pathetic struggle until he was suddenly borne up by a pair of massive hands and carried over the wall like a child.

Cryer set him down none too gently on the other side, then slid over himself.

Ord bent at the waist, panting. "There were"—pant, pant, pant—"more than a dozen of them."

He managed to stand himself upright, at which point Hotsteel thrust a Leveler into his chest. Shocked, Ord stared at it, his hands not quite willing to accept the offering.

"Take it, Ord," Hotsteel growled. "We all have to fight this time."

"But . . ." Ord stammered. "I don't . . . I can't . . ." But he did. His hands reaching up and taking the ugly weapon, caving to the pure immensity of Hotsteel's will.

Hotsteel spun on the rest of them, rapidly passing out Levelers. "Everyone get down. We're going to let the fuckers get in close—real close, and then we're all going to open up on them at once. We only got a few charges left, so choose your shots and make 'em count." He looked right at Ord. "If you can take out one Ticker, that's good, but if you can take out two or three with a single blast, that's even better."

Ord had fixated more on the command to get down. His back hit the cold, wet, stone wall, and he slid down, still trying to catch his breath, still trying to come to terms with the enormity of what was being asked of him.

No one else seemed to give a shit. They didn't seem to register the pure, unadulterated terror all over Ord's face—and he was taking no pains to hide it—so he had to conclude they just didn't care.

"Six against a dozen or so," Hotsteel said, clutching his own Leveler while he squatted and waddled like a duck to the far corner of the redoubt.

"*More* than a dozen," Ord huffed.

Hotsteel gave no response to that. He propped his Leveler up against the wall, then fished about in a satchel at his side, coming up with his spyglass. Their position was toward the edge of the Ruins so that only the remnants of the tower blocked their view from the rolling fields aright.

Ord watched the captain with a morbid sort of fascination, hoping against hope that something would miraculously change. Maybe Hotsteel would discover that they weren't Tickers at all, only scouts from Gunnar Thaersh's detachment. Which would be highly unlikely, as Ord had relatively good vision and had spotted the naked, olive skin. But such was the depth of his desperation at the moment.

Hotsteel extended the spyglass and eased the top of his head over the wall, peering through the instrument into the fields. "They're coming from arights, you said?"

Ord hadn't said, but they were. "Yes."

Hotsteel didn't move. Still as a spider in a web, waiting, observing.

Cryer had his scaef pouch out. Crammed his mouth full. Passed it around. Ponts took some. Lochled took some. Rony declined but took a long draft from her flask and passed it to Lochled. Everyone getting their minds right, which apparently meant addling them to the point that they weren't afraid of what was coming.

"Ord." Cryer was holding the flask out to him.

Ord stared at it for a moment, a handful of ridiculous things coming to the edge of his tongue but not quite making it out. He wasn't a priest right now, was he? Because priests don't go about with Levelers in their hands. Priests aren't called upon to kill—only to help justify others' killing.

No, he had to act like a soldier now, apparently. And, taking a cue from the others, figured maybe a stiff nip was called for.

He snatched the flask. Put it to his lips and drank it like it would grant him immortality. It burned his mouth, burned his throat, left it feeling chapped and raw when he came up for air.

Cryer took the flask back. "Say a prayer for us?"

A prayer? Ord stared blankly. How could he say a prayer? He wasn't a priest right now. Had just taken a massive slug of drips. Had a Leveler in his hands. And now they wanted a prayer?

They did. Cryer's expression was earnest. As was Ponts's and Rony's and—most shocking of all—Lochled's.

"Uh. Right, then." Ord blinked a few times. "Feor . . . uh . . . Feor intercede for us. Protect your servants"—*Servants of what*— "in the hour of our need"—*Need to murder? Need to survive?*—"as we attempt to faithfully carry out your will." *Will for what? What does Feor even want from us? Why has Feor even put us in this position?* "Swearnsoot. Swearnfire. Swearnchild. Light unto light."

"Light unto light," the others murmured.

And right on the tail of that prayer, Hotsteel broke in: "There those fuckers are."

Ord found his thighs clenching together against a sudden urge to piss himself. The prayer was forgotten. All eyes turned on Hotsteel now. All hands grasping weapons.

"I count fourteen," Hotsteel murmured. "Running that first hill, about five hundred strides out and closing. They're moving with purpose." A pause. A glance over his shoulder at the remains of his soldiers. "They got two stone-throwers with them."

"Don't give 'em a chance to use 'em," Lochled whispered, face scrunching down, eyes like an animal peering out from a clouded brow, all his top hair a shambles and hanging in his bloody face. A nightmare made flesh.

"Looks like they're planning to skirt the edge of the Ruins, right past us," Hotsteel said, motioning with one hand to the right of their position. "We'll need to wait until they're right on us. No one trigger off until I do. We'll hit them all at once, right in the flank, dump as many push charges as we can, and then take them with steel."

"Can't get too close," Lochled said. "You get too close, they can use their powers to toss you around."

Hotsteel shimmied about irritably. "Then I guess we'll just have to hit them faster than they can react, uh?"

"Will they be close enough to topple stones on us?" Rony worried.

Lochled shrugged. "Seems to me they got to be right on top of the stone to hurl it. So don't let them get too close to stones either. Tricksy bastards."

Cryer scrunched a little closer to Ord. "Is it charged?"

"Is it charged?" Ord repeated dumbly. He stared down at the thing in his hands, realizing again what a ghastly foreign object it was to him. He fumbled about at the brass fittings, trying to mimic what he'd seen others do, and was almost glad that he managed to break the thing open. Then he wished he hadn't. Maybe if he demonstrated more ignorance, they'd decide to simply let him hide.

Cryer pointed to the breech. "Spent. Take that out."

Ord's fingers trembled so bad that he could hardly get a grip on the spent charge. Finally managed to get his fingernails on it and yanked, cracking them. Another reminder that he wasn't supposed to be doing this.

"Here." Cryer held out a fresh push charge. "Put that in and close it up."

Ord obeyed, completely numb. Seemed his hands and feet weren't sensing like they should. All he seemed to be able to feel was fear. He closed the Leveler.

"Watch out for that trigger bar," Cryer said, almost as an afterthought. "Don't trigger it into the middle of us. Can't afford any mistakes now."

No mistakes. Right. As if Ord could do anything without cocking it up. Didn't they realize he was more of a hazard than an asset?

"Wait," Hotsteel breathed out, long and slow and unhappy sounding.

Silence. Everyone holding their breath.

"They've stopped," Hotsteel whispered. "About two hundred strides out. Shit."

"What are they doing?" Ord eked out.

"Don't know. They're all just standing there now, like spooked deer."

"Do they know we're here?"

"How'm I supposed to know what the fuck they know?" Hotsteel snarled under his breath. "They shouldn't. They *shouldn't* know a fucking thing. Fuck . . ." Hotsteel stayed fixed to his spyglass, his chest starting to heave more rapidly now. Was that fear? Was Hotsteel afraid? Oh, Feor. How bad was it when Hotsteel was afraid?

Bad. So bad.

"You're breathing too hard," Cryer whispered to Ord, not even looking at him. "Steady on. Deep, slow breaths."

Ord tried. Failed miserably. Couldn't catch his breath, like his lungs were being crushed under the weight of his terror.

"Fuck, fuck, fuck." Hotsteel suddenly ducked behind the wall, snapping his spyglass closed. He spun, putting his back to the wall, wide eyes slashing across his tiny squad. "They know something. They're setting up their stone-throwers." Hotsteel glared at Cryer. "Did you hide the fucking horses?"

"Yes, hef." Cryer looked fearful too.

"Right then," Hotsteel snarled. "Shields it is. Cryer and Ponts—"

Thwack!

Ord let out a high-pitched yelp as stone dust blasted his face. "Stones! They're throwing stones!"

And then the air was filled with buzzing bees and exploding stone and dust and tiny pebbles that stung at Ord's face no matter how small he made himself. Realized he was wailing, all curled up into a ball. Caught himself only at the last second from hitting the trigger bar with his knee.

Hotsteel screaming at them: "Cryer! Lochled! Take the right! Ponts and Rony! Take the left! Advance!"

Advance?

Ord let out a mad shriek with the last of his air and tried to rise up, but was grabbed by the collar of his shirt and yanked back down, face-to-face with Hotsteel.

"Not you, you daft twank!" Hotsteel roared in his face. "You stay with me!"

Up and over.

And just like on the boat, Rony felt herself carried over the wall as though by a force beyond her comprehension—because she sure as shit wouldn't have chosen to do it herself. But Ponts was going over, his massive greatshield clattering and scraping across the stone, and she'd been told to follow, so follow she did.

"You with me, Rony?" Ponts yelled over a sudden cacophony of strikes against his shield, like a hundred blacksmiths hammering at once.

"Here!" Rony gasped, finding herself hugging Ponts's back end, smelling his sweat and his sodden clothes.

"Moving!" Ponts shouted and began to surge forward, the muscles in his arms and back writhing and bulging as he carried the greatshield just a thumb or two from the ground. All Rony could do was stay stuck to his hind end, trying to time her feet with his so they didn't trip each other.

She couldn't see shit. Didn't know where the fuck they were going except that they'd been told to go left. Was Ponts even going left? It didn't matter. She had a hard time caring about anything but staying as small as possible behind the shield while the air all around her whistled and whined and menaced, promising instant death if she made so much as a single misstep.

Cobbles under her feet. Then moss. Then grass. Then cobbles again.

She managed a glance to the right, saw Cryer and Lochled moving just the same as she and Ponts. Then they disappeared—a wall of mean gray stone separating them.

The tower. Were they already at the tower? She looked up and saw the half-toppled height of it. Dared to feel a glimmer of hope that they were making good progress before a shotstone smacked the wall and she felt needles across the side of her face and neck.

"Fuck!" she shouted, hand snapping up and feeling the bleeding, puckered flesh, little bits of rock stuck in her.

"Y'all right?" Ponts yelled. "You with me?"

"Here!" she said again. "Fine!"

"We're clearing the corner in three paces. Two paces. One pace." The wall of the tower fell away, and she spotted Cryer and Lochled again, a little farther out this time, as they continued to the right under a hailstorm of shotstones. "Give 'em something to think about! Give me a fucking breath!"

Rony didn't know exactly what that meant, but felt she could intuit it well enough, so she thrust her Leveler out and triggered it with a big bone-jarring eruption of yellow.

"Forward!" Ponts shouted, surging into a weight-hobbled jog, Rony barely able to stay with him, nearly falling on her face, only pure panic animating her feet to catch up. "Stopping!" Ponts slammed the shield down, chest heaving. "Again!"

Rony recharged her Leveler with a quickness born only from complete lack of thought—fingers moving on terror-fueled instinct. Snapped it closed. Thrust it out—

Whap!

She screamed, watching the two outermost fingers of her left hand fly off her, the flesh beneath showing pale and pink and then rapidly welling with red. "Fuck! My hand!" She jerked the appendage back into cover, hissing and spitting until frothy drool came dribbling down her chin.

"Bastard!" Ponts yelled, and Rony didn't know if it was directed at her or the Tickers. "Never come out the same side, Rony! Never!"

"My hand!" she repeated, somehow indignant that Ponts didn't seem to care.

Ponts twisted around and fixed her with a look entirely foreign to his usual gormless state. "Will you live?"

"Yes!" As she stared at the shaking, bleeding remains of her hand.

"Then fucking shoot them!" Ponts bellowed, spit speckling her face.

"Ahh!" she screamed back at him, even as she switched her grip on her Leveler—wounded hand now on the trigger bar—and thrust her Leveler out, this time on the opposite side of the shield. The jar when she let loose sent a shock of pain through her wounded hand that made her vision sparkle and her head swim.

"Moving!" And Ponts was off again, no time for pity, no time for fixing wounds, it was only fight or die now.

Reason fled. Fear and aggression reigned supreme. She had no sense of esteem, no sense of shame. She made weird noises, just for the fact that they seemed to make the pain more bearable, seemed to enable her to keep putting one foot in front of the other. Her whole arm feeling on fire now. Another spent charge tossed off. Another fresh one seated.

"Don't stop!" she shouted in Ponts's ear, barely even heard herself for all the sounds in her head and all around her, the rattle of shotstones against the greatshield sending tremors all through Ponts's big body so that she could feel them on the other side. "Going over!"

"What?"

Rony didn't explain—no time for explanations either. She went high with her Leveler, having to stand on tiptoe to get it over the top of the shield, and then triggered it again.

A brief respite in the rate of fire—had she actually hit one of them?

"Gotta stop!" Ponts panted, groaning, straining at the weight of the greatshield.

"Don't you fucking stop, you feebling!"

A cry of rage from Ponts, or maybe it was the pain in his arms and back, but he kept it moving for another ten strides before he nearly toppled them all in a heap. Sank the bottom of the shield into soupy mud, gasping.

Another recharge. More meaningless noises from her throat. Off to the right again, this time, and then she realized she was running out of charges fast.

"Only two more charges in my loop!" she yelled. "Where are we?" She looked around, her whole body shaking now, knees quaking and threatening to give out. She could see Cryer and Lochled, maybe a hundred strides from them, still moving, starting up the rise of the hill.

Ponts unhooked his left arm from the shield and shook it out. Rony could actually see the cramps seizing his forearms so hard that his big hands had contorted into gnarled claws.

"Gotta keep moving, Ponts!"

"I fucking know!" He didn't seem to be able to ease the cramps, but if she could fight with a hand half blown off, this big bastard could manage a fucking cramp. So she started smacking him on the hind end like a horse that needed spurring.

He swore at her something fierce but locked himself into the shield again and forward they went, out of the sloggy mud and onto the rise of the hill.

One foot in front of the other. Recharge. Come out a different side. Trigger.

Again.

CHAPTER 36

This isn't so bad, Ord thought, huddled behind the stone wall.

Not so bad, so long as the fighting stayed out there and Ord stayed in here with Captain Hotsteel.

Ord prayed fervently for the safety of the soldiers trying to get up that hill. But more because he was worried about what might happen to him if they failed. He knew this was crass and selfish—unseemly for a priest—but he wasn't particularly interested in self-betterment at the moment. Self-preservation would do just fine.

"Get 'em!" Hotsteel urged from behind the wall, just his eyes taking a peek over every once in a while. "Get 'em!"

"Are they getting them?" Ord worried.

"Not quite. But . . ." A pause.

"What?" Ord twisted around, but he wasn't anywhere near brave enough to stick his head up, so he tried his best to surmise what was happening from the look on Hotsteel's face. And it wasn't good.

"Bastard fucks," Hotsteel seethed, snatching up his Leveler. "Ten of 'em, cutting a line around the back of the hill, trying to flank." He seemed to thrash about for a minute as though caught in a dilemma. Then he stuck his head up, one hand cupped to his mouth and bellowed, "Lochled! Watch your flank!"

Did he really think he was going to be heard over all that racket? Ord's ears were still ringing with the din of those shot-stones clattering off the metal shields—couldn't imagine what it was like to be right behind them.

Breathless moments passed where Ord's panicking need to know what was happening battled with his desire not to make the man beside him too angry. Hotsteel seemed like the type that could get dangerous rather quickly.

"Shit," Hotsteel whispered. "Shit and fuck. They're not even . . . shit." He ducked back behind cover, putting his back to the wall. Started grabbing up spare charges and cramming them into the loop around his neck. "They're not even interested in Lochled and Cryer. They're coming for us."

"For us?" Ord squeaked.

After all that prayer too. Maybe he should've offered a few up for his own self-preservation. Decided that there's no time like the present and bowed his head, but only got as far as, "Feor—" before Hotsteel smacked him on the shoulder.

"No time for prayers now!" Hotsteel had five charges in his loop. Grabbed a spare loop with three left in it and slung it over Ord's head. He didn't particularly want them, but it seemed a poor time to say so. "We're going to have to take them out ourselves. Look at me."

It was a needless command, as Ord was already looking at him, so he did his best to comply by widening his eyes and looking more intense, though it felt more fearful than anything else.

"The others won't make it back to us in time, you hear me?" Hotsteel was nodding, his mouth in something between a grin and a grimace. "No one's coming to help. It's down to us."

Perhaps the precise words Ord had been hoping *not* to hear. But he found himself nodding, even as he let out a little mewl of terror.

"With me," Hotsteel snapped, then turned and did that little duck waddle until he was against the wall facing the flanking Tickers.

Ord went with a more basic approach and simply crawled on hands and knees.

Hotsteel took big, deep breaths. Steadying himself. Leveler held to his chest. "Good thing is, none of 'em have weapons, and we do. Bad thing is, they have powers. So you'd best kill them before they get close enough to use them."

Ord's head was bobbing again in a nonsensical nod, even as, inwardly, he wondered if he could actually do it. It was so much simpler to point the way and give blessings and assure men that they were doing Feor's will and count the bodies afterward. But this? This was entirely different. Now *he* was going to be required to kill.

They're just fucking animals, he tried to tell himself, but it tasted like lies, and he knew it.

All of a sudden, Ord's dogma for Church doctrine seemed a flimsy thing. Had he ever really believed them? Or had he simply never been in a situation dire enough to make him confront his conscience over it?

Hotsteel squirmed around until he faced the wall, then eased up, tilting his head over to one side so it was just a single eye and the side of his face that peered over the broken stone wall. He sat there for a time, a torturous time of indecision, so many thoughts whirling through Ord's head, doubts about everything from what he actually believed, to who he actually was, to what he could actually do.

Possibly the worst time to have doubts, but there they were all the same.

Hotsteel made a little chuffing noise. "What're they doing?" he murmured. To himself? To Ord?

"I don't know," Ord offered in a fit of unhelpful confusion.

"They're passing us by." Hotsteel had a mystified tone to his voice.

"Oh, thank Feor," Ord gasped.

"Where the fuck are they going?"

"Away? Are they running away?"

"No, they're not running away, you—" Seemed Hotsteel had bitten off an insult. "They're skirting around towards the back of the Ruins."

Fresh horror struck Ord in a gut-melting wave. "Do you think they have more stone-throwers stashed somewhere?"

"Doesn't matter," Hotsteel decided. "We've gotta stop them anyhow. Gotta cut them off before they get in the Ruins with us." He eyed Ord up and down. "You ready?"

No! And yet Ord's head nodded.

Hotsteel clapped him on the shoulder. "Good man." And with that, he vaulted over the wall and took off running toward the hill with a surprising agility that Ord envied to his core in that moment, left him thinking how he might've traded a few hours of study here and there for some running and weapons training.

But then his own feet hit the slippery cobbles on the other side of that wall.

Feor, help me . . .

Ord was in it, and there was no way out.

"They're slowing!" Cryer shouted over his shoulder.

Lochled could hear it, and it sounded like victory. The

Tickers had given them a good whopping only a few breaths before, but that seemed to have sapped them hard, and now the shots were coming only once every few seconds.

Lochled checked his loop. Nothing left. Only what he had in his Leveler. He'd have to make it count for everything. After that, it would be axes and knives, and even with Lochled's daemons running amok in his veins, making his blood sing, he knew that a close-in fight with these warrior-Tickers was a bad bet.

"Right, then," he grunted, shuffling in place as Cryer took a few more strides. "How close are we?"

"Fuck if I know," Cryer bit back. "Can't see shit but shield!"

Lochled glanced to his left, to where Rony and Ponts were. The big boy looked exhausted. Rony was being ginger with one of her hands, and he glimpsed that it was all marred and bloody.

Lochled leaned out of cover just enough to spot the stone-thrower Ponts was facing down and realized with a jolt of dread that they were less than fifteen strides apart. Hadn't they heard him say not to get too close? Maybe they didn't even know—probably couldn't see any better than Lochled and Cryer.

"They're getting too close," Lochled said, then grabbed Cryer by his belt and pulled on him. "Stop here! Don't get any closer!" Then he raised a hand to his mouth, took a big breath, and shouted to Ponts and Rony so hard that his vision sparkled: "*Don't get too close!*"

Ponts must've heard him, because his face whipped around, all confused and questioning. And then he suddenly exploded off the earth like he'd been yanked up by an invisible giant. Shield went whizzing through the air like a thrown plate, and Ponts flailed as he seemed to accelerate skyward nearly thirty strides and then abruptly changed course and plummeted back to the ground.

Lochled's breath caught in his chest as Ponts slammed into

the earth so hard that Lochled swore he could feel the impact in his feet.

Rony was standing there, all alone and uncovered, and it was by pure force of instinct that Lochled lurched toward her, unthinking, moved only by a sudden and irresistible urge not to see the girl get shredded, not after coming so far, not after all he'd done to try to keep her alive.

Rony snapped her Leveler up and triggered it. Lochled watched the two Tickers manning the stone-thrower go spinning, blood jetting from a dozen wounds.

Lochled realized his error in a terrific flash of horror—he was two strides out of cover now. Spun to his right, bringing his Leveler up, gut tightening as he fully expected to be lanced with shotstones for his foolishness.

The Tickers manning the second stone-thrower were pivoting—not toward Lochled, but toward Rony.

He pulled his trigger bar, yellow dust spewing from his very last push charge, and lurched back toward the cover of Cryer's shield. Through the mist of yellow, he caught sight of one Ticker sagging bonelessly over the stone-thrower so that the long, brass barrel of it suddenly jerked skyward. But the second Ticker was still alive, grabbing at its downed comrade, trying to shove its body off the contraption, attention now moving to Lochled.

Lochled screamed like all the daemons in him and threw his Leveler carelessly to the side as he charged, leg muscles tightening painfully, hands snatching at his axe and knife. Cryer yelled something at him, but he was too far gone by then. Sometimes when you make a fast decision, you just have to bear it out and deal with the consequences.

The live one gave the dead one a final shove. Freed the contraption. Seized the handles of it, started to bring it around.

Lochled would never make it in time—still five strides off.

But five strides was the distance he would stand from a block of wood and hurl his axe for practice. So he snapped his arm up and flung the axe with everything he had.

It whirled through the air. The Ticker watched it coming, cringing. It smacked him on the face, but the blade didn't bite—only left a gash across the thing's bald skull. But Lochled hadn't stopped moving. Four strides—the Ticker reared back on instinct, clutching its head as rivulets of red streamed through its fingers. Two strides—Lochled leapt, knife up.

He fell a tad short and landed on the Ticker's legs. Felt the body topple even as he rolled through the dirt and grass, then found his arms and legs scrambling forward, reaching for that Ticker as it struggled to right itself, bringing its hands up, hands that could push things and pull things and throw them all about . . .

Lochled just started stabbing. Couldn't think about where best to actually land a killing blow. All he could think was that he needed to keep it from using its powers on him. So he stabbed it in the leg. Clawed his way up its body. Stabbed it in the groin. Thrust himself further. Stabbed it in the chest—felt the blade nick off a rib, opening the thing's side. Stabbed once more, right below the thing's armpit—

And then he was flying.

Rony watched Lochled go catapulting into the air and was stuck in a threadbare moment of indecision—run to Ponts, or run to Lochled, or run toward the last Ticker?

Her hands were already moving, even as her feet danced, undecided. She broke her Leveler open and batted about her loops for a spare charge, confused at the emptiness until she realized she'd spent her last one.

Lochled hit the ground with a grunt, about five strides from the Ticker he'd knifed, then went tumbling a few more.

She couldn't go to Ponts, couldn't go to Lochled—not with the Ticker still breathing. So she screamed up a war cry that broke her throat and charged at it, dropping her Leveler and ripping her steels out.

Cryer had released his greatshield, letting it topple to the ground with a faint metallic thunk, pulling his own steels out.

The Ticker still had Lochled's knife buried in its armpit. Blood was spouting from the wound, covering the thing's side, but it somehow managed to haul itself to its feet, swaying and stumbling. Saw Cryer coming at it and raised a single hand. Cryer jolted to a stop, like he'd run face-first into a stone wall, and toppled backward. But he didn't go flying.

It's weak, Rony thought, and that was all the thinking she needed to convince her feet to keep moving—a tiny shred of hope that she could get to it without it pummeling her into the ground like it'd done to Ponts.

She realized she'd run out of air with that last scream of hers, was running with her mouth gaping and her teeth bared like a savage, lungs aching for air. Sucked it in, parching her already dry throat. She was close, so close—ten strides away and closing.

The Ticker whirled on her, head bobbling like it was barely keeping itself upright. Raised a hand, and she cringed, but didn't stop running at it. Something struck her, like being battered by waves in the surf, but she didn't lose her feet, hunched down into the force of that invisible blow, feeling the flesh of her face and arms pressed tight against it.

And then she was free, running again, the wave of power depleted.

She made it another three strides before the Ticker raised its hand again, and she prepared to hold fast and charge after its next assault on her, but it never got that far. Hand hanging in the air, palm out toward her. The Ticker's head lolled on its shoulders and tilted backward, eyes going up to the heavens as its body went limp.

Rony's steps were already slowing from exhaustion by the time she clattered her way over the contraption and the dead Ticker next to it. She stumbled to a stop right over the one with the knife still stuck in its armpit.

Rony didn't think it even saw her. Eyes had already gone sightless, staring at the gray skies over their heads, though its chest still hitched, hitched . . . and hitched again, one final time before it let out a grinding breath of air—no voice for the pain it might've felt, just wind in its throat, and then nothing at all.

Rony's own breath rattled in her throat. Rage and worry pouring over her. Thinking she might just hack its skull to bits for the fuck of it, but her eyes were pulled back around to the slope of the hill. Cryer already up and running again. Lochled struggling to his feet, looking woozy.

Which only left Ponts.

"Ponts!" she yelled, as though screaming his name would make him pop up lively and smiling. Her eyes tore around her, trying to see where his body had fallen. The run, the dodging, the fighting—she was all disoriented.

There. A big shape of tangled brown limbs in matted wet grass.

"Ponts!" she yelled again, less energetically, worry turning to downright dread. She wanted to run to him, but her legs, even as good a runner as she was, were tired and unwieldy. She forced them on anyway, hips screaming with the effort of stepping high over all that grass that clung to her like thousands of tiny fingers trying to hold her back.

Ponts was laid out, limbs all twisted and wrong. Hips facing one way. Shoulders facing the other. Head cranked around in still another direction, so he was looking right at her when she collapsed at his side.

He blinked. *Still alive!*

"Ponts . . ." she huffed out. "What's wrong? Where are you hurt?"

Ponts blinked again, eyes swimming down in the direction of his body. "I don't know," he said, his words thin and breathy. "I don't . . . I don't hurt at all."

Rony's eyes tracked over his twisted body. How the hell could he not be hurting? One of his leg bones was sticking out his thigh, she realized with a start. He should be feeling *that* at the very least.

"Rony," Ponts wheezed out. "I think . . . my back's broke."

Rony seized one of his hands. The way it was all tangled up, she couldn't even tell if it was his right or left hand. It was cold and limp, like a dead fish. She squeezed it hard, only thinking to elicit some sort of response. "Can you feel that?"

"Feel what?"

"I'm squeezing your hand."

"I can't . . ." It looked like he tried to shake his head, but all he managed was a minimal twitch. "Can't feel nothin' at all."

"Squeeze my hand. Just think about squeezing my hand." She waited for it, prayed for it, hoped for it. Ponts looked like he was trying, his face all pained and grimacing, but his hand never even gave the slightest tremor.

Ponts's face relaxed, giving up.

"Don't give up!" Rony snarled at him.

"Rony, listen—"

"Rony!" Cryer's voice bellowed.

She whipped around, still clutching Ponts's hand. Spotted

Cryer and Lochled moving back down the hill, Cryer waving hastily at her.

"Come on!" he screamed at her.

"Rony."

But she was already rising, already releasing that hand. A painful glance back at Ponts. "I'll come back, I swear!" she said, taking a hesitant step away from Ponts.

"Rony, you have to tell . . ." He struggled for more air.

"With us!" Cryer screamed at her. "Rony, you fucking rot-slit! With us!"

Lochled and Cryer were halfway back to the Ruins now.

"I've got to go," Rony said, taking another step away—that same sense of being pulled by something beyond her control.

"Tell my father . . ." Ponts groaned, then fought for breath again.

"I'll be back!" she cried out, feet moving her away now, as inexorable as the tide. "Just . . . just . . ." She meant to say *hang on*, but it all seemed so ridiculous that she simply turned and ran.

Realized halfway down the hill that she was sobbing. Tears in her eyes as unbidden and unfelt and buried beneath the savagery as the ones she'd watched stain Lochled's eyes earlier.

CHAPTER 37

Ord had no idea how he'd gotten separated from Hotsteel. If he could have retraced his steps and rectified that mistake, he certainly would have. They'd jumped the wall and started running, and then Hotsteel had cut around one side of a pillar, and Ord the other.

At which point, Ord realized it wasn't a pillar, but the end of a wall.

And yet he kept on going because he was too scared to think. Wound up taking a few turns through the maze of tumbledown structures, and only realized he'd become thoroughly separated after he caught the tail end of the column of Tickers slipping around a corner ahead of him.

He'd plastered himself to the nearest wall, looked behind him, and realized he was utterly alone.

He opened his mouth to cry out for Hotsteel, but then snapped it shut again. If he yelled, the Tickers would know he was there.

Leveler clutched in both hands and held to his chest. The big, heavy barrel of the thing pressed against his face. He needed to breathe but was terrified it would be too loud, so he was taking these tiny little whiffs of air that weren't enough and made his skin prickle, vision all clouded down to a single pinpoint.

There were many prayers to Feor for salvation, but all Ord's mouth could work out was "Feor."

He slid along the wall, in more or less the direction he felt he should have been going. That slide was about all he could manage amid a perilous hope that he might be able to break his fear-born paralysis and find Hotsteel again.

"Feor." Not even a whisper—just his lips moving.

He reached the corner. Did he dare turn it?

Through a strength of willpower heretofore unknown to Ord, he squirmed his way in a tight circle so he was facing the wall, and leaned out, tiny breaths buffeting the cold wall smelling of stone and, now, his own sour breath.

He couldn't see the Tickers anymore.

"Feor," he whined, then thrust himself around the corner, but wasn't quite ready to relinquish the paltry sense of safety he got from the stone, so he moved with his shoulder sliding along the wall. Feet moving down this narrow lane through the Ruins, along which he'd last spotted the Tickers—oh, why were his feet moving this way? Why couldn't he go the *other* way?

Leveler at his hip, trembling fingers tense upon the trigger bar, further down the lane he went. Grass and weeds sprouting from between mossy stones. Unsteady feet negotiating the unlevel ground. No strength in them. Barely even any feeling in them.

He reached another tumbledown intersection of ancient alleys and stopped, looking over his shoulder. He was surprised to find that he'd successfully navigated a whole twenty strides. He realized he was immensely proud of himself for this feat. Hell, he might actually be getting a bit *brave* . . .

He turned back forward, and that concept died, stillborn.

A Ticker, not five strides from him, stood in the middle of the intersection.

"Feor!" Ord yelped, yanking his Leveler up from where he'd unconsciously let it sag, finger scrambling about for the trigger bar—damn it, where was the fucking trigger bar?

The Ticker's face snarled silently at him, rows of blunt little teeth bared, its hands snatching out, fingers clawing, and Ord felt the Leveler wrenched out of his grasp by an invisible hand . It went spinning away, slammed into a wall, and went off with a great plume and scattering of shotstones.

"Ah!" Ord yipped, empty hands reaching out for his lost Leveler, feet dancing, and warm wetness cascading down his thighs.

The Ticker stood there, glaring at him, not a shred of clothing on its wiry frame, only a necklace of bright blue beads hanging low on its chest.

Ord waved his hands, mind feeling like it'd been struck by lightning. "Wait-wait-wait! We don't need to fight! We can—"

The Ticker took a step toward him, making him cringe back into the wall, whimpering. Its hand came up, finger's closing into a fist and Ord felt a crushing pressure all around him, encompassing every inch of his body, and his feet left the ground as he was born up into the air, screaming—

FWOOM!

The Ticker came apart.

Ord tumbled to the ground, hit a stone, and rolled, pain lancing through his ankle, then an impact to his forehead that turned the world as white as staring into the sun and a horrendous ringing in his ears.

There was all sorts of yelling that bled through the ringing, but Ord could make no sense of any of it, only that it must've been people, because Tickers don't talk. He could feel his hands grasping at wet stone, wet grass, his fingernails scraping and filling up with dirt.

Chaos enveloped him. The chaos of his own shocked body, the chaos of his mind all torn to tatters, and the chaos without: booming Levelers, screaming and cursing, clattering shotstones, and a huge, heavy impact of stone on stone that he felt through his hands and knees.

He realized he was crawling. Didn't really know what he was crawling for until his vision cleared and he saw that he was scrabbling toward his Leveler. It seemed absolutely foolhardy, but for some reason he needed to get that thing back in his hands . . . a little closer, a little closer.

Another eruption. A gout of red mist went swimming over Ord, making him blink and spit. A tickle on the side of his face, something wet going into his right eye. Redness. He whimpered, trying to blink it out, but there was too much of it.

A stone bigger than he was slammed into the earth right in front of him, dirt and mud spraying his face, filling his mouth so that he gagged and coughed and spat. The stone tumbled past. But Ord never stopped crawling. Found himself in the middle of the crater that the stone had left and thought about just curling up there for a final prayer, but by the time he'd decided to do so, he was already clambering out.

Leveler. There. Almost within reach. Loop with three spare charges bouncing around his neck, clattering across the ground, clattering against his knees.

A big brown-skinned body landed right in front of him. No head on it, so that Ord didn't recognize it until he heard a voice scream its name: "Cryer!" Blood squirting from a neck that'd been smashed flat, body convulsing in a strange way that made it look like the big man was trying to rise again, head or not.

Ord crawled heedlessly over the body, mewling and spitting and blubbering. "Feor. Feor. Feor."

Leveler.

The wooden butt of it was shattered to splinters, but Ord had neither the knowledge nor the inclination to assess its mechanical soundness. Clumsy hands battered at it. Managed to grab it. Shards of wood sinking deep into his palms, but for once the pain was so distant as to be rendered insensible. He cradled the thing like a lost child, then rolled, gibbering nonsense. His back against a stone wall again. Vision fuzzy with mud and blood, but he could see the shapes of Tickers all clustered around the corner, taking turns snatching at stones and hurling them at their attackers, and for some reason, none of them seemed to give a shit about Ord, or maybe didn't even notice him there.

Leveler.

Whimpering with every feathery breath, Ord strangled the Leveler with confused hands, squeezing this and that, completely forgetting how the damn thing worked, all the while the carnage continued on, the stones whirling back and forth, yellow dust, red mist, screams and cries and shouts—

The Leveler broke open. For a dismaying beat of his heart, Ord was convinced he'd simply broken the stupid thing until he saw the spent charge staring him in the face and remembered that that was how it worked.

Darkness was creeping into his vision again, chest feeling hot, skin feeling cold. He was breathing too hard, too rapidly. What was it that poor, headless Cryer had said? Don't breathe so hard?

Ord pressed the wind out of his chest until it was all empty, then sucked in a great breath and held it. Fingers clasping the spent charge. Extracting it. Dropping it. Fingers grasping a new charge. Get it into the breech. Damn it! Get it into the breech! But it just kept slipping around, not seating—and then it did. Slid in, so perfect and snug.

"Uh?" Ord gasped, as though questioning what the hell he was supposed to do now.

Oh, yes. He snapped it closed. Turned it on the Tickers.

If you can take out one Ticker, that's good, but if you can take out two or three with a single blast, that's even better.

Ord took the smallest of moments to register where most of the Tickers were huddled at that corner and did his best to point his Leveler right into the middle of them, then, without a second thought, he pulled the trigger bar.

At the same moment that he watched them splatter to gristle, he wished he'd never done it. Wished he could suck those shotstones back into the maw and drop the thing and run, run for the hills and never look back. But he couldn't.

"I killed," Ord said, numb and sick and terrified of this dark new frontier. "I—"

"Get the fuck up!" Hotsteel, dragged him to his feet. "We got 'em on the run!"

"We got 'em on the run!" Lochled heard Hotsteel caterwaul, and that was all his singing blood needed to hear.

He was running with the daemons now. Again. Forever.

Yowling, Lochled threw himself around the corner, bloody axe, bloody knife that he'd plucked from the dead Ticker's armpit. On the other side of that corner, the dreary gray stones were indeed livened up by the bright crimson spray. And the bright shreds of greenish flesh. And the bright speckles of white brain and bone.

Feet stamping heedlessly through a muck of gore.

How many dead? How many left? Didn't really matter.

Three ahead, running. One turned, saw Lochled. Batted at the air, and Lochled went hurtling sideways into the wall. Bone-jarring crunch. Bounce. But he landed on his feet, even madder than before, and hurled his axe with an uncanny accuracy he'd never thought himself capable of.

The axe smacked the thing in the back, and this time it stuck. The Ticker arched, spinning in a circle, clawing at its back, and by that moment, Lochled had reached it, grabbed it by the head when it was facing the other way, and opened its throat with one strong swipe, snatching his axe from its back as it fell.

Another Ticker, maybe five strides away, goggling at him, a mix of terror and determination in its hard little eyes.

Lochled thrust his knife at it. "You!"

It spun away from him and ducked into the door of a roofless structure, not dissimilar to their redoubt before, but this one had higher walls.

"Lochled, wait!"

He couldn't even tell who'd hollered at him, but didn't really care. There was no waiting, there was no stopping. The daemons only ran one way, and that was forward, always seeking more, more life to liberate from its fleshy prison.

"Don't go in there!"

But Lochled was already going in.

He burst through the arched doorway, arms tucked tight, spring-loaded, ready to lash out. Two Tickers straight ahead, facing him, backs to a corner. He reared back to throw his axe, but they both rammed their hands at him and sent him smashing into the doorframe, feeling a dull crackling through his spine.

"Look out!" Definitely Hotsteel now. And just as Lochled

had the presence of mind to realize that the warning was meant for him—at which point he tucked himself into a ball—a thunderhead of yellow came rolling through the door.

Lochled waited for the clatter of shotstones, rolled out of his tucked position, and came up to one knee before realizing that the two Tickers still had their hands out, both of them as though they were trying to carry a bushel basket at arm's length. Then Lochled wondered why the hell they were still standing instead of being lathered all over the walls.

He got his answer a split second later as his eyes snapped to the center of the room, not making sense of what he was seeing, struggling to focus on it. What the hell . . . ?

Twenty shotstones. Hovering in midair. Each of them trembling. Like each polished rock was bursting with some inner energy—except it wasn't their energy. It was the Tickers'. And Lochled thought he knew what they meant to do with it.

"Aw, fuck!" Lochled simply let his knees go out. Wasn't sure if that was going to do a damn bit of good, but neither was charging, and neither was falling back, and there wasn't any cover in this empty, stone-walled room.

There was no explosion to let him know when it'd happened—just the zip of things splitting the air all around him, followed by the smash and clatter of twenty impacts.

But nothing hit him.

And now he was pissed off something fierce. Didn't even want his weapons anymore. He wanted to rip those fuck Tickers apart with his hands, get their blood under his fingernails and sticky in the webbing of his fingers.

He swam to his feet, steels striking high-pitched sparks from the stones. Saw a blur to his right—Rony coming in, hacking and slashing and screaming like a hellcat.

The Tickers shrank back but weren't giving up. They both

reached for her at the same time. Maybe it was just instinct, because they were so focused on her. Maybe it was because they'd barely any experience in fighting wars. Regardless, they didn't pay attention to the madman coming at their side.

Rony was launched into the air with a jerk, and Lochled used the Tickers' momentary distraction to its full extent. He didn't yell. Didn't scream at them, or any of that other barbarity—just clenched his breath and gritted his teeth and took the last stride swinging.

Came pretty close to lopping one Ticker's head right off, except for the fact that Rony slammed into him right as he was closing and they both went blasting into the wall, Lochled hitting first, then Rony right after, a double punch that felt like it might've crumpled his whole rib cage and tenderized his innards.

Guess they saw him coming after all—he didn't so much think it as feel the disappointment of it.

He and Rony hit the ground in a jumble, knives and axes nicking each other.

Rony came up first, spry as a leafhopper, tried a hurl of her axe, but it caught in midair and went spinning—right past the nose of Hotsteel as he came roaring through the door, steels swinging. The axe clanged off the wall and bounced to the floor, right at the feet of a sodden, daemon-possessed . . .

Priest. Though you wouldn't think it to see him. Pale Fen skin made all the more horrific by the slashes of red across his face. Eyes somehow both pinched and wide—both trying to see everything and cringing away from it all at once. Mouth open in a ghastly grimace, stringy spit or snot connecting his emotion-wrinkled lips in a glistening strand.

Leveler.

"Bastards!" Ord screeched.

Hotsteel, who had skidded to a halt after the axe nearly

grazed him, had only time to dive to the side, yelling, "No, don't!"

Too late.

The room filled with yellow again. Ord still screaming something between a war cry and a terrorized wail. And again Lochled saw all twenty stones stopped in midair, though they swirled unsteadily this time.

The Tickers were getting tired.

Lochled bounded for the nearest one, spittle seething from his clenched teeth. The thing looked up at him with the apathy of the absolutely exhausted, and Lochled sank his knife down deep, right inside its collar bone. Its knees went out immediately, Lochled riding it to the ground, already bringing his axe around, gripping it high in the haft for slashing.

The shotstones started splitting the air, not all at once, but in succession, like the last Ticker was trying his hardest to contain them but rapidly failing. Lochled registered this only as a buzz right behind him, and then the crack of a stone's impact, just in front.

He hit the ground. Ripped the knife out. Slashed with his axe. Its blade connected with the Ticker's neck at the same moment the thing weakly pushed its hand up and Lochled felt his knife go flying out of his grip. But by then his axe blade had slit its throat.

Lochled felt a snatch at his side, and thought it was someone slapping him, except that it was damn hard—harder even than Cryer could have . . .

And his only real thought in that moment, as he pitched sideways, was *Cryer.*

Funny, he didn't see his life flash before him like some of the men said. He saw Cryer flashing before him. Hadn't really even considered that his friend's head had been crushed only a minute or two ago. Strange how this fact chose now to hit him full force, like it'd somehow gotten attached to that shotstone that'd just gouged its way through him.

"Oof!" Lochled toppled to the ground.

The Ticker he'd just been shot off of gave one last lurch toward him—mouth dribbling red so bright it seemed pink, neck spurting out the same—and then collapsed, looking right into Lochled's eyes. Dead. Or close enough anyway. And so was Cryer. And probably, so was Lochled.

No point to any of it.

That damn circle. He never had been able to get free of it.

Something was making crunchy wet noises, and someone was saying, "Yah! Yah! Yah!" over and over. Lochled tore his eyes off the dead Ticker and looked to his left to find Hotsteel straddling the last one, hacking its face off with his axe.

Someone else was making fluttery squeaking noises, and when Lochled looked into the middle of the room, he found Ord lying on his side, hand clutching his calf, which had a big red hole bored through the middle of the meat. Shoulders shaking. Looking like he'd damn near lost his mind.

And someone else was sobbing quietly.

Honestly, Lochled assumed it was himself, given his performance earlier. But he realized his chest was still and dead cold. Hurt like shit in his side, though. Even the tiniest breath sent branding-iron pain through him.

He looked to the right, and found the final living member of their party: Rony. Little Roan. Young lady Hirdman, down to save her family's farm and free her brothers from debtors' prison. Now with a face that looked like she might've wiped her sleeve across it, but all the red about her ears and neck and shoulders told the true story.

And her eyes. Those told it too.

She wasn't hysterical about it. Just stood there, straight as a board with gory steels in gory hands, sobbing. In fact, she seemed a bit confused about it too.

All of this happened in the few tiny seconds between the shock of having been shot and the pain coming on strong.

Lochled's whole body twisted up, but the contortions only made the pain worse. It started to center itself, right there under his arm, and went through his back. There was something worse to it this time, something on the inside.

"Aw, swearnsoot . . ." He tried to sit up but couldn't quite. Hands trying to cover the wounds. He could reach the hole in his side where the stone had gone in but not the one in his back where it'd come out.

Rony looked at him. Didn't move toward him, but said, "You need help?"

Lochled, teeth grinding, nodded hastily and held out his hand, already preparing for the agony of standing.

Rony stared at his outstretched hand for a moment, then stuck her axe back in her belt and limped forward, favoring her left leg. She grasped his hand, blood sticky between them. Made Lochled want to wash his hands. In fact, he'd never wanted to wash after a battle so bad as he did now.

Rony set her face as though she were preparing for pain of her own, then hauled on him. Both of them moaned and snarled, Rony leaning back, and Lochled coming upright with a stagger.

Curses abounded, Rony clutching shoulder and hip, Lochled clutching his punched-out ribs, and Ord clutching his calf.

Seemed only Hotsteel had made it through unscathed. He'd finished hacking the last Ticker's head to fragments and had stood up, gasping for air, grinning through his bloody face. Snorted up a gob of snot and spat it on the body, looking as pleased as a man can be.

"That's how it's fucking done!" He shook his axe at them, as though expecting a mighty cheer of victory. But who in the hell could cheer at this point? Four bloody bastards, three of them wounded, and all of them lost, even in their triumph.

Lochled frowned around the room. Frowned at the ruined bodies of the two Tickers. It wasn't that he felt bad about it all. Not at the moment, anyway. It was just that once his blood stopped singing and the daemons retreated back from whence they came, none of it seemed to make any sense.

Like he'd just paid a golden whale for a day-old haddock.

Like waking up next to a ghastly whore and wondering what in the world you'd found attractive about her the previous night.

"You been shot in the side," Rony said.

Lochled looked down at himself as though he'd forgotten. "Seems that way."

Rony fixed him with a curiously emotionless look. "You gonna die?"

Lochled gave a facial shrug—a real shrug would have hurt his ribs. "Can't really say."

"What I wanna know," Hotsteel spoke—entirely too loud, Lochled thought—"is why in the fuck these bastards came here?"

Oh. For some reason, Lochled had expected his captain to show some concern for his three wounded soldiers. But that was all right. He had captainly things to worry about. Can't go about coddling your soldiers after every skinned knee and pricked finger.

Hotsteel circled the room, working the steels in his grip, hunching with tension as he glowered at the walls as though he intended to frighten each and every stone into giving up its secrets. "There's nothing even here! Why in the fuck would they come into the Ruins—which they *knew* we were defending—just to hole up in some random fucking room?"

"For all the fucking mercy of Feor," Ord snapped. "I've been shot in the fucking leg!"

Hotsteel looked at him. Chuffed softly. "Then fucking wrap it up, Theynen." Then Hotsteel turned back to intimidating the walls.

But Lochled was still looking at Ord. Well, not exactly at Ord, but at the circular stone on which he sat. Something different about it. All the other stones looked like they'd toppled or, in the case of cobbles, grown over with moss and grass.

But this one was clean all across its surface, and the moss and grass hadn't even started to encroach on the edges, giving a defined seam all the way around.

Lochled limped forward, and Rony limped with him. Felt like they were kind of attached now, somehow. Lochled flicked a finger at Ord. "Stand up, Theynen."

Ord stared at him, indignant. Lochled didn't think spooky blues could flare that hot. "I can't fucking stand!" he snapped. "I've been shot!"

"Give the priest a break," Hotsteel said, distractedly. "This is his first battle."

"It's the stone you're sitting on," Lochled said to him, having to speak each word a little slower and quieter than usual, as deep breaths made his ribs crackle and his lungs rattle. He wondered absently if he had a hole in his lung. That'd be a finishing blow for sure.

Ord looked down at the stone. Scanned its edges, at first looking irritable, but then starting to look a little curious. He clambered onto his hands and knees, and then, unwilling to put any pressure on his wounded leg, he reached out for help. Lochled obliged him, though he barely had strength to spare.

Ord got to one foot and hopped on it until he was off the stone.

Hotsteel had gotten interested and was circling and glaring at the stone now instead of the walls. "Well, lookit that, Lochled. I think you might be onto something."

"Think there's a passage underneath it?" Rony wondered.

"No handholds," Ord murmured. "No way to lift it."

"Tickers don't lift with their hands, now do they?" Hotsteel said, then crouched. Stuck fingers experimentally into the space between stone and grass. Wiggled them about, as though searching for the bottom of the stone. Dropped his steels, then went at it with both hands, straining a bit. The stone moved, but not much.

"Oh, there's definitely something there," Hotsteel said, voice heady with a sort of lusty excitement. He stood up quickly, glanced around. "Need a lever or—" He looked at the half-broken Leveler lying off to the side of the stone. "There we are." He snatched it up, returned to his original spot, and jammed the splintered end of the stock in where he'd been jamming his fingers. Then looked up, a little irritably. "A little help? Or are you all too wounded?"

Rony didn't respond. Nor did Ord. But just before Hotsteel might've started to get pissed about it, Lochled grunted and shuffled forward. "Yes, hef. Wounded, but not *too* bad, I think. I can help."

"You been shot through the side," Rony said to him.

Lochled waved her off—painfully—as he took a place next to Hotsteel. "Been shot in the *ribs*, Rony. Let's not be dramatic."

Rony just leaned over and spat.

Ord was still balancing on one leg, but to his credit, seemed to have overcome his pain with fascination.

"Ready?" Hotsteel grunted.

Lochled wasn't ready at all. Knew there was a strong possibility that trying to lever the damn stone was going to make his ribs hurt so bad he might pass out. "Ready."

"Heave!"

Hotsteel heaved. Lochled groaned and tried his best.

The stone quaked, rattled, then lifted.

Darkness beneath.

"Ah! Push it, push it!" Hotsteel ordered, and Lochled obediently did his best to push the thing to the side, swiveling it out of the way and exposing half of a wide circular hole with a pair of steps descending in a single flight . . .

And a cluster of greenish-skinned faces staring up at them.

CHAPTER 38

"Oh-ho!" Hotsteel leapt backward, fumbling with the Leveler, then realizing it was empty and hurling it off to the side and snatching up his steels instead. "What the fuck is this?"

"Wait!" Ord shouted, waving his arms, so distracted that he hadn't realized he'd put his wounded foot down. "Don't kill them!"

Hotsteel had his weapons ready. Lochled stood there, only his axe still in his hand, staring into that collection of fearful expressions and not feeling the tiniest note of violence in his blood.

"Why the fuck not?" Hotsteel demanded, eyes slashing back and forth between Ord and the Tickers below.

Five of them, it looked like. Two older ones, male and female. Two younger ones, both males. And the youngest of all, a female.

If Lochled had considered them people, he might've looked at them and seen a family. Mother and father. Two strapping older boys. One young daughter. A brood any man would be proud of.

"Just, just, just wait!" Ord stammered out, pumping his hands in the air. "They're not dangerous!"

"How the fuck you know that?" Hotsteel seethed, staring at them with a weird hunger, like a dog being told not to chew a bone.

"Well, they're not throwing stones, for fucking starters!" Ord snapped back.

Lochled tensed, half expecting them to suddenly correct Ord on that point and smash them all, but they just kept staring up, the little female squirming against the older female like she couldn't get close enough, the older female clutching at the younger.

"Plus," Ord went on, speaking faster and faster now as he tried to convince Hotsteel not to start mincing them up. "They're hiding! Why would they be hiding if they were warrior-Tickers like the others? I don't think these ones even have powers, or they would have used them already. And, and, and—look!" Ord pointed rapidly to the oldest pair. "What's all this jewelry? All these necklaces and earrings?"

Hotsteel twisted his head, a bit confused.

Lochled scoffed in soft amazement. "Almost looks like a chief and his wife."

Hotsteel snapped him a nasty look. "Not like that at all, Lochled. Don't go down that road."

"I think," Ord struggled on, "what Lochled is trying to say, is that this might be . . . might be . . . like the Brannen or something. The leaders of the Tickers, maybe. Or some sort of special family. Why else would they hide them away like this? Why else would they be protected by the warrior-Tickers? Come on, Captain, you know it makes sense! The way the Tickers ran back right to this spot—because they weren't trying to fight us, they were trying to protect this family!"

"And what fucking difference does that make?" Hotsteel suddenly roared, drooping steels snapping erect again. "Who gives a fuck if they got a Brannen or a chief or a fucking green-skinned Steadman?"

Ord's mouth worked silently for a few desperate moments. Then he blurted, "I want to see if they'll talk!"

"Again with this?" Hotsteel cried.

Ord managed to stand as straight as he could, summon up some semblance of priestly authority. Didn't do a half-bad job of it, Lochled thought, all things considered. "Captain Hotsteel, it is the Church's interest to see if these beings are capable of speech and thought."

Well, that was a damn lie, Lochled thought, but he found a sliver of respect for Ord in trying.

"Now," Ord continued, "I will conduct a necessary experiment to that effect. So . . . have them come up here."

Hotsteel stood there, somewhat hunched, somewhat sulky, glaring at Ord, then at the Tickers, then back at Ord. "All right," he said, low and dangerous. "Have it your way, Theynen. An experiment it is." He snapped to the Tickers, waved his axe at them. "Come on, then! Out! Out-out!"

All the Tickers glanced around at each other. Except for the little girl. She was staring at Hotsteel, eyes wide and wet with tears. Now, what kind of animal sheds tears? Isn't that a human thing? Or course, Lochled had heard that the jackals in Drugoth could imitate a crying baby and lure people to their deaths. Maybe this was just imitation.

Right about when Hotsteel was sucking in a breath to shout at them again, the oldest male and female turned, hands linked, and strode up the stairs. Carefully. Haltingly. Like the steps were covered in broken glass—except that they weren't looking where they were going. They were focused on Hotsteel. That was the real danger.

"Did you see that?" Ord pointed, as the younger males

started up the steps, holding the youngest female between them protectively. "They understood!"

Lochled knew what Hotsteel was going to say before he even opened his mouth.

"I made a motion to move." A scoff. "Even my hounds know what that means."

The oldest pair reached the top, still pressed tight. Looking around them and shuffling a little this way, then a little that way. Taking in this strange audience they now found themselves in front of. Ord, staring in an odd, feverishly eager way. Rony, dull as slate, save for the very slightest squint of her eyes, like she might be interested, but only a small fraction's worth. Hotsteel, slavering at them with his eyes, barely restraining himself from murder.

And Lochled himself, whose mouth was hanging open, he realized. He couldn't seem to tear his eyes off the girl-Ticker as she reached the top of those old stairs. Her tears welled up even harder as she saw all these gore-stained figures hovering around them, two cut-up Ticker bodies off to the side.

Did she recognize those dead Tickers? Had she known them?

"Do your experiment then," Hotsteel grunted, leaving all the rest blank for the imagination. And no matter how you imagined it, it was ugly.

Ord clapped his hands and gained some flinching attention from the group of five Tickers. He sought desperately for eye contact, and when he finally found it, it seemed to be one of the younger males. Ord smiled, and the male Ticker squinted at him, looking uncertain.

"Will you speak to me?" Ord said slowly, evenly, perhaps a little loudly.

The male's eyes narrowed further, then flashed to the side, to the oldest ones.

Ord waved his hands, sweat trickling down his face, leaving tiny pinkish streaks in the blood. "No, no. You need to . . ." He seemed to expend some effort getting himself under control. "You need to pay attention to *me*!"

Hotsteel sighed raspily. "They don't talk, Theynen. The Church has already established that."

Ord snapped a look like an arrow at Hotsteel. "And I'm confirming it! You have to . . . to *confirm* things! In science," he added. Then back to the Ticker. "Uh . . . uh . . . let's try this: *friend*."

He was pointing to his lips.

Another sideways glance. The Ticker frowning and worried looking. Chest heaving. Sweating.

"Friend!" Ord nearly shouted at it. Fingers jabbing the air in front of his mouth. "Say it!" Then he jabbed his fingers manically in front of the Ticker's mouth. "Now you say it: *friend*!"

The Ticker did a strange thing with its mouth. Bared its teeth. Moved its mouth around, all exaggerated. Took Lochled a moment to realize it was just mimicking Ord's mouth. Or trying to anyway. And doing a poor job.

"No, no," Ord said, his voice cracking. "You have to say what I say. With your voice." Pointing at his throat. Then reaching over to point at the Ticker's throat, but it jerked back and swatted Ord's hand away.

Then snapped at him with its teeth.

Ord jumped back, surprisingly nimble for having a hole in his calf.

Hotsteel was laughing. But Lochled didn't feel much like joining in.

"You poor, dumb bastards!" Hotsteel exclaimed. "You and Lochled both. Sorry, Theynen, but it's true. You got good hearts, I'll give you that. Wanted to give the little beasties a chance.

But you see for yourself now, don't you? Fucker would've probably gnawed your arm off if we hadn't been here to convince it otherwise."

Ord looked at Hotsteel, hands still clutched to his chest. "It was just the one. I didn't try to talk to the others."

The oldest male stepped forward, causing Rony to snap her axe upright and slide up next to Ord. The male froze, eyes darting. Its hands came up, slow, and Lochled tensed, couldn't decide if it looked like the thing was about to spring for Rony or if it was moving slow to put her at ease. Then it started pointing at stuff. Fingers moving around. This and that. It and Ord. Rony and Ord.

None of it made the least bit of sense. Lochled felt his stomach sink even further. It looked like the Ticker was just mimicking again. Just pointing at things the way Ord had pointed at them.

But did it really matter? What about all the other things? What about the contraptions? And the medicine? What about the forests full of food and tended like a garden? What about all the trinkets that the Church claimed were left over from the Old Ones, but Lochled knew—somehow just knew—that they weren't? What about all that?

A noise lilted to them over the air, distant and sad.

A horn blowing. One blast. Then two. Then silence.

Hotsteel straightened. Pointed a finger of his knife hand to the sky. "You hear that?" he asked Ord. "That'll be Gunnar Thaersh. Now, imagine if he were to see this foolfuckery and report it back to the Church?" Hotsteel shook his head. "Be my head and yours, Ord. Come on, then. We all saw you try." He leaned forward, enunciating his words. "Tickers. Don't. Fucking. Talk. They don't talk"—poking at his temple—"because they don't got minds to think."

Hotsteel grabbed the loop from around his neck, two charges dangling. "You saw it. We all saw it. Time to end this fucking stage show and get back to war." He tossed the loop at Lochled, and he caught it, his ribs shaking and quaking, tremors of pain rolling through him just from that tiny movement. Hotsteel gave him a dismissive nod and a wave. "Sergeant Thatcher, dispose of these Tickers."

And right there, Lochled watched them all draw up.

Like they *knew*. Like they understood *that* perfectly well.

"Did you see that?" Lochled mumbled, fingering one of the push charges.

"What?" Hotsteel grimaced. "Them jump? They reacted to me throwing something at you is all. Feor help me, man! Could you stop?" Hotsteel's face reddened as he spoke. "Can we *fucking* stop? Can we just do our fucking jobs? Is it so much to ask that a soldier fucking obey his orders? That is the fucking point, isn't it? Uh? The Brannen tells the general, the general tells the captain, the captain tells the sergeant, and *THE SERGEANT FUCKING OBEYS!* That's how the military works, Lochled! That's how law and order works!" He thrust a finger at the Tickers. "So kill those fucking Tickers!"

Lochled's mouth had gone dry. Gut twisted. Heart thudding hard. Kept thinking about disobeying orders, but fuck, that felt terrifying. Then he'd think about obeying them, and he might not like it, might have regrets about it, but at least he wouldn't be terrified.

"With the Leveler?" Lochled croaked out. Wasn't even sure why he asked the question. Maybe he was just stalling.

Hotsteel clutched the air in frustration. "I don't give a fuck how you kill 'em! You can drown 'em in your own piss if you like—just get it done!"

Lochled turned stiffly. Fingers still feeling their way around that push charge. Oh, Feor. How many of those had he spent today? How many of those had he spent since hitting the beaches? Twenty? Fewer? More?

Almost sounded like a joke to Lochled, as he bent over, hissing in pain, and scooped up the Leveler. How many Tickers have to be burned to make twenty push charges?

How many of our own sons and daughters?

Lochled straightened with the Leveler. Felt woozy all a sudden and almost staggered. And when he regained himself, he breathed hard, and it turned into a nasty cough. Felt it spew up into the back of his mouth, and when he swallowed it, he knew it wasn't phlegm. Tasted like copper.

Fuck. So I'm done then anyways, uh?

He turned around, saw Hotsteel frowning at him. "You all right, Lochled?"

"Yes, hef," Lochled managed to get out without sounding as bad as he suddenly felt. He fingered the latch on the busted-up weapon and opened the breech. Was staring at his work while his mind ran furiously. If you'd have looked at his slow, steady hands, you'd have thought his mind was just as slow and steady, but it was racing about, trying to find an answer.

He was going to die anyway. Was there much point in making a final stand about some shit like this? How long did he have? A few days, maybe? If he was lucky. Wouldn't he rather spend those in a bed, being looked after and honored as a good soldier to the end? But men that don't follow orders don't get that treatment. No, they swing at the end of a rope, or maybe they're just executed by their captain on the spot.

Somehow he'd gotten the Leveler recharged and closed. Didn't even remember doing it.

Rony and Ord, shuffled to one side, out of the way of Lochled's aim.

"Haven't got all day, Lochled," Hotsteel muttered, glancing away.

Lochled had looked in the one place he knew he shouldn't have—the little girl-Ticker's eyes. Had been trying to avoid looking *any* of them in the eye as he pointed the Leveler at them. But his eyes seemed to have a mind of their own.

But she wasn't staring at him. Even though he was the one that had the Leveler trained on them. She was looking at Hotsteel. And she was terrified. Same face you'd give a ravenous bear, or something even worse—something black and evil that had crawled out from under a bridge or a cleft in a damp cave. Her fear of him was absolute.

Lochled followed her gaze to Hotsteel's face, and found him looking right back at the girl-Ticker, with absolutely no expression. No more emotion in his eyes than he would have if he'd asked someone to shuck some corn for supper.

That horn blasted again, slightly closer.

And then Hotsteel did have an expression: impatience.

"Lochled—"

"I can't do it."

Hotsteel's eyes widened. "What do you mean you can't do it?" He glanced at the Leveler, like perhaps it was malfunctioning.

"I mean I won't," Lochled said. Lowering the Leveler. The little girl's eyes on him now. And they didn't look scared at all. They looked pleading. Wanting. Kind of how Libby's eyes had looked before she knew that her father was going to take a step back and let the Seeker do his job. Because those were the rules, and these were the orders, and orders is orders.

Fuck. Lochled didn't know which hurt worse—the hole in his side, or the girl's eyes.

Girl-TICKER! His mind tried to emphasize, but that skin wouldn't hold wine no more. It'd gone and popped. Worn straight through. That's how lies are, sometimes. They can be useful for a while, but eventually they wear through. Truth is like steel, though. It can last forever if you take care of it.

"Lochled," Hotsteel said, his voice even, but only just, a threat of pure rage bumping at it from underneath like a blackfish thinking of tipping a small boat. "You've been faithful all along. And now you're at the end. Finish your race with honor, Lochled. Finish it the *right way*. Be a *good man*."

"I'm not a good man," Lochled said, hands working unsteadily at wood and bronze. Then harsher, louder: "I'm not a fucking *good man*! I'm a good *soldier*, and there's a fucking difference! A good *man* don't let his daughter get taken from him! A good *man* don't believe things just because men in fine robes tell him! A good *man* trusts his own fucking morals and doesn't obey an order unless he knows it's *good*! And this?" Lochled thrust a bloody hand at the five Tickers. "This is not good!"

Hotsteel's face went through a strange evolution as Lochled spoke. At first, confused and frustrated. Then almost fascinated. Then hardening. Freezing. Falling. Until it was just this nasty, cold grimace.

"Oh?" Hotsteel turned around, took a step toward the Tickers. "I'm a good man, Lochled. I've done my fucking duty—with honor. I've been exemplary. And yet, I'm still capable of doing *this*." He stabbed the oldest male Ticker. Not hard. Not even fast. Just kind of slid the knife in, all casual, then pulled it out. The Ticker's eyes bulged, body curling around the wound. Not making a damn sound. The others' hands grasping all over him as he sank to his knees.

"See, that's the problem with you, Lochled," Hotsteel shook his head, pointing the bloody knife at him. "My father warned me that you always thought you were smarter than everyone else. But I thought, he's Redskin! I'll give him some rope and see what he does. Fucking mistake."

A quick slash as he said the last word, and the woman-Ticker's hands shot to her throat, blood already pouring.

"Stop," Lochled said, but it was barely a whisper.

"No!" Hotsteel snapped, as he reached into the pile of limbs, the man-Ticker having fallen, then the woman-Ticker on top of him, both of them bleeding and squirming, the two young males' hands hovering all over them like they couldn't decide what to do. The girl-Ticker standing there, all alone, hands clenched at her breast, eyes squinched up tight and leaking out the sides. "You don't get to give me orders, even if you are Redskin!" He hauled one of the younger males up and kind of hugged him into his knife. Held him there thrashing for a moment before letting him drop. "That's not how it fucking works!"

"Captain," Ord squeaked, and was completely ignored.

Rony hadn't moved. Hadn't spoken. But her knuckles were ashy and bloodless around her steels.

"I'm the fucking captain!" Hotsteel bellowed, snatching for the other male, but he darted out of reach, silently crying now, just as hard as the girl-Ticker was. Hotsteel let him go, like he didn't care, knew he'd get around to him eventually—not like he had anywhere to go. "I give the orders! And the sergeant—that's you, Lochled—fucking obeys them!"

"There's no fucking point to any of it!" Lochled suddenly screamed at Hotsteel.

But Hotsteel just looked at him with pitiless, sardonic eyes. "Are you just now figuring that out?" And then he reached for the nearest Ticker at hand—the little girl.

"*No*," Lochled spoke in thunder, and his breath was yellow dust.

CHAPTER 39

Ashes.

Ashes alchemized. Harnessed. Yoked by science. By progress.

Ashes distilled, extracted, changed, and metered into a single push charge that could splatter a man's body. The ashes of the innocent, twisted and warped into doing bloody deeds. But that's alchemy for you. That's science. That's progress.

But that last one? That last push charge that he'd triggered off?

Out of all of the push charges he'd detonated—the hundreds that he'd done in his lifetime—that was the one Lochled regretted the least.

Part of him felt a tiny jolt of grief at the loss. But even that was so small. And it couldn't bear up against the weight of truth: Hotsteel had never been his friend. Crushing that grief right to dust, Othis hadn't been his friend either. Father and son, spitting images of each other—they'd only ever been his handlers. The ones who held the leash of the fighting dog. The stupid, ravenous dog that was fed scraps and misconstrued it as love and caring. The dumb, bloody dog that gets a pat on the head when he rips another to shreds and thinks that it's mutual respect.

Good man.

Good boy.

Good dog.

That's not a friend at all. That's a master.

Lochled sucked in a sharp breath of air that tasted of everything he hated and nothing he loved. Blood and bowels and yellow dust that stank of soot—stank of the person it'd been before.

The storm of yellow receded, dissipated, and Lochled saw the ruins of his superior, painted across the stone wall, and there wasn't much left of him but a tatter of a captain's tunic, and a hand—the hand that fed him, but also the hand that pointed, and beat, and mocked him. The hand that *used*.

"I'll fucking split your head right down the middle," Rony said.

Lochled dragged his weary eyes over to hers. Rony stood there, stiff and ready, steels bared. Ord huddled behind her, face all agog at what had happened, still staring at the visceral remnants of Captain Hotsteel, with fresh bits of that same captain all over him.

"You know you can't move fast enough to stop me," she said. "Not with that hole in your side." Her voice was quiet. Not that Lochled doubted her. Seemed she'd come to the realization that you don't have to be loud to be heard. You just have to mean what you say.

His thumb caught the latch on the broken Leveler in his hand, and he let it open. Showing he had no intent to use it. His other hand he held open at his side, showing his palm.

Rony's jaw muscles were pulsing rapidly. A snarl starting to curl her nostrils. "The fuck'd you do that for, uh?"

"I don't mean you any harm," Lochled said, letting the Leveler drop from his hands.

The second it hit the ground, the young male Ticker bolted, snatching up the little girl in his arms, and making for the door, but Lochled swept up in front of them, blocking their path.

"No," he said, hands up.

The male Ticker peered at him, backing up a single step. The girl watched him too. But they didn't seem terrified of him like they had been of Hotsteel. Only cautious. Eager to get away.

"There's an army out there," Lochled said to them, pointing back behind him. "And if you go out there alone, they'll track you down and kill you." He brought that hand back to his chest. "I can help you."

"Lochled, what are you doing?" Rony hissed. "Fucking Thaersh'll hang you for sure now!"

Lochled shook his head. "I'm doing something good for once in my life, Rony. And I don't intend to—" His chest bucked, ribs seizing up, lungs burning and scraping. He hacked out a cough. Tasted blood again. "Fuck." Tears in his eyes. "I don't intend to be here when he arrives."

Rony took a step forward, her steels lowering just a hair. "Where the fuck do you think you're going to go, Lochled?"

He nodded to the two Tickers in front of him. "I'm going to get these two to safety. Or as close as I can. And then . . ." He looked down at his side. Couldn't even see the wound for all the blood coating it. "Then I suppose I'm going to die."

"Lochled," Rony urged, stepping closer, steels drooping. "We can fix this. We can say Hotsteel died in the fight! Ord will back us up—won't you, Ord?"

Ord looked shocked to be called upon. Or maybe he was still in shock. But he must've at least understood her, because he nodded his head. Understood her, or he just agreed to treason without thinking about it.

"There, see?" Rony looked back at Lochled, pleading. "You don't have to run away—you can get help for that wound!"

"Uh," Lochled half cleared his throat. "There's no helping me at this point, Rony. And besides, what would become of them?"

Rony looked at the two Tickers for a long time, her eyes switching between the girl and the young male. Lochled could see the struggle in her, one he knew intimately. Knew she was thinking of just solving this with violence.

Lochled reached out and touched her elbow—the one with the axe in its hand. "Rony. I'll be the first to admit there's a lot of situations can be solved by violence." He waited until her eyes flitted to his, then gently shook his head. "But this idn't one of them. This one . . . this one needs to be done right. For once, I gotta do something right. Something good. Just let me do it. Let me go."

She peered at him. "Saving them won't bring back Libby."

Lochled gave an involuntary wince. "I know that." He let his hand fall away from Rony's arm. "But if I do this, at least I can know that I'm not the shitheel I was."

Rony coughed a sudden, inexplicable laugh.

And, inexplicably, Lochled found himself smiling. "Came a bit late, I guess. But I suppose it's better than never. Least this way I can die having done *one* thing that a good man would do." He grimaced against a wave of faintness, hot-cold across his scalp. "Ah, fuck. You think it'll be enough?"

Rony wasn't laughing anymore. She nodded, eyes brimming. "Yes, hef."

"Don't call me that anymore," Lochled said. "And if you'd listen to me one more time, Rony, don't call *anyone* that anymore, uh? Be your own. Don't let anyone else own you."

That horn again, bleating out its miserable refrain. So much closer now. They must've been marching double-quick.

"Well, if you're gonna do it, then fucking do it!" Rony snapped, angrily flicking tears off her cheeks. "Get gone before someone sees you."

"Hold a moment." Lochled reached into his scaef pouch. Dug around. Pulled out the phial of yellow powder. Pressed it into her hands. "That's ten golden whales, right there. And, guess what."

Rony stared at the phial. Lifted her eyes to his. Raised her brow in question.

Lochled smiled sadly. "You're the only member of the squad left. That means you're the only one that'll get the commission on those stone-throwing contraptions. Between the medicine and the contraption, I think you'll have your farm paid for." He leaned in closer to her. "I know you might think you had brothers here in Leftland, blood bound and all that brownspill. But even if that was true, they're all dead now, aren't they, cully? So go back to your real brothers. Go back to your real family. Forget about this fucking nightmare, Little Roan." He winked tiredly at her. "Go home and wake up."

Rony closed her hand around the phial. Drew back a step.

"Right then," Lochled glanced around. Hand touched his scaef pouch. It only had a bit left in it, but he only had a bit left in him, so that worked out. Had already sheathed his knife and axe. After all, you never knew when violence might be the good man's answer, like it had been today. "I'm gonna steal two horses," he said absently. "Don't think they'll be missed."

The horns again. And now, faintly, the tramp of feet.

"Go," Rony urged.

Lochled nodded. Looked at the two Tickers. Didn't really know what to say, or how much they understood. But he knew that they thought, that they felt, just the same as any man, even if they couldn't speak the words to prove it. They could prove it in other ways. And there are ways of communicating that are universal.

Lochled held out his hand. Jerked his head toward the door. A gentle beckoning.

Neither of them grabbed it. They were cautious, and Lochled guessed he could understand that. So he looked at that little girl-Ticker, and he imagined that it was that little Fen girl from the House of Draeids and that he'd saved her from her doom. Barged right through those iron gates, cut down the guards, and pulled her right out of there. And then he imagined that it was Libby, and he hadn't let her slip out of his hands, that he'd held onto her when the Seeker came, and he'd looked at that Seeker and told him, straight and true, that if he tried to even reach for his daughter, he'd maul him dead, right there on the doorstep.

He imagined these thing so hard he could almost feel Libby's hand in his. Then he realized he wasn't imagining that bit—the little girl-Ticker had reached out and wrapped her fingers around his. He just couldn't see past all the damn water in his eyes.

"Steady on, then," Lochled croaked. "Let's go."

CHAPTER 40

It was quite a time waiting for the army to get there.

It'd seemed they were approaching so fast earlier. But Rony had been sitting on this rock for the last ten minutes, and they were just now coming into view.

She kept having the urge to look behind her, but she'd already done it twice and knew what she'd see: Ponts's cold corpse, ten strides behind her. She knew he was dead because she'd checked on her way up the hill. Thought maybe she'd hear those last words that he'd asked her to hear—something to tell his father. But by the time she made it back to him, he wasn't going to speak those words anymore, and his father wasn't going to hear them.

She kept telling herself it was just one more body out of dozens—maybe even hundreds of others. Why should it be special? Why should it hurt her any more than the others had? But for some reason it did. It put ideas in her head about what she could've done differently, and how she might not feel like she did now if she'd just sat there for another handful of seconds to hear him out, even with Hotsteel bellowing at her.

She took a pull from a flask. She'd taken it from a dead body that she'd passed on her way out here. One of Breakwood's men, she thought. She didn't want to steal from any of her dead squadmates but didn't feel bad at all about taking it from one of those fuckers.

"We make up some really strange rules for ourselves, don't we?" Rony asked, passing the flask to her left.

Ord sat there with her. Legs up on the stone, arms resting on his knees, just as pensive and silent as a man could be. Thickly wrapped cloth around the wound in his calf, starting to spot through. He glanced at the flask. Glanced at Rony. Then took it and pulled long and hard from it.

"There are no rules," he husked as he pulled the flask away. "We're trained, I think—maybe by our parents, or maybe it's in our blood, I don't know. But we're trained to think of these rules as these great, infallible cornerstones of our existence. But really, they're all just made up, aren't they? They don't mean anything." He scoffed bitterly. "They never benefit the people that have to follow them. Have you ever noticed that? They only ever benefit the people that make them up."

"Huh." Rony took the flask back. Her eyes ranged up to the top of the hill, where Gunnar Thaersh's detachment had come to a stop, and the horn was bleating out a bunch of pathetic noises, like an old beggar on a corner shouting at carts.

A few figures on horseback came melting out of all the men on foot. Three of them: two in front, one behind, holding a banner. The Brytan Company banner. One of the ones in the front seemed a mite small compared to the others, and he seemed to be holding a spyglass on them. Rony assumed it was Gunnar Thaersh. So she raised a hand and waved it slowly back and forth.

"Think they're going to come themselves," Ord asked, "or just pound the whole area to dust with their siege cannons?"

Rony snorted half-heartedly. "Maybe you've a future as a general."

"Ah, a fucking future," Ord mumbled. Blew dissatisfied air between his lips. "What am I going to do now that I know about all the lies?"

Rony looked sidelong at him. Took another mouthful of drips. Shrugged. "Suppose you could run away. Suppose you could stay."

Ord grimaced. "If I leave the Church, I can't *affect* the Church. I lose any voice I might ever have."

"Hmm." Rony frowned out at the hill. Put her flask away. "Well, here he comes."

Gunnar Thaersh and two of his attendees, followed by an entire squad of mounted heavies, cantered their way down the slope toward the Ruins.

Rony and Ord didn't say anything else to each other. Just sat there with distant eyes, watching the riders approach, shoulders all slumped, lips loose, brows tweaked like they'd found a mystery that always seemed to elude an answer.

Gunnar Thaersh pulled to a stop, his hand up in a fist. Very martial. Every bit the Steadman. Except for being so damn small. Still, everyone's big on a horse. Rony had to look up, squinting against the sun.

Gunnar had a half smile on his lips as he peered around at the Ruins. "Well. Given the fact that I don't see stones flying every which way, I'm guessing the Tickers skirted right past this position." He frowned, let his hand flop to his lap. "Well, fuck."

Rony hiked a thumb over her shoulder. "They're in the Ruins."

Gunnar lifted his brow. "You mean your captain?"

"I mean the Tickers. Dead. All of them."

Gunnar blinked a handful of time, but the smile was returning to his face. "You don't say. So your little detachment of three squads managed to take them out, uh? I must say. That's some fine soldiering. Where's your captain and the others?"

Rony almost laughed. Managed to restrain herself as she hiked her thumb over her shoulder again. "They're in the Ruins. Dead. All of them."

She wasn't really sure why she'd had the urge to laugh. Seemed everything was just a little disjointed, like this was her first day as a human being, and she wasn't quite sure what was normal.

Gunnar was very still. Except for his thumb, which rubbed manically at the reins in his hand. "You are, then, the only survivors?"

Rony gave a single nod.

Another man—someone Rony didn't recognize, and immediately didn't care about—came bustling forward, his plump, pink lips flapping in indignation. "That's about enough insolence out of you. You're talking to the fucking Steadman! How's about you stand the fuck up?"

Rony just about did. Right along with her axe and knife and her own question in turn: *How's about I axe your fucking head in two?*

But she remained still, staring coldly up at the lip-flapper, and she only got away with it because Gunnar waved an irritable hand at the man. "Swearnsoot, man! I don't need you snapping away at everyone. Now go froth back there if you can't control yourself."

The man looked briefly sad, like a kicked dog. Managed to give Rony a last, baleful look before pulling his horse around and retreating a very minimal distance.

Gunnar turned back to Rony, eyes narrowed and teeth showing. "All right, cully. You can squeeze off the brownspill, I've got no use for it. What the fuck happened here? What happened to the rest of your detachment? Where's Captain Hotsteel?"

"Captain Hotsteel was splattered by a Leveler," Rony said, looking off at the rolling grass, because she didn't want to look at Gunnar, and she certainly didn't want to look at Lip-Flapper, but mostly she didn't want to look at the army cresting that hill. "By one of Sergeant Breakwood's men, I believe. They mutinied when we arrived at the Ruins. We fought them—Lochled's squad that is—us against Breakwood's squad and Hamfist's squad. Right after that, we got hit by the Tickers. We killed them. They killed us. That part's somewhat mixed together. But all of them are dead now, and not all of us are dead, so I guess we won."

Gunnar's lips had pursed as she talked. Everything about him was stiff and brooding. Staring at her with those spooky blues of his, like they could peel her skin off and see what was really beneath.

"What's your name, soldier?" Gunnar asked quietly.

"Rony Hirdman." And she almost said *hef* but held back at the last second.

Gunnar didn't seem to notice or care. He looked at Ord. "And you, soldier?"

Ord straightened, looked a little confused. "Ord Griman?" A pause. "Priest of the Third Order? We've met."

Gunnar leaned in close, then seemed to recoil in shock. "My fuck! Theynen! It is you! What the hell happened?"

Ord nodded in Rony's direction. "What she said."

Gunnar looked rapidly between them. Then settled on Rony. "Tell it true, cully. I know you're no fighter. I heard all about the fucking debacle on the boat over. And now you want me to believe you hacked all the Tickers to bits by yourself?"

"Never said I hacked 'em to bits by myself."

"Did you do any fighting at all, or did you just hide until all your squad was dead so you could take the glory? Uh?" He seemed mad about it. Rony couldn't tell if he was working himself up or fucking with her. Again she felt lost. No, not lost. Newly born somehow. Or newly dead? Risen *from* the dead, perhaps?

"If I may, Steadman Thaersh," Ord raised his hand.

Gunnar looked at him. "Of course, Theynen."

"Rony didn't fight them all single handed. We all had to fight—myself included. But I can tell you for sure and certain she didn't hide. She did as much as anybody else. I myself, however, did very little."

"Not true," Rony said, patting him on the back. "You took four or five at that corner. We'd've been pinned down all day if it wasn't for you."

Ord shook his head. "It was only four."

"Well, you tried to get the one in the room too. Would've worked, but who'd've known they could catch the shotstones?"

Ord chuffed. "One of my own damned shotstones caught me in the leg, you know? After the Ticker took 'em and fired 'em back."

Rony shook her head, mournfully. "That's when all them shotstones hit Lochled. Ripped him right to shreds. Wasn't even anything left to identify him by."

Ord hung his head. "My fault."

"You were doing the best you could, Theynen."

Gunnar watched the exchange like a dog watches a ball being tossed back and forth. Then held up a hand. "All right. I've heard enough." He waved a hand, and Lip-Flapper, along with several of the mounted heavies, came trotting eagerly forward. "Get this cully and Theynen Griman back to our outpost and see that they're treated. Then have the Ruins there checked over thoroughly and report back to me." He leaned forward in the saddle. "And anything that doesn't match up with your story, young cully, is going to be a big fucking problem."

CHAPTER 41

Lochled didn't know how far he'd ridden. Only that he hadn't stopped until the graylit hours. And at that point, he figured he was close to dead. Maybe that's why he'd kept on going—last sunset and all that.

He'd stolen two horses, as he'd said he would. He on one, and the male Ticker on the other, with the girl nestled against his chest. They seemed to be close to each other. Maybe brother and sister. Maybe they really had all been a family.

Riding seemed a touch awkward for them, but the young male got the gist of it fairly quickly. Seemed alternately terrified and thrilled. When he first saw the horse, Lochled thought he might up and run and realized, if they didn't have horses over here in Leftland, then these poor, gentle beasts had probably become daemons in the minds of Leftlanders—seeing as how every time they saw one it carried a man trying to murder them.

It was just like Trut had said. Men had taken a beautiful thing and made it do ugliness.

When they finally stopped, Lochled stared down at the ground, as though it were too far away to possibly reach. He felt weak and shaky. Didn't trust himself to even get out of the saddle without collapsing. Could've done for a fire, though he couldn't quite decide if he was hot or cold. He felt cold, yet he couldn't stop sweating.

He glanced over to the young male and the little girl. They'd already dismounted and were standing there, watching him with blank faces.

Lochled licked his lips, but everything was pasty dry. Damn. And there hadn't even been any water to steal. The barrel had been crushed to splinters outside the Ruins. They'd passed several streams, but Lochled could no more bend to get the water than he could dismount.

"It's fine," Lochled wheezed, just a hot wind through Drugothan sands. "I'll be fine."

He maneuvered his body into a dismount position. And almost got it done with something akin to grace, but right as he was trying to ease himself down, his leg went wonky in the stirrup, and his hands didn't quite have the strength to hold to the saddle, so down he went.

As he fell, he thought, *This is going to hurt*, and it did. Bad.

He lay there in the grass—everything was grass, seas and seas of it, it seemed—staring up into the darkening sky, just the first few stars making their entrance. His breath was coming in, rapid and shallow. He could feel the fluid in his lungs. They were slowly filling up. Rattling on the exhales.

He'd fully intended to try to call out for help, but apparently he hadn't made it that far, because then he woke up and it was full dark, and he was propped on his side. He glanced about, confused, bleary, not quite fully there.

There was a fire. Someone had built a fire.

The little girl was there. She had his flask in her hand. Pushed it toward his face.

"Probably not a good idea," he whispered. But he took it. Damn, but his hands were shaky. Grip weak. Could barely even hang onto the flask. "But then again, I'm dead anyways, so why not?" And he put the flask to his lips.

It was water. They'd gone and got water for him.

He was almost disappointed.

The little girl leaned forward and took the flask from him. He watched her for a moment. Their faces, they didn't show much at all, did they? Looking at this girl-Ticker in front of him, her face was so level he couldn't tell at all what might be going on beneath. Compared to Tickers, people were open and easy to read.

"Do you understand anything I'm saying?"

The girl looked at him. Stared for a moment. At his eyes. Then at his lips. Then reached out and grabbed his mouth and smooshed it, working his mouth like a puppet. Then she looked expectantly at him.

He frowned. "The fuck's that supposed to mean?"

She turned and looked at the male Ticker, who was squatting by the fire. They held each other's gazes for a moment, then his went back to the fire, and hers went back to Lochled's, this time with the slightest crease to her brow—what Lochled could only interpret as consternation. Then she leaned forward and mushed her hand across his face, fingers wiping his eyes closed.

"You want me to sleep, then?" Lochled murmured, not bothering to open his eyes again. "Might not wake up."

Then he felt her hand on his wound and started, eyes popping open and flinching away from her touch. "Whassat then?"

She seemed unperturbed by his reaction. Simply reached forward and tried to brush his eyelids closed again, but he wasn't having it.

"No. No. You gonna go prodding around in my wounds?" Lochled glanced at the male Ticker, but he was looking intensely at the girl. The girl's face flashed angrily for half a second, and she turned and looked at the male. Then back at Lochled. She pointed quite emphatically to his head, then to the ground, then to the wound, and then reached forward and brushed his eyelids closed again.

"Persistent cully, aren't you?" Lochled grumbled, allowing his head to be pressed back into the ground, his eyes to stay closed. "Just . . . don't poke around too hard."

Turned out she didn't do much at all. Just laid her hand there for a while. At first the salt of her skin stung it, but that passed, and afterward it just felt somewhat numb. Numb enough that he slipped off to sleep again, wondering if he was ever going to wake up, and not all that troubled about it.

Later that night, Rony was escorted into Gunnar Thaersh's command tent. She'd gotten her blown-off fingers wrapped up and all her cuts either stitched or bandaged. Cleaned up. Washed her clothes and put them back on wet because she didn't have any others.

Sore and dripping and cold, she hobbled her way into the tent. Hip aching something fierce from being thrown into the wall, and her shoulder too, if she moved it a certain way. The guards that had escorted her remained outside, and the tent flap was left open.

Gunnar was the only one in the tent. She'd been expecting more grandness, but he'd kept things simple and utilitarian. One woven rug to keep the mud down. One pine table, on which sat his maps and a single candle in a stand. A dark brazier with no coals in it. A cot in the corner. A satchel, not unlike the ones most soldiers would carry, stowed under the cot.

Gunnar was standing with his fists on the table, propping him up. One of those old maps of Leftland laid out before him, with a few stones to weigh down the corners. He watched her as she limped to a stop on the other side of the table.

"You wanted to see me, hef?" She almost didn't say it again, but the circumstances had become more formal now. Dirty and bloody and only one of two survivors on a rock with death behind you? Any decent man would forgive you some lack of discipline in that moment. But she'd been watered, fed, stitched, and cleaned. She had no excuses anymore.

Gunnar sniffed. "You skipped the part where your Seeker was killed."

"Don't know that she was, hef. Did you find her body?"

He glanced sharply up at her. Considered her for a moment. Then shook his head. "No sign of her. What happened?"

"They went after her, and she done ran off."

"You saw this happen? Why didn't you mention it?"

"Yes, hef. Didn't seem pertinent at the time."

"And does it seem pertinent now?"

"To be honest, hef, I don't know what's pertinent anymore. Perhaps you could tell me."

"Who went after Seeker Kayna Redstone, and why?" Gunnar didn't demand it, but the authority in his voice was strong enough that it made little difference.

"Breakwood, hef. And I suppose he intended to cut her to bits. So she couldn't get a message to you about the mutiny." Rony tilted her head. "Has she been in contact?"

His eyes narrowed a smidge. "No. Which she should have, and I find it troubling that she has not." He straightened up. Rolled his stocky shoulders. "That is, perhaps, the only real item in question. But I've no reason to disbelieve you. The theynen has already vouched for everything you claimed." A long pause, like maybe he was getting around to something he didn't want to say. "And your fighting prowess."

Rony didn't know what to say to that, so she chose to say nothing at all. That seemed a good strategy, most of the time.

Gunnar crossed his arms over his chest. "There's three barques, already loaded to bear our harvest, setting off back to Bransport tomorrow. You've done far more than anyone could have expected of you. A cully and a swineherd. Yes, you've been most impressive. So I'm going to grant you permission to return to Bransport tomorrow on one of those barques."

Rony waited to feel something about that. Wanted to feel relief. But really, all she felt was a little miffed. "You're sending me back?"

He looked sharply at her. "That depends."

"On what, hef?"

"On whether you want to go back." One eyebrow arching. "Do you?"

Rony blinked. Looked down at her feet. Wondering if this was some sort of trick. Wondering what she actually felt about it in her gut. It was all so mixed up that she was having a hard time telling which feelings were true and which were false. Which were hers and which were simply born out of the nightmare of the last several days?

And why was she even having to think about this? Of course she wanted to go home! She'd been wanting to go home since she stepped off the docks in the first place! And now she had a fucking chance to do it. Why was she hesitating?

She swallowed. "I don't know, hef. What . . . what if I stayed?"

"If you stayed?" Gunnar looked shocked, and she realized in a sudden flash that he hadn't been trying to ship her back to get rid of her. He'd assumed her frail woman's mind had cracked under the pressure of combat, much like the Mad Queen's. He looked down at his table. Had another roll of parchment that he extended with a finger, briefly reading something. "I have . . . approximately . . . twenty-seven fractions of squads that would be far more effective combined into whole squads. Which means that I find myself suddenly in the need of eight new sergeants. Now, the vast majority of men who had a viable reputation are either dead or already in other positions. The rest of these bastards I don't know from Feor's Golem. And I don't know you either, but at least you've got a reputation that's been vouched for." He laughed. "And by a priest, no less. Not many Steadmen can even say that, uh?"

Rony stared at him. Seemed she was doing a lot of that lately. It was just that lag between what was happening and the point at which she finally arrived at the right way to respond. Seemed like that had been so easy when it'd been the old Rony. But this was the new Rony. She'd drowned in fire and blood and come out the other side something else entirely. And like a foal with its gangly, wobbly legs, she was having to learn everything afresh.

Everything except fighting, that is. When she thought of fighting, that seemed pretty doable. Seemed like she could slip back into that role pretty fucking easy. It was just all the other parts of being a human being that seemed difficult.

"Are you offering me a sergeant's commission?" she asked, voice blank.

Gunnar nodded. "Seems that way. But . . ." He held up a hand. "You look half-dead. Now's not the time to decide if you want to fight or rest. That's like going to the butcher's when you haven't eaten in a week. So go and sleep the night. Get your head back on straight. You'll feel more like yourself in the morning." His eyes avoided hers for a moment. "Trust me, cully, we've all been there. You can give me your answer then."

Rony nodded. Then remembered: "Yes, hef." She turned and headed out. Thinking about how she felt like she could never do anything but fight now. How close she'd felt to those boys on her squad. Closer than she'd ever felt to her own brothers. To her own father. Accepted. A part of something. And more than that, *valued.*

And here, she was, valued again. By the Steadman himself.

Steadman Gunnar Thaersh had *valued* her enough to offer her a sergeant's commission.

Long way from a father who thought of her as "in the way." Thought of her as "one of those people that adds to others' weight."

Yes, she'd truly been born anew. And she wanted that position, wanted other people to value her. Wanted her own squad. Wanted to keep them protected. Wanted to be blood bound to them. Wanted them to call her hef.

Yes, she wanted the sergeant's commission something fierce.

So why did it feel like dying?

CHAPTER 42

Ord watched Rony exit the Steadman's tent. He hadn't been intending to spy on her, and he wasn't taking any pains to hide himself, but he felt like a sneak anyway since she didn't see him. She seemed wrapped up in some hard thoughts.

Ord shifted the crutch beneath his armpit, aching leg now aching even more from having to be held up off the ground, and this stupid stick the doctor had given him was an uncomfortable bastard. The cloth tied to the top did little to relieve the chafing in his armpit.

All the technology they had now, and they still used sticks to hobble around on lame legs. Seemed a bit ridiculous. Like there should be some sort of alchemy-powered apparatus for getting around. And he was tempted to start thinking about how he could make that happen but wound up only feeling sour about the whole thing. Could he ever use alchemy again after what he'd seen?

Then again, he'd never had qualms about all the little draeids back in Eormun, ripped from their parents' arms and sent to live like orphans in one House of Draeids or another.

Now that he thought about it, that had soured too.

Everything had soured. His whole life had soured.

His perceptions had changed, and everything he thought he knew was uprooted. Couldn't look at alchemy the same. Couldn't look at the Church the same. Couldn't look at himself the same either.

He sighed and muttered a few curses under his breath as he watched Rony trundle off into the darkness. He looked at Gunnar Thaersh's tent, knew he should just go in and stop stalling, but at the moment, he didn't want to talk to the Steadman. Barely knew what he was supposed to say to the man. Knew he'd be asked questions he didn't have good answers for.

No. What he wanted now was to talk to the only other person who might understand his strange new burgeoning of conscience.

So he followed after her, at a distance, not really able to catch up, even as slow as she seemed to be moving. She was making her way toward the edge of the encampment, and after a time of his hobbling after her, she disappeared, so he just kept heading in the last direction he'd seen her moving.

He found her sitting at the coals of an abandoned watch fire, staring into the orange embers. She glanced up when he finally struggled his way into the dim circle of light—just enough to see each other's faces—and she didn't seem surprised to see him.

"Theynen," she murmured, looking back to the embers.

He eyed the stones around the fire for a place to sit, but then decided it would be easier to stay standing than to have to struggle to his feet again. So he slouched against his crutch. Looked up at the night sky. A patch of stars twinkling between blankets of black clouds.

"How's the leg?" she asked him.

"It'll heal. How's your thinking?"

"Difficult."

"Are you in trouble?"

She scoffed. "You could say that."

Ord grimaced. "Fah. It's unjust, Rony. I've a meeting with the Steadman shortly. I'll reiterate that you did your best. I still have some sway in these matters."

Rony didn't take her eyes off the coals. Tan face lit umber, dark eyes reflecting the light. "He offered me a sergeant's commission."

Ord raised his eyebrows. "Oh."

She reached around and pulled her little satchel off her shoulder. Extracted some odd little box that Ord had never seen before. "That, or a trip back to Bransport tomorrow."

Ord frowned. "Why would you not take it?"

She glanced up at him again, thumbs plucking at little metal tines on the box, making wonderful, musical notes. "The commission or the trip back home?"

"I thought you wanted to be free of this place as soon as possible."

She nodded. Stared at the box in her hands as she made the notes. A melody coming out of them now, a song he'd heard before but couldn't really place. "Yes, that's what I thought too. Lochled would have wanted me to go, that's for sure. He didn't want war to ruin me. But I wonder if it already has? Seeing as how I can't decide what to do."

Ord stretched a kink out of his back. Brought the crutch out from under his armpit and wobbled a bit getting it situated so he was leaning on it with both hands. "I don't think it's ruined you, Rony. I'm not sure it really can. Not if you're a good person. And you are. Even Lochled, after all the war he'd been in, still was able to make a right decision."

Rony peered at him skeptically. "So you think he made the

right decision, then? What's that mean for you? What's that mean for your belief in the Church?"

Ord sighed heavily. Shook his head. "Perhaps it's folly to believe in an institution of men. What gives us the right to speak for Feor? Just because I believe in Feor, does that mean I have to believe in every man who claims to know Feor's thoughts? Perhaps they have their own, human motives, just like every human does. Perhaps the Church has made a mistake."

Rony clucked her tongue at him. "That's unseemly for a priest to say, you know."

Ord nodded. "Yes. I know."

They were silent for a moment after that. Ord wrestling with himself, with his faith, with his duties, with whether or not to say the thing that he felt Rony needed to hear. Didn't even know why he felt compelled to tell her. Only that . . . he knew what it was to be stuck in a dilemma. And if someone around him could have clarified his own, he sure would have liked them to speak up.

"Rony, I'm going to tell you something that you shouldn't repeat to anyone."

Her eyes were sharp and curious when they caught his again. Ord found it easier to look away from her. Made it seem less like he was being treasonous, and more like he was just speaking his thoughts into the darkness.

"You may not be able to escape war, Rony. Even if you go back to Brymsland."

"What do you mean?"

Still staring out into the night of a foreign land. "Annistis Fyrngelt has escaped with some loyalists. There is some suspicion that she may attempt to get to Leftland to recruit this crusade to fight against her cousin Morric's claim to the title of Brannen. But whether she stays there in Brymsland or comes here doesn't really matter, does it?"

He realized he felt sad. Like he was watching a dream wilt and wither. A dream of peace and prosperity. Promises of progress, now turning slowly to omens of blood and ash.

"War is coming, Rony. The fragile alliances between Morric and his chiefs will splinter, some siding with Annistis, and others with Morric. And in amongst all of that, there will be those who see this as a chance to divest the Church of its power and seize the secrets of alchemy for themselves. They've been biding their time for years, but Annistis will cause it all to come crashing down. She's tilted the gameboard, and now the pieces will fall, but we won't know where they will land until they hit the ground. All I know for certain, is that war is coming for all of us, and there won't be a place you can go in all of Eormun that it won't touch you. Go or stay. But you won't escape it. None of us will."

When he finally looked back at Rony, he found her frowning into the embers again. Silent. Brooding. Perhaps he hadn't clarified her choices at all. Perhaps he'd only confused her thoughts with this knowledge and killed her hopes just as sure as his had been.

"Well." He cleared his throat. Stuffed the wretched crutch back under his armpit. "I'm sorry." Wasn't sure what he was sorry for. Maybe everything. "I've a meeting that I can't delay any longer. But . . ." His eyes strayed to the musical box in her hands. She wasn't making it sing anymore, which was a pity. "That box. Might be worth something, you know."

She turned it slowly over in her hands. "Doesn't matter if it is. I think I'll keep this one for myself."

"Good. You play it well." He turned away from the coals.

"What will you do?" her voice said at his back. "Knowing what you know? About the Tickers?"

He stopped, but didn't turn. Just craned his neck to look over his shoulder, but only caught the orange light in the edge of his vision. "I'll complete my mission, and find how deep Leftland goes. And I'll tell the Church. And I'll tell them about the stone-throwing contraptions they built. And I'll tell them about the cannons they had in Halun's Landing. And the medicine. And the fact that they do understand, even if they can't speak. And maybe that'll be the end of me. But at least I'll have done the right thing."

"They won't listen," she said, quietly. Truthfully. "And they'll never accept you after that."

Ord simply shrugged. Smiled. "I'm a Fen, Rony. They were never going to accept me anyways."

Kayna sat in the darkness of a new-fallen night, alone in an alien land. She had no fire for light or warmth. But the night was not cold, and the stars provided just enough light that she could see the line of glass phials laying on the ground before her crossed legs.

She raised her eyes and scanned the terrain around her. Even if the night had been cold and too black to see, she would not have lit a fire. Firelight can be seen for many thousands of strides, and she didn't think there were many friendly eyes out there right now.

Somewhere behind her, she could hear the steady breathing and chomping of her horse as it cropped grass. She could feel its mind, and it was calm. Alert, as any animal would be at night. But not alarmed by anything. She trusted the horse's senses over her own. It would catch the smell of an intruder long before she caught its ill intents.

It struck her that she was as far aleft as any human had ever been on this strange continent.

But then she realized that wasn't true.

Lochled was farther aleft than she was. If he wasn't already dead.

She'd ridden hard to escape Breakwood, but when she'd seen that she'd lost him, she'd doubled back and witnessed the fight within the Ruins. Every bit of it. Down to the last moment when she'd watched Lochled leave on horseback, heading aleft, accompanied by two young Leftlanders.

She'd followed for a time, but stopped when night fell. Lochled was now too far away for her to sense, but she was confident that she could find him again in the morning.

If it was required of her.

She returned her attention to the phials. Each one snugged into a leather strap, and each strap attached to a leather sleeve so the whole thing could be rolled into a tight bundle. She selected the rightmost phial and pulled it from its place. Held it up and stared at the starlit glass and the clear liquid within.

If it had been any other night, she would have put it back. She was not a woman easily frightened, but the events of the day had been . . . unsettling. And now she craved the comfort of that warm, euphoric embrace. She did not like to take gest when she was craving it so fiercely.

But . . . what else was she to do? She could not go forward, and she could not go back. Not until she found out what they wanted her to do.

So, knowing there was nothing to be done for it, she plucked the cork from the top and upended the phial into her mouth. The feel of it sliding down her throat—somehow both oily and sharp. The taste of it like honey and soot.

Then the warmth. Hot and stinging at first, then settling into a milder burn that seemed to coalesce in her stomach and slowly, ever so slowly, leak into her veins, spreading through her midsection, through her chest, through her arms and her legs, and up into her head, until she was swallowed whole by it.

Distantly, the feeling of sweat began to prickle her skin.

All around her, the night vanished, and her mind flew through a place indescribable. A place made of light and mist and strange interwoven patterns.

Master Tior, she beckoned into the abyss, and found him waiting, as he always was. He who remained in that place, his mind aloft, even as his body withered from neglect.

You are alive, he replied, pleased but not entirely surprised. *I know of the mutiny and your escape. Are you wounded?*

No, I am well, she said truthfully. For nothing could bother her when she was in this place. *I am alone, several thousandstride from the ruins where the mutiny took place.* She paused, but perceived that Tior wished her to continue, so she did. *Something occurred in the ruins that I was not able to ascertain. I was not close enough to sense it. But when it was finished, only five walked out.*

I know of only two, Tior said, curiously. *Ord, the priest, and a girl named Rony. Who are the other three?*

The sergeant, Lochled Thatcher, and two Leftlander children.

Together?

Yes. They fled alefts, and I followed them until nightfall.

There came a long pause, and Kayna saw that Tior had pulled back from her to mull this over in the privacy of his mind. When he spoke again, he was cautious.

The girl and the priest reported that Sergeant Thatcher had been killed.

That is very odd, Kayna mused. *But I am not mistaken. It was Lochled Thatcher, and he was very much alive, although he did appear to be badly wounded.*

And with two Leftlander children, you say?

A girl and a boy. A brother and sister, I sensed.

And what did you sense of Sergeant Thatcher?

He was too addled by drips and his injuries. His thoughts were too muddled to make sense of. Only . . . he wished to save the children.

Did he, now?

Another pause, longer than the first.

Would you have me continue to follow them? Kayna prompted. *Or shall I return to the army?*

Tior's response was slow and thoughtful. *And what of these children, Seeker Kayna? Did they go with Sergeant Thatcher willingly? Did they . . . trust him?*

I believe they sensed that he meant them no harm. Whether they trust him I cannot say. But they went willingly.

Do you think they can be brought to trust him? Can they be brought to trust any man?

Perhaps.

Can they be brought to trust you?

Strange. She'd believed that nothing could bother her in this place. Yet, with that question, a tiny sliver of dread pierced her veil of ecstasy. It was so unexpected that she didn't have time to pull back from Tior's mind before he perceived it.

I sense that this question disturbs you. Why?

I do not know. Perhaps I am disturbed more that I felt anything at all.

Much has changed for you. But your mission has not changed, Seeker Kayna. Though perhaps the method by which you may take to fulfill it has changed. If they can be brought to trust a man who has killed so many of them—a fact which I'm sure they have already perceived—then I must believe they can be brought to trust you as well. The question is, Can you bring yourself to gain their trust?

I can communicate with them, which Lochled cannot do. But

can I hide from them my true purpose? If they can perceive thoughts as readily as I, won't they see what we intend?

Have any Leftlanders managed to probe that deeply into your mind?

I am sure they are capable. But all the ones that got close enough to perceive my thoughts were killed.

Then guard your thoughts against them, Seeker Kayna. Be, in your mind, who they would want you to be, and think only of what you want them to believe about you. When the time comes for you to act upon your true nature . . . well, then it will be too late.

This time Kayna had the sense to pull back from Tior so that the little note of unease that wriggled through her mind passed by undetected. He would have noticed that she'd pulled back, but such a thing was not uncommon. And she was quick to open up to him again.

Still, Tior commented on it. *I hope the conflict within you is not so strong that you cannot overcome it. Is it wise for you to continue on your course? Perhaps I should have you return to the army. There are other Seekers that can be sent . . .*

No. And Kayna did exactly what Tior had just instructed her to do: She guarded her thoughts. She became, in her mind, a woman who was unconflicted. She thought only of completing her mission. *I will go.*

One final pause, during which Kayna continued to think only of what Tior wanted to believe about her. The mind is a funny thing. Desire often clouds it from true perception. And Seekers were no different.

And, as it turned out, neither was the Master.

Very well, Seeker Kayna. Follow them. Speak with them. Gain their trust. You know that the survival of our kind depends upon you. We are, all of us, depending upon you.

CHAPTER 43

What's this? Lochled thought, groggy and reeling, eyes jerking through the graylit dawn. *I get another fucking day? Really?*

Yes, really. And his body felt bad enough to prove it to him. He'd lasted through the night, but it seemed for no apparent reason. The wound across his face was leaking yellow shit, and the hole in his side gave him no relief from the pain. When he looked at it and touched it now with a ginger fingertip, he could see that it was sickly red and hot.

"There's the corruption," he whispered. Hell, he'd known it was setting in halfway through the night when he'd started to get that feverish feeling. Wished he hadn't given that last little bottle of medicine away. But then again, the world needed more Ronys in it and fewer Redskins.

He fully expected the Tickers to have abandoned him to his death in the night—he wouldn't even have blamed them. But when he fought his way into a sitting position, gasping and cursing, there they were. Standing with the horses, like they were ready to ride.

"Well, I'll be fucked," Lochled mumbled, a careworn smile

twitching one corner of his mouth. "What are you two still doing around me? Just waiting to watch me die, uh? Don't worry. It won't be long." He ran out of breath surprisingly fast and then started coughing. Tasted like blood again, but more bitter this time. Reminded him of the smell of the drains in Rotsbottom.

He waited to get his breath back.

Felt a hand on his shoulder. Warm and small.

Looked with his bleary, watering eyes. The little girl stood there, two fingers pointing to her two eyes. Then she turned and pointed them aleft. Looked back at him, patiently waiting.

He managed a small smile for her. Then realized he'd never seen any of the Tickers smile—not that he'd given them much cause to—and wondered if it even meant anything to them. They seemed entirely bereft of all but the most basic facial expressions.

"You're trying to say something to me," Lochled said, his voice soft and phlegmy.

The girl pointed to him, very insistently, then again at her eyes, and again out aleft.

"You want me to see something?" Lochled guessed.

The little girl looked at the male again. They made eye contact but there wasn't anything else that you might've found in human communication. No questioning brows. No expressive eyes. No twisting of the lips to display this emotion or that.

Just staring. Like two kids waiting to see who would blink first.

After a moment of this, the girl looked back to him. And then stretched her mouth open wide, showing all her teeth clenched together.

Lochled couldn't help but lean away from her. "Whoa, now. Is that supposed to be a smile?"

But at that point, both the little girl and the younger male were taking him by the arms and pulling him upright, them silent and implacable, him cursing and spitting and calling them all kinds of names. It didn't seem to offend them.

Getting on the damned horse was like being asked to climb a mountain, but mount it he did. Breathless and pouring sweat and sick to his stomach but, oh, so terrified of spewing on account of his ribs. Lochled swayed in the saddle, praying for Feor to clear his poor bubbling head and keep him from toppling.

And on they went, this time with the brother and sister—he was getting surer that's what they were—up in front and Lochled following.

Reality melted and rebuilt itself many times as the sun came up and the day dragged on. They never went faster than a walk. The brother and sister brought him water several times, but that was it. They seemed to have someplace to be, and they wanted to get there.

Lochled wasn't even sure why he was going along with it. He'd gotten them out of there. He'd saved them from being murdered—his tiny little stamp of goodness on the world before he left it. Why keep going at all? Why not stop at the next forest they found and lie in the shade and let himself drift off peacefully, dreaming of green hills and blue skies, a girl that would have a chance to grow to a woman, and a woman who still had enough love in her heart to give him because it hadn't all been stripped away by grief . . .

When reality rebuilt itself again, Lochled smelled it.

Salt. Ocean.

They were cresting a hill. Distantly, Lochled could hear the cries of gulls carried on the wind. He blinked some sense back into his eyes—getting harder and harder to do—and squinted in the direction of the sun. It was right where it should be—they were still going aleft. Had been going aleft the whole time since the Ruins.

How long had it been? Things were fuzzy, but Lochled was still pretty sure it had only been one day. Maybe a day and a half at the outside.

And that made Leftland less than four days' ride, from coast to coast.

No. Couldn't be that damn small. Could it? Maybe this wasn't the ocean he was smelling. Maybe it was . . . a salt lake, or something.

But when they reached the top of the hill, and he looked out at the great, flat, blue expanse, and traced his eye from one end to the other, it sure looked to him like what he'd thought it was.

"Well, I'll be damned," Lochled wheezed. Coughed. "It's the fuckin' ocean."

The brother and sister wrangled their horse up beside him—the male still a bit clumsy with the reins. The girl looked at Lochled with that same, direct, intense look. Pointed to him. Pointed to her eyes. Pointed to the ocean.

Lochled nodded. "Yes, cully. I see the ocean."

Then she did something different: brought both her hands up, palms facing each other. Then squished them together so there was only a slim gap between them. Looked at the gap. Looked at him.

It wasn't that Lochled was dense. It was just that he didn't expect the girl to be so sharp. So it took him a moment to really reconcile himself to what the girl was telling him.

"Leftland," he said. "Is small. Is that it?"

She gave him a full set of teeth again. Seemed they thought a smile was some sort of affirmative answer. Lochled took it as "Yes."

He leaned on his saddle horn to get some weight off his aching side. Stared out at the ocean. Chuffing softly in amazement. Followed the coastline with his eyes, all the way nyhtside, until he saw a little something in the distance that didn't quite look like it belonged.

"That a city?" he asked, thinking he should point, but didn't have the strength to raise his arm. He did manage to turn his head to look at whatever they might offer as an answer.

The male was the communicator this time: pointing to himself and to the girl, then pointing to that little something in the distance. White stones, Lochled supposed. That's what he'd seen sitting out there on the coast. Just like Halun's Landing. Another city, on the opposite side of a very narrow continent. One that couldn't possibly hold all that many Tickers.

"Church'll be disappointed," Lochled grunted, then clicked his mouth and set his horse in motion again. "Shame I won't live to see it."

Down the hill the horse went, heading for the ocean. And when Lochled managed to twist far enough to look behind him, he saw the brother and sister still standing at the crest. They hadn't moved. Didn't intend to follow. As though they knew he was going someplace they could not follow.

He was glad for them—that brother and sister. Glad they at least had a chance to grow old now.

Might only be one good deed, but one's better than none.

He closed his eyes and let himself slump in the saddle. Swaying gently to the rhythm of the horse as it meandered its way toward the beach. That swaying almost like being on a boat. The sea breeze in his face. The gulls overhead. A beach like the one he'd imagined, but never found in Brymsland. A place that didn't smell of soot and sewage.

Just wind and water and salt.

The ocean.

Maybe he could get down in the sand one last time. Maybe

he could walk himself into the surf, let that brine soak his skin, soak his befouled wounds. Clean all this blood and dust from him. Clean him up so that you could actually see the man underneath.

The ocean heals all wounds, after all.

That's what Marna used to say.

ACKNOWLEDGMENTS

As I often say in my video series, Lessons in Writing, stories are both an art and a craft. The artistry happens in solitude, and that solitude is sacred. But the craftsmanship is much more of a group effort. Here's some folks I must give huge thanks to for helping me craft this chunk of raw art into something worthy of being read . . .

First off, all my beta readers. There were more than forty of you, so I'll spare the reader a long list of names. You all know who you are, and I am indebted to you for taking the time to read this story in one of its much rougher drafts and offering me all those incredible insights that helped me mold it into what you now hold in your hands. You guys are awesome!

To my good friend Jon; my wife, Tara; and my father, Brad (a.k.a. Pops—who still reads everything I write): thanks for sitting with me, listening to my constant second-guessing, and always encouraging me to keep going when the going got tough.

Diana Gill, you were an amazing editor. Your feedback was incisive and undeniable, and working with you was a real pleasure. I hope we can do it again soon!

Blackstone Publishing fielded an entire platoon of folks for this book, so if I don't get your name in here, know that I still appreciate your peerless work in making the complicated process of bringing a book to market so painless. To Sarah Bonamino, Rachel Sanders, Francie Crawford, Isabella Bedoya, and Gabrielle Grace: If a tree falls in the forest, and no one is there to hear it, does it make a sound? Similarly, if an artist writes a book, but no one sees it, is it even art? Thanks for making sure my art was seen and heard. My infinite gratitude also goes to Kathryn English for her fantastic art and design work. And to my copyeditor, M.K.: Please edit these acknowledgments so they look as good as you made the book. And I'm sorry I still don't know how to properly use a hyphen.